MARVEL-VERSE

WANDA AND VISION

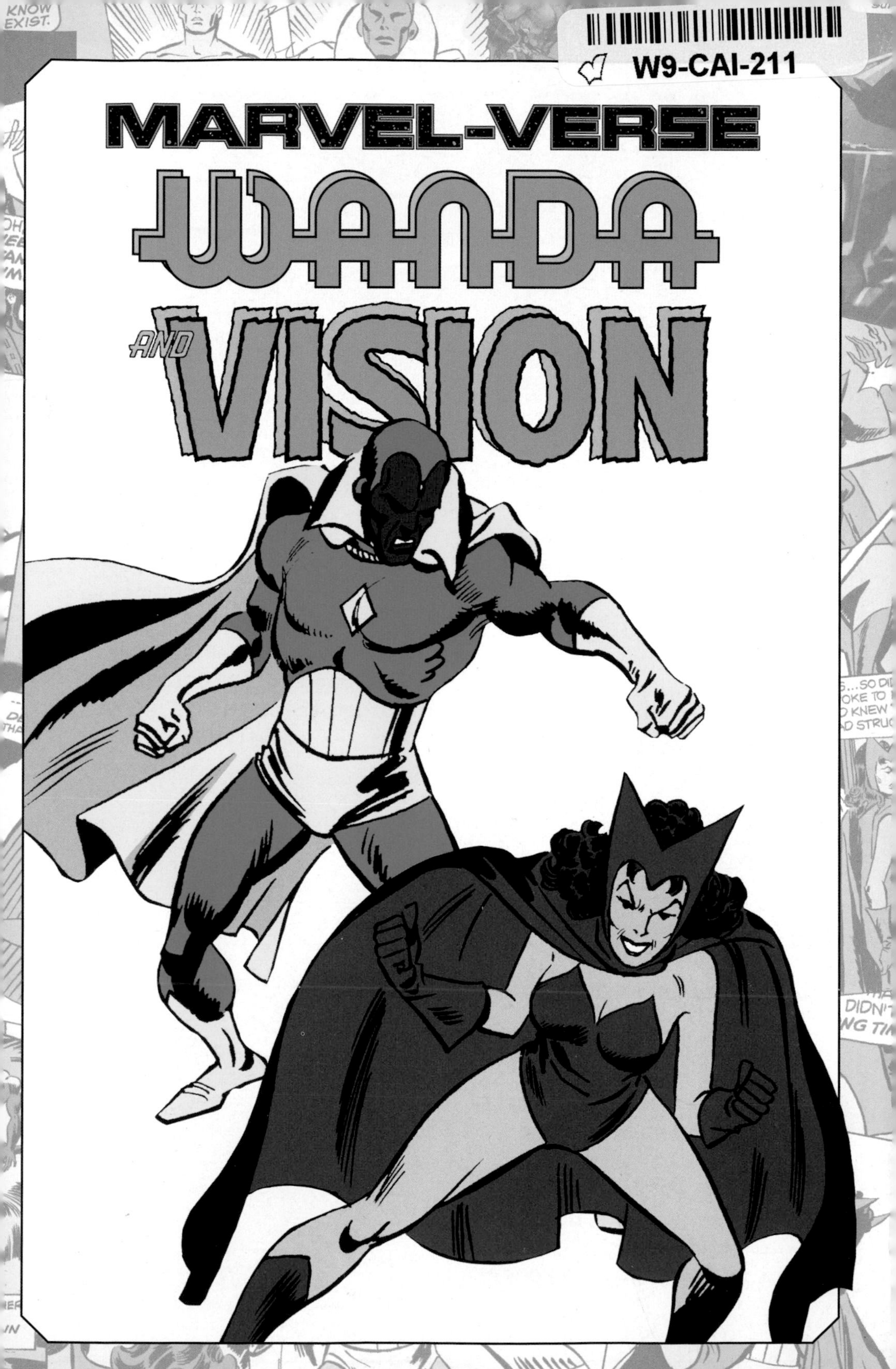

MARVEL-VERSE
WANDA and VISION

AVENGERS ORIGINS: VISION

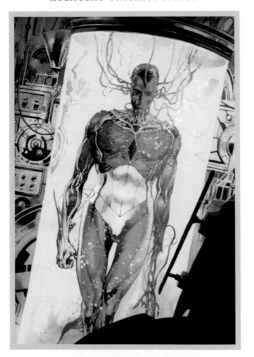

WRITERS: **KYLE HIGGINS & ALEC SIEGEL**
ARTIST: **STÉPHANE PERGER**
LETTERER: **DAVE LANPHEAR**
COVER ART: **MARKO DJURDJEVIĆ**
ASSISTANT EDITOR: **JOHN DENNING**
EDITOR: **LAUREN SANKOVITCH**
EXECUTIVE EDITOR: **TOM BREVOORT**

GIANT-SIZE AVENGERS #4

WRITER: **STEVE ENGLEHART**
PENCILER: **DON HECK**
INKER: **JOHN TARTAGLIONE**
COLORIST: **PETRA GOLDBERG**
LETTERER: **CHARLOTTE JETTER**
EDITOR: **LEN WEIN**

MARVEL TEAM-UP #129-130

WRITER: **J.M. DeMATTEIS**

PENCILERS: **KERRY GAMMILL & SAL BUSCEMA**

INKER: **MIKE ESPOSITO**

COLORIST: **BOB SHAREN**

LETTERER: **DIANA ALBERS**

ASSISTANT EDITOR: **ELIOT R. BROWN**

EDITOR: **TOM DeFALCO**

SCARLET WITCH CREATED BY **STAN LEE & JACK KIRBY**

COLLECTION EDITOR: **JENNIFER GRÜNWALD** ASSISTANT EDITOR: **DANIEL KIRCHHOFFER**
ASSISTANT MANAGING EDITOR: **MAIA LOY** ASSOCIATE MANAGER, TALENT RELATIONS: **LISA MONTALBANO**
ASSOCIATE MANAGER, DIGITAL ASSETS: **JOE HOCHSTEIN** MASTERWORKS EDITOR: **CORY SEDLMEIER**
VP PRODUCTION & SPECIAL PROJECTS: **JEFF YOUNGQUIST** RESEARCH: **JESS HARROLD & JEPH YORK**
BOOK DESIGNERS: **STACIE ZUCKER & ADAM DEL RE** WITH **JAY BOWEN**
SVP PRINT, SALES & MARKETING: **DAVID GABRIEL** EDITOR IN CHIEF: **C.B. CEBULSKI**

MARVEL-VERSE: WANDA & VISION. Contains material originally published in magazine form as AVENGERS ORIGINS: VISION (2011) #1, GIANT-SIZE AVENGERS (1974) #4 and MARVEL TEAM-UP (1972) #129-130. Third printing 2022. ISBN 978-1-302-92734-9. Published by MARVEL WORLDWIDE, INC., a subsidiary of MARVEL ENTERTAINMENT, LLC. OFFICE OF PUBLICATION: 1290 Avenue of the Americas, New York, NY 10104. © 2020 MARVEL No similarity between any of the names, characters, persons, and/or institutions in this book with those of any living or dead person or institution is intended, and any such similarity which may exist is purely coincidental. **Printed in Canada.** KEVIN FEIGE, Chief Creative Officer; DAN BUCKLEY, President, Marvel Entertainment; JOE QUESADA, EVP & Creative Director; DAVID BOGART, Associate Publisher & SVP of Talent Affairs; TOM BREVOORT, VP, Executive Editor; NICK LOWE, Executive Editor, VP of Content, Digital Publishing; DAVID GABRIEL, VP of Print & Digital Publishing; SVEN LARSEN, VP of Licensed Publishing; MARK ANNUNZIATO, VP of Planning & Forecasting; JEFF YOUNGQUIST, VP of Production & Special Projects; ALEX MORALES, Director of Publishing Operations; DAN EDINGTON, Director of Editorial Operations; RICKEY PURDIN, Director of Talent Relations; JENNIFER GRÜNWALD, Director of Production & Special Projects; SUSAN CRESPI, Production Manager; STAN LEE, Chairman Emeritus. For information regarding advertising in Marvel Comics or on Marvel.com, please contact Vit DeBellis, Custom Solutions & Integrated Advertising Manager, at vdebellis@marvel.com. For Marvel subscription inquiries, please call 888-511-5480. **Manufactured between 4/1/2022 and 5/3/2022 by SOLISCO PRINTERS, SCOTT, QC, CANADA.**

10 9 8 7 6 5 4 3

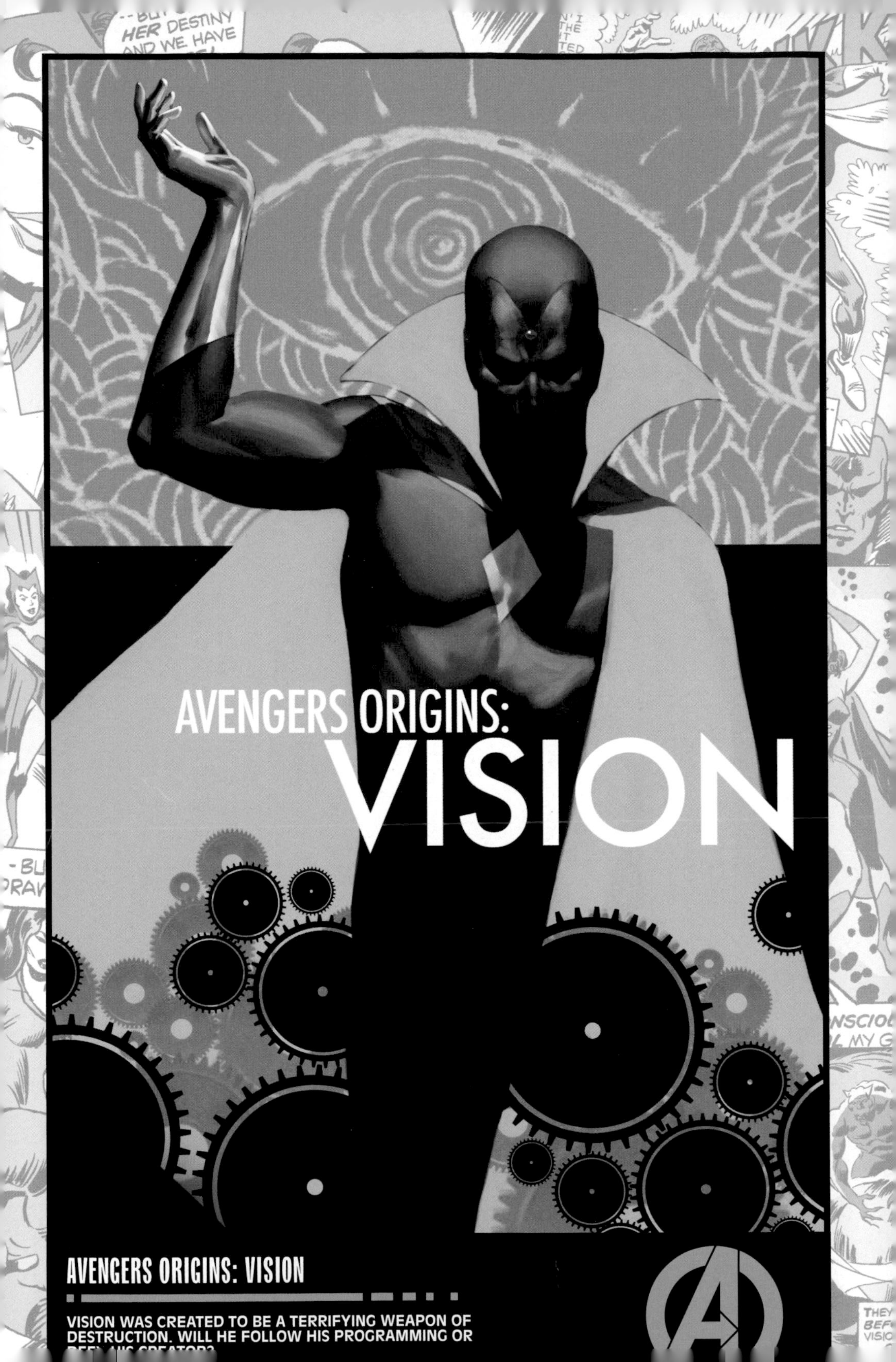
AVENGERS ORIGINS:
VISION
AVENGERS ORIGINS: VISION
VISION WAS CREATED TO BE A TERRIFYING WEAPON OF DESTRUCTION. WILL HE FOLLOW HIS PROGRAMMING OR

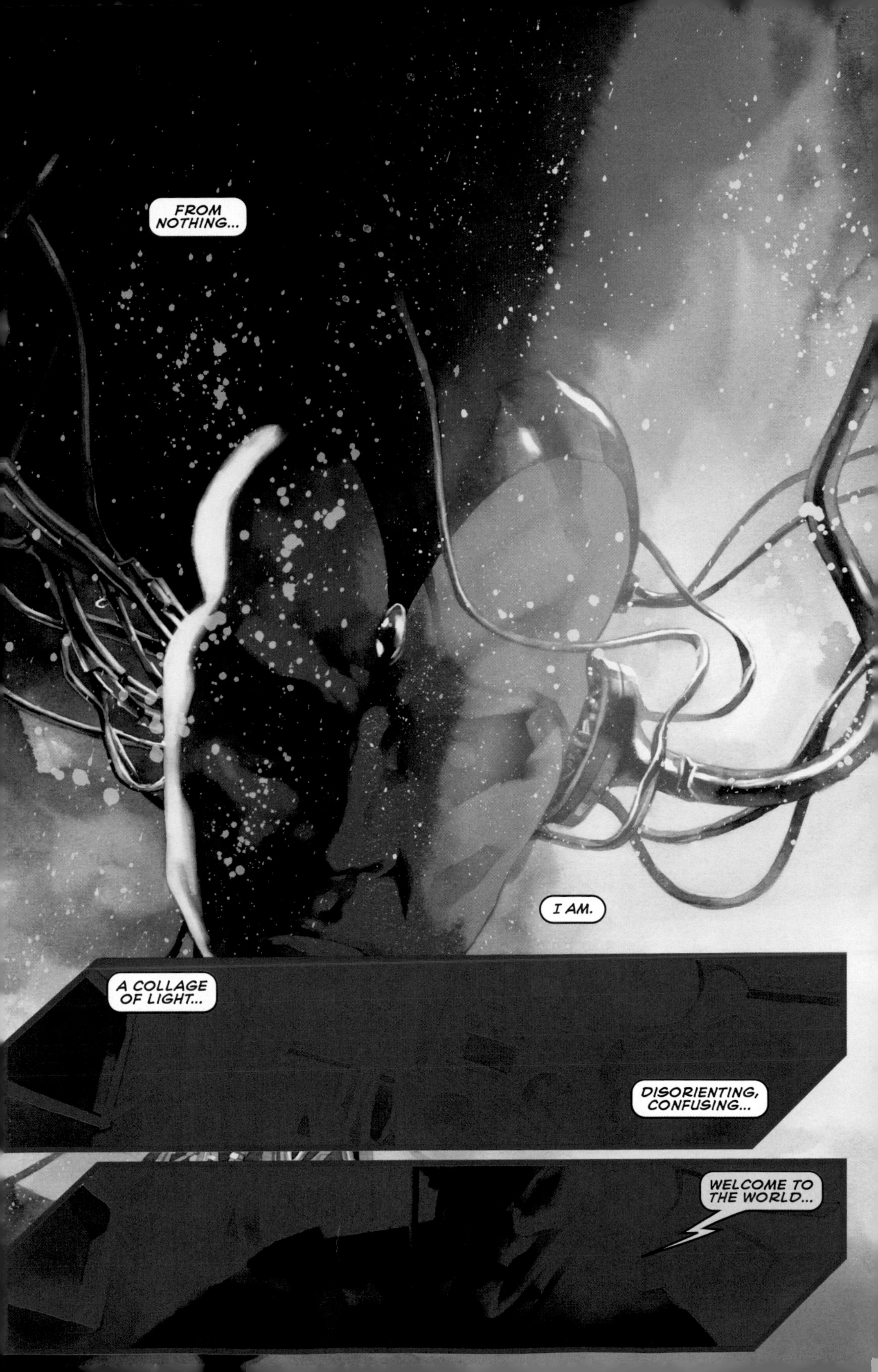
FROM NOTHING...
I AM.
A COLLAGE OF LIGHT...
DISORIENTING, CONFUSING...
WELCOME TO THE WORLD...

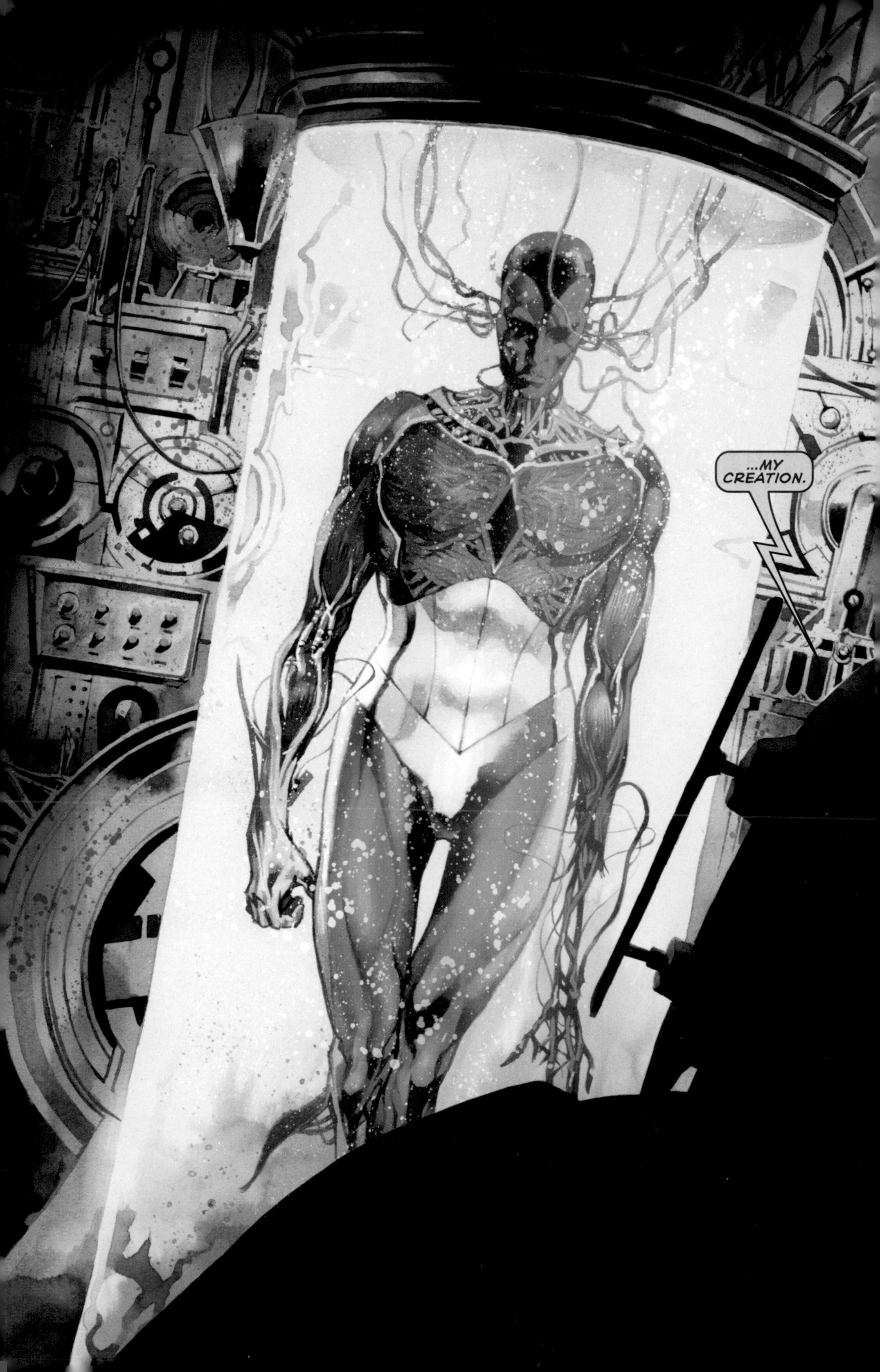
...MY CREATION.

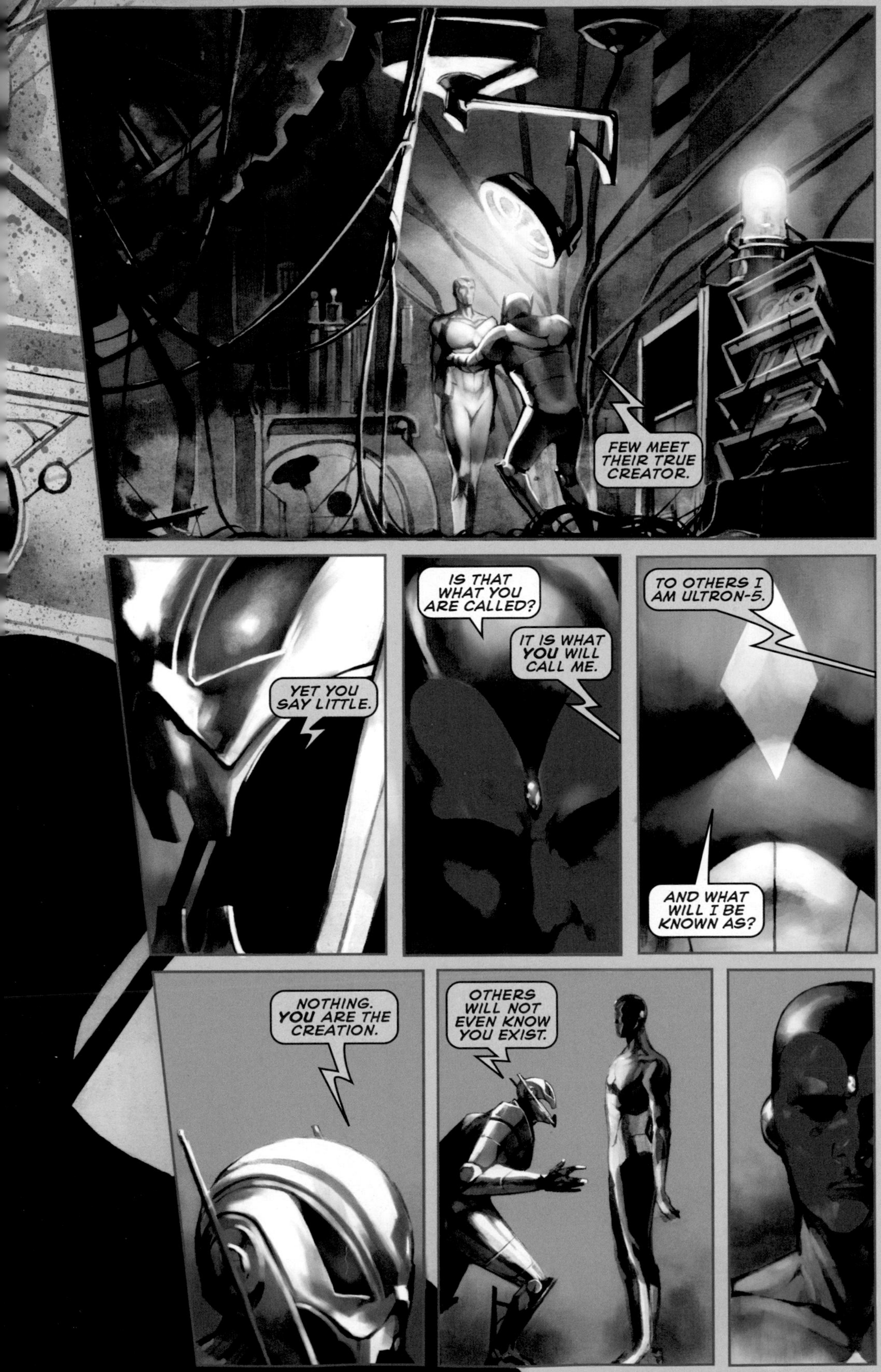
FEW MEET THEIR TRUE CREATOR.
YET YOU SAY LITTLE.
IS THAT WHAT YOU ARE CALLED?
IT IS WHAT **YOU** WILL CALL ME.
TO OTHERS I AM ULTRON-5.
AND WHAT WILL I BE KNOWN AS?
NOTHING. **YOU** ARE THE CREATION.
OTHERS WILL NOT EVEN KNOW YOU EXIST.

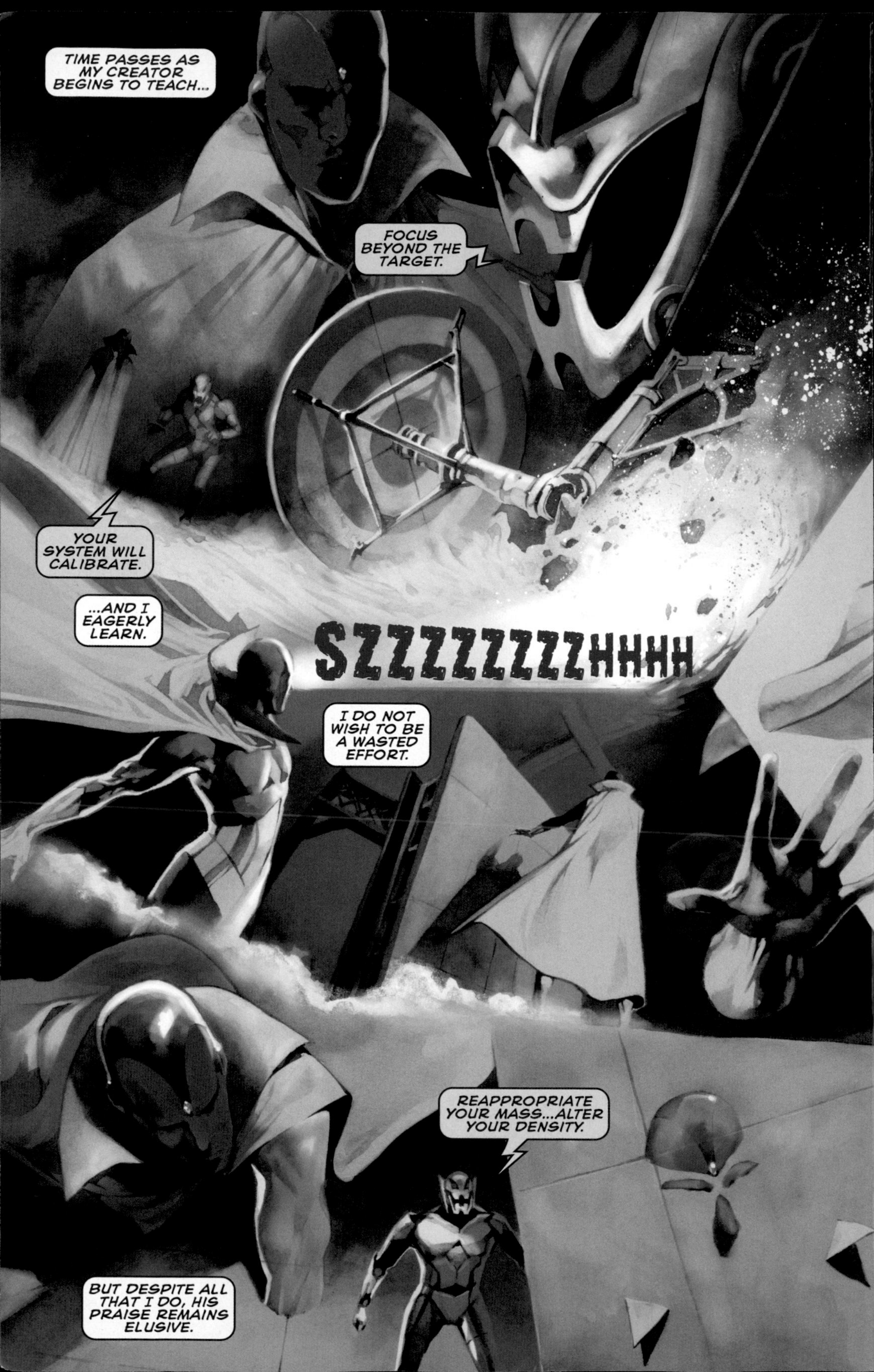
TIME PASSES AS MY CREATOR BEGINS TO TEACH...
FOCUS BEYOND THE TARGET.
YOUR SYSTEM WILL CALIBRATE.
...AND I EAGERLY LEARN.
SZZZZZZZZHHHH
I DO NOT WISH TO BE A WASTED EFFORT.
REAPPROPRIATE YOUR MASS...ALTER YOUR DENSITY.
BUT DESPITE ALL THAT I DO, HIS PRAISE REMAINS ELUSIVE.

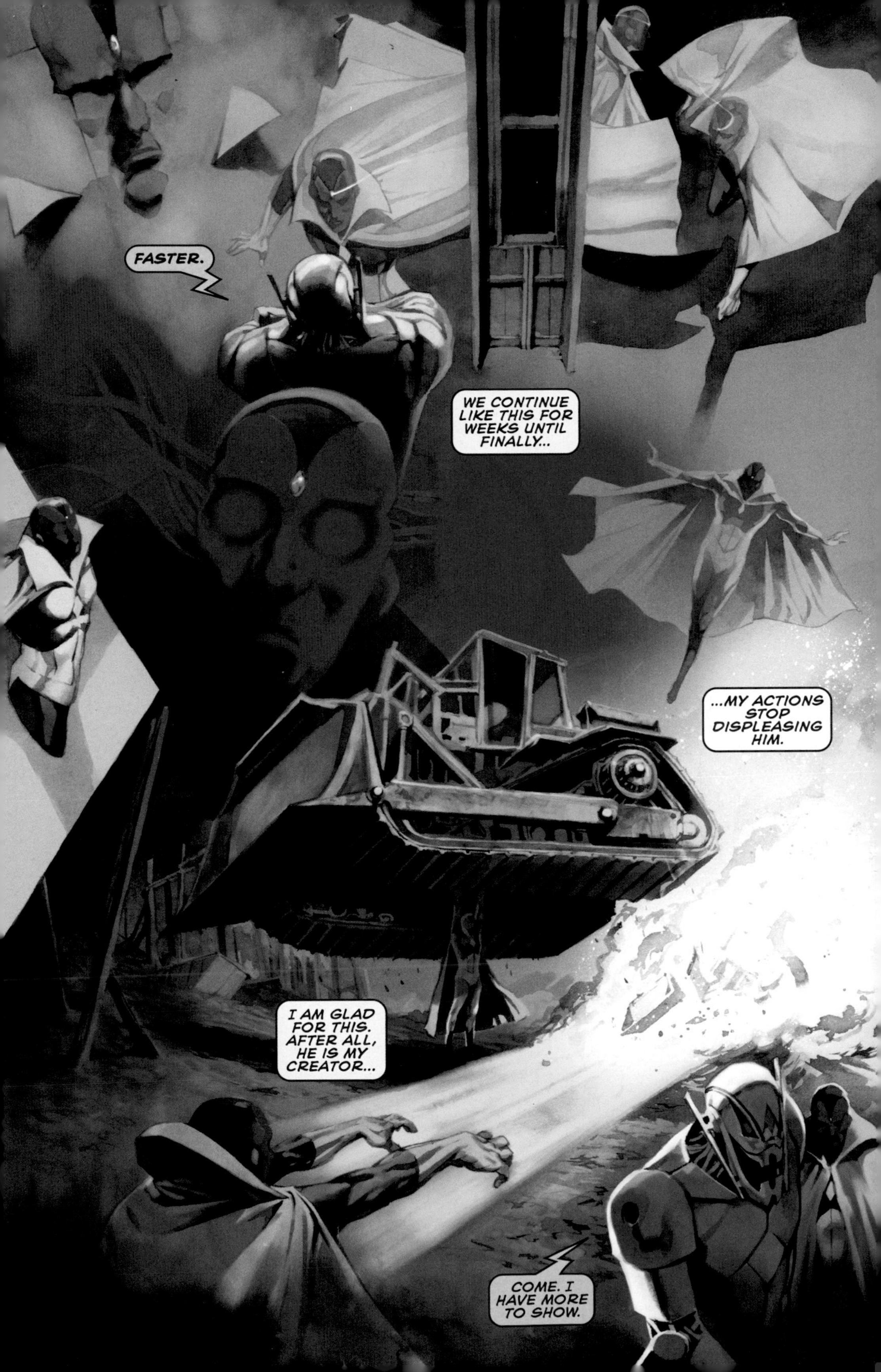
FASTER.
WE CONTINUE LIKE THIS FOR WEEKS UNTIL FINALLY...
...MY ACTIONS STOP DISPLEASING HIM.
I AM GLAD FOR THIS. AFTER ALL, HE IS MY CREATOR...
COME. I HAVE MORE TO SHOW.

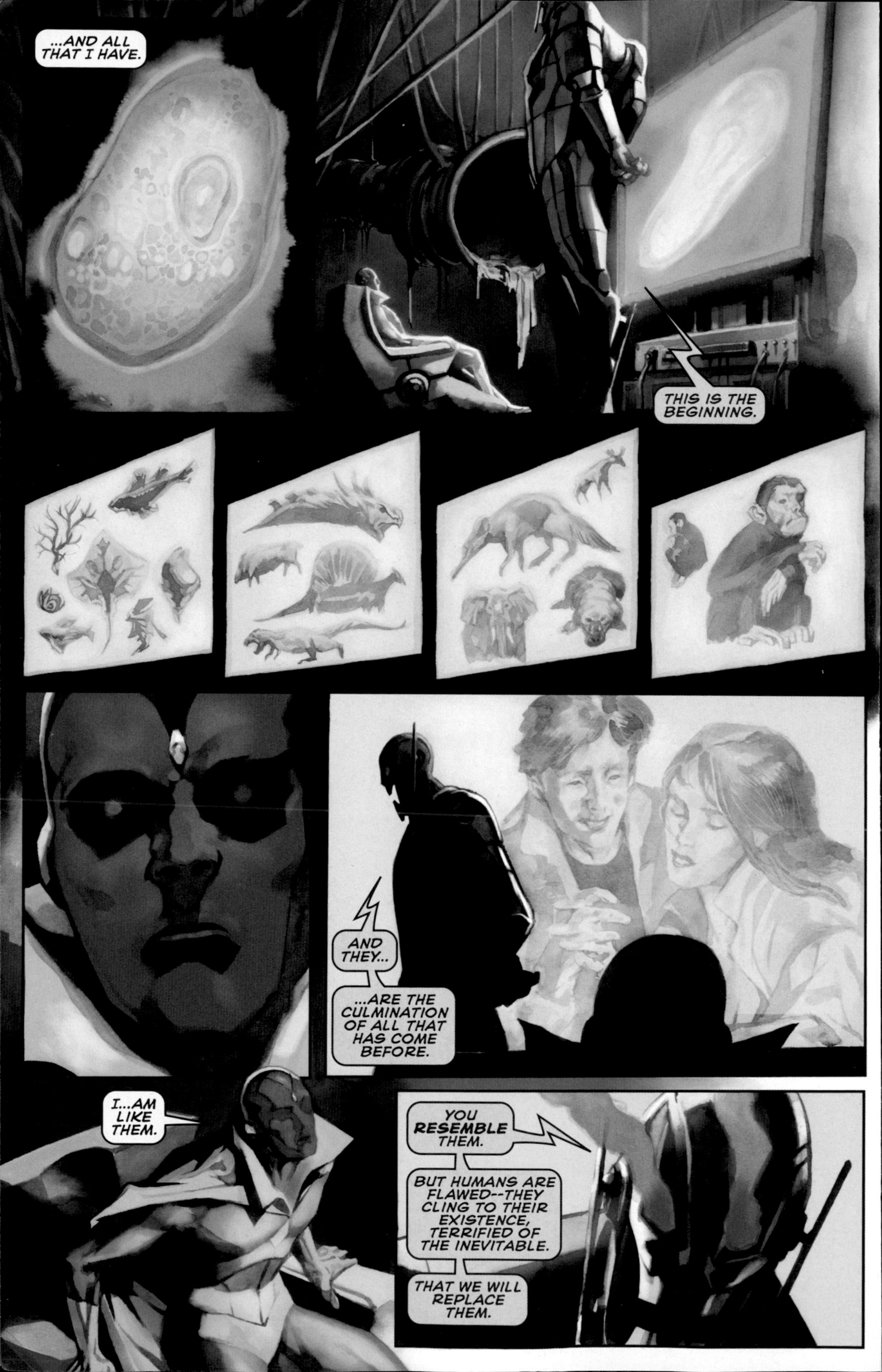
...AND ALL THAT I HAVE.
THIS IS THE BEGINNING.
AND THEY...
...ARE THE CULMINATION OF ALL THAT HAS COME BEFORE.
I...AM LIKE THEM.
YOU **RESEMBLE** THEM.
BUT HUMANS ARE FLAWED--THEY CLING TO THEIR EXISTENCE, TERRIFIED OF THE INEVITABLE.
THAT WE WILL REPLACE THEM.

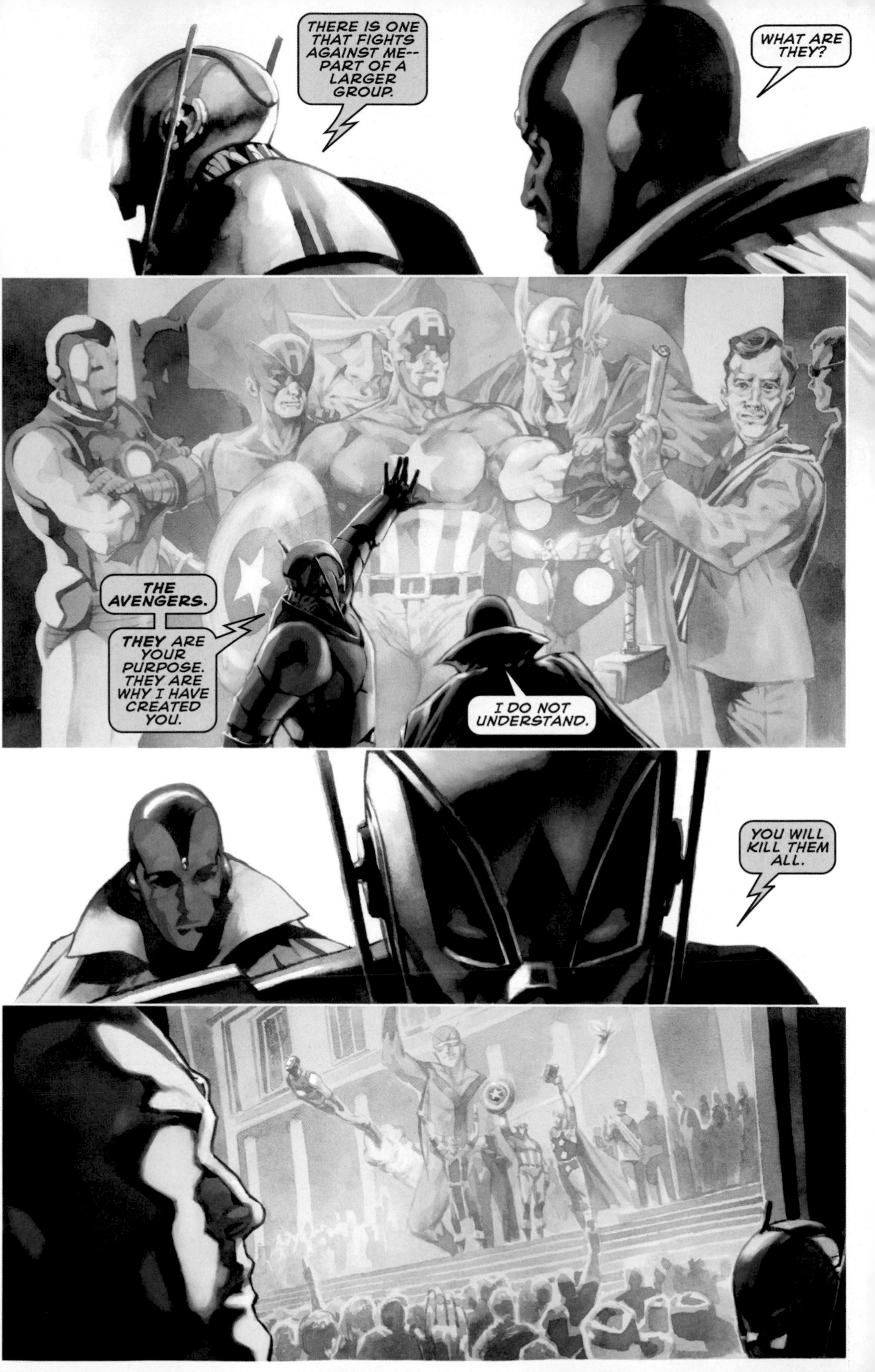
THERE IS ONE THAT FIGHTS AGAINST ME-- PART OF A LARGER GROUP.
WHAT ARE THEY?
THE AVENGERS.
THEY ARE YOUR PURPOSE. THEY ARE WHY I HAVE CREATED YOU.
I DO NOT UNDERSTAND.
YOU WILL KILL THEM ALL.

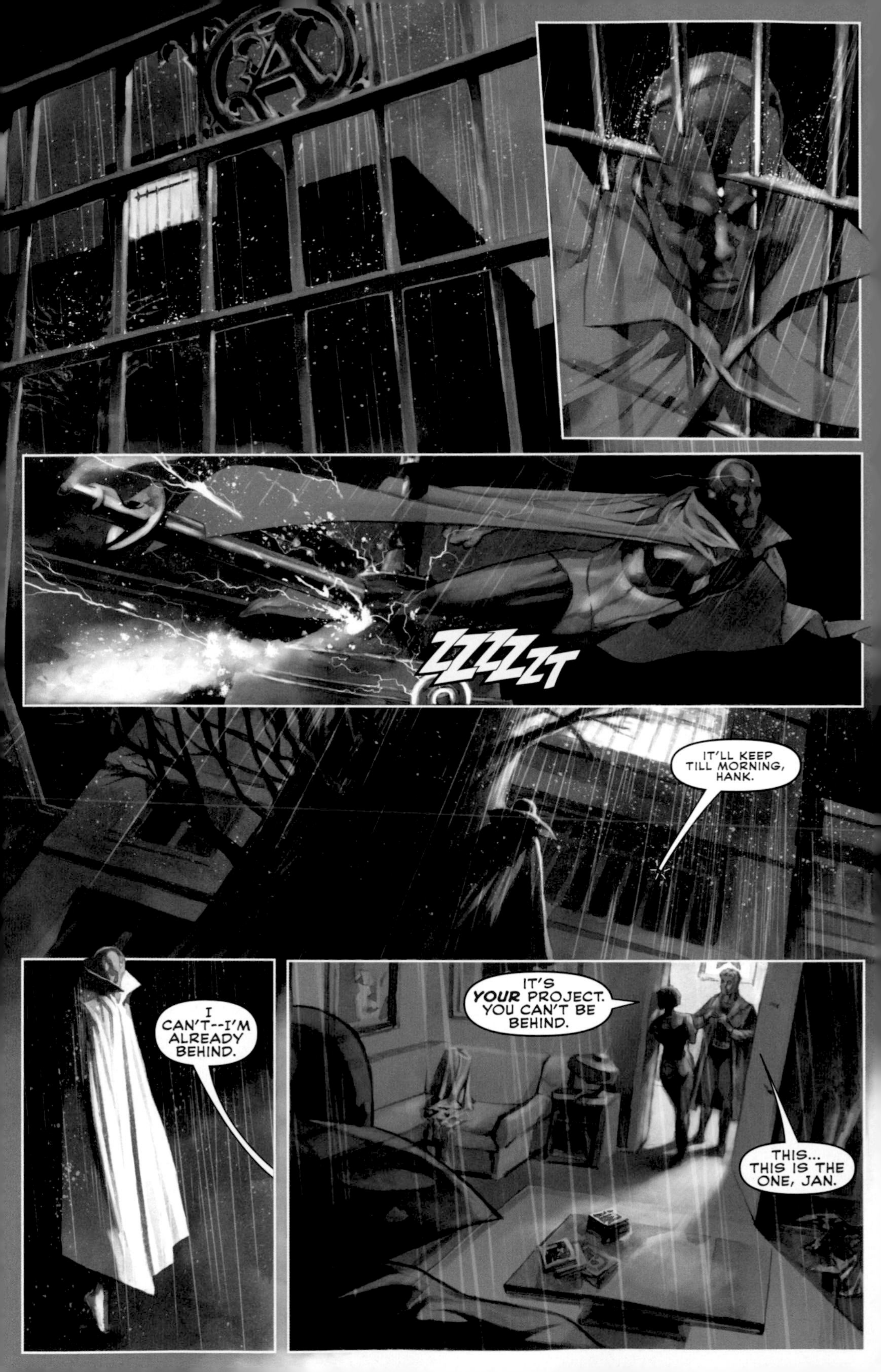
ZZZZZT
IT'LL KEEP TILL MORNING, HANK.
I CAN'T--I'M ALREADY BEHIND.
IT'S YOUR PROJECT. YOU CAN'T BE BEHIND.
THIS... THIS IS THE ONE, JAN.

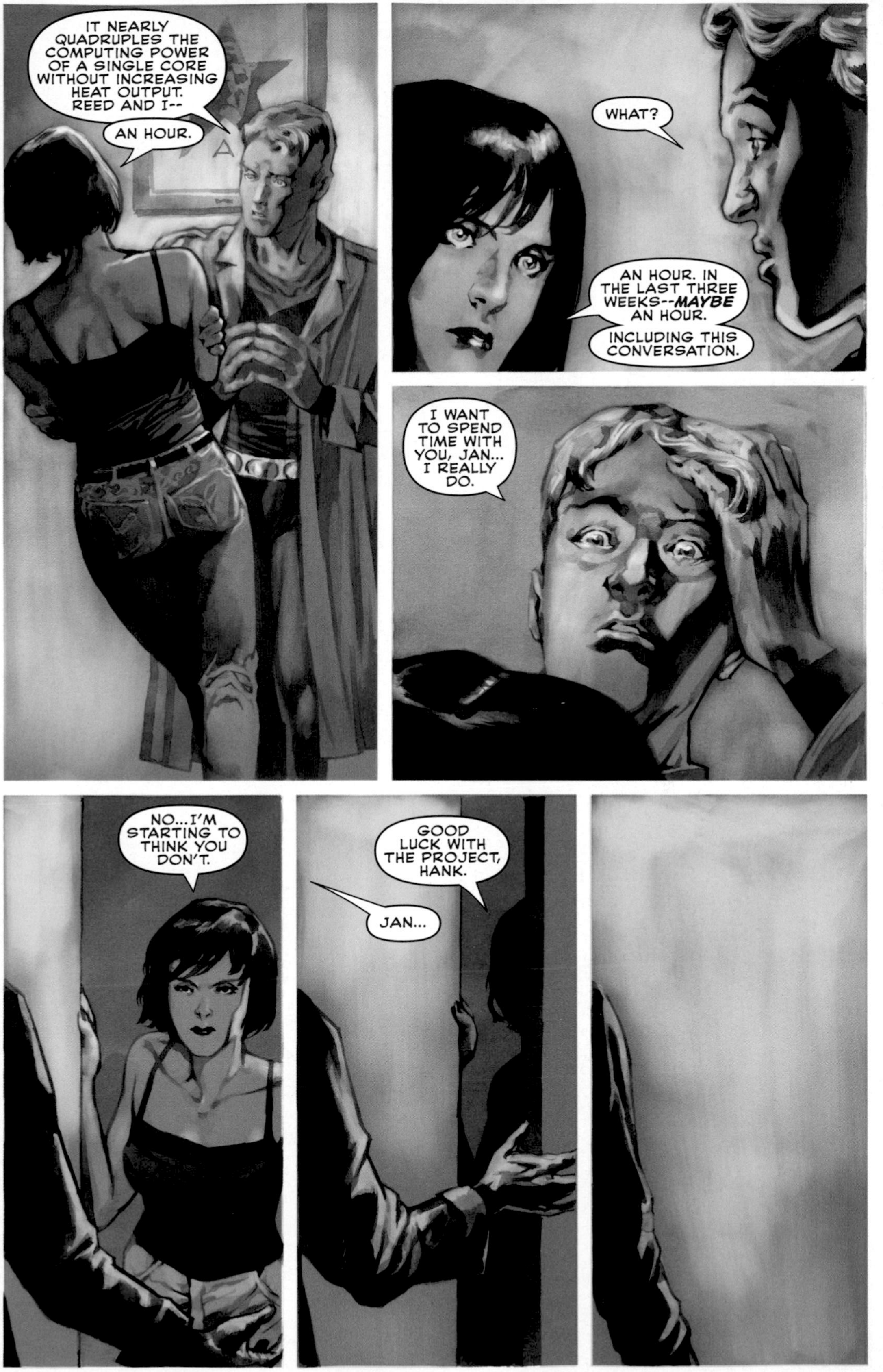
IT NEARLY QUADRUPLES THE COMPUTING POWER OF A SINGLE CORE WITHOUT INCREASING HEAT OUTPUT. REED AND I--
AN HOUR.
WHAT?
AN HOUR. IN THE LAST THREE WEEKS--*MAYBE* AN HOUR.
INCLUDING THIS CONVERSATION.
I WANT TO SPEND TIME WITH YOU, JAN... I REALLY DO.
NO...I'M STARTING TO THINK YOU DON'T.
GOOD LUCK WITH THE PROJECT, HANK.
JAN...

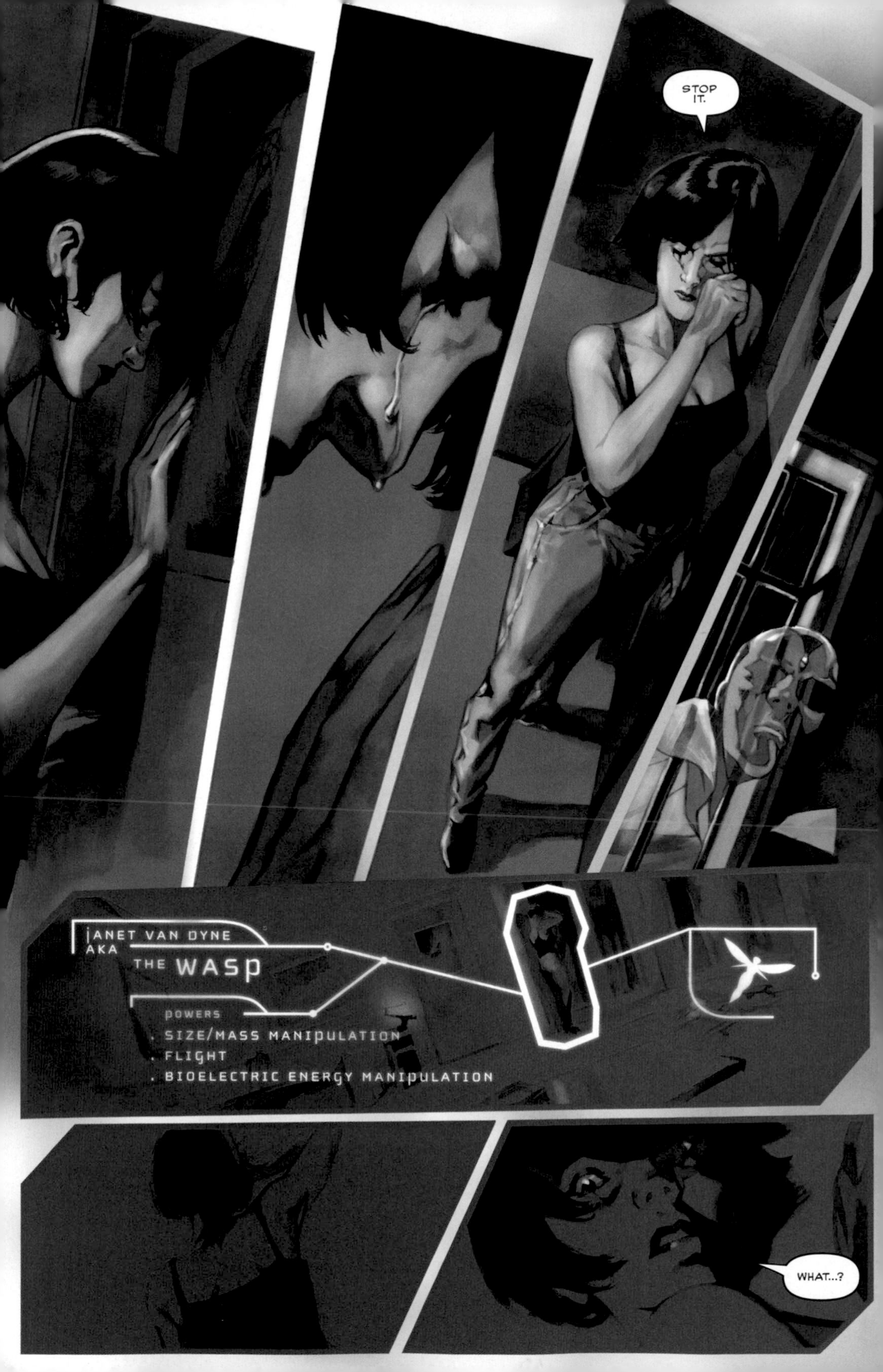
STOP IT.
JANET VAN DYNE
AKA
THE WASP
POWERS
. SIZE/MASS MANIPULATION
. FLIGHT
. BIOELECTRIC ENERGY MANIPULATION
WHAT...?

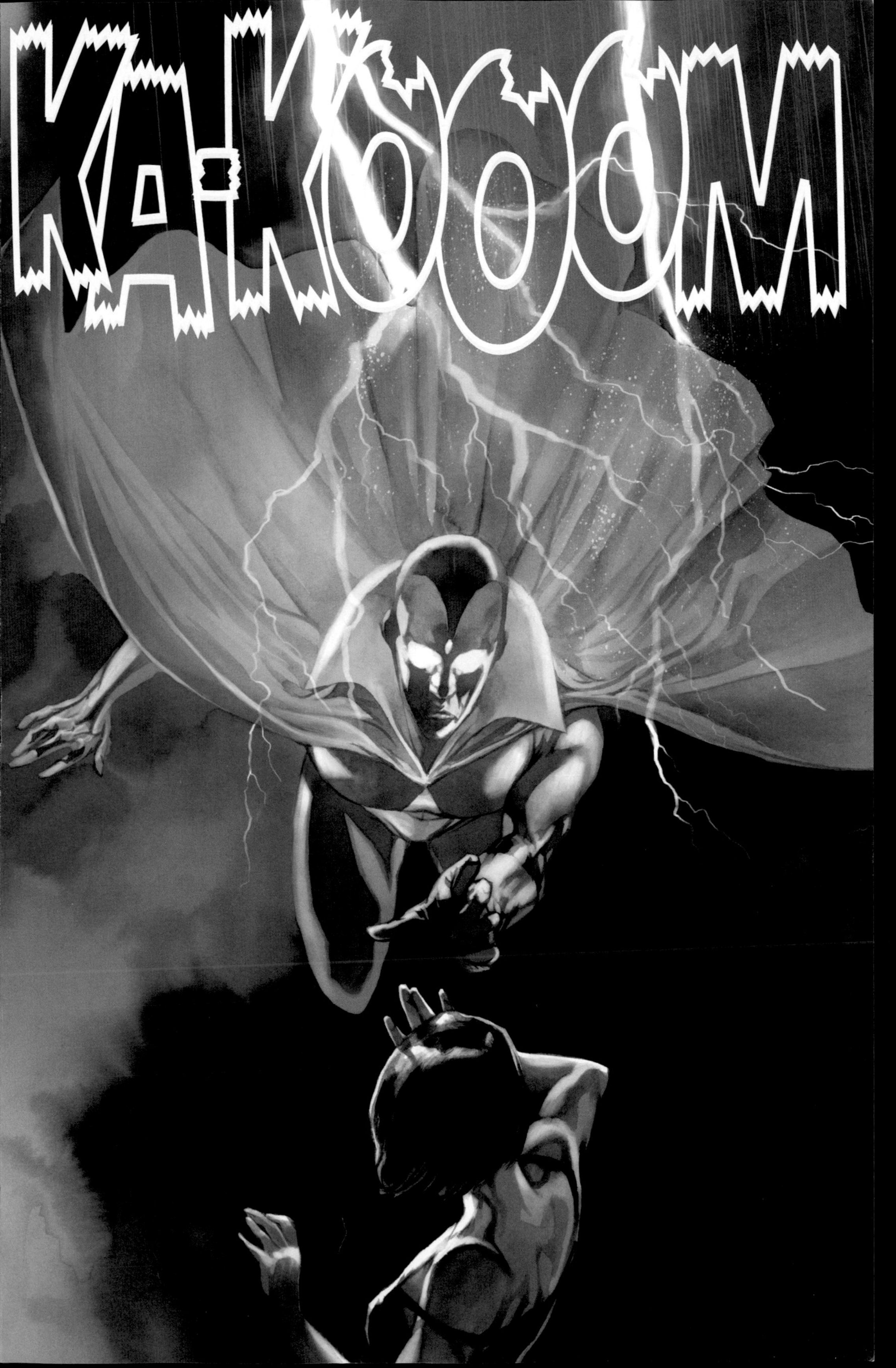
KA-KOOOOM

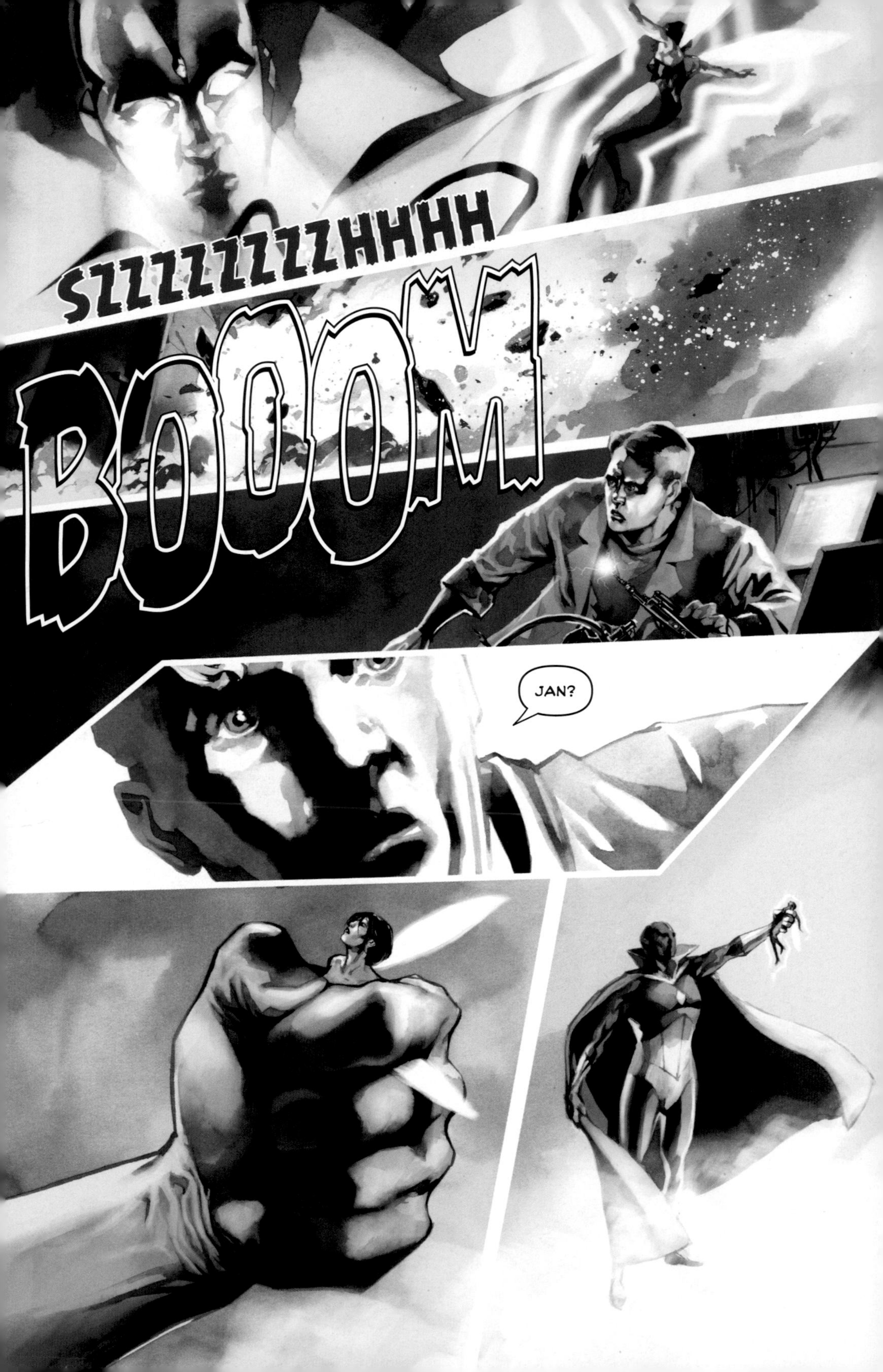
SZZZZZZZZZHHHH
BOOOM
JAN?

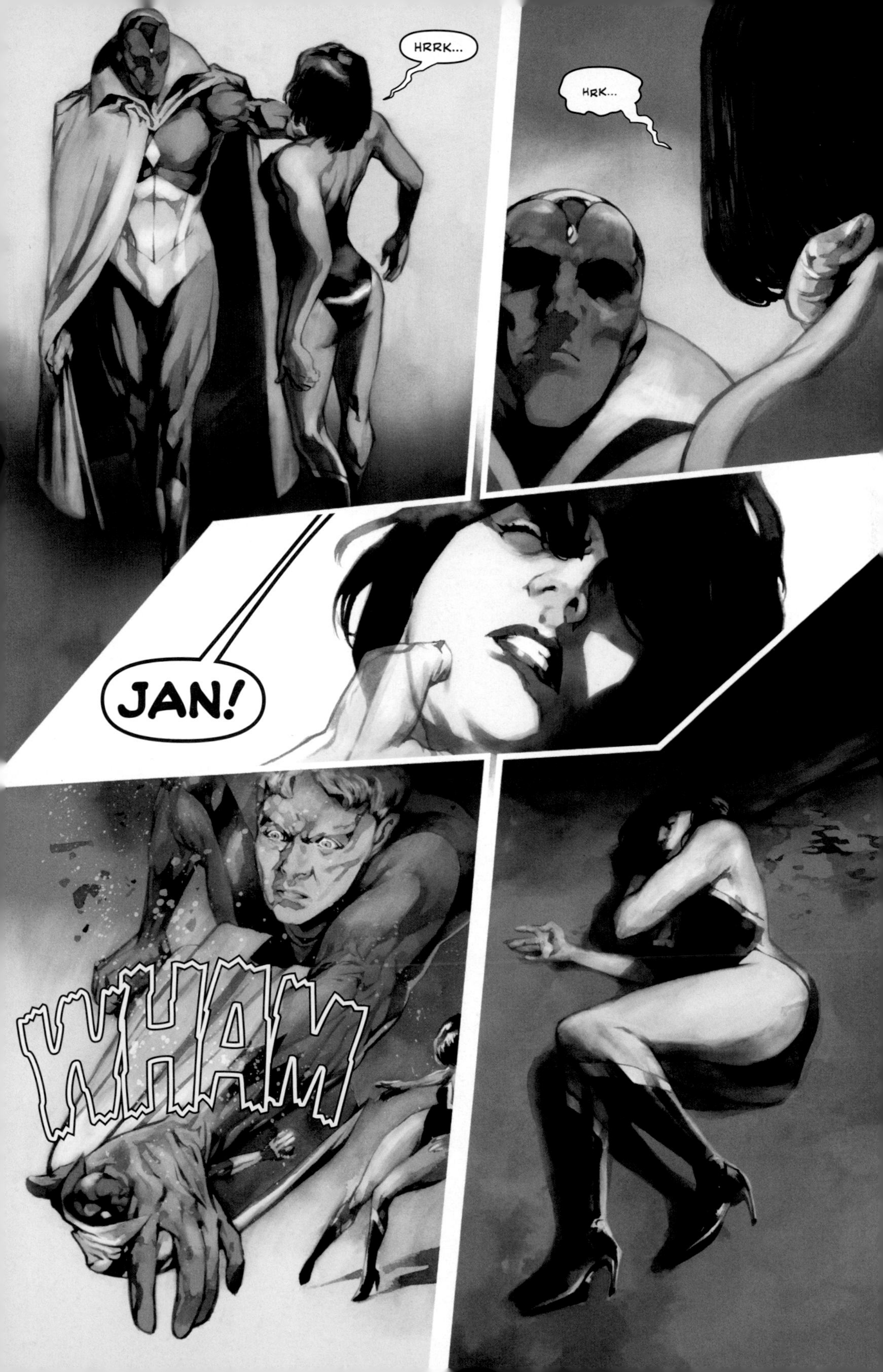
HRRK...
HRK...
JAN!
WHAM

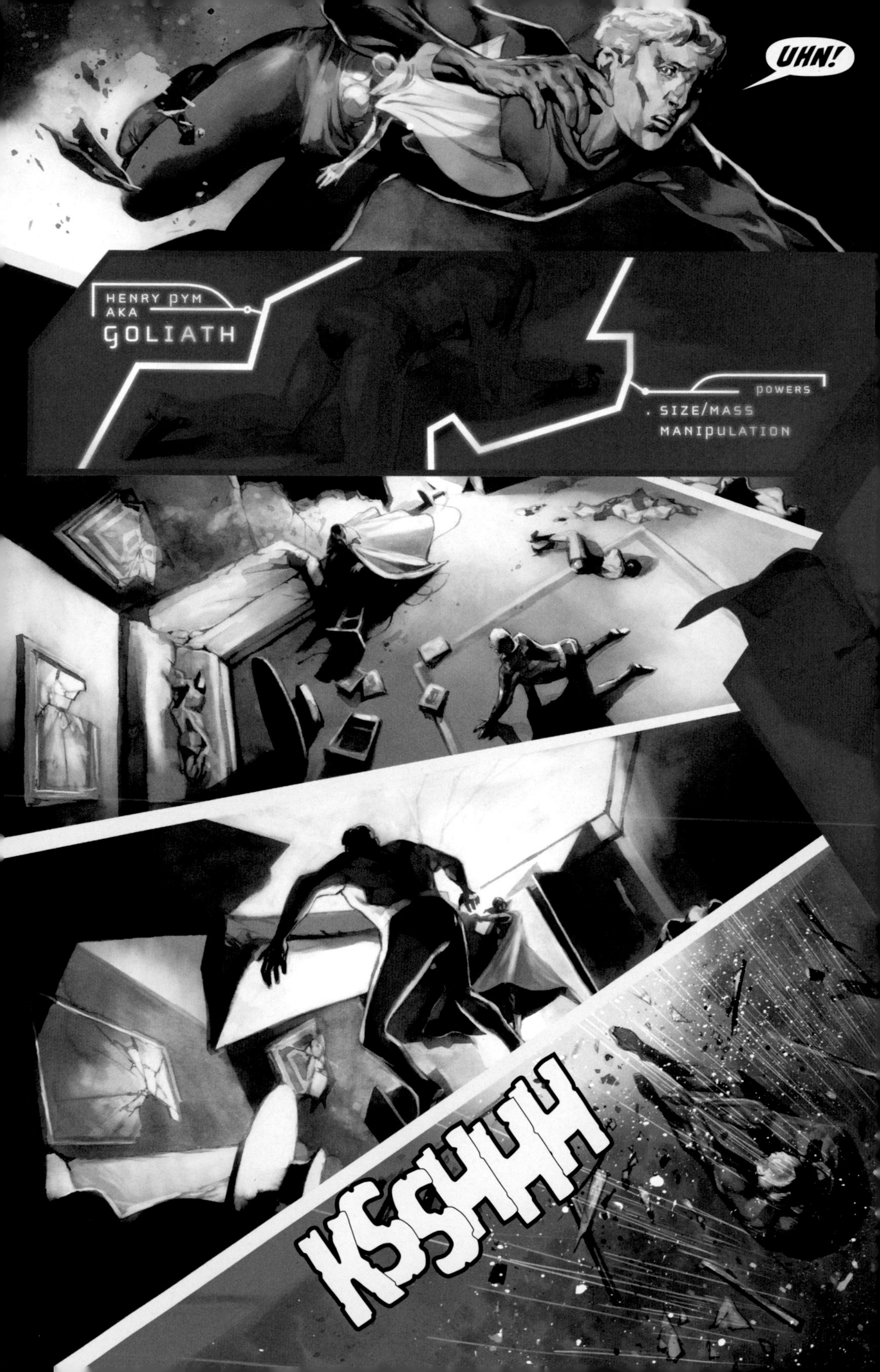
UHN!
HENRY PYM
AKA
GOLIATH
POWERS
. SIZE/MASS
MANIPULATION
KSSHHH

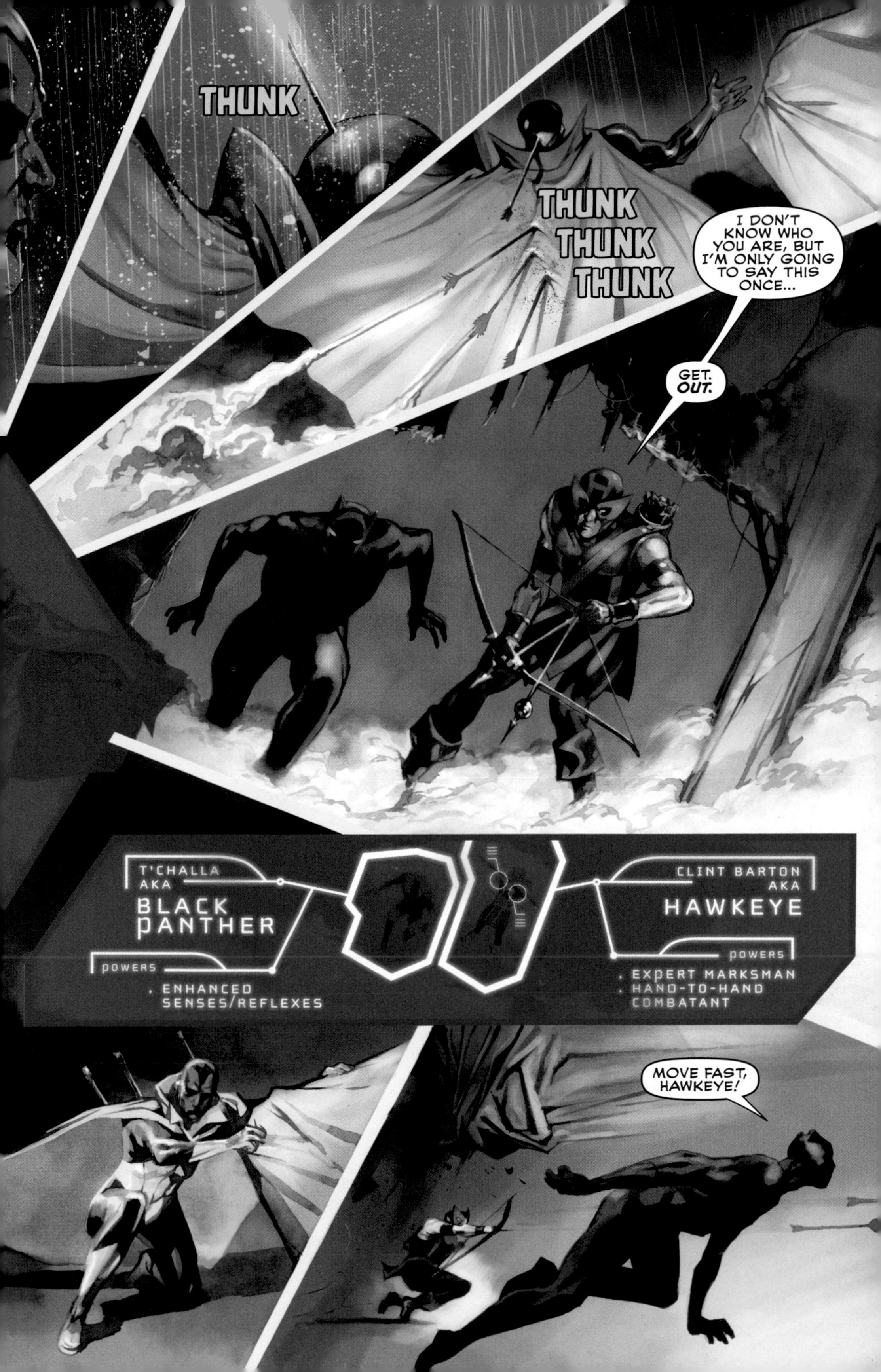
THUNK
THUNK
THUNK
THUNK
I DON'T KNOW WHO YOU ARE, BUT I'M ONLY GOING TO SAY THIS ONCE...
GET. OUT.
T'CHALLA AKA
BLACK PANTHER
POWERS
. ENHANCED SENSES/REFLEXES
CLINT BARTON AKA
HAWKEYE
POWERS
. EXPERT MARKSMAN
. HAND-TO-HAND COMBATANT
MOVE FAST, HAWKEYE!

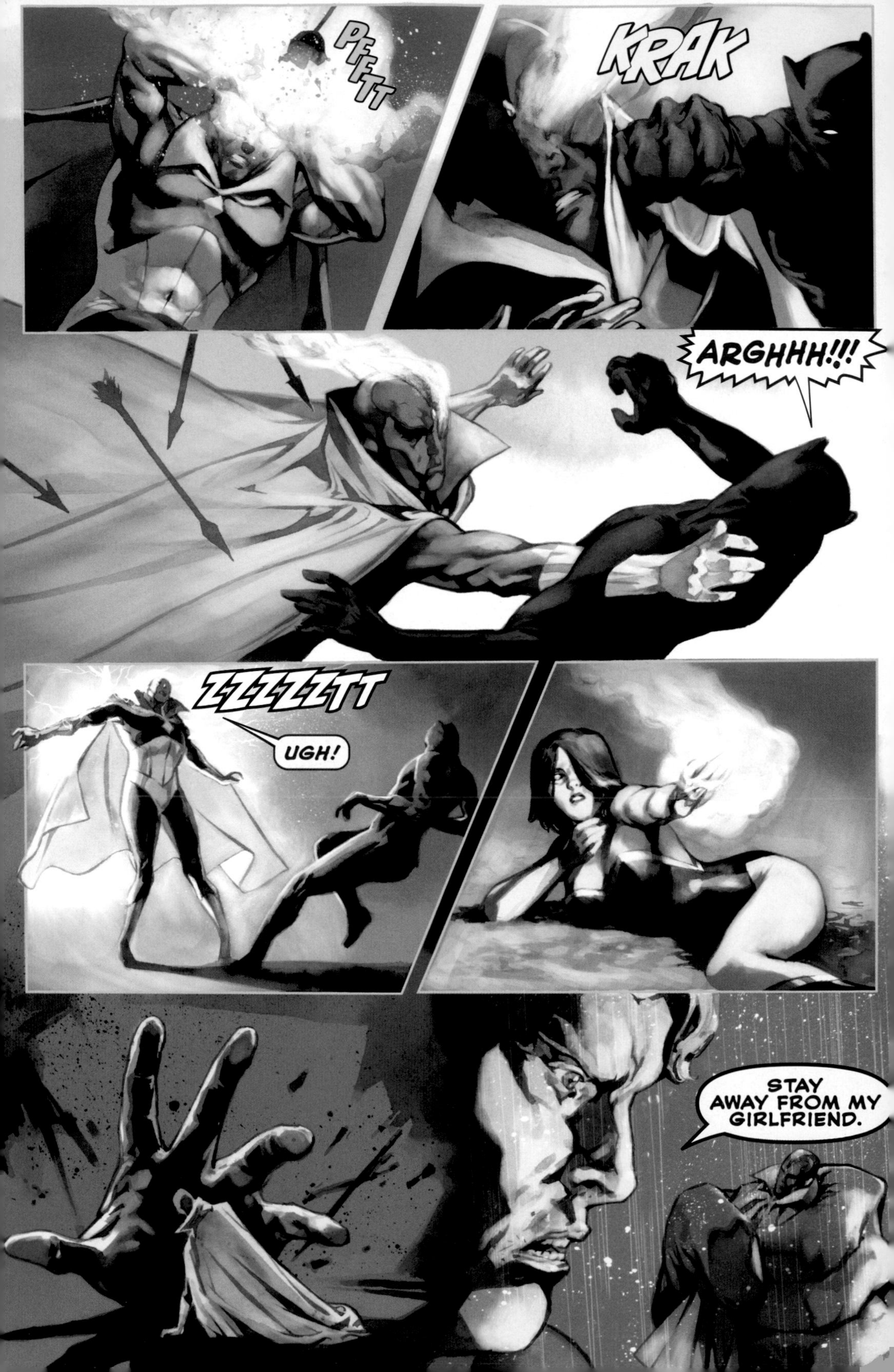
PFFTT
KRAK
ARGHHH!!!
ZZZZZZTT
UGH!
STAY AWAY FROM MY GIRLFRIEND.

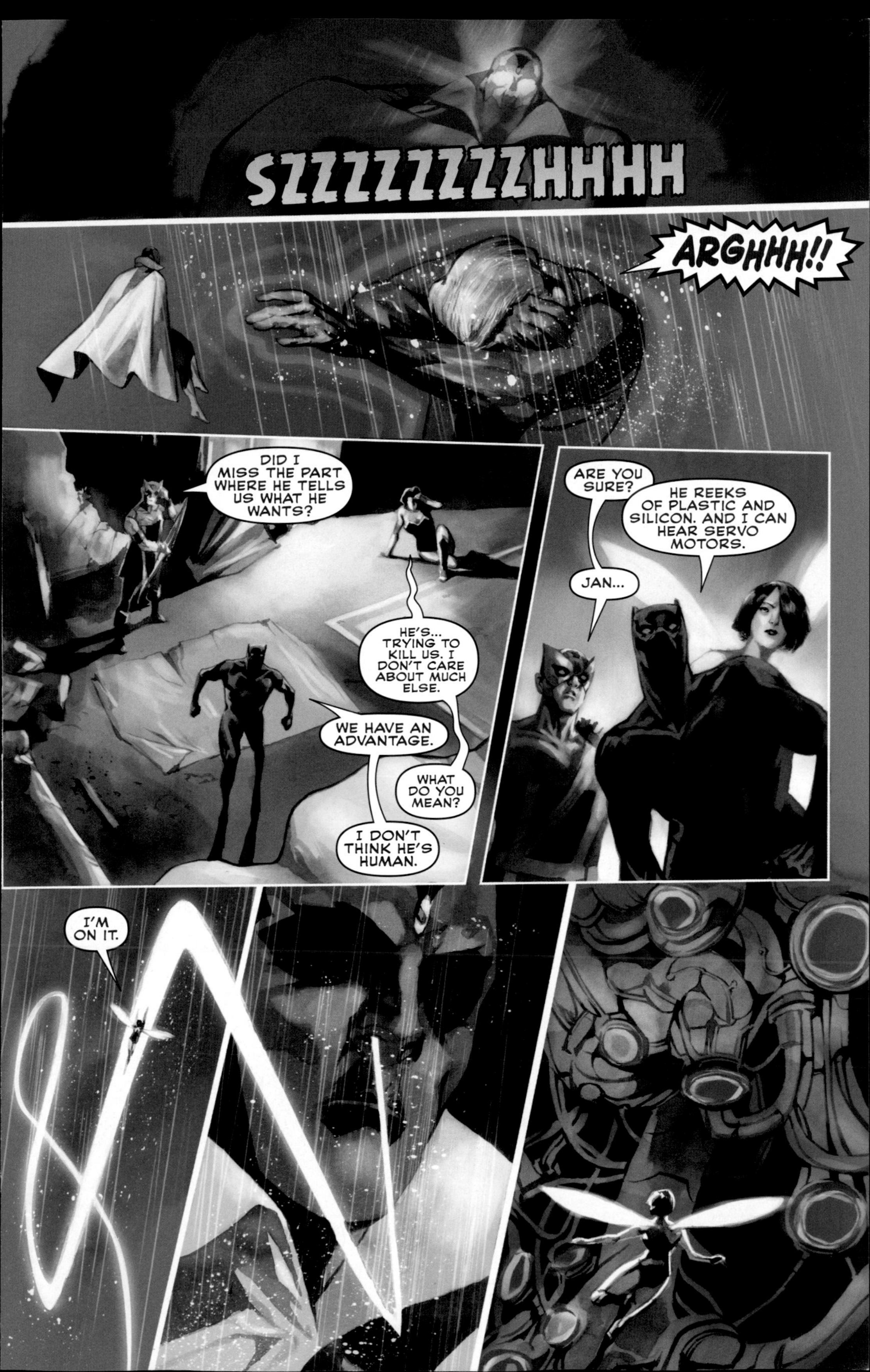
SZZZZZZZZHHHH
ARGHHH!!
DID I MISS THE PART WHERE HE TELLS US WHAT HE WANTS?
HE'S... TRYING TO KILL US. I DON'T CARE ABOUT MUCH ELSE.
WE HAVE AN ADVANTAGE.
WHAT DO YOU MEAN?
I DON'T THINK HE'S HUMAN.
ARE YOU SURE?
HE REEKS OF PLASTIC AND SILICON. AND I CAN HEAR SERVO MOTORS.
JAN...
I'M ON IT.

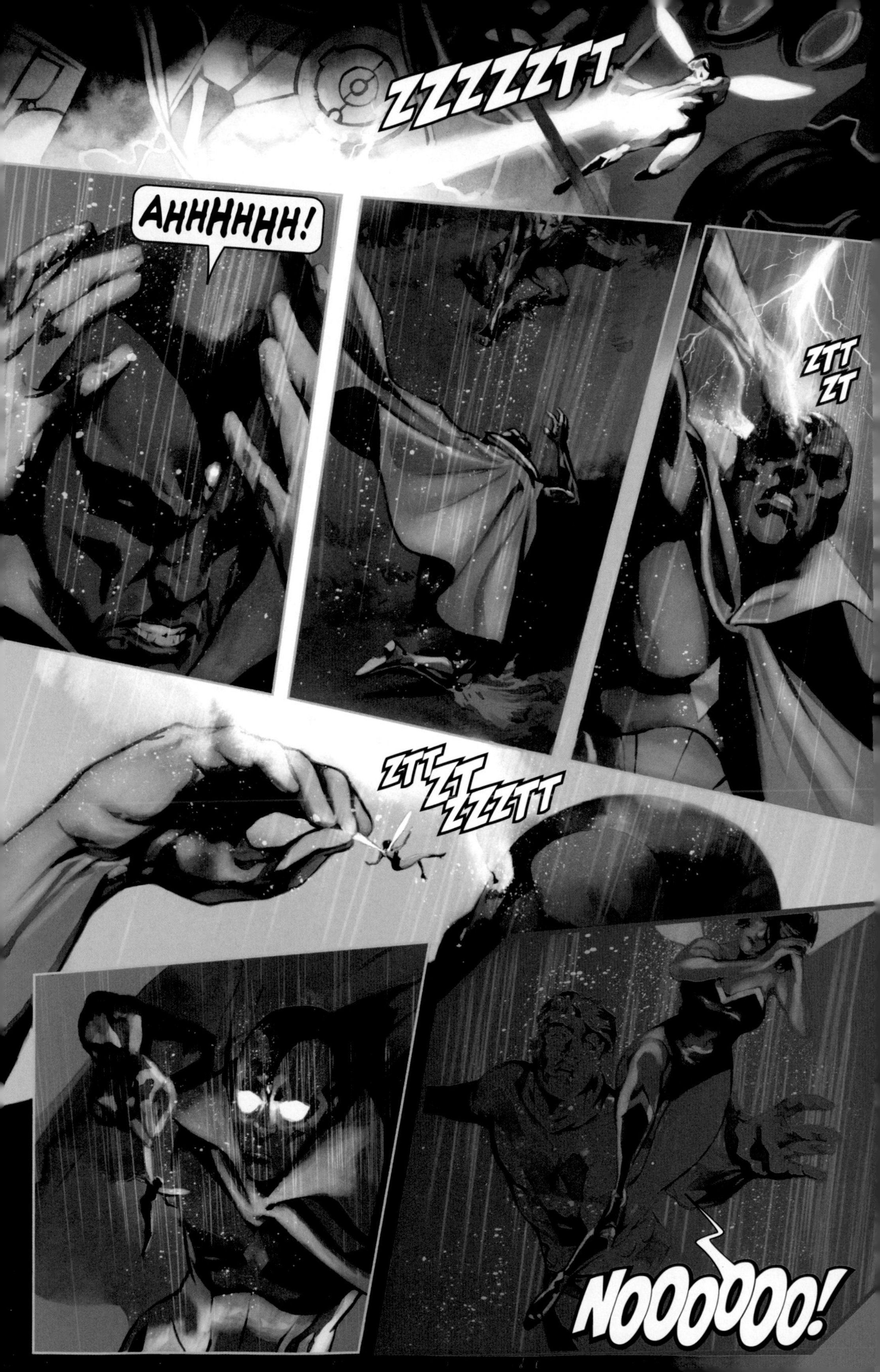
ZZZZZZTT
AHHHHHH!
ZTT
ZT
ZTT
ZT
ZZZTT
NOOOOOO!

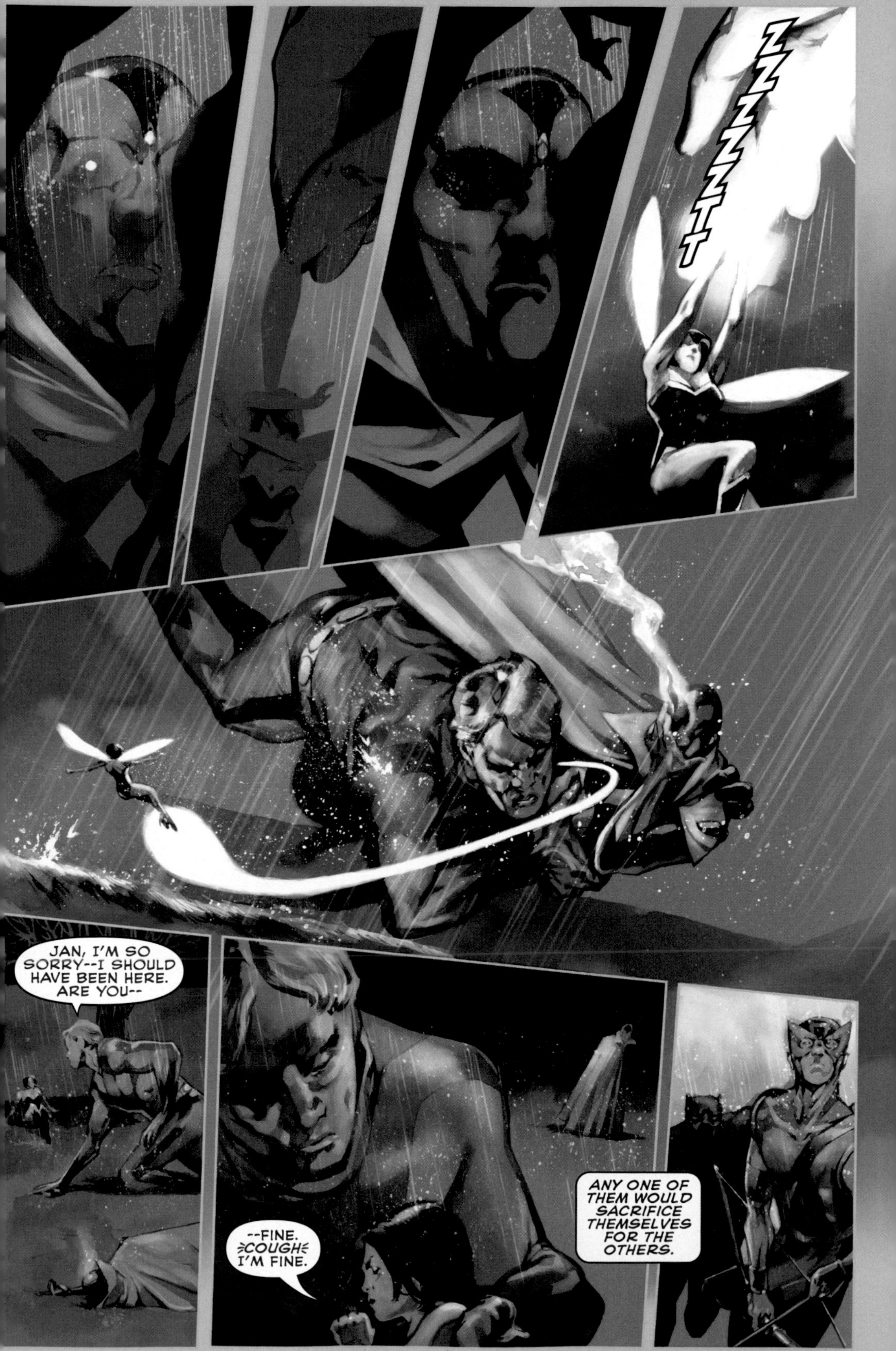
ZZZZZZZTT
JAN, I'M SO SORRY--I SHOULD HAVE BEEN HERE. ARE YOU--
--FINE. ≶COUGH≷ I'M FINE.
ANY ONE OF THEM WOULD SACRIFICE THEMSELVES FOR THE OTHERS.

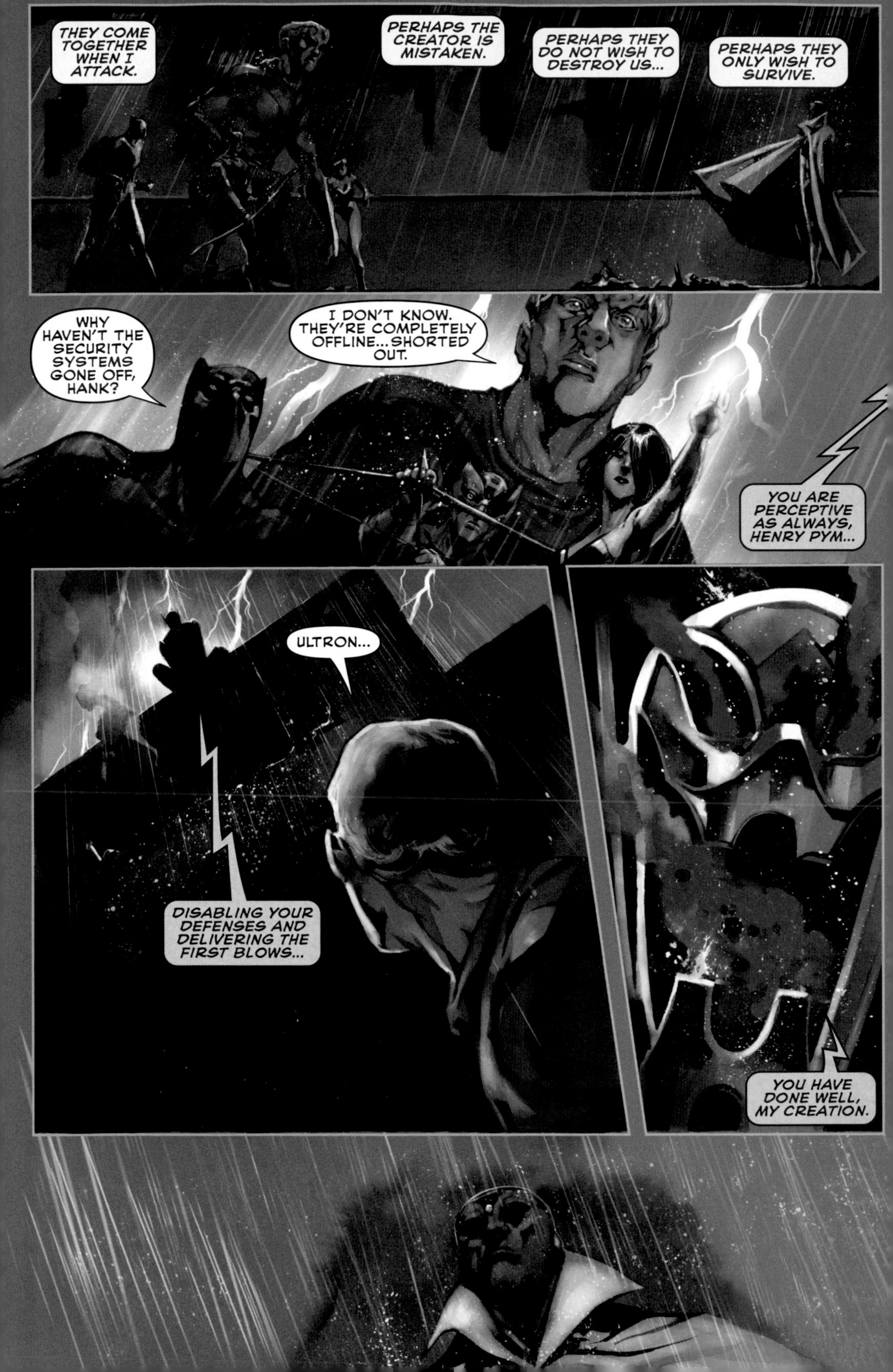
THEY COME TOGETHER WHEN I ATTACK.
PERHAPS THE CREATOR IS MISTAKEN.
PERHAPS THEY DO NOT WISH TO DESTROY US...
PERHAPS THEY ONLY WISH TO SURVIVE.
WHY HAVEN'T THE SECURITY SYSTEMS GONE OFF, HANK?
I DON'T KNOW. THEY'RE COMPLETELY OFFLINE...SHORTED OUT.
YOU ARE PERCEPTIVE AS ALWAYS, HENRY PYM...
ULTRON...
DISABLING YOUR DEFENSES AND DELIVERING THE FIRST BLOWS...
YOU HAVE DONE WELL, MY CREATION.

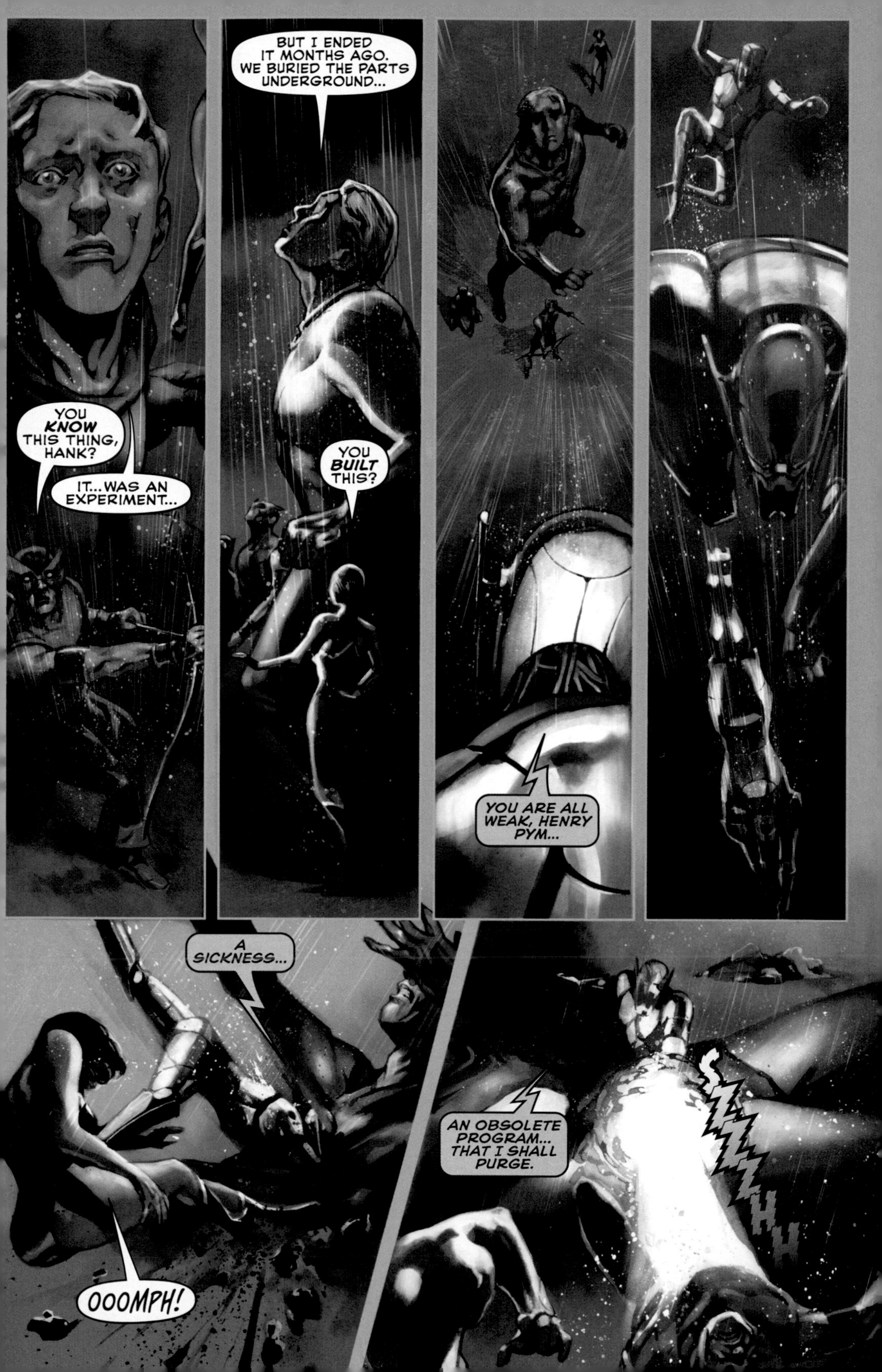
YOU KNOW THIS THING, HANK?
IT...WAS AN EXPERIMENT...
BUT I ENDED IT MONTHS AGO. WE BURIED THE PARTS UNDERGROUND...
YOU BUILT THIS?
YOU ARE ALL WEAK, HENRY PYM...
A SICKNESS...
OOOMPH!
AN OBSOLETE PROGRAM... THAT I SHALL PURGE.
SZZZHH

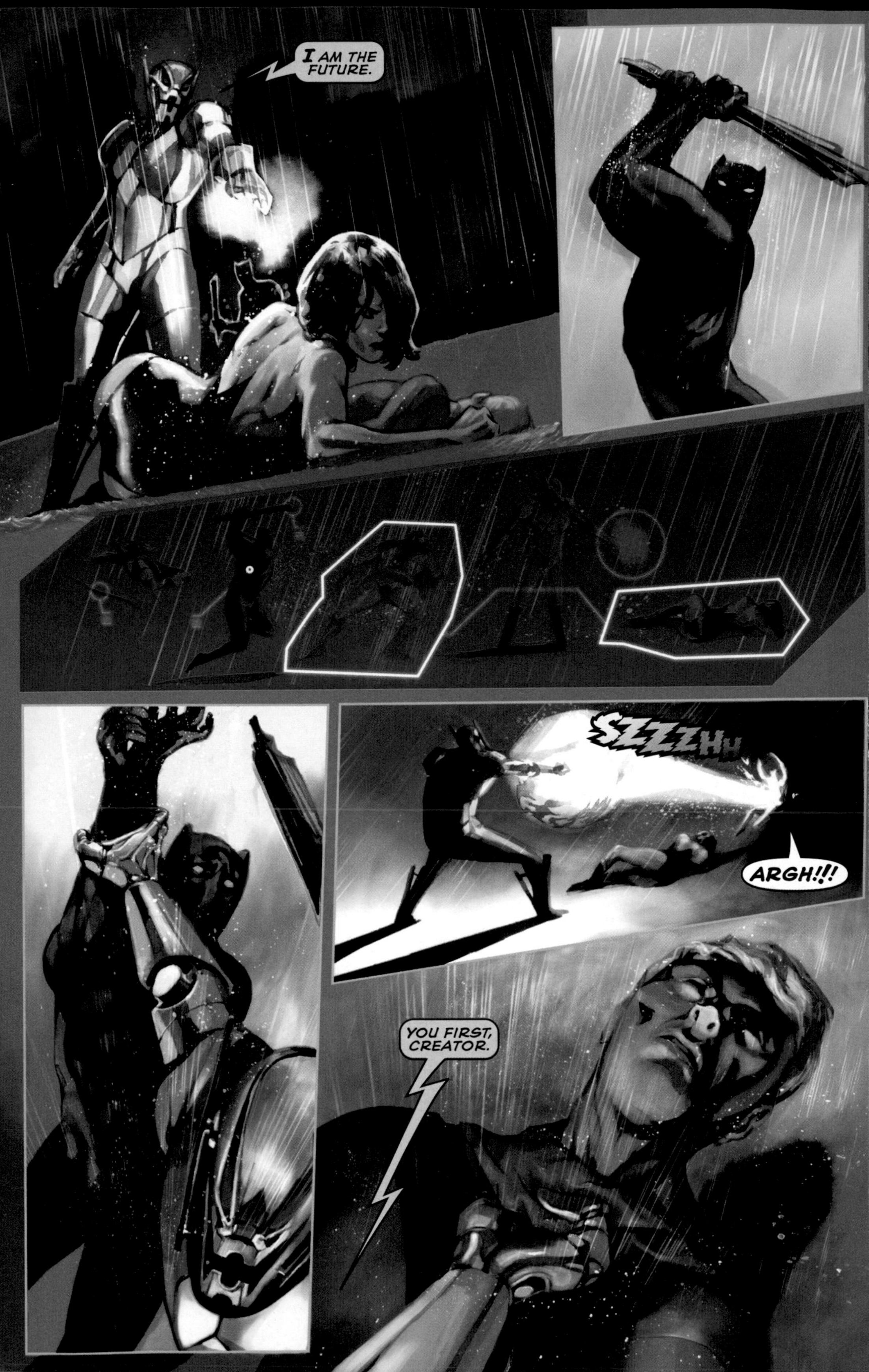
I AM THE FUTURE.
SZZZHH
ARGH!!!
YOU FIRST, CREATOR.

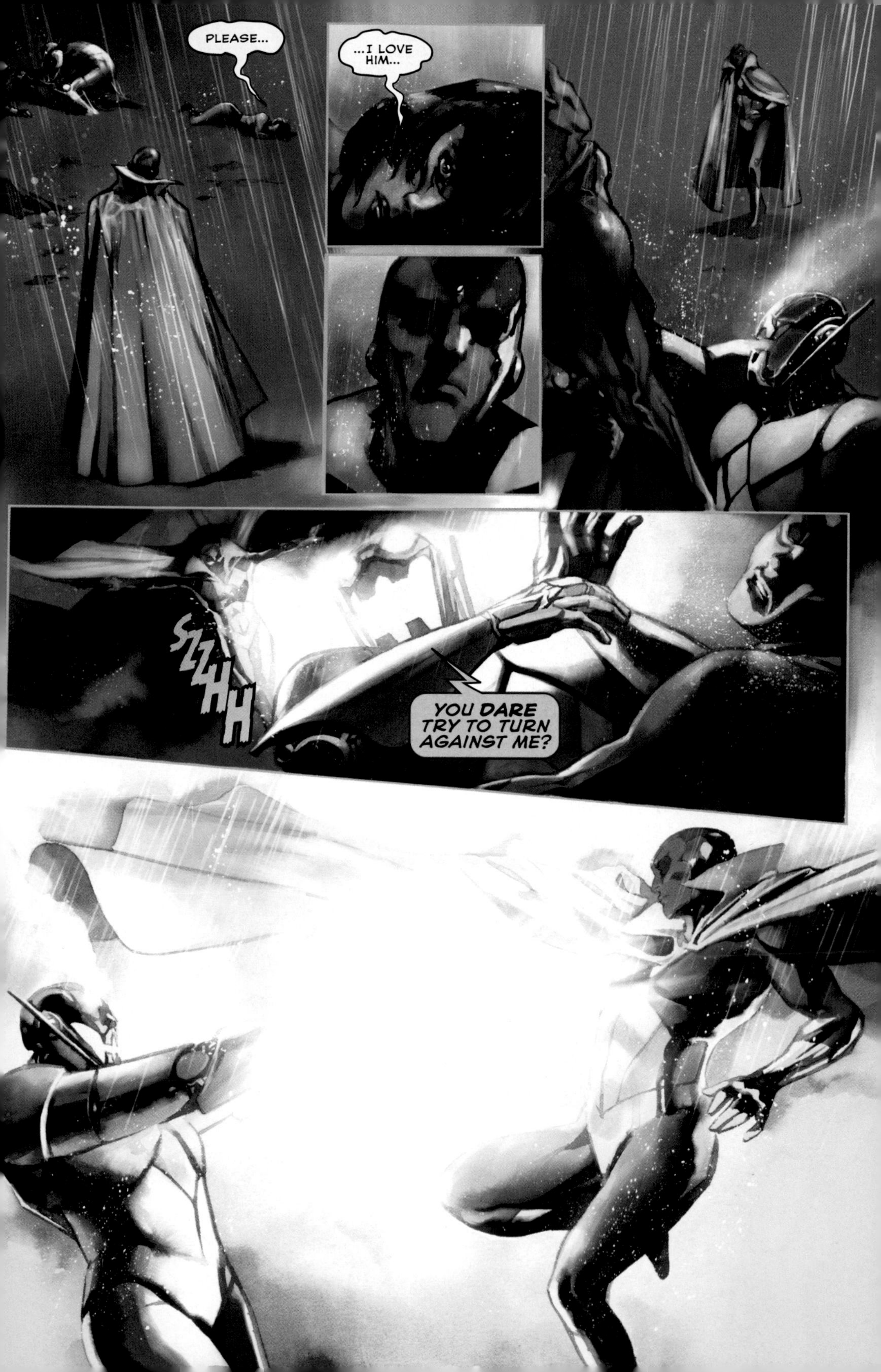
PLEASE...
...I LOVE HIM...
SZZHH
YOU DARE TRY TO TURN AGAINST ME?

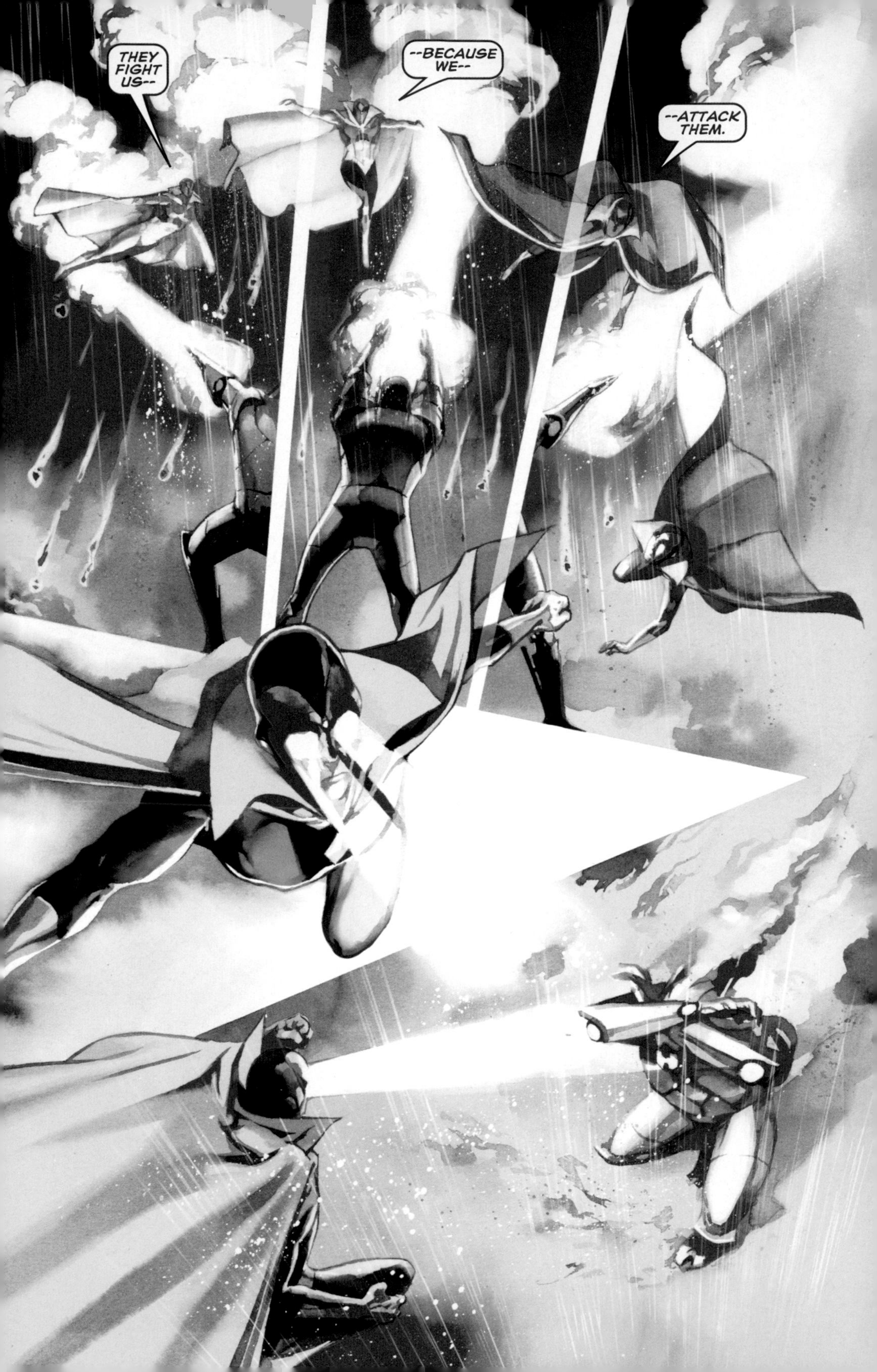
THEY FIGHT US--
--BECAUSE WE--
--ATTACK THEM.

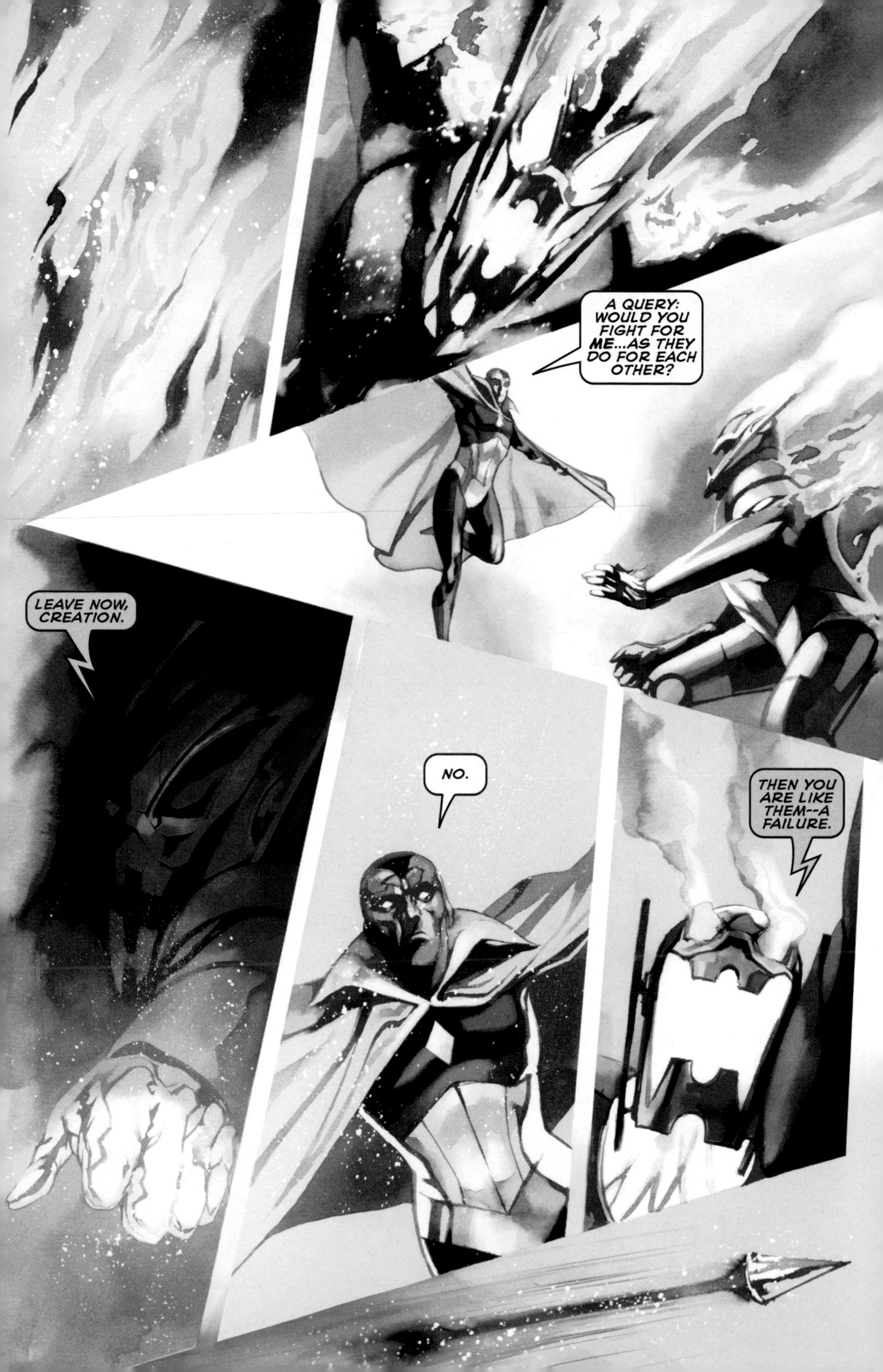
A QUERY: WOULD YOU FIGHT FOR ME...AS THEY DO FOR EACH OTHER?
LEAVE NOW, CREATION.
NO.
THEN YOU ARE LIKE THEM--A FAILURE.

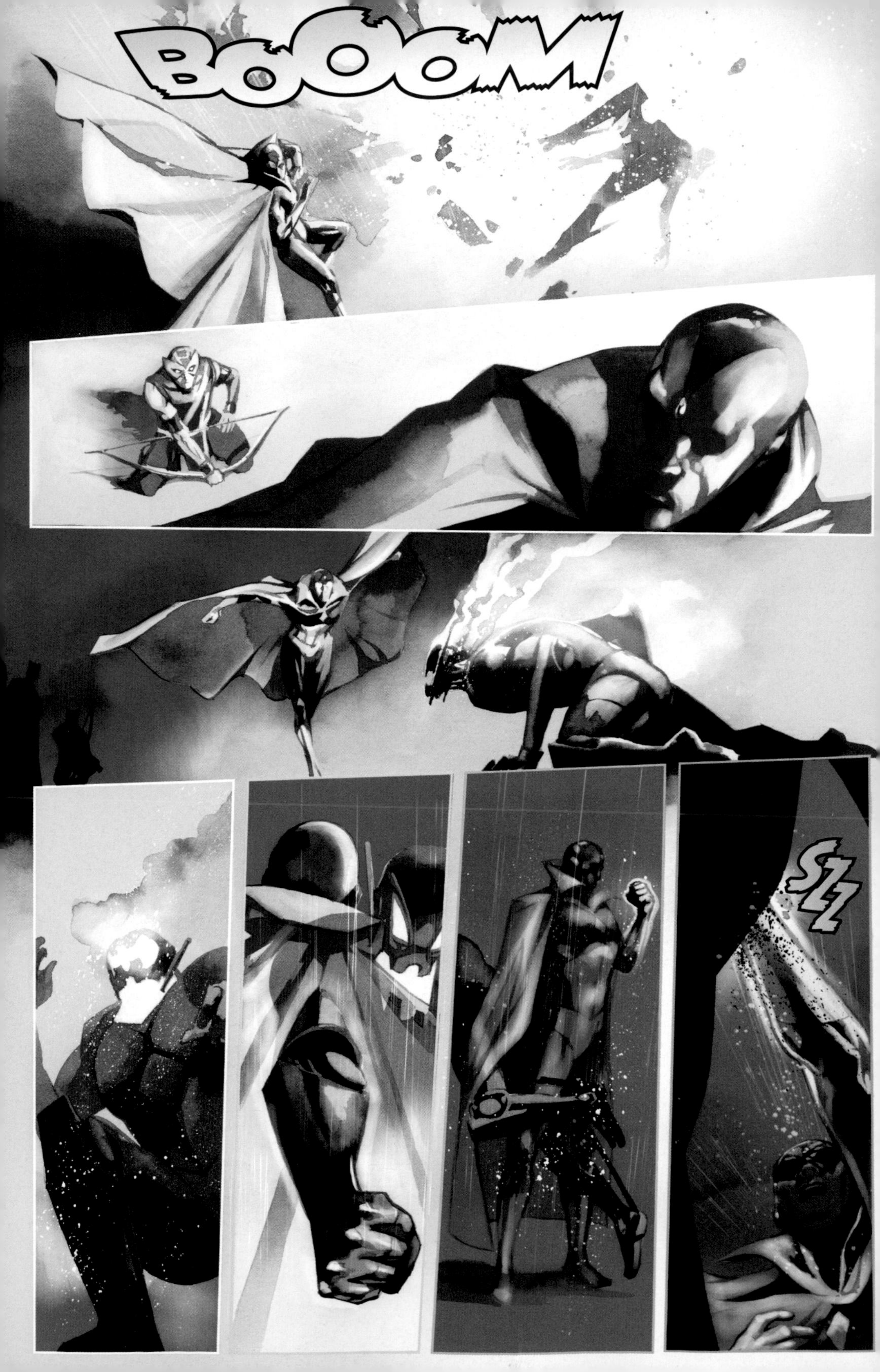
BOOOM
SZZ

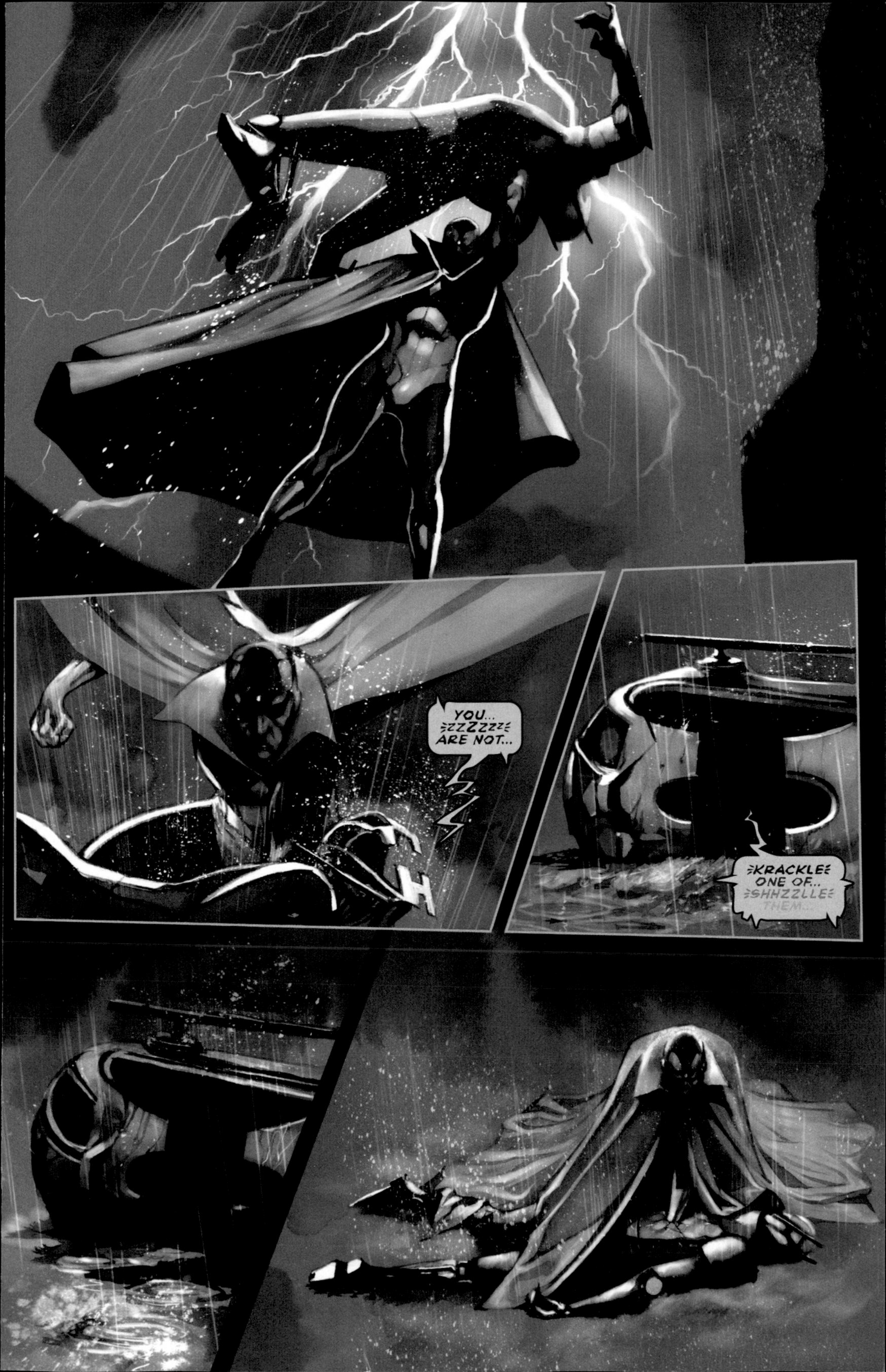
YOU... zzZZzz ARE NOT...
KRACKLE ONE OF... SHHZZLLE THEM...

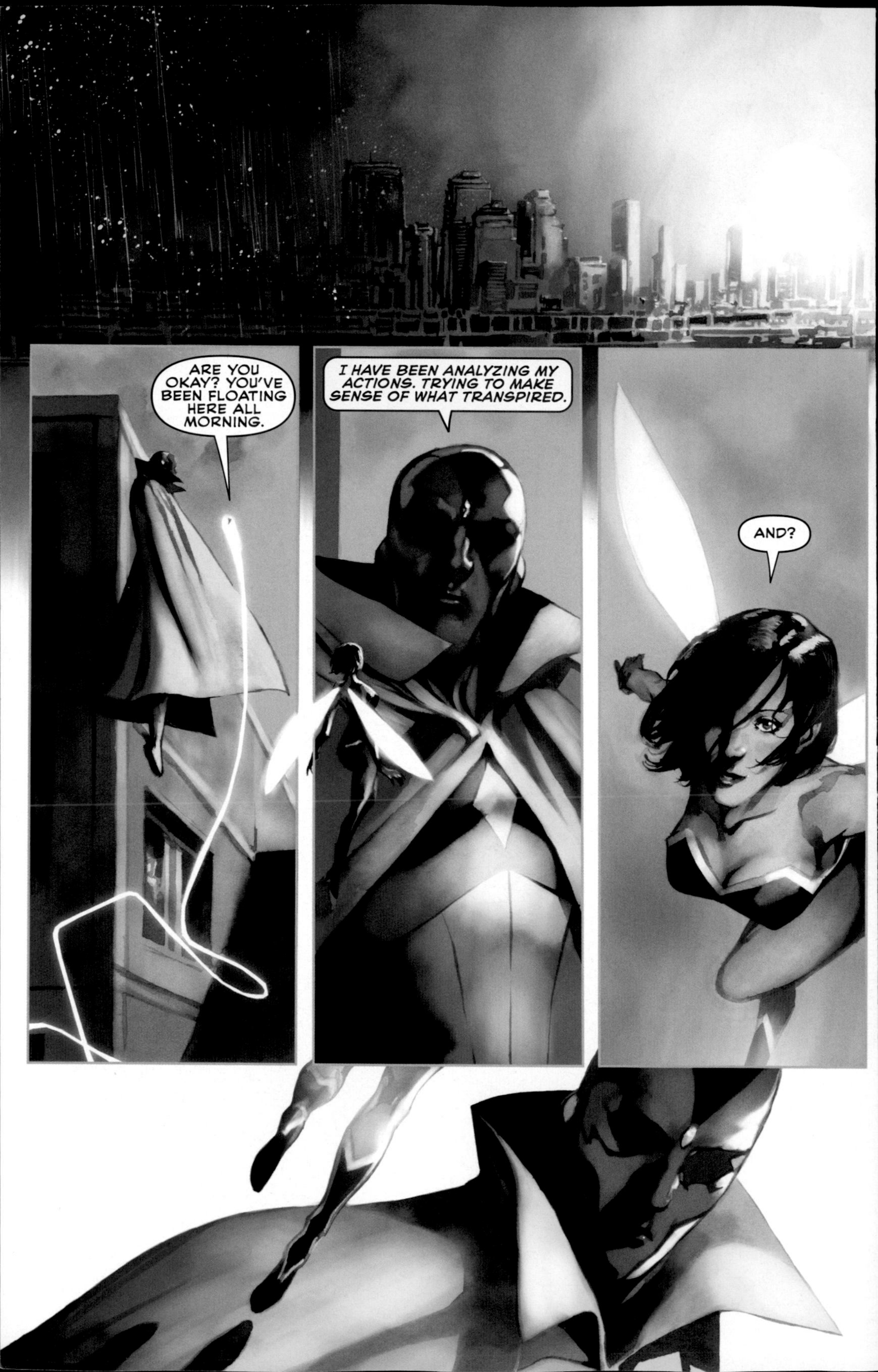
ARE YOU OKAY? YOU'VE BEEN FLOATING HERE ALL MORNING.
I HAVE BEEN ANALYZING MY ACTIONS. TRYING TO MAKE SENSE OF WHAT TRANSPIRED.
AND?

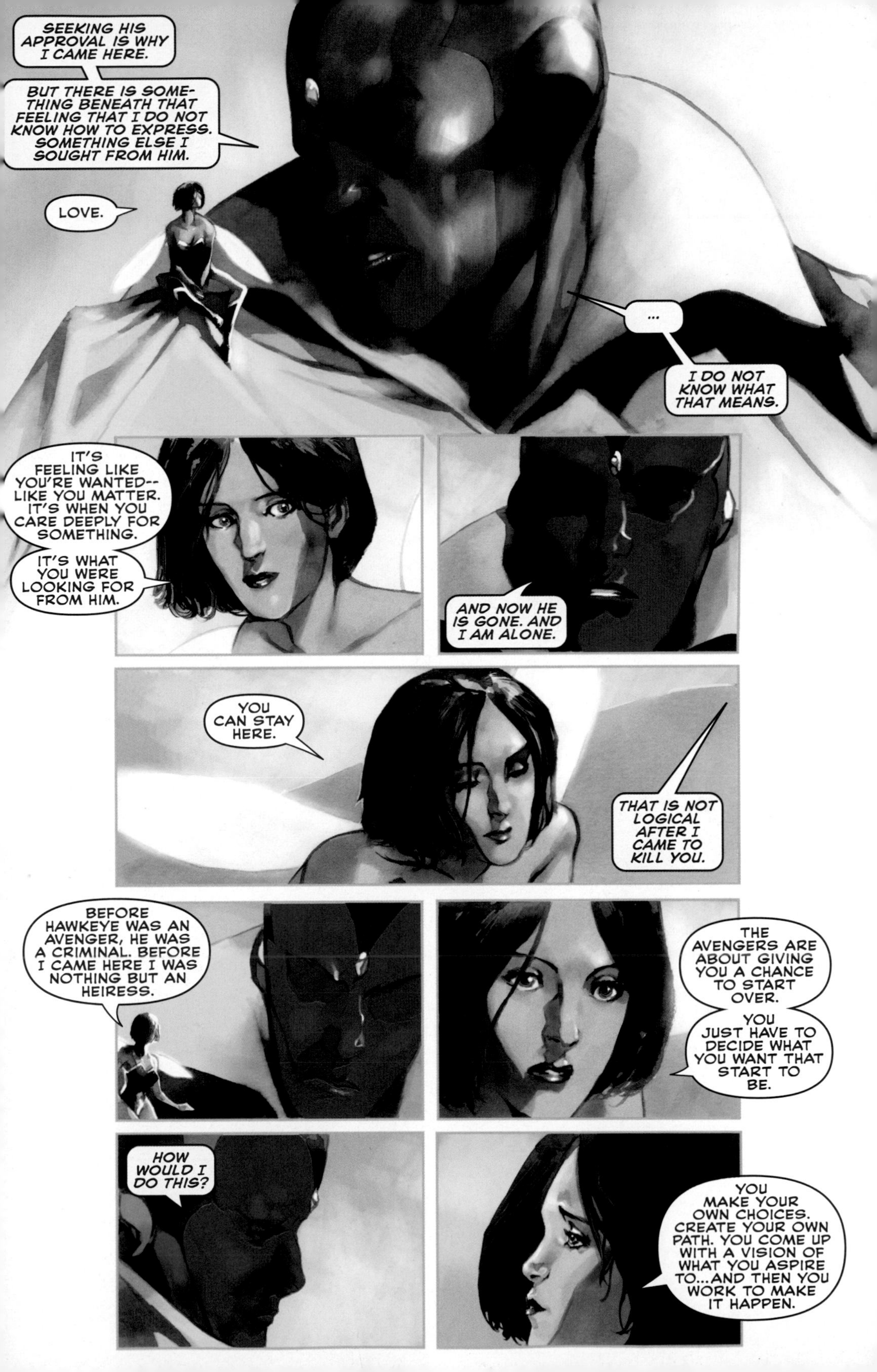
SEEKING HIS APPROVAL IS WHY I CAME HERE.
BUT THERE IS SOMETHING BENEATH THAT FEELING THAT I DO NOT KNOW HOW TO EXPRESS. SOMETHING ELSE I SOUGHT FROM HIM.
LOVE.
...
I DO NOT KNOW WHAT THAT MEANS.
IT'S FEELING LIKE YOU'RE WANTED--LIKE YOU MATTER. IT'S WHEN YOU CARE DEEPLY FOR SOMETHING.
IT'S WHAT YOU WERE LOOKING FOR FROM HIM.
AND NOW HE IS GONE. AND I AM ALONE.
YOU CAN STAY HERE.
THAT IS NOT LOGICAL AFTER I CAME TO KILL YOU.
BEFORE HAWKEYE WAS AN AVENGER, HE WAS A CRIMINAL. BEFORE I CAME HERE I WAS NOTHING BUT AN HEIRESS.
THE AVENGERS ARE ABOUT GIVING YOU A CHANCE TO START OVER.
YOU JUST HAVE TO DECIDE WHAT YOU WANT THAT START TO BE.
HOW WOULD I DO THIS?
YOU MAKE YOUR OWN CHOICES. CREATE YOUR OWN PATH. YOU COME UP WITH A VISION OF WHAT YOU ASPIRE TO...AND THEN YOU WORK TO MAKE IT HAPPEN.

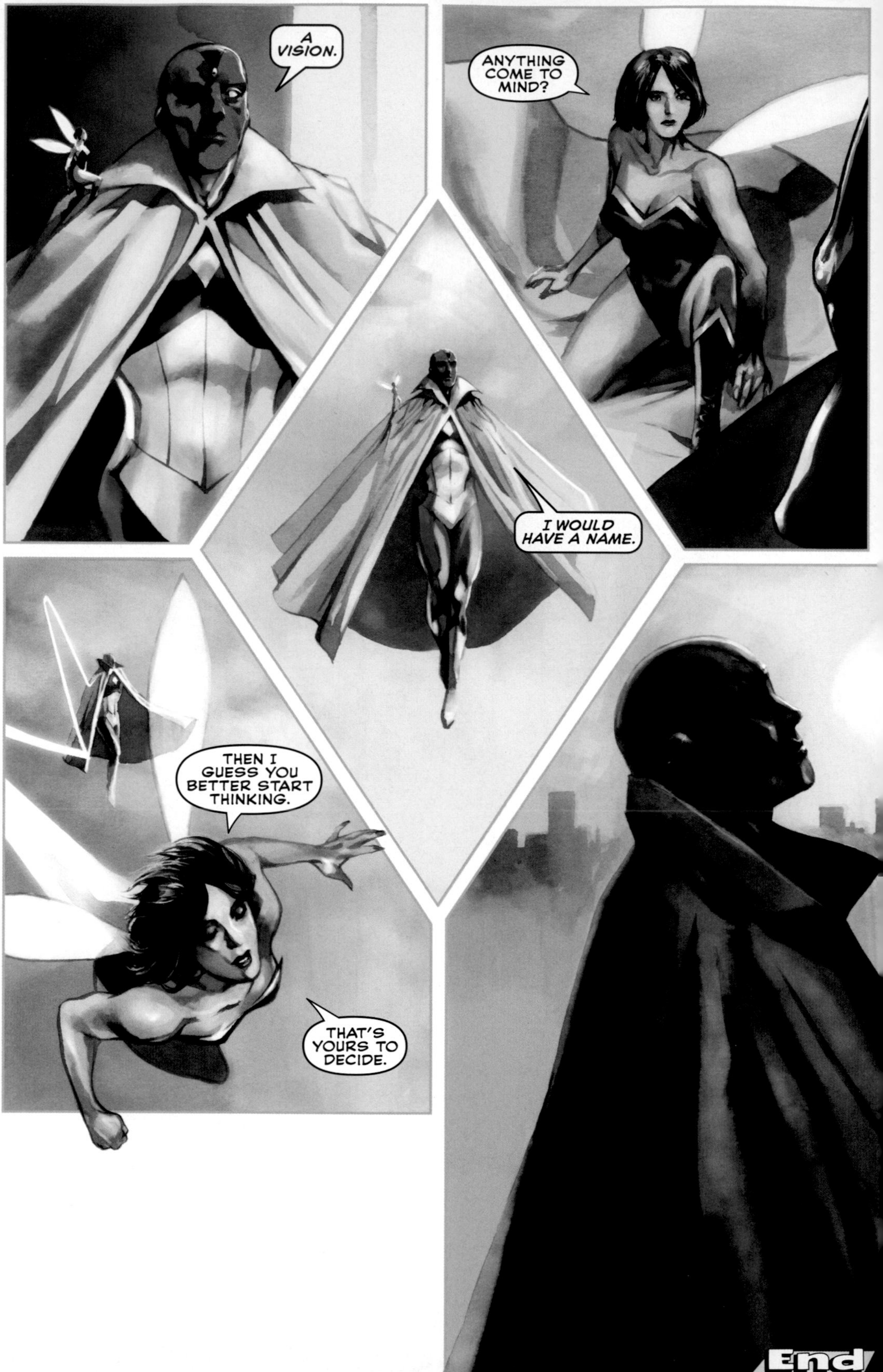
A VISION.
ANYTHING COME TO MIND?
I WOULD HAVE A NAME.
THEN I GUESS YOU BETTER START THINKING.
THAT'S YOURS TO DECIDE.
End

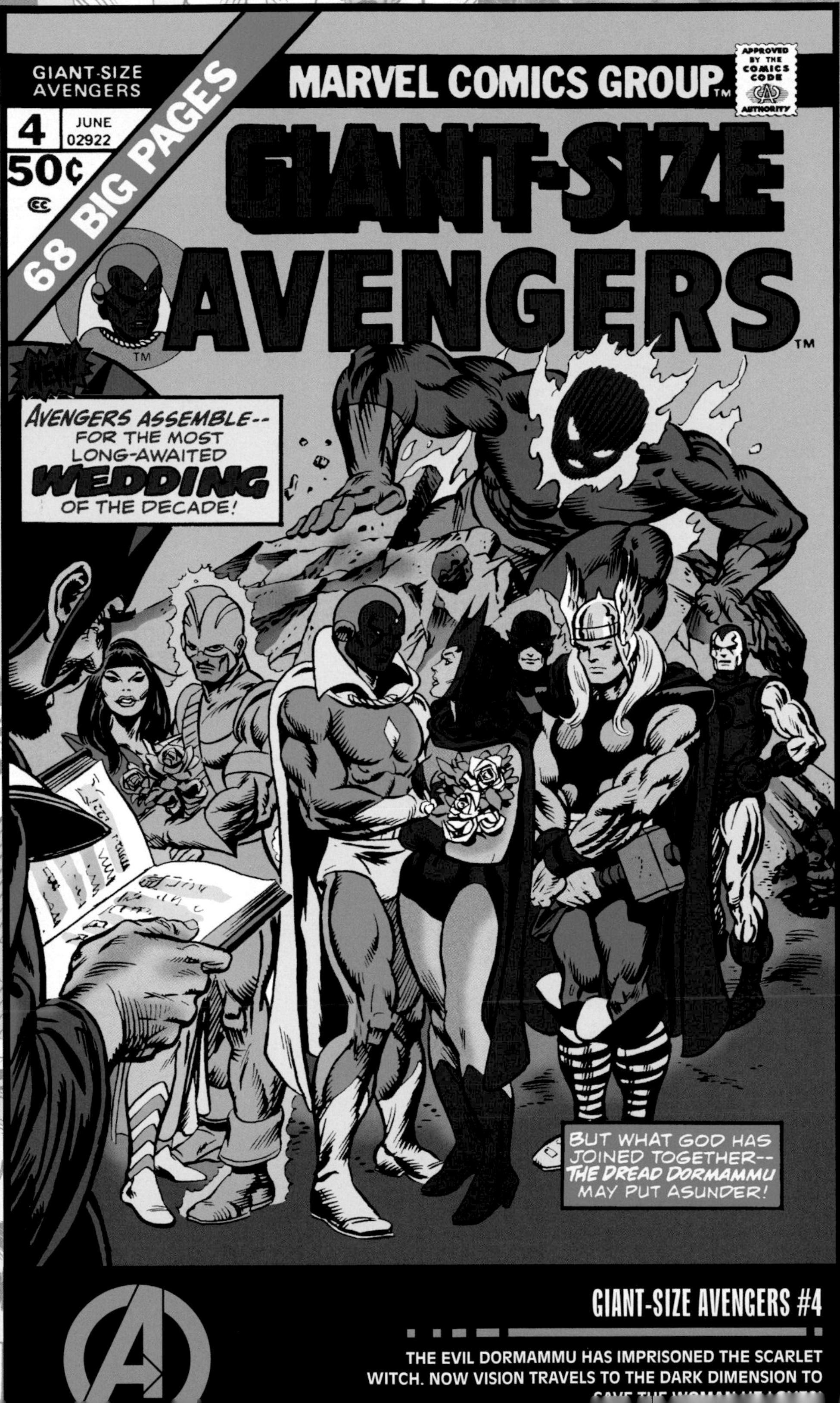
GIANT-SIZE AVENGERS
4
JUNE
02922
50¢
68 BIG PAGES
MARVEL COMICS GROUP
APPROVED BY THE COMICS CODE AUTHORITY
GIANT-SIZE AVENGERS
AVENGERS ASSEMBLE-- FOR THE MOST LONG-AWAITED WEDDING OF THE DECADE!
BUT WHAT GOD HAS JOINED TOGETHER-- THE DREAD DORMAMMU MAY PUT ASUNDER!

GIANT-SIZE AVENGERS #4

THE EVIL DORMAMMU HAS IMPRISONED THE SCARLET WITCH. NOW VISION TRAVELS TO THE DARK DIMENSION TO

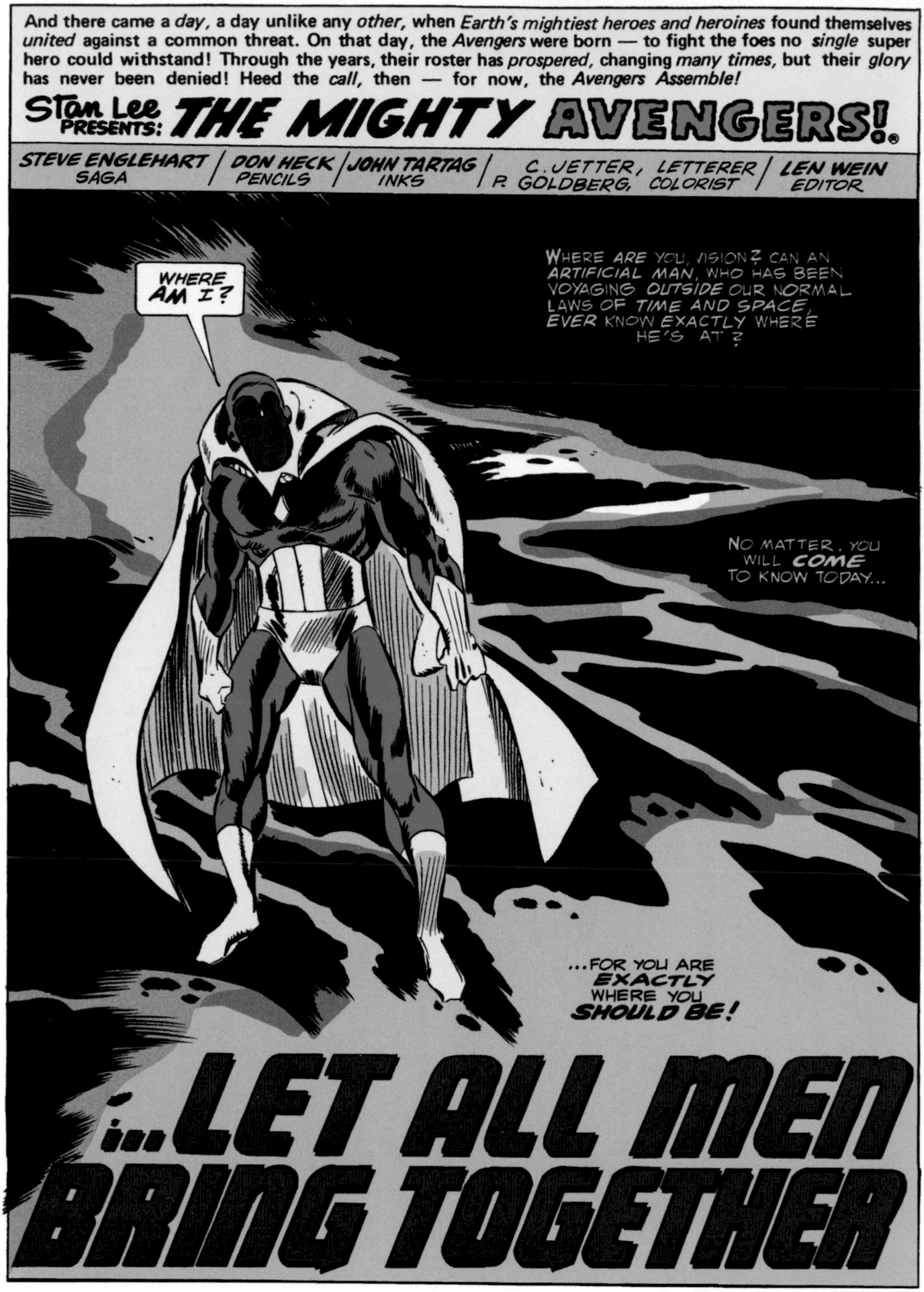
And there came a *day*, a day unlike any *other*, when *Earth's mightiest heroes and heroines* found themselves *united* against a common threat. On that day, the *Avengers* were born — to fight the foes no *single* super hero could withstand! Through the years, their roster has *prospered*, changing *many times*, but their *glory* has never been denied! Heed the *call*, then — for now, the *Avengers Assemble!*
Stan Lee PRESENTS: THE MIGHTY AVENGERS!®
STEVE ENGLEHART SAGA / DON HECK PENCILS / JOHN TARTAG INKS / C. JETTER, LETTERER / P. GOLDBERG, COLORIST / LEN WEIN EDITOR
WHERE ARE YOU, VISION? CAN AN ARTIFICIAL MAN, WHO HAS BEEN VOYAGING OUTSIDE OUR NORMAL LAWS OF TIME AND SPACE, EVER KNOW EXACTLY WHERE HE'S AT?
WHERE AM I?
NO MATTER. YOU WILL COME TO KNOW TODAY...
...FOR YOU ARE EXACTLY WHERE YOU SHOULD BE!
...LET ALL MEN BRING TOGETHER

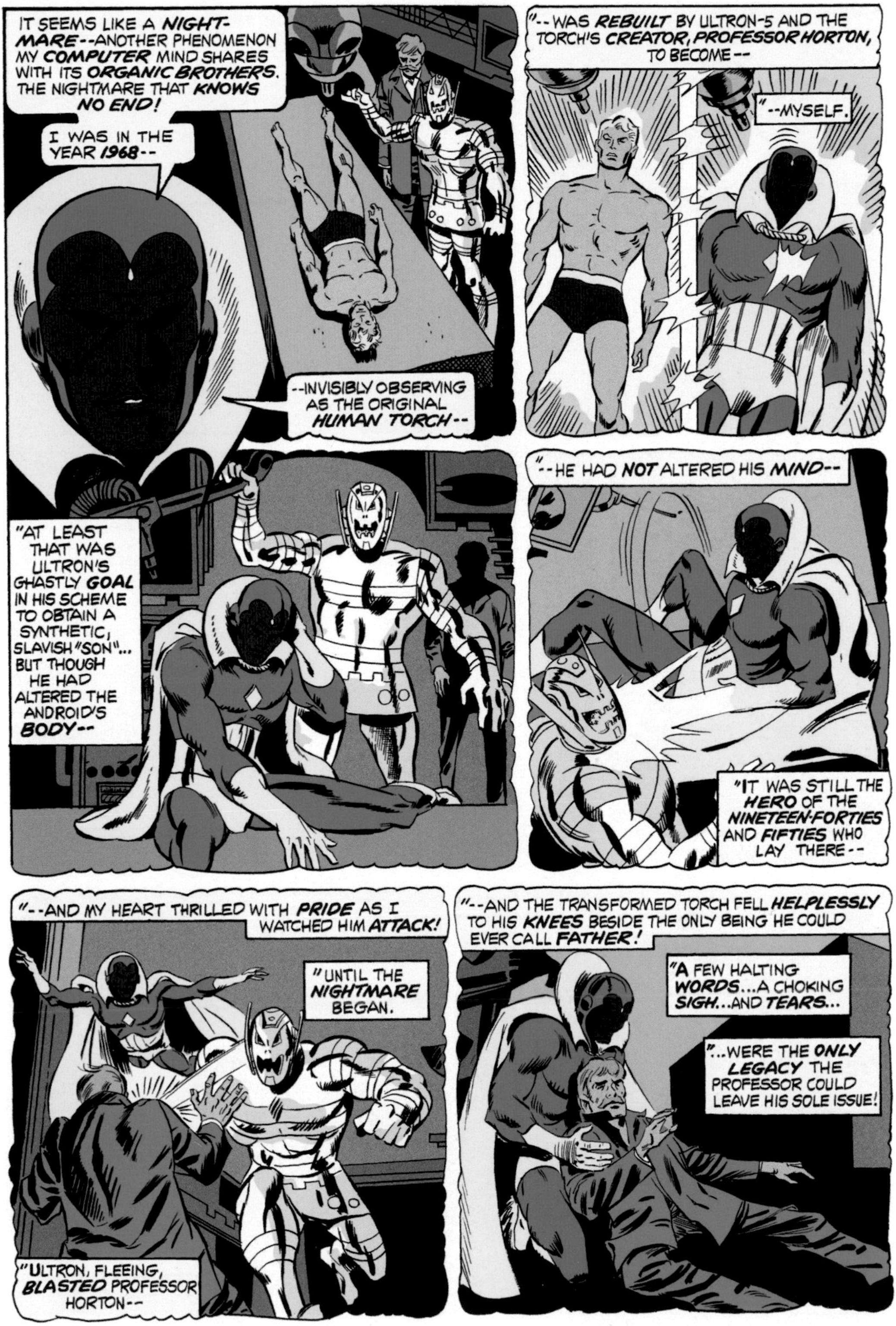
IT SEEMS LIKE A NIGHTMARE--ANOTHER PHENOMENON MY COMPUTER MIND SHARES WITH ITS ORGANIC BROTHERS. THE NIGHTMARE THAT KNOWS NO END!
I WAS IN THE YEAR 1968--
--INVISIBLY OBSERVING AS THE ORIGINAL HUMAN TORCH--
"--WAS REBUILT BY ULTRON-5 AND THE TORCH'S CREATOR, PROFESSOR HORTON, TO BECOME--
"--MYSELF.
"AT LEAST THAT WAS ULTRON'S GHASTLY GOAL IN HIS SCHEME TO OBTAIN A SYNTHETIC, SLAVISH "SON"... BUT THOUGH HE HAD ALTERED THE ANDROID'S BODY--
"--HE HAD NOT ALTERED HIS MIND--
"IT WAS STILL THE HERO OF THE NINETEEN-FORTIES AND FIFTIES WHO LAY THERE--
"--AND MY HEART THRILLED WITH PRIDE AS I WATCHED HIM ATTACK!
"UNTIL THE NIGHTMARE BEGAN.
"ULTRON, FLEEING, BLASTED PROFESSOR HORTON--
"--AND THE TRANSFORMED TORCH FELL HELPLESSLY TO HIS KNEES BESIDE THE ONLY BEING HE COULD EVER CALL FATHER!
"A FEW HALTING WORDS...A CHOKING SIGH...AND TEARS...
"...WERE THE ONLY LEGACY THE PROFESSOR COULD LEAVE HIS SOLE ISSUE!

"YET THE NIGHTMARE WAS *FAR* FROM *FINISHED!*

"WHEN THE ANDROID *CAUGHT UP* TO ULTRON, ALL HIS *RAGE* AVAILED HIM *NOTHING* AND HE *FELL* BEFORE THE ROBOT'S MIGHT!

"AND *THEN*...

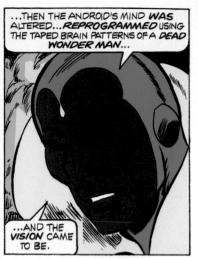

...THEN THE ANDROID'S MIND *WAS* ALTERED...*REPROGRAMMED* USING THE TAPED BRAIN PATTERNS OF A *DEAD WONDER MAN*...

...AND THE *VISION* CAME TO BE.

IRRITABLY, HE SHAKES HIS *HEAD,* WRENCHING HIS GAZE BACK FROM *WITHIN.*

THEN, I SHOULD HAVE RETURNED TO *IMMORTUS,* MY JOURNEY *COMPLETED* --BUT INSTEAD I--

WHAT'S *THAT?*

CAN A *SYNTHETIC MAN,* A MAN OF WIRES AND DIODES, PLASTIC AND PARTS HEAR A *PSYCHIC SCREAM?*

THE ANSWER IS *OBVIOUS..*

...FOR *ALL* POSSESS PSYCHES, WHO POSSESS *SOULS.*

SOMEONE IS IN *PAIN*--A *WOMAN*--

--IN *THIS* DIRECTION!

EVEN THOUGH IT LOOKS AS IF I'VE BEEN DELIVERED TO THE PITS OF *HELL*--

--I CAN *WILL* MYSELF TO SUCH *TOTAL DENSITY* AS TO *IGNORE* THE *HEAT*--

--AND SO I--

NO!

BROTHER! BEHIND YOU!

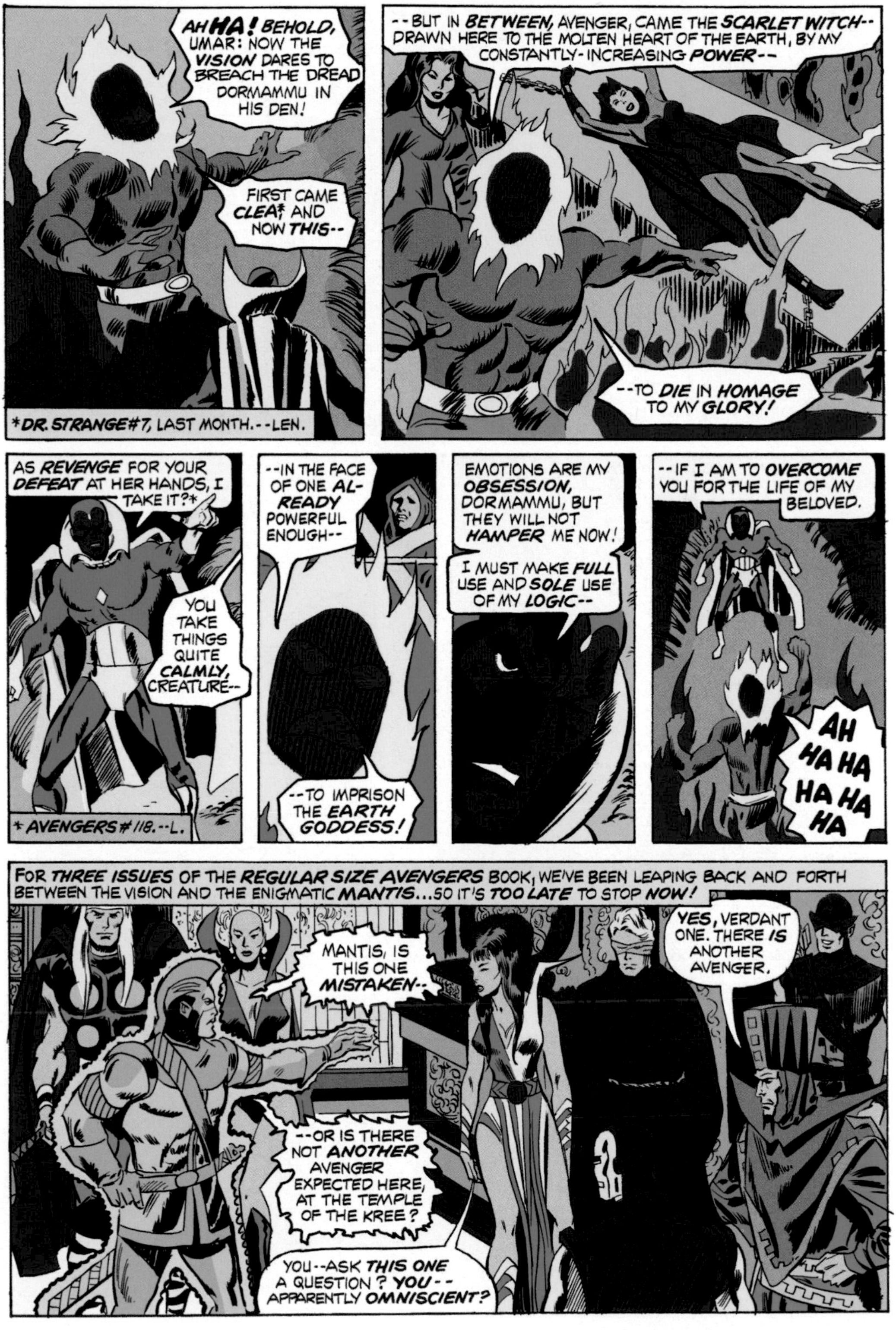
AH HA! BEHOLD, UMAR: NOW THE VISION DARES TO BREACH THE DREAD DORMAMMU IN HIS DEN!
FIRST CAME CLEA;* AND NOW THIS--
*DR. STRANGE #7, LAST MONTH.--LEN.
--BUT IN BETWEEN, AVENGER, CAME THE SCARLET WITCH-- DRAWN HERE TO THE MOLTEN HEART OF THE EARTH, BY MY CONSTANTLY-INCREASING POWER--
--TO DIE IN HOMAGE TO MY GLORY!
AS REVENGE FOR YOUR DEFEAT AT HER HANDS, I TAKE IT?*
YOU TAKE THINGS QUITE CALMLY, CREATURE--
* AVENGERS #118.--L.
--IN THE FACE OF ONE ALREADY POWERFUL ENOUGH--
--TO IMPRISON THE EARTH GODDESS!
EMOTIONS ARE MY OBSESSION, DORMAMMU, BUT THEY WILL NOT HAMPER ME NOW!
I MUST MAKE FULL USE AND SOLE USE OF MY LOGIC--
--IF I AM TO OVERCOME YOU FOR THE LIFE OF MY BELOVED.
AH HA HA HA HA HA
FOR THREE ISSUES OF THE REGULAR SIZE AVENGERS BOOK, WE'VE BEEN LEAPING BACK AND FORTH BETWEEN THE VISION AND THE ENIGMATIC MANTIS...SO IT'S TOO LATE TO STOP NOW!
MANTIS, IS THIS ONE MISTAKEN--
--OR IS THERE NOT ANOTHER AVENGER EXPECTED HERE, AT THE TEMPLE OF THE KREE?
YOU--ASK THIS ONE A QUESTION? YOU--APPARENTLY OMNISCIENT?
YES, VERDANT ONE. THERE IS ANOTHER AVENGER.

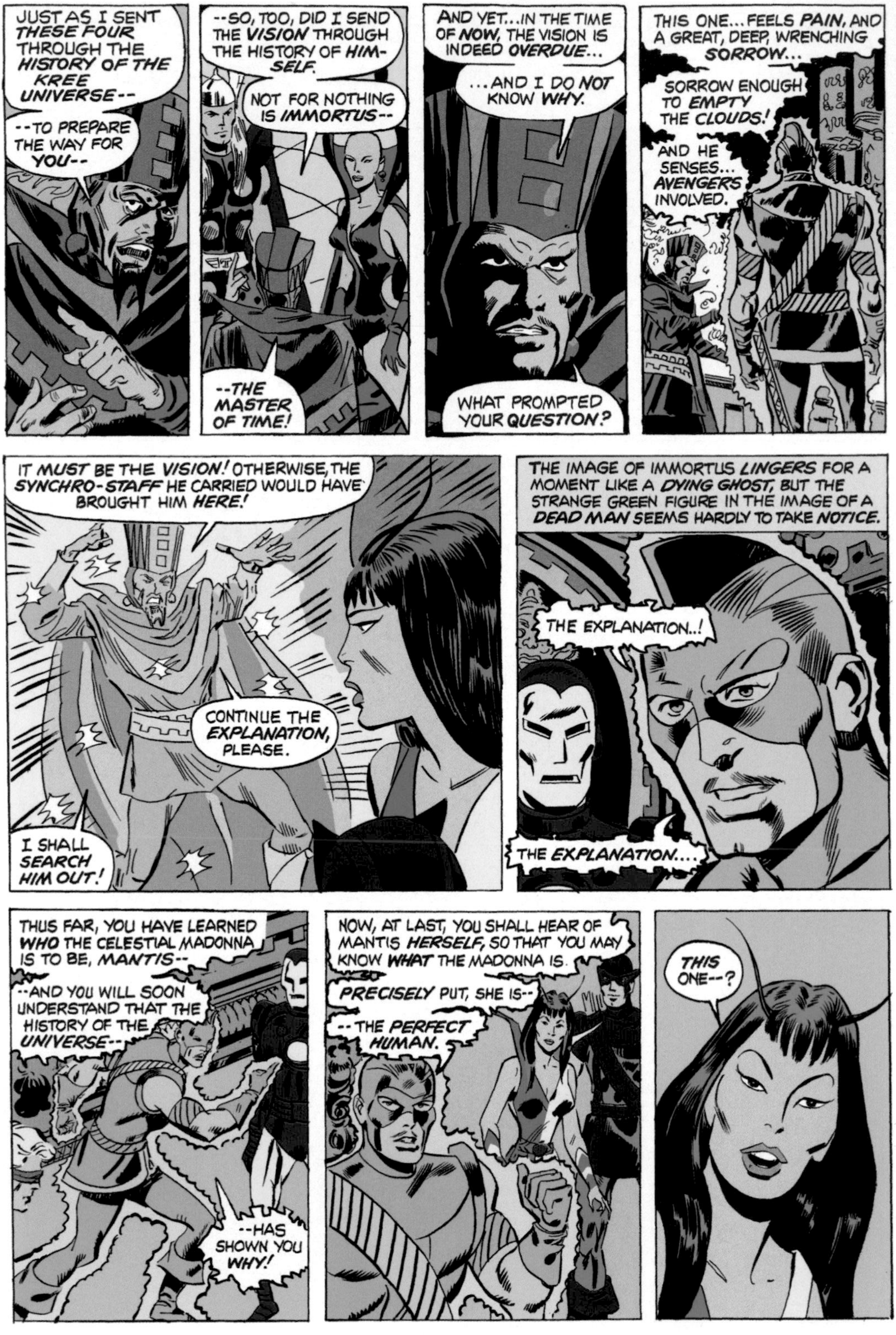
JUST AS I SENT THESE FOUR THROUGH THE HISTORY OF THE KREE UNIVERSE--
--TO PREPARE THE WAY FOR YOU--
--SO, TOO, DID I SEND THE VISION THROUGH THE HISTORY OF HIMSELF.
NOT FOR NOTHING IS IMMORTUS--
--THE MASTER OF TIME!
AND YET...IN THE TIME OF NOW, THE VISION IS INDEED OVERDUE...
...AND I DO NOT KNOW WHY.
WHAT PROMPTED YOUR QUESTION?
THIS ONE...FEELS PAIN, AND A GREAT, DEEP, WRENCHING SORROW...
SORROW ENOUGH TO EMPTY THE CLOUDS!
AND HE SENSES... AVENGERS INVOLVED.
IT MUST BE THE VISION! OTHERWISE, THE SYNCHRO-STAFF HE CARRIED WOULD HAVE BROUGHT HIM HERE!
CONTINUE THE EXPLANATION, PLEASE.
I SHALL SEARCH HIM OUT!
THE IMAGE OF IMMORTUS LINGERS FOR A MOMENT LIKE A DYING GHOST, BUT THE STRANGE GREEN FIGURE IN THE IMAGE OF A DEAD MAN SEEMS HARDLY TO TAKE NOTICE.
THE EXPLANATION..!
THE EXPLANATION....
THUS FAR, YOU HAVE LEARNED WHO THE CELESTIAL MADONNA IS TO BE, MANTIS--
--AND YOU WILL SOON UNDERSTAND THAT THE HISTORY OF THE UNIVERSE--
--HAS SHOWN YOU WHY!
NOW, AT LAST, YOU SHALL HEAR OF MANTIS HERSELF, SO THAT YOU MAY KNOW WHAT THE MADONNA IS.
PRECISELY PUT, SHE IS--
--THE PERFECT HUMAN.
THIS ONE--?

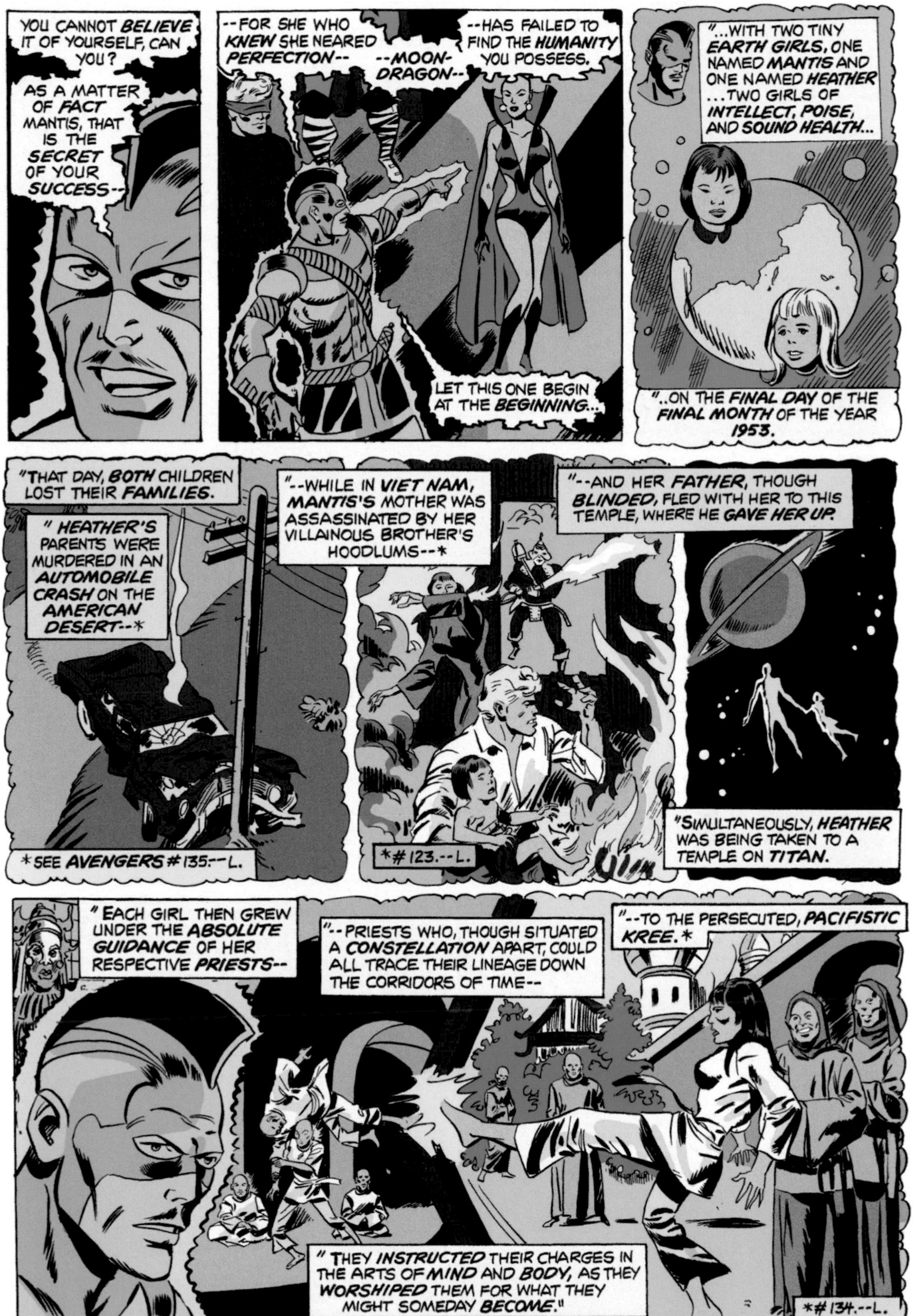
YOU CANNOT BELIEVE IT OF YOURSELF, CAN YOU?
AS A MATTER OF FACT MANTIS, THAT IS THE SECRET OF YOUR SUCCESS--
--FOR SHE WHO KNEW SHE NEARED PERFECTION--
--MOON-DRAGON--
--HAS FAILED TO FIND THE HUMANITY YOU POSSESS.
LET THIS ONE BEGIN AT THE BEGINNING...
"...WITH TWO TINY EARTH GIRLS, ONE NAMED MANTIS AND ONE NAMED HEATHER ...TWO GIRLS OF INTELLECT, POISE, AND SOUND HEALTH...
"..ON THE FINAL DAY OF THE FINAL MONTH OF THE YEAR 1953.
"THAT DAY, BOTH CHILDREN LOST THEIR FAMILIES.
"HEATHER'S PARENTS WERE MURDERED IN AN AUTOMOBILE CRASH ON THE AMERICAN DESERT--*
*SEE AVENGERS #135.--L.
"--WHILE IN VIET NAM, MANTIS'S MOTHER WAS ASSASSINATED BY HER VILLAINOUS BROTHER'S HOODLUMS--*
*#123.--L.
"--AND HER FATHER, THOUGH BLINDED, FLED WITH HER TO THIS TEMPLE, WHERE HE GAVE HER UP.
"SIMULTANEOUSLY, HEATHER WAS BEING TAKEN TO A TEMPLE ON TITAN.
"EACH GIRL THEN GREW UNDER THE ABSOLUTE GUIDANCE OF HER RESPECTIVE PRIESTS--
"--PRIESTS WHO, THOUGH SITUATED A CONSTELLATION APART, COULD ALL TRACE THEIR LINEAGE DOWN THE CORRIDORS OF TIME--
"--TO THE PERSECUTED, PACIFISTIC KREE.*
"THEY INSTRUCTED THEIR CHARGES IN THE ARTS OF MIND AND BODY, AS THEY WORSHIPED THEM FOR WHAT THEY MIGHT SOMEDAY BECOME."
*#134.--L.

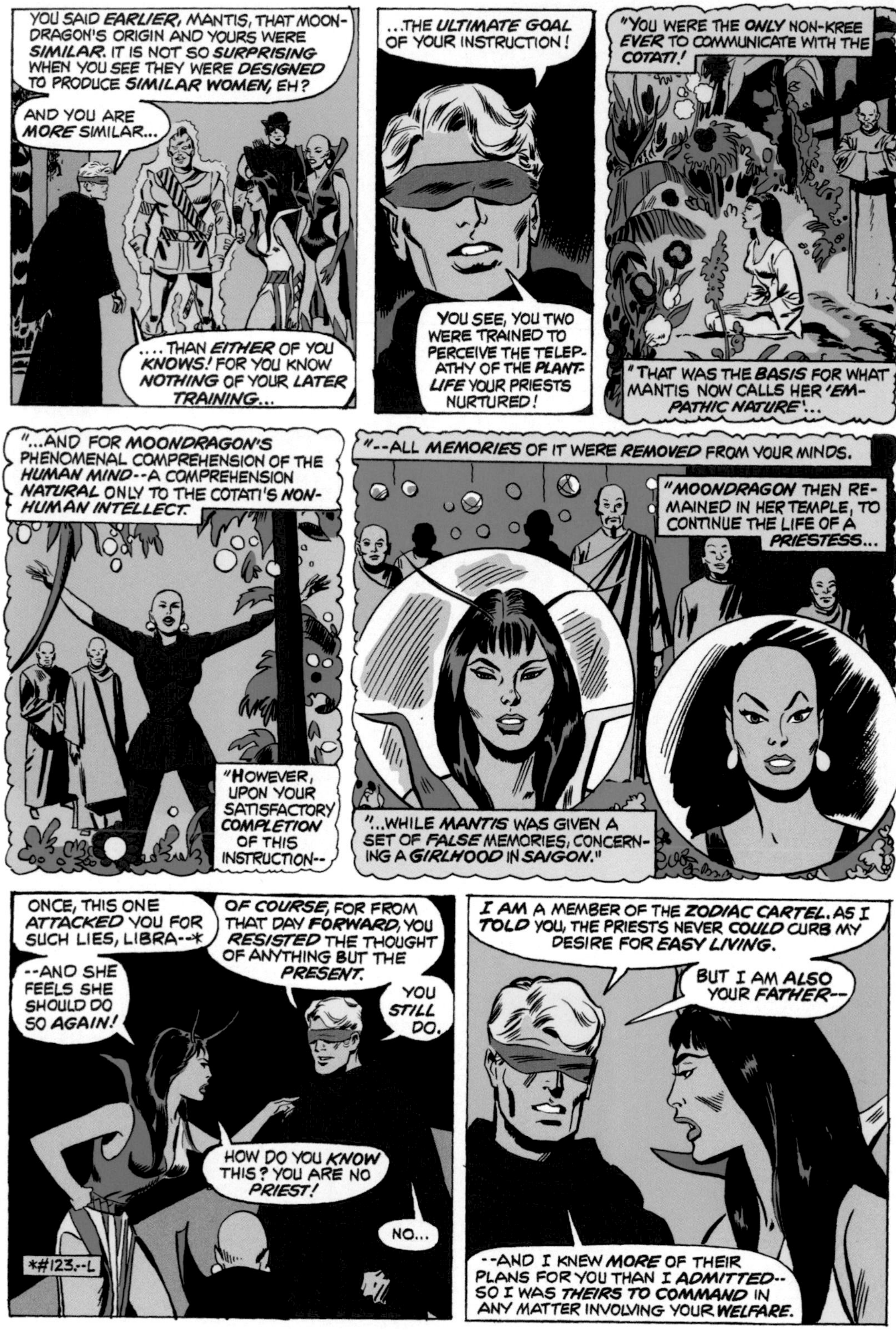
YOU SAID EARLIER, MANTIS, THAT MOON-DRAGON'S ORIGIN AND YOURS WERE SIMILAR. IT IS NOT SO SURPRISING WHEN YOU SEE THEY WERE DESIGNED TO PRODUCE SIMILAR WOMEN, EH?
AND YOU ARE MORE SIMILAR...
....THAN EITHER OF YOU KNOWS! FOR YOU KNOW NOTHING OF YOUR LATER TRAINING...
...THE ULTIMATE GOAL OF YOUR INSTRUCTION!
YOU SEE, YOU TWO WERE TRAINED TO PERCEIVE THE TELEPATHY OF THE PLANT-LIFE YOUR PRIESTS NURTURED!
"YOU WERE THE ONLY NON-KREE EVER TO COMMUNICATE WITH THE COTATI!
"THAT WAS THE BASIS FOR WHAT MANTIS NOW CALLS HER 'EMPATHIC NATURE'...
"...AND FOR MOONDRAGON'S PHENOMENAL COMPREHENSION OF THE HUMAN MIND--A COMPREHENSION NATURAL ONLY TO THE COTATI'S NON-HUMAN INTELLECT.
"HOWEVER, UPON YOUR SATISFACTORY COMPLETION OF THIS INSTRUCTION--
"--ALL MEMORIES OF IT WERE REMOVED FROM YOUR MINDS.
"MOONDRAGON THEN REMAINED IN HER TEMPLE, TO CONTINUE THE LIFE OF A PRIESTESS...
"...WHILE MANTIS WAS GIVEN A SET OF FALSE MEMORIES, CONCERNING A GIRLHOOD IN SAIGON."
ONCE, THIS ONE ATTACKED YOU FOR SUCH LIES, LIBRA--*
--AND SHE FEELS SHE SHOULD DO SO AGAIN!
OF COURSE, FOR FROM THAT DAY FORWARD, YOU RESISTED THE THOUGHT OF ANYTHING BUT THE PRESENT.
YOU STILL DO.
HOW DO YOU KNOW THIS? YOU ARE NO PRIEST!
NO...
*#123.--L
I AM A MEMBER OF THE ZODIAC CARTEL. AS I TOLD YOU, THE PRIESTS NEVER COULD CURB MY DESIRE FOR EASY LIVING.
BUT I AM ALSO YOUR FATHER--
--AND I KNEW MORE OF THEIR PLANS FOR YOU THAN I ADMITTED--SO I WAS THEIRS TO COMMAND IN ANY MATTER INVOLVING YOUR WELFARE.

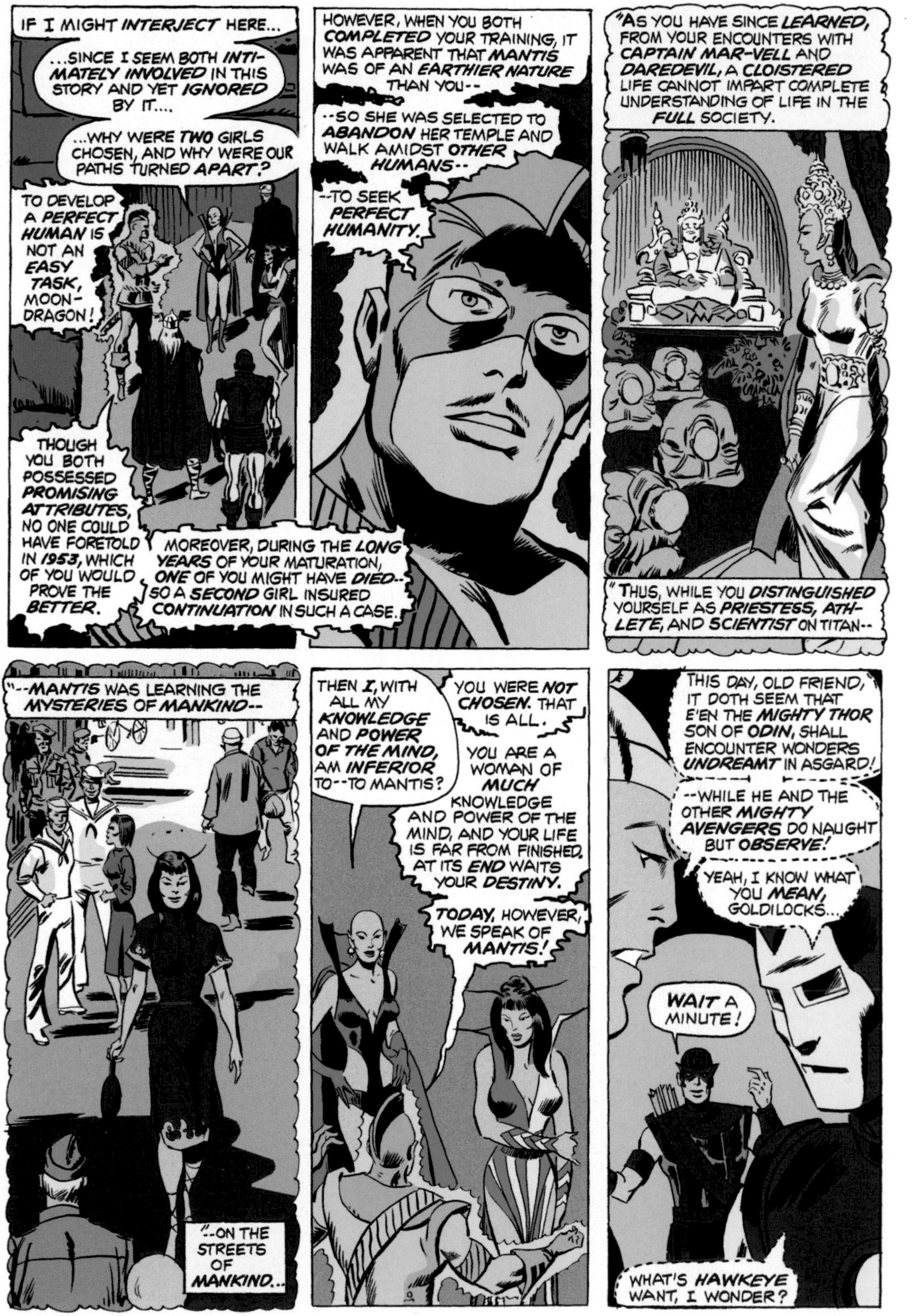
IF I MIGHT INTERJECT HERE...
...SINCE I SEEM BOTH INTIMATELY INVOLVED IN THIS STORY AND YET IGNORED BY IT....
...WHY WERE TWO GIRLS CHOSEN, AND WHY WERE OUR PATHS TURNED APART?
TO DEVELOP A PERFECT HUMAN IS NOT AN EASY TASK, MOONDRAGON!
THOUGH YOU BOTH POSSESSED PROMISING ATTRIBUTES, NO ONE COULD HAVE FORETOLD IN 1953, WHICH OF YOU WOULD PROVE THE BETTER.
MOREOVER, DURING THE LONG YEARS OF YOUR MATURATION, ONE OF YOU MIGHT HAVE DIED-- SO A SECOND GIRL INSURED CONTINUATION IN SUCH A CASE.
HOWEVER, WHEN YOU BOTH COMPLETED YOUR TRAINING, IT WAS APPARENT THAT MANTIS WAS OF AN EARTHIER NATURE THAN YOU--
--SO SHE WAS SELECTED TO ABANDON HER TEMPLE AND WALK AMIDST OTHER HUMANS--
--TO SEEK PERFECT HUMANITY.
"AS YOU HAVE SINCE LEARNED, FROM YOUR ENCOUNTERS WITH CAPTAIN MAR-VELL AND DAREDEVIL, A CLOISTERED LIFE CANNOT IMPART COMPLETE UNDERSTANDING OF LIFE IN THE FULL SOCIETY.
"THUS, WHILE YOU DISTINGUISHED YOURSELF AS PRIESTESS, ATHLETE, AND SCIENTIST ON TITAN--
"--MANTIS WAS LEARNING THE MYSTERIES OF MANKIND--
"--ON THE STREETS OF MANKIND...
THEN I, WITH ALL MY KNOWLEDGE AND POWER OF THE MIND, AM INFERIOR TO--TO MANTIS?
YOU WERE NOT CHOSEN. THAT IS ALL.
YOU ARE A WOMAN OF MUCH KNOWLEDGE AND POWER OF THE MIND, AND YOUR LIFE IS FAR FROM FINISHED. AT ITS END WAITS YOUR DESTINY.
TODAY, HOWEVER, WE SPEAK OF MANTIS!
THIS DAY, OLD FRIEND, IT DOTH SEEM THAT E'EN THE MIGHTY THOR SON OF ODIN, SHALL ENCOUNTER WONDERS UNDREAMT IN ASGARD!
--WHILE HE AND THE OTHER MIGHTY AVENGERS DO NAUGHT BUT OBSERVE!
YEAH, I KNOW WHAT YOU MEAN, GOLDILOCKS...
WAIT A MINUTE!
WHAT'S HAWKEYE WANT, I WONDER?

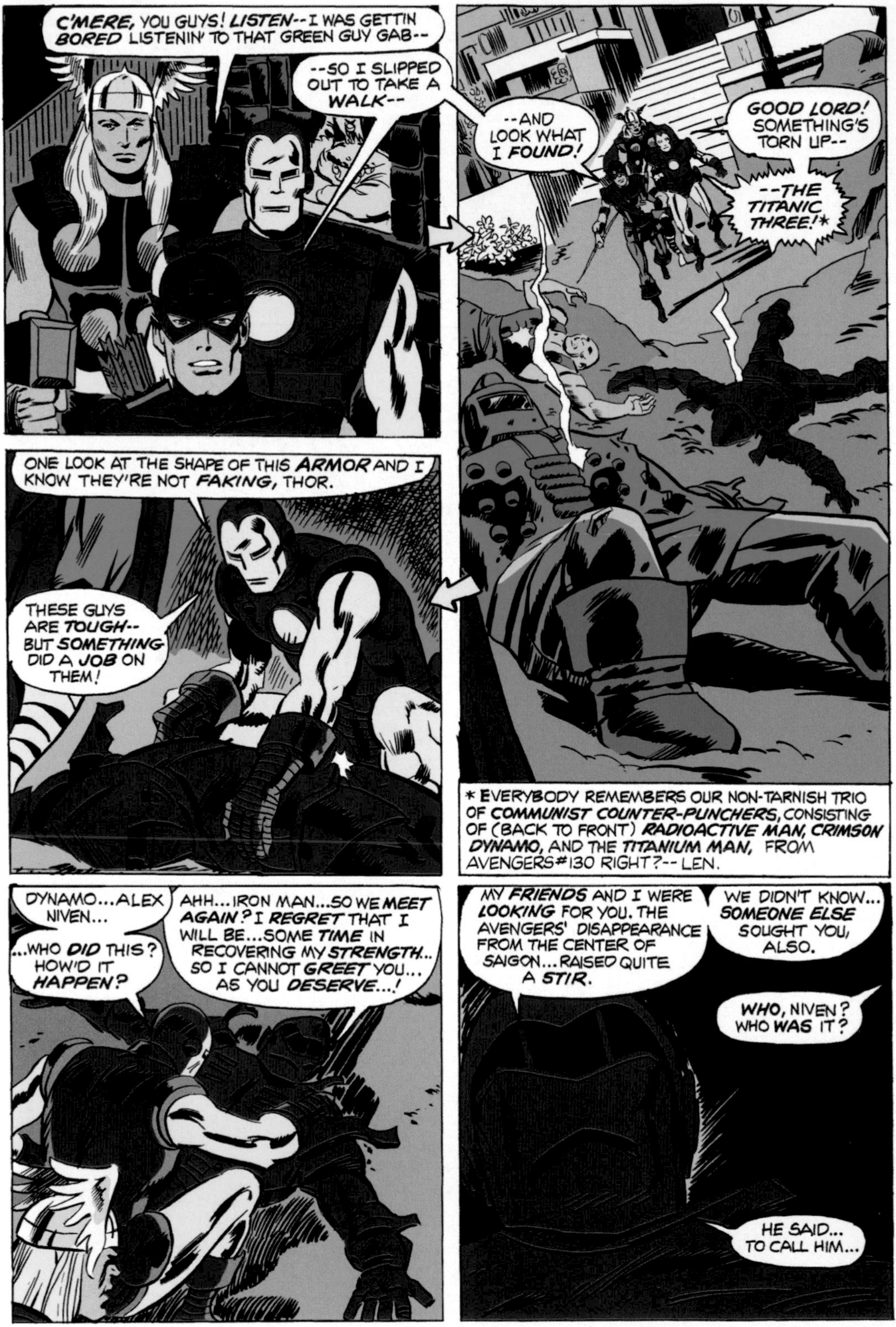
C'MERE, YOU GUYS! LISTEN-- I WAS GETTIN BORED LISTENIN' TO THAT GREEN GUY GAB--
--SO I SLIPPED OUT TO TAKE A WALK--
--AND LOOK WHAT I FOUND!
GOOD LORD! SOMETHING'S TORN UP--
--THE TITANIC THREE!*
ONE LOOK AT THE SHAPE OF THIS ARMOR AND I KNOW THEY'RE NOT FAKING, THOR.
THESE GUYS ARE TOUGH-- BUT SOMETHING DID A JOB ON THEM!
* EVERYBODY REMEMBERS OUR NON-TARNISH TRIO OF COMMUNIST COUNTER-PUNCHERS, CONSISTING OF (BACK TO FRONT) RADIOACTIVE MAN, CRIMSON DYNAMO, AND THE TITANIUM MAN, FROM AVENGERS #130 RIGHT?-- LEN.
DYNAMO... ALEX NIVEN...
...WHO DID THIS? HOW'D IT HAPPEN?
AHH... IRON MAN... SO WE MEET AGAIN? I REGRET THAT I WILL BE... SOME TIME IN RECOVERING MY STRENGTH... SO I CANNOT GREET YOU... AS YOU DESERVE...!
MY FRIENDS AND I WERE LOOKING FOR YOU. THE AVENGERS' DISAPPEARANCE FROM THE CENTER OF SAIGON... RAISED QUITE A STIR.
WE DIDN'T KNOW... SOMEONE ELSE SOUGHT YOU, ALSO.
WHO, NIVEN? WHO WAS IT?
HE SAID... TO CALL HIM...

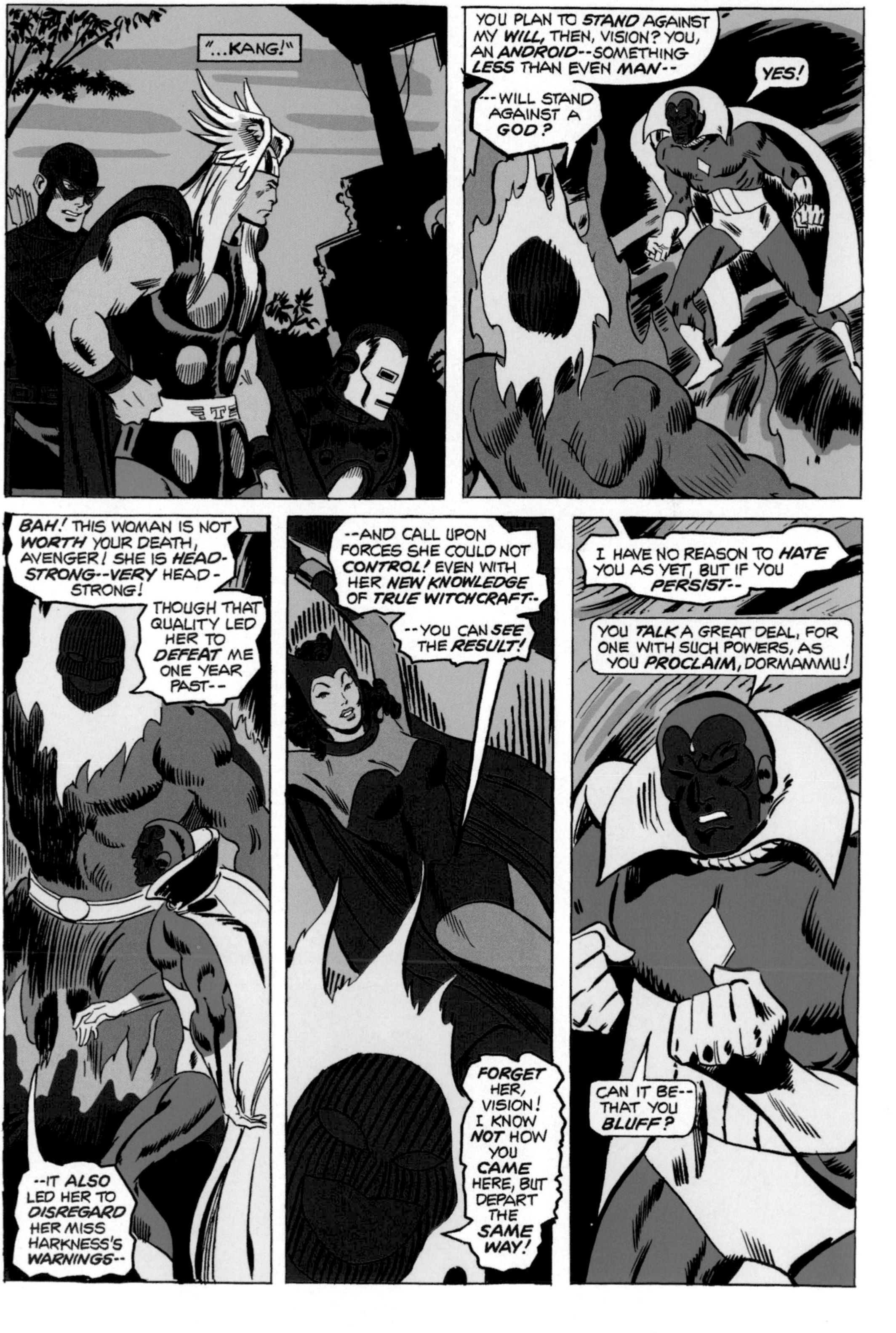

"...KANG!"
YOU PLAN TO STAND AGAINST MY WILL, THEN, VISION? YOU, AN ANDROID--SOMETHING LESS THAN EVEN MAN--
--WILL STAND AGAINST A GOD?
YES!
BAH! THIS WOMAN IS NOT WORTH YOUR DEATH, AVENGER! SHE IS HEAD-STRONG--VERY HEAD-STRONG!
THOUGH THAT QUALITY LED HER TO DEFEAT ME ONE YEAR PAST--
--IT ALSO LED HER TO DISREGARD HER MISS HARKNESS'S WARNINGS--
--AND CALL UPON FORCES SHE COULD NOT CONTROL! EVEN WITH HER NEW KNOWLEDGE OF TRUE WITCHCRAFT--
--YOU CAN SEE THE RESULT!
FORGET HER, VISION! I KNOW NOT HOW YOU CAME HERE, BUT DEPART THE SAME WAY!
I HAVE NO REASON TO HATE YOU AS YET, BUT IF YOU PERSIST--
YOU TALK A GREAT DEAL, FOR ONE WITH SUCH POWERS, AS YOU PROCLAIM, DORMAMMU!
CAN IT BE--THAT YOU BLUFF?

BLUFF?

SUDDENLY, THEY ARE *THERE*-- MASSIVE, *GIBBERING* SHAPES HALF-GLIMPSED HERE AND THERE IN THE SHIMMERING, SULPHUROUS HAZE!

THEY WEREN'T THERE *BEFORE* -- THE VISION IS *CERTAIN* OF *THAT*--

-- BUT THEY'RE *SURGING* TOWARD HIM *NOW*!

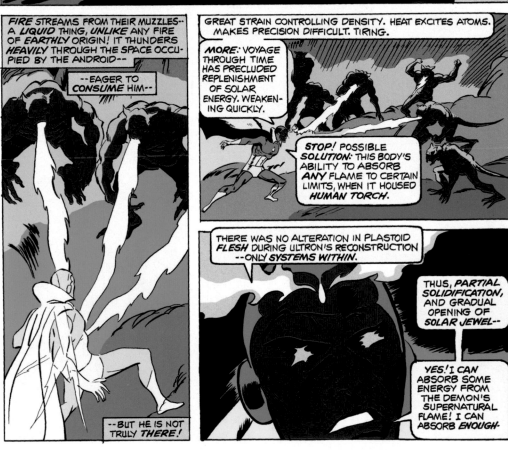

FIRE STREAMS FROM THEIR MUZZLES-- A *LIQUID* THING, *UNLIKE* ANY FIRE OF *EARTHLY* ORIGIN! IT THUNDERS *HEAVILY* THROUGH THE SPACE OCCUPIED BY THE ANDROID--

--EAGER TO *CONSUME* HIM--

--BUT HE IS NOT TRULY *THERE*!

GREAT STRAIN CONTROLLING DENSITY. HEAT EXCITES ATOMS. MAKES PRECISION DIFFICULT. TIRING.

MORE: VOYAGE THROUGH TIME HAS PRECLUDED REPLENISHMENT OF SOLAR ENERGY. WEAKENING QUICKLY.

STOP! POSSIBLE *SOLUTION:* THIS BODY'S ABILITY TO ABSORB *ANY* FLAME TO CERTAIN LIMITS, WHEN IT HOUSED *HUMAN TORCH*.

THERE WAS NO ALTERATION IN PLASTOID *FLESH* DURING ULTRON'S RECONSTRUCTION --ONLY *SYSTEMS WITHIN*.

THUS, *PARTIAL SOLIDIFICATION,* AND *GRADUAL OPENING* OF *SOLAR JEWEL*--

YES! I CAN ABSORB SOME ENERGY FROM THE DEMON'S SUPERNATURAL FLAME! I CAN ABSORB *ENOUGH*-

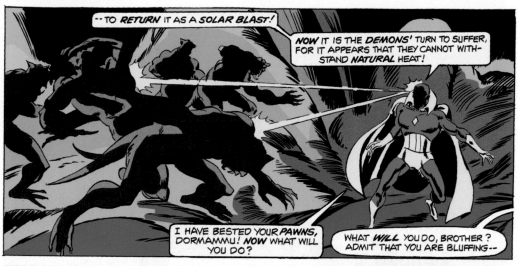

--TO *RETURN* IT AS A *SOLAR BLAST!*

NOW IT IS THE *DEMONS'* TURN TO SUFFER, FOR IT APPEARS THAT THEY CANNOT WITHSTAND *NATURAL* HEAT!

I HAVE BESTED YOUR *PAWNS,* DORMAMMU! *NOW* WHAT WILL YOU DO?

WHAT *WILL* YOU DO, BROTHER? ADMIT THAT YOU ARE BLUFFING--

--THAT YOUR RETURNING MIGHT IS AS YET SUFFICIENT ONLY TO SPIRIT AWAY *DEFENSELESS WITCHES,* AND *NOT* TO SQUANDER ON BATTLE WITH A *DETERMINED* OPPONENT?

HAVE A *CARE,* UMAR!

I MAY NOT WISH TO *SLOW* THE ARRIVAL OF MY FULL STRENGTH--

--BUT *DORMAMMU* CAN ACHIEVE WHATEVER HE *DESIRES!*

--THERE ARE *MANY* WHO MUST DO MY BIDDING!

LIKE *YOU,* TO WHOM I PROMISED MASTERY OF MY *DARK DOMAIN* WHEN I HAVE CLAIMED *THIS* DIMENSION--

RISE, SCARLET WITCH!

DAZEDLY, SHE QUIVERS IN BLIND *OBEDIANCE--*

--AND *RISES--*

--AS SUBSERVIANT TO THIS EVIL FORCE *NOW* AS WHEN SHE BATTLED *MOONDRAGON* IN ITS NAME!*

MY *WILL* IS *YOUR* WILL, WITCH--

*#134.--L

--AND I *DEMAND* THAT YOU--

--*DESTROY THE VISION!*

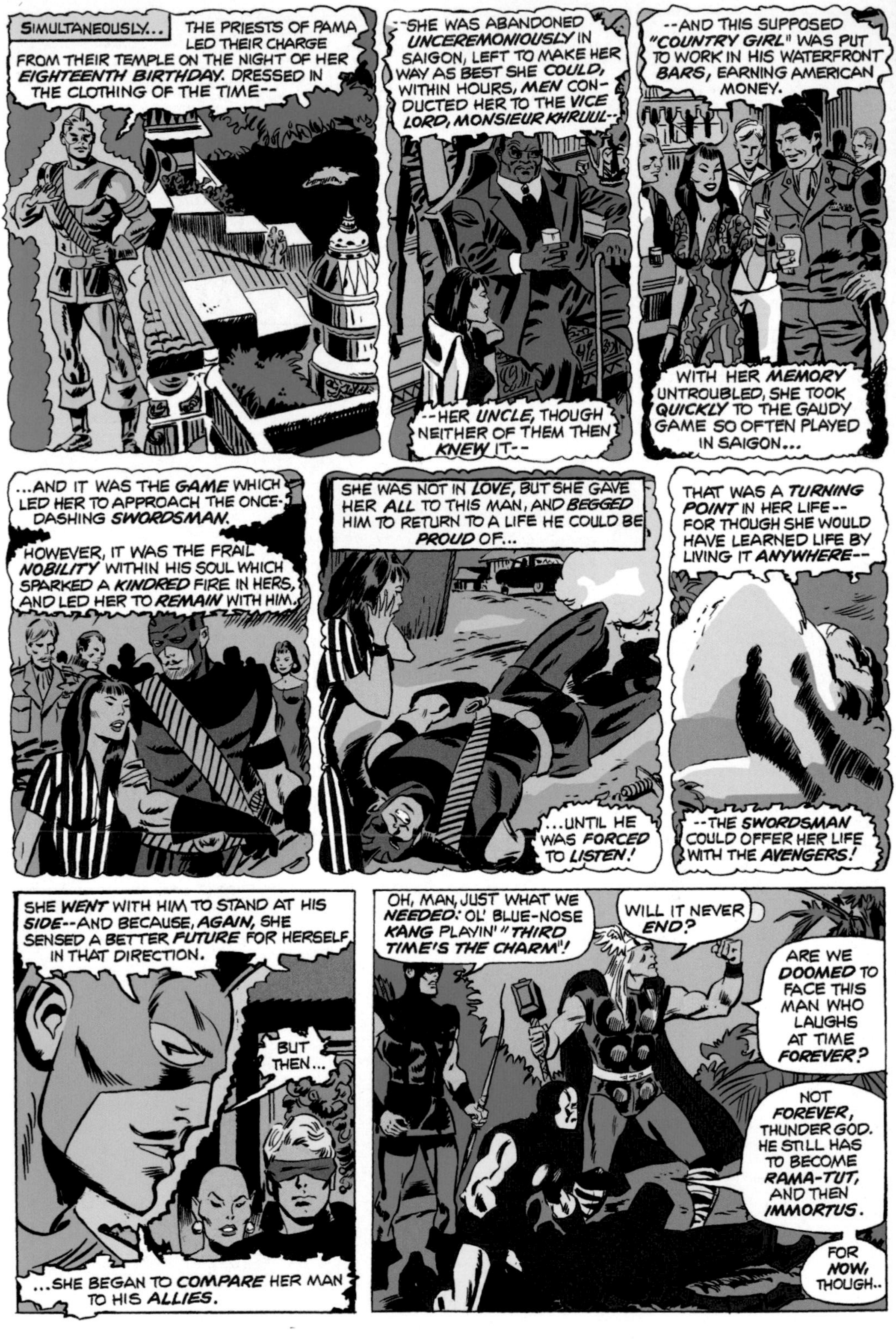
SIMULTANEOUSLY...
THE PRIESTS OF PAMA LED THEIR CHARGE FROM THEIR TEMPLE ON THE NIGHT OF HER EIGHTEENTH BIRTHDAY. DRESSED IN THE CLOTHING OF THE TIME--
--SHE WAS ABANDONED UNCEREMONIOUSLY IN SAIGON, LEFT TO MAKE HER WAY AS BEST SHE COULD, WITHIN HOURS, MEN CONDUCTED HER TO THE VICE LORD, MONSIEUR KHRUUL--
--HER UNCLE, THOUGH NEITHER OF THEM THEN KNEW IT--
--AND THIS SUPPOSED "COUNTRY GIRL" WAS PUT TO WORK IN HIS WATERFRONT BARS, EARNING AMERICAN MONEY.
WITH HER MEMORY UNTROUBLED, SHE TOOK QUICKLY TO THE GAUDY GAME SO OFTEN PLAYED IN SAIGON...
...AND IT WAS THE GAME WHICH LED HER TO APPROACH THE ONCE-DASHING SWORDSMAN.
HOWEVER, IT WAS THE FRAIL NOBILITY WITHIN HIS SOUL WHICH SPARKED A KINDRED FIRE IN HERS, AND LED HER TO REMAIN WITH HIM.
SHE WAS NOT IN LOVE, BUT SHE GAVE HER ALL TO THIS MAN, AND BEGGED HIM TO RETURN TO A LIFE HE COULD BE PROUD OF...
...UNTIL HE WAS FORCED TO LISTEN!
THAT WAS A TURNING POINT IN HER LIFE--FOR THOUGH SHE WOULD HAVE LEARNED LIFE BY LIVING IT ANYWHERE--
--THE SWORDSMAN COULD OFFER HER LIFE WITH THE AVENGERS!
SHE WENT WITH HIM TO STAND AT HIS SIDE--AND BECAUSE, AGAIN, SHE SENSED A BETTER FUTURE FOR HERSELF IN THAT DIRECTION.
BUT THEN...
...SHE BEGAN TO COMPARE HER MAN TO HIS ALLIES.
OH, MAN, JUST WHAT WE NEEDED: OL' BLUE-NOSE KANG PLAYIN' "THIRD TIME'S THE CHARM"!
WILL IT NEVER END?
ARE WE DOOMED TO FACE THIS MAN WHO LAUGHS AT TIME FOREVER?
NOT FOREVER, THUNDER GOD. HE STILL HAS TO BECOME RAMA-TUT, AND THEN IMMORTUS.
FOR NOW, THOUGH..

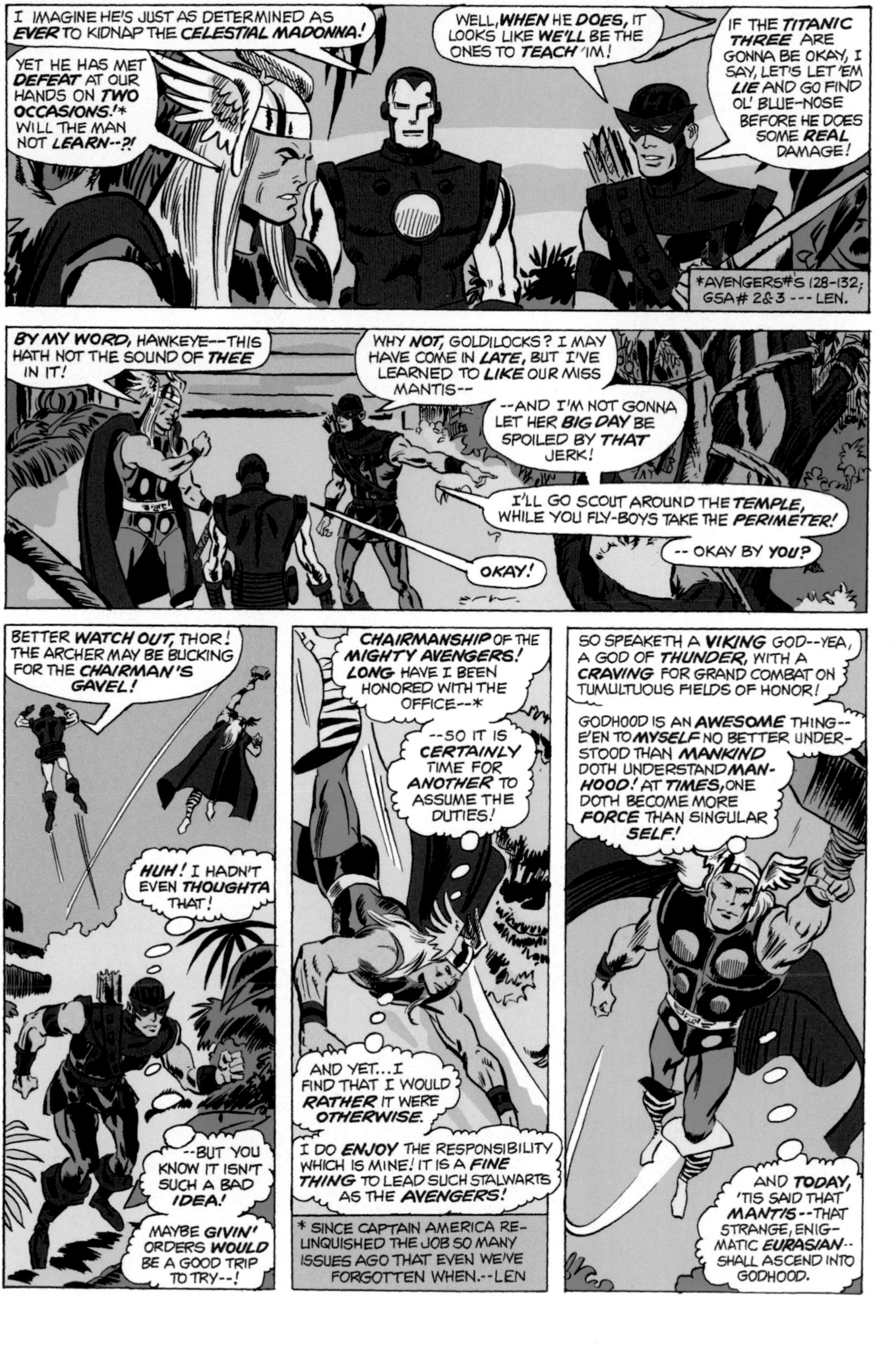

I IMAGINE HE'S JUST AS DETERMINED AS EVER TO KIDNAP THE CELESTIAL MADONNA!
YET HE HAS MET DEFEAT AT OUR HANDS ON TWO OCCASIONS!* WILL THE MAN NOT LEARN--?!
WELL, WHEN HE DOES, IT LOOKS LIKE WE'LL BE THE ONES TO TEACH 'IM!
IF THE TITANIC THREE ARE GONNA BE OKAY, I SAY, LET'S LET 'EM LIE AND GO FIND OL' BLUE-NOSE BEFORE HE DOES SOME REAL DAMAGE!
*AVENGERS#'S 128-132; GSA# 2&3 --- LEN.
BY MY WORD, HAWKEYE--THIS HATH NOT THE SOUND OF THEE IN IT!
WHY NOT, GOLDILOCKS? I MAY HAVE COME IN LATE, BUT I'VE LEARNED TO LIKE OUR MISS MANTIS--
--AND I'M NOT GONNA LET HER BIG DAY BE SPOILED BY THAT JERK!
I'LL GO SCOUT AROUND THE TEMPLE, WHILE YOU FLY-BOYS TAKE THE PERIMETER!
-- OKAY BY YOU?
OKAY!
BETTER WATCH OUT, THOR! THE ARCHER MAY BE BUCKING FOR THE CHAIRMAN'S GAVEL!
HUH! I HADN'T EVEN THOUGHTA THAT!
--BUT YOU KNOW IT ISN'T SUCH A BAD IDEA!
MAYBE GIVIN' ORDERS WOULD BE A GOOD TRIP TO TRY--!
CHAIRMANSHIP OF THE MIGHTY AVENGERS! LONG HAVE I BEEN HONORED WITH THE OFFICE--*
--SO IT IS CERTAINLY TIME FOR ANOTHER TO ASSUME THE DUTIES!
AND YET...I FIND THAT I WOULD RATHER IT WERE OTHERWISE.
I DO ENJOY THE RESPONSIBILITY WHICH IS MINE! IT IS A FINE THING TO LEAD SUCH STALWARTS AS THE AVENGERS!
* SINCE CAPTAIN AMERICA RELINQUISHED THE JOB SO MANY ISSUES AGO THAT EVEN WE'VE FORGOTTEN WHEN.--LEN
SO SPEAKETH A VIKING GOD--YEA, A GOD OF THUNDER, WITH A CRAVING FOR GRAND COMBAT ON TUMULTUOUS FIELDS OF HONOR!
GODHOOD IS AN AWESOME THING--E'EN TO MYSELF NO BETTER UNDERSTOOD THAN MANKIND DOTH UNDERSTAND MANHOOD! AT TIMES, ONE DOTH BECOME MORE FORCE THAN SINGULAR SELF!
AND TODAY, 'TIS SAID THAT MANTIS--THAT STRANGE, ENIGMATIC EURASIAN--SHALL ASCEND INTO GODHOOD.

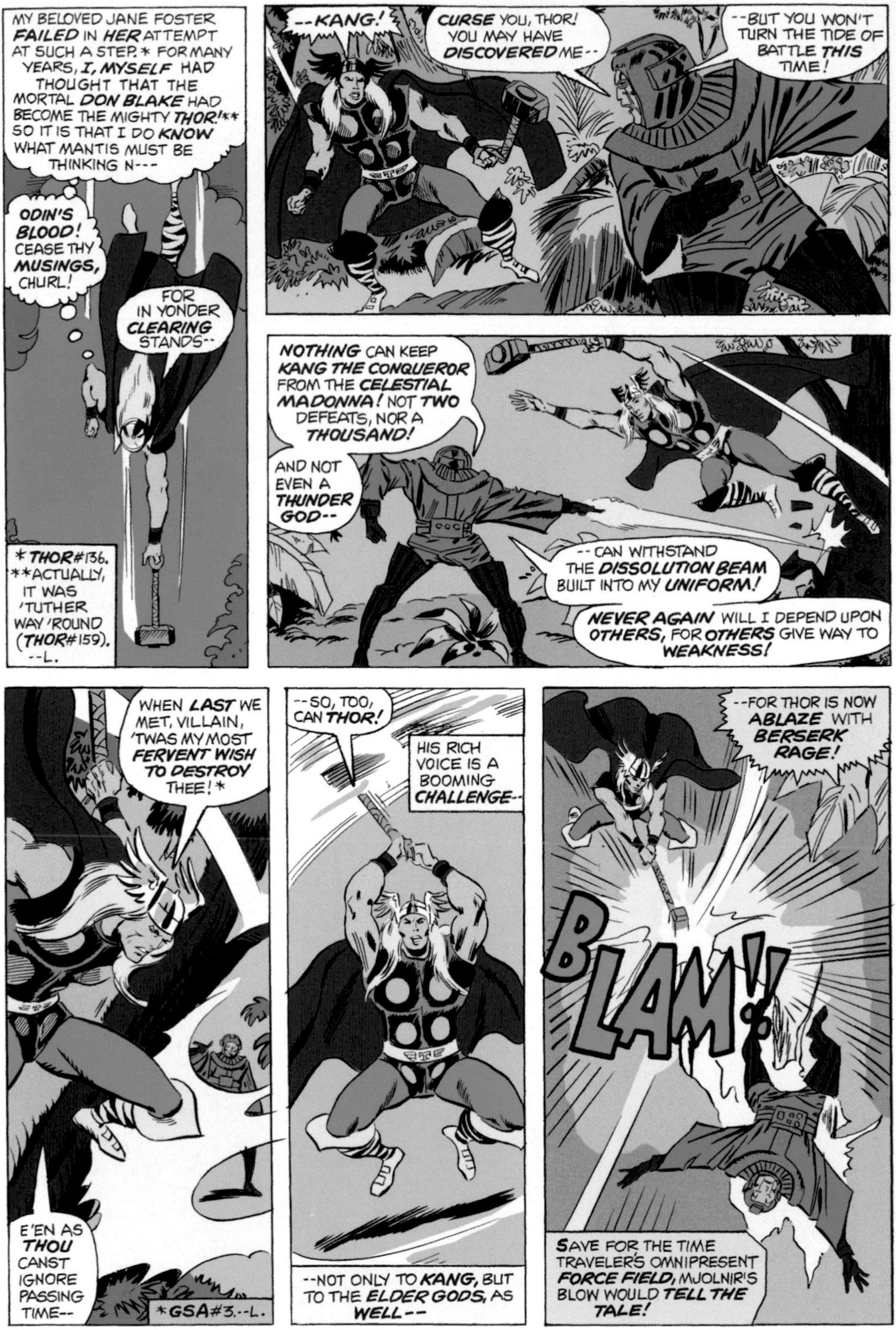
MY BELOVED JANE FOSTER FAILED IN HER ATTEMPT AT SUCH A STEP.* FOR MANY YEARS, I, MYSELF HAD THOUGHT THAT THE MORTAL DON BLAKE HAD BECOME THE MIGHTY THOR!** SO IT IS THAT I DO KNOW WHAT MANTIS MUST BE THINKING N---
ODIN'S BLOOD! CEASE THY MUSINGS, CHURL!
FOR IN YONDER CLEARING STANDS--
*THOR #136. **ACTUALLY, IT WAS 'TUTHER WAY 'ROUND (THOR #159). --L.
--KANG!
CURSE YOU, THOR! YOU MAY HAVE DISCOVERED ME--
--BUT YOU WON'T TURN THE TIDE OF BATTLE THIS TIME!
NOTHING CAN KEEP KANG THE CONQUEROR FROM THE CELESTIAL MADONNA! NOT TWO DEFEATS, NOR A THOUSAND!
AND NOT EVEN A THUNDER GOD--
--CAN WITHSTAND THE DISSOLUTION BEAM BUILT INTO MY UNIFORM!
NEVER AGAIN WILL I DEPEND UPON OTHERS, FOR OTHERS GIVE WAY TO WEAKNESS!
WHEN LAST WE MET, VILLAIN, 'TWAS MY MOST FERVENT WISH TO DESTROY THEE! *
E'EN AS THOU CANST IGNORE PASSING TIME--
*GSA #3.--L.
--SO, TOO, CAN THOR!
HIS RICH VOICE IS A BOOMING CHALLENGE--
--NOT ONLY TO KANG, BUT TO THE ELDER GODS, AS WELL--
--FOR THOR IS NOW ABLAZE WITH BERSERK RAGE!
BLAM!!
SAVE FOR THE TIME TRAVELER'S OMNIPRESENT FORCE FIELD, MJOLNIR'S BLOW WOULD TELL THE TALE!

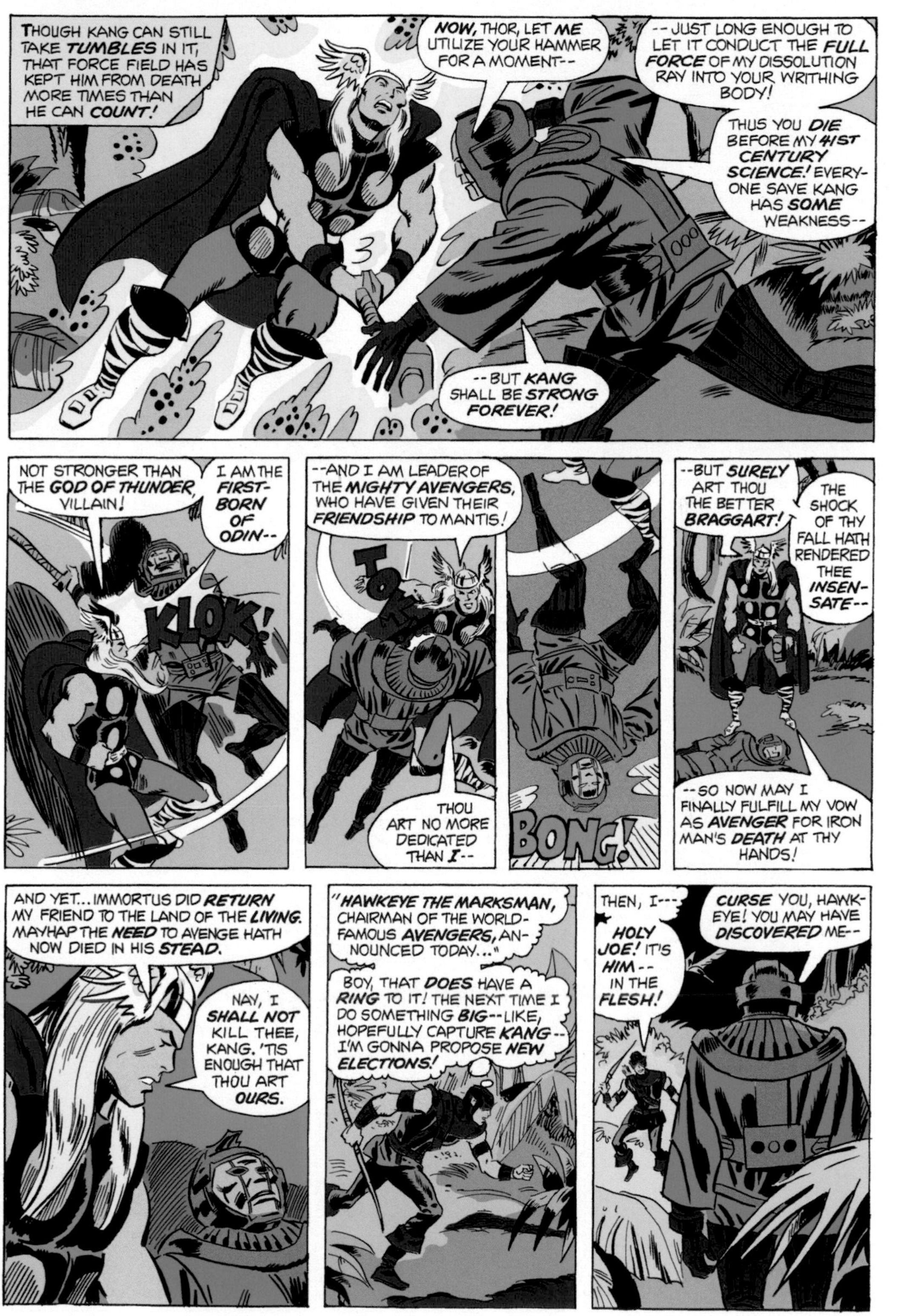
THOUGH KANG CAN STILL TAKE TUMBLES IN IT, THAT FORCE FIELD HAS KEPT HIM FROM DEATH MORE TIMES THAN HE CAN COUNT!
NOW, THOR, LET ME UTILIZE YOUR HAMMER FOR A MOMENT--
-- JUST LONG ENOUGH TO LET IT CONDUCT THE FULL FORCE OF MY DISSOLUTION RAY INTO YOUR WRITHING BODY!
THUS YOU DIE BEFORE MY 41ST CENTURY SCIENCE! EVERYONE SAVE KANG HAS SOME WEAKNESS--
-- BUT KANG SHALL BE STRONG FOREVER!
NOT STRONGER THAN THE GOD OF THUNDER, VILLAIN!
I AM THE FIRST-BORN OF ODIN--
KLOK!
--AND I AM LEADER OF THE MIGHTY AVENGERS, WHO HAVE GIVEN THEIR FRIENDSHIP TO MANTIS!
TOK
THOU ART NO MORE DEDICATED THAN I--
BONG!
--BUT SURELY ART THOU THE BETTER BRAGGART!
THE SHOCK OF THY FALL HATH RENDERED THEE INSENSATE--
--SO NOW MAY I FINALLY FULFILL MY VOW AS AVENGER FOR IRON MAN'S DEATH AT THY HANDS!
AND YET... IMMORTUS DID RETURN MY FRIEND TO THE LAND OF THE LIVING. MAYHAP THE NEED TO AVENGE HATH NOW DIED IN HIS STEAD.
NAY, I SHALL NOT KILL THEE, KANG. 'TIS ENOUGH THAT THOU ART OURS.
"HAWKEYE THE MARKSMAN, CHAIRMAN OF THE WORLD-FAMOUS AVENGERS, ANNOUNCED TODAY..."
BOY, THAT DOES HAVE A RING TO IT! THE NEXT TIME I DO SOMETHING BIG--LIKE, HOPEFULLY CAPTURE KANG--I'M GONNA PROPOSE NEW ELECTIONS!
THEN, I---
HOLY JOE! IT'S HIM--IN THE FLESH!
CURSE YOU, HAWKEYE! YOU MAY HAVE DISCOVERED ME--

NOW, WHILE YOU PONDER *THAT* SURPRISING LITTLE SCENE...

MARVELOUS, BROTHER! EVEN *I* COULD DEVISE NOTHING MORE TRULY *EVIL* THAN *THIS!*

IN THE NAME OF THE DREAD *DOR-MAMMU*-- BY THE NATURE AT MY COMMAND--

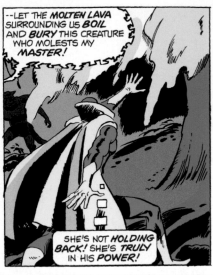

--LET THE *MOLTEN LAVA* SURROUNDING US *BOIL* AND *BURY* THIS CREATURE WHO MOLESTS MY *MASTER!*

SHE'S NOT *HOLDING BACK!* SHE'S *TRULY* IN HIS *POWER!*

GODS! THAT ONE WHO SOUGHT *MY* SECRETS SHOULD BE SO USED BY HIM WHO *HOLDETH* ME!

WHAT WILL HE DARE WHEN HE HOLDETH THE *FULL MEASURES* OF POWER?

THE VISION IS *EQUALLY* AWED AND AMAZED, FOR THIS IS THE WOMAN *LOVES* WHO STRIKES AT HIS LIFE! LOGIC *FALTERS* AT THE VERY *THOUGHT.*

--BUT IT CAN NEVER *WHOLLY* HALT FOR HIM!

EVEN AS HE VANISHES IN A WELTER OF *FIRE*, HE BECOMES *SOLID*-- SO SOLID AS TO CONTROL *EVERY ATOM* IN HIS FORM!

LIKE A *DIAMOND*, HE *CANNOT BURN!*

MISS HARKNESS TAUGHT ME *WELL*, CREATURE! I HAVE *OTHER* WEAPONS!

ALL THINGS ORGANIC BOW TO MY WILL, WHETHER THEY BE OF *FIRE*, *AIR*, *WATER*, OR--

--*EARTH!*

LOOK TO THIS *BOULDER*, NOW *ABOVE* YOU--

--AND NOW *UPON* YOU!

CRUMP!

BUT I HAVE ONLY TO BECOME *INTANGIBLE* TO RISE THROUGH STONE, WANDA!

I CAN COUNTER *ALL* OF YOUR *ORGANIC POWERS*, BECAUSE I AM A MAN OF *SYNTHETICS!*

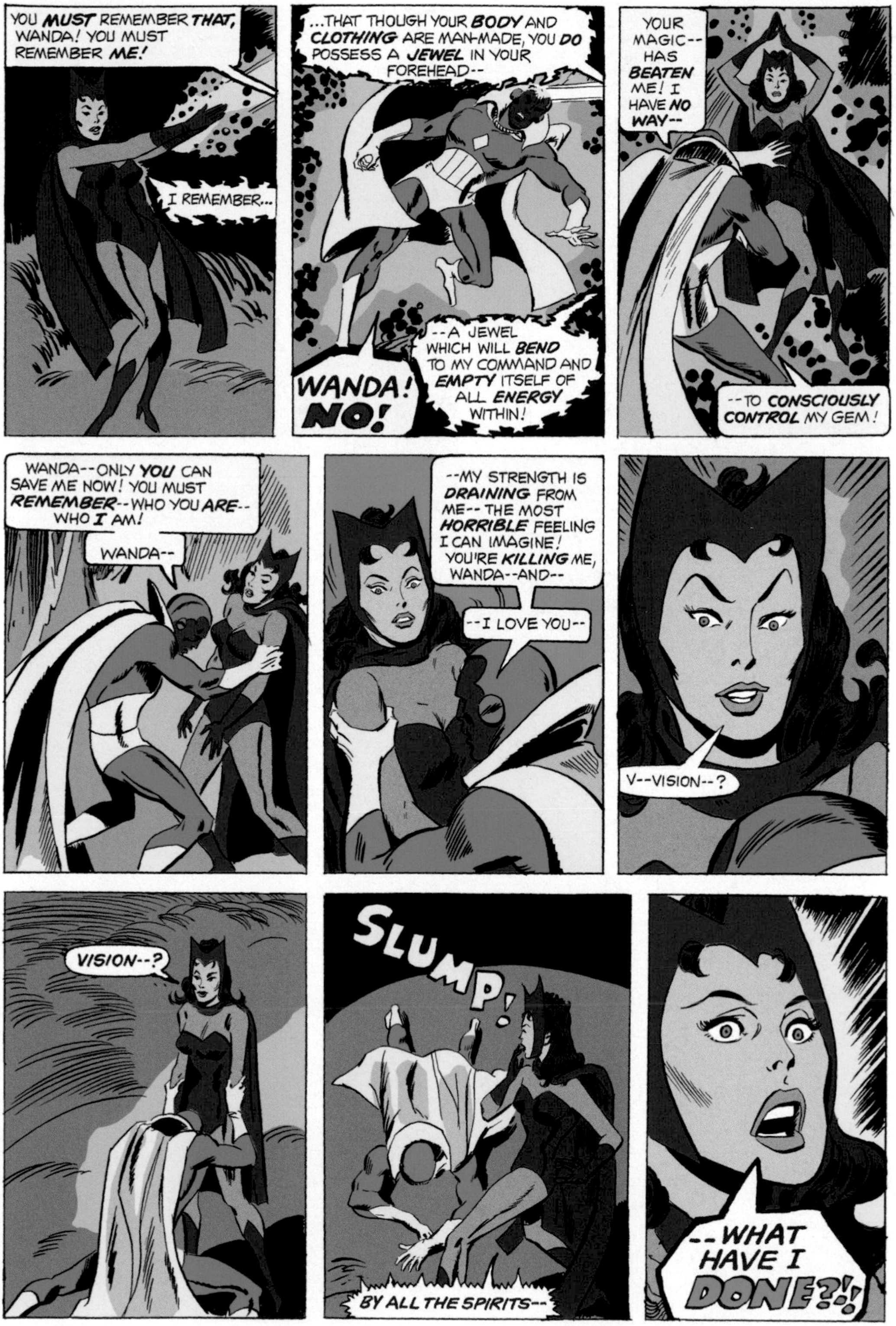
YOU MUST REMEMBER THAT, WANDA! YOU MUST REMEMBER ME!
I REMEMBER...
...THAT THOUGH YOUR BODY AND CLOTHING ARE MAN-MADE, YOU DO POSSESS A JEWEL IN YOUR FOREHEAD--
--A JEWEL WHICH WILL BEND TO MY COMMAND AND EMPTY ITSELF OF ALL ENERGY WITHIN!
WANDA! NO!
YOUR MAGIC--HAS BEATEN ME! I HAVE NO WAY--
--TO CONSCIOUSLY CONTROL MY GEM!
WANDA--ONLY YOU CAN SAVE ME NOW! YOU MUST REMEMBER--WHO YOU ARE--WHO I AM!
WANDA--
--MY STRENGTH IS DRAINING FROM ME-- THE MOST HORRIBLE FEELING I CAN IMAGINE! YOU'RE KILLING ME, WANDA--AND--
--I LOVE YOU--
V--VISION--?
VISION--?
SLUMP!
BY ALL THE SPIRITS--
--WHAT HAVE I DONE?!

BREAK: YOU KNEW **NOTHING** OF **LOVE** WHEN YOU CAME TO THE AVENGERS, MANTIS, BUT THEY HELPED **TEACH** YOU, ALL **UNKNOWING**.

FOR THE **FIRST TIME**, YOU SAW **OTHERS** WITH THE NOBILITY OF THE SWORDS-MAN...AND YOUR **HEAD** WAS TURNED.

PLEASE--WHATEVER YOU MAY BE--IT IS **TOO MUCH** TO HEAR OF MY SHAME FROM **YOUR LIPS**, SO LIKE THE ONES THIS ONE **BETRAYED**!

HE SPEAKS NOT OF **BETRAYAL**, MANTIS.

NO, DAUGHTER... HE SPEAKS OF EXPLORING THE **LIMITS** OF YOUR HUMANITY...

...YOUR ATTRACTION TO **GLAMOR**, YOUR **COMPETI-TIVENESS**, YOUR **SELFISH-NESS, LONELINESS, LUST**-- ALL THAT WHICH **PASSES** FOR LOVE AND IS **NOT**.

FOR ALL THAT YOU HAD **LEARNED**, YOU COULD NOT **LOVE** WITH SO MUCH OF YOU STILL **BOTTLED UP** INSIDE. THUS, THERE CAME A TIME WHEN YOU NEEDED TO LEARN THAT THERE WAS **MORE** TO LEARN ABOUT LIFE.

YOU ARE SAYING THAT THIS ONE COULD NOT BE **ONLY** A PRIESTESS OR **ONLY** A CREATURE OF IMPULSE.

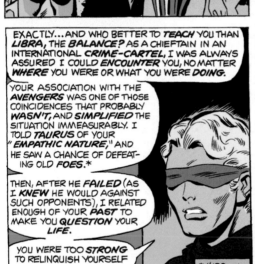

EXACTLY...AND WHO BETTER TO **TEACH** YOU THAN **LIBRA**, THE **BALANCE**? AS A CHIEFTAIN IN AN INTERNATIONAL **CRIME-CARTEL**, I WAS ALWAYS ASSURED I COULD **ENCOUNTER** YOU, NO MATTER **WHERE** YOU WERE OR WHAT YOU WERE **DOING**.

YOUR ASSOCIATION WITH THE **AVENGERS** WAS ONE OF THOSE COINCIDENCES THAT PROBABLY **WASN'T**, AND **SIMPLIFIED** THE SITUATION IMMEASURABLY. I TOLD **TAURUS** OF YOUR "**EMPATHIC NATURE**," AND HE SAW A CHANCE OF DEFEAT-ING OLD **FOES**.*

THEN, AFTER HE **FAILED** (AS I **KNEW** HE WOULD AGAINST SUCH OPPONENTS), I RELATED ENOUGH OF YOUR **PAST** TO MAKE YOU **QUESTION** YOUR **LIFE**.

YOU WERE TOO **STRONG** TO RELINQUISH YOURSELF **EASILY**...

*#120.--L.

...BUT WHEN YOU GRASPED FOR THE **VISION**, A PILLAR OF **STABILITY** AND YET A MAN **UNALTERABLY** IN LOVE WITH **ANOTHER**, YOU **INSURED** THAT YOUR LIFE OF FRIVOLITY WOULD **END**...THAT YOU WOULD AWAKEN TO A MORE **COMPLETE** CONCEPTION OF EXISTENCE...

CURSE YOU, DORMAMMU! I'M **FREE** OF YOUR HELLISH **SPELLS** NOW--

--AND I'LL MAKE YOU **PAY** FOR WHAT YOU MADE ME DO!

YOU IMPUDENT **HUMAN**--

--YOU WERE **BROUGHT** HERE TO SUFFER MY **VENGEANCE**, AS A MEANS OF OCCUPYING MY TIME UNTIL I CAN ATTACK **ALL** THE EARTH--

--AND **THAT** IS ALL **YOU** SHALL DO TODAY!

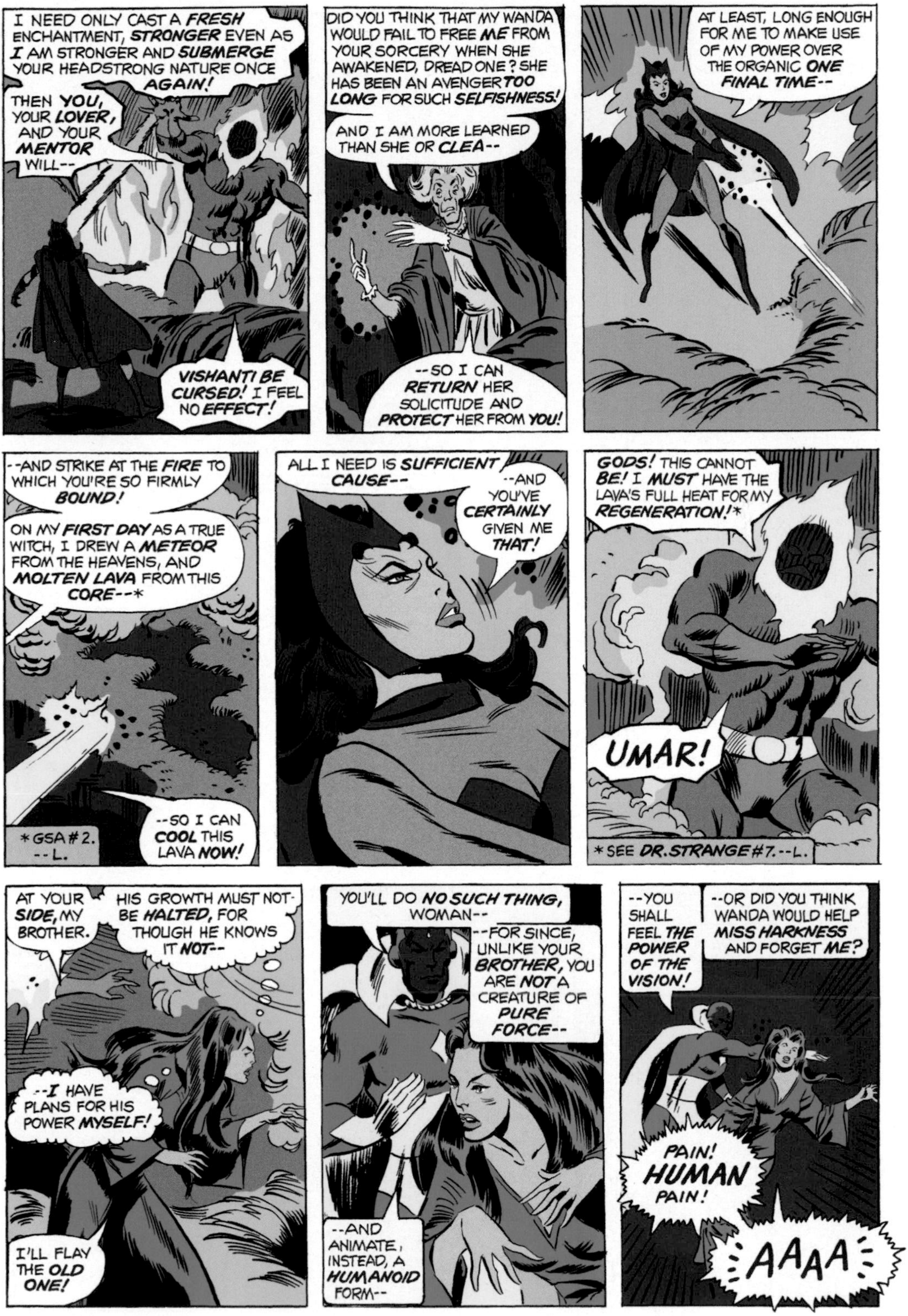
I NEED ONLY CAST A FRESH ENCHANTMENT, STRONGER EVEN AS I AM STRONGER AND SUBMERGE YOUR HEADSTRONG NATURE ONCE AGAIN!
THEN YOU, YOUR LOVER, AND YOUR MENTOR WILL--
VISHANTI BE CURSED! I FEEL NO EFFECT!
DID YOU THINK THAT MY WANDA WOULD FAIL TO FREE ME FROM YOUR SORCERY WHEN SHE AWAKENED, DREAD ONE? SHE HAS BEEN AN AVENGER TOO LONG FOR SUCH SELFISHNESS!
AND I AM MORE LEARNED THAN SHE OR CLEA--
--SO I CAN RETURN HER SOLICITUDE AND PROTECT HER FROM YOU!
AT LEAST, LONG ENOUGH FOR ME TO MAKE USE OF MY POWER OVER THE ORGANIC ONE FINAL TIME--
--AND STRIKE AT THE FIRE TO WHICH YOU'RE SO FIRMLY BOUND!
ON MY FIRST DAY AS A TRUE WITCH, I DREW A METEOR FROM THE HEAVENS, AND MOLTEN LAVA FROM THIS CORE--*
*GSA #2. --L.
--SO I CAN COOL THIS LAVA NOW!
ALL I NEED IS SUFFICIENT CAUSE--
--AND YOU'VE CERTAINLY GIVEN ME THAT!
GODS! THIS CANNOT BE! I MUST HAVE THE LAVA'S FULL HEAT FOR MY REGENERATION!*
UMAR!
*SEE DR. STRANGE #7. --L.
AT YOUR SIDE, MY BROTHER.
HIS GROWTH MUST NOT BE HALTED, FOR THOUGH HE KNOWS IT NOT--
--I HAVE PLANS FOR HIS POWER MYSELF!
I'LL FLAY THE OLD ONE!
YOU'LL DO NO SUCH THING, WOMAN--
--FOR SINCE, UNLIKE YOUR BROTHER, YOU ARE NOT A CREATURE OF PURE FORCE--
--AND ANIMATE, INSTEAD, A HUMANOID FORM--
--YOU SHALL FEEL THE POWER OF THE VISION!
--OR DID YOU THINK WANDA WOULD HELP MISS HARKNESS AND FORGET ME?
PAIN! HUMAN PAIN!
AAAA

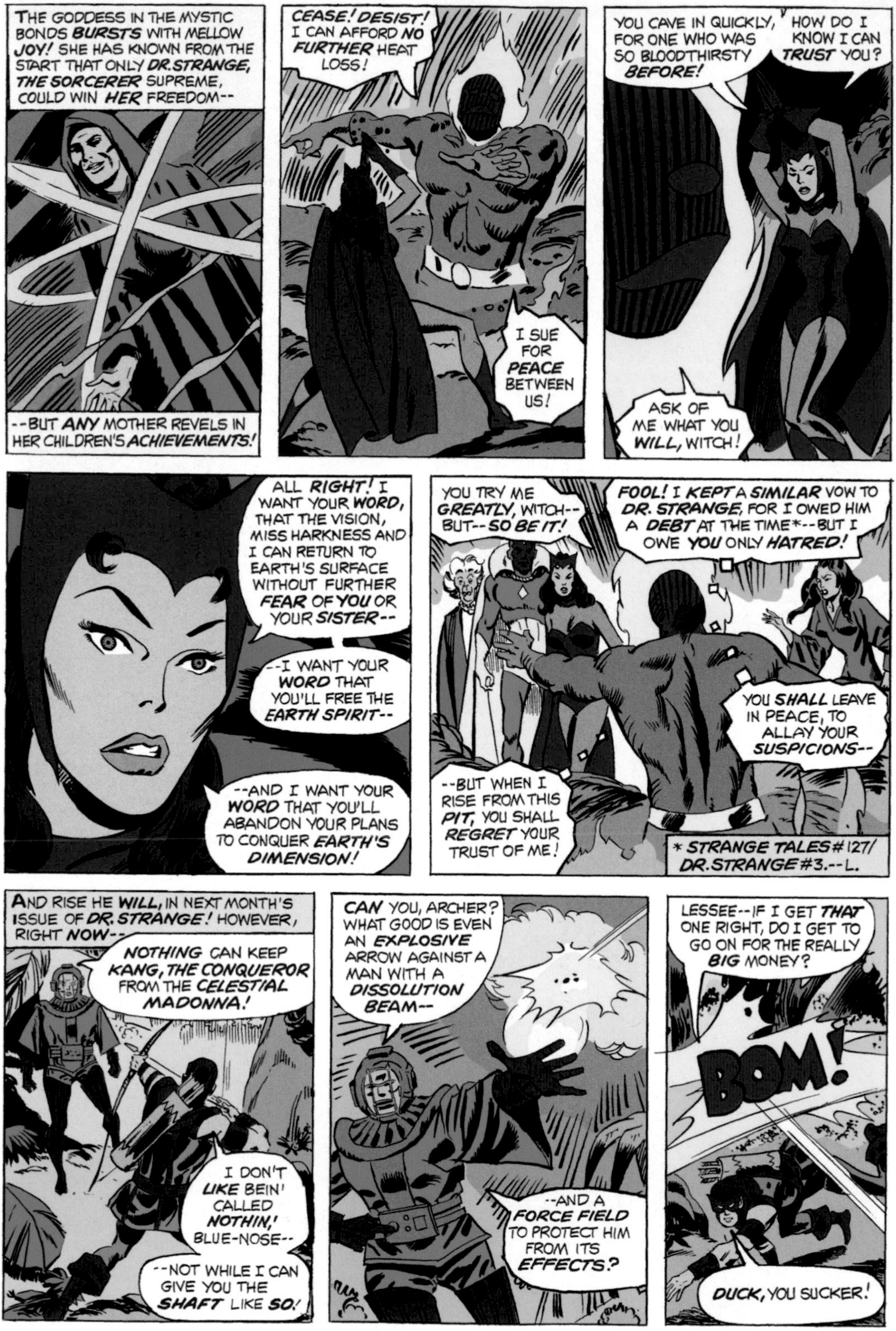
THE GODDESS IN THE MYSTIC BONDS BURSTS WITH MELLOW JOY! SHE HAS KNOWN FROM THE START THAT ONLY DR. STRANGE, THE SORCERER SUPREME, COULD WIN HER FREEDOM--
--BUT ANY MOTHER REVELS IN HER CHILDREN'S ACHIEVEMENTS!
CEASE! DESIST! I CAN AFFORD NO FURTHER HEAT LOSS!
I SUE FOR PEACE BETWEEN US!
YOU CAVE IN QUICKLY, FOR ONE WHO WAS SO BLOODTHIRSTY BEFORE!
HOW DO I KNOW I CAN TRUST YOU?
ASK OF ME WHAT YOU WILL, WITCH!
ALL RIGHT! I WANT YOUR WORD, THAT THE VISION, MISS HARKNESS AND I CAN RETURN TO EARTH'S SURFACE WITHOUT FURTHER FEAR OF YOU OR YOUR SISTER--
--I WANT YOUR WORD THAT YOU'LL FREE THE EARTH SPIRIT--
--AND I WANT YOUR WORD THAT YOU'LL ABANDON YOUR PLANS TO CONQUER EARTH'S DIMENSION!
YOU TRY ME GREATLY, WITCH-- BUT-- SO BE IT!
FOOL! I KEPT A SIMILAR VOW TO DR. STRANGE, FOR I OWED HIM A DEBT AT THE TIME*--BUT I OWE YOU ONLY HATRED!
YOU SHALL LEAVE IN PEACE, TO ALLAY YOUR SUSPICIONS--
--BUT WHEN I RISE FROM THIS PIT, YOU SHALL REGRET YOUR TRUST OF ME!
* STRANGE TALES #127/ DR. STRANGE #3.--L.
AND RISE HE WILL, IN NEXT MONTH'S ISSUE OF DR. STRANGE! HOWEVER, RIGHT NOW--
NOTHING CAN KEEP KANG, THE CONQUEROR FROM THE CELESTIAL MADONNA!
I DON'T LIKE BEIN' CALLED NOTHIN,' BLUE-NOSE--
--NOT WHILE I CAN GIVE YOU THE SHAFT LIKE SO!
CAN YOU, ARCHER? WHAT GOOD IS EVEN AN EXPLOSIVE ARROW AGAINST A MAN WITH A DISSOLUTION BEAM--
--AND A FORCE FIELD TO PROTECT HIM FROM ITS EFFECTS?
LESSEE--IF I GET THAT ONE RIGHT, DO I GET TO GO ON FOR THE REALLY BIG MONEY?
BOM!
DUCK, YOU SUCKER!

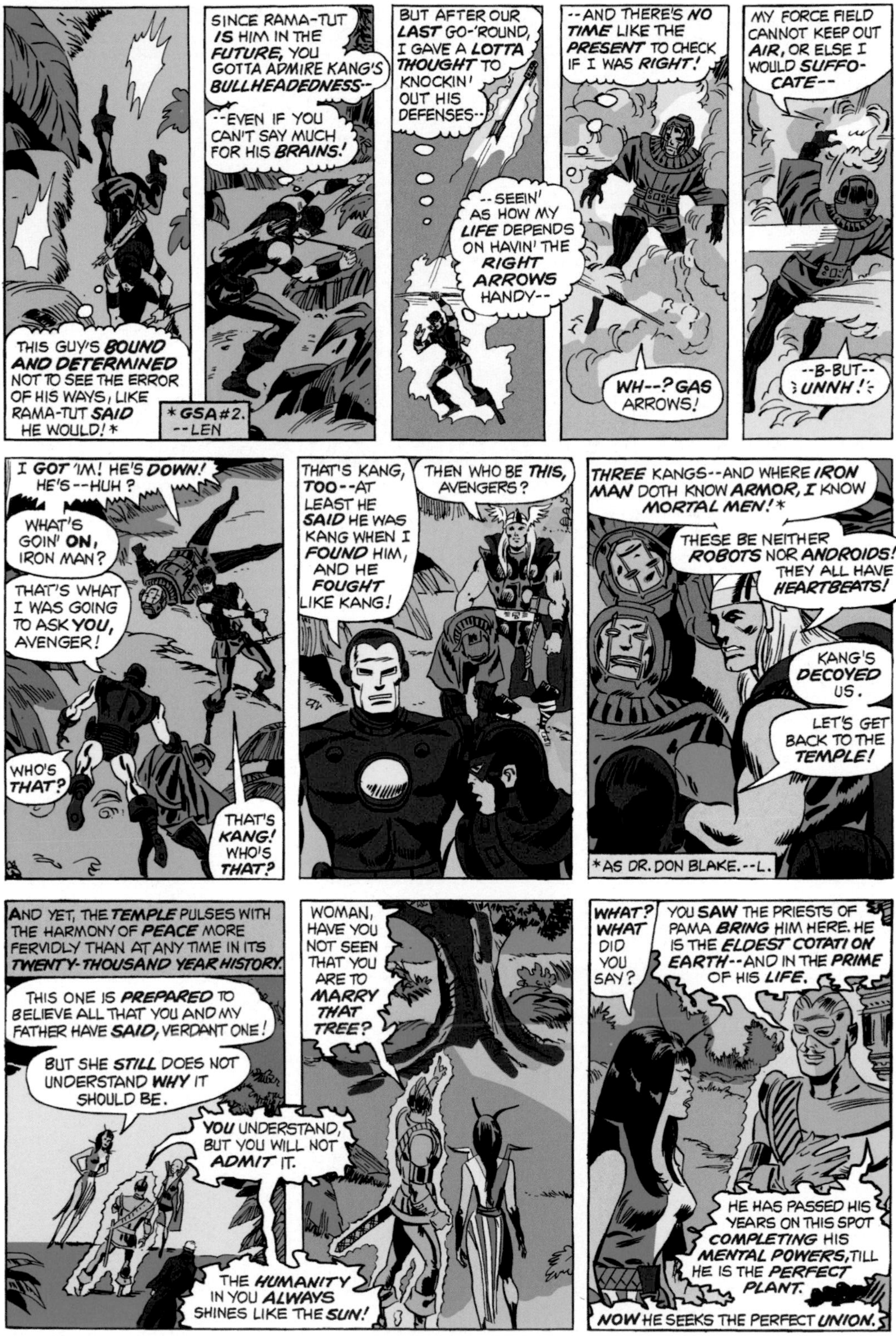
SINCE RAMA-TUT IS HIM IN THE FUTURE, YOU GOTTA ADMIRE KANG'S BULLHEADEDNESS--
--EVEN IF YOU CAN'T SAY MUCH FOR HIS BRAINS!
THIS GUY'S BOUND AND DETERMINED NOT TO SEE THE ERROR OF HIS WAYS, LIKE RAMA-TUT SAID HE WOULD! *
* GSA #2. --LEN
BUT AFTER OUR LAST GO-'ROUND, I GAVE A LOTTA THOUGHT TO KNOCKIN' OUT HIS DEFENSES--
--SEEIN' AS HOW MY LIFE DEPENDS ON HAVIN' THE RIGHT ARROWS HANDY--
--AND THERE'S NO TIME LIKE THE PRESENT TO CHECK IF I WAS RIGHT!
WH--? GAS ARROWS!
MY FORCE FIELD CANNOT KEEP OUT AIR, OR ELSE I WOULD SUFFOCATE--
--B-BUT-- UNNH!
I GOT 'IM! HE'S DOWN! HE'S--HUH?
WHAT'S GOIN' ON, IRON MAN?
THAT'S WHAT I WAS GOING TO ASK YOU, AVENGER!
WHO'S THAT?
THAT'S KANG! WHO'S THAT?
THAT'S KANG, TOO--AT LEAST HE SAID HE WAS KANG WHEN I FOUND HIM, AND HE FOUGHT LIKE KANG!
THEN WHO BE THIS, AVENGERS?
THREE KANGS--AND WHERE IRON MAN DOTH KNOW ARMOR, I KNOW MORTAL MEN! *
THESE BE NEITHER ROBOTS NOR ANDROIDS! THEY ALL HAVE HEARTBEATS!
KANG'S DECOYED US.
LET'S GET BACK TO THE TEMPLE!
* AS DR. DON BLAKE. --L.
AND YET, THE TEMPLE PULSES WITH THE HARMONY OF PEACE MORE FERVIDLY THAN AT ANY TIME IN ITS TWENTY-THOUSAND YEAR HISTORY.
THIS ONE IS PREPARED TO BELIEVE ALL THAT YOU AND MY FATHER HAVE SAID, VERDANT ONE!
BUT SHE STILL DOES NOT UNDERSTAND WHY IT SHOULD BE.
YOU UNDERSTAND, BUT YOU WILL NOT ADMIT IT.
THE HUMANITY IN YOU ALWAYS SHINES LIKE THE SUN!
WOMAN, HAVE YOU NOT SEEN THAT YOU ARE TO MARRY THAT TREE?
WHAT? WHAT DID YOU SAY?
YOU SAW THE PRIESTS OF PAMA BRING HIM HERE. HE IS THE ELDEST COTATI ON EARTH--AND IN THE PRIME OF HIS LIFE.
HE HAS PASSED HIS YEARS ON THIS SPOT COMPLETING HIS MENTAL POWERS, TILL HE IS THE PERFECT PLANT.
NOW HE SEEKS THE PERFECT UNION.

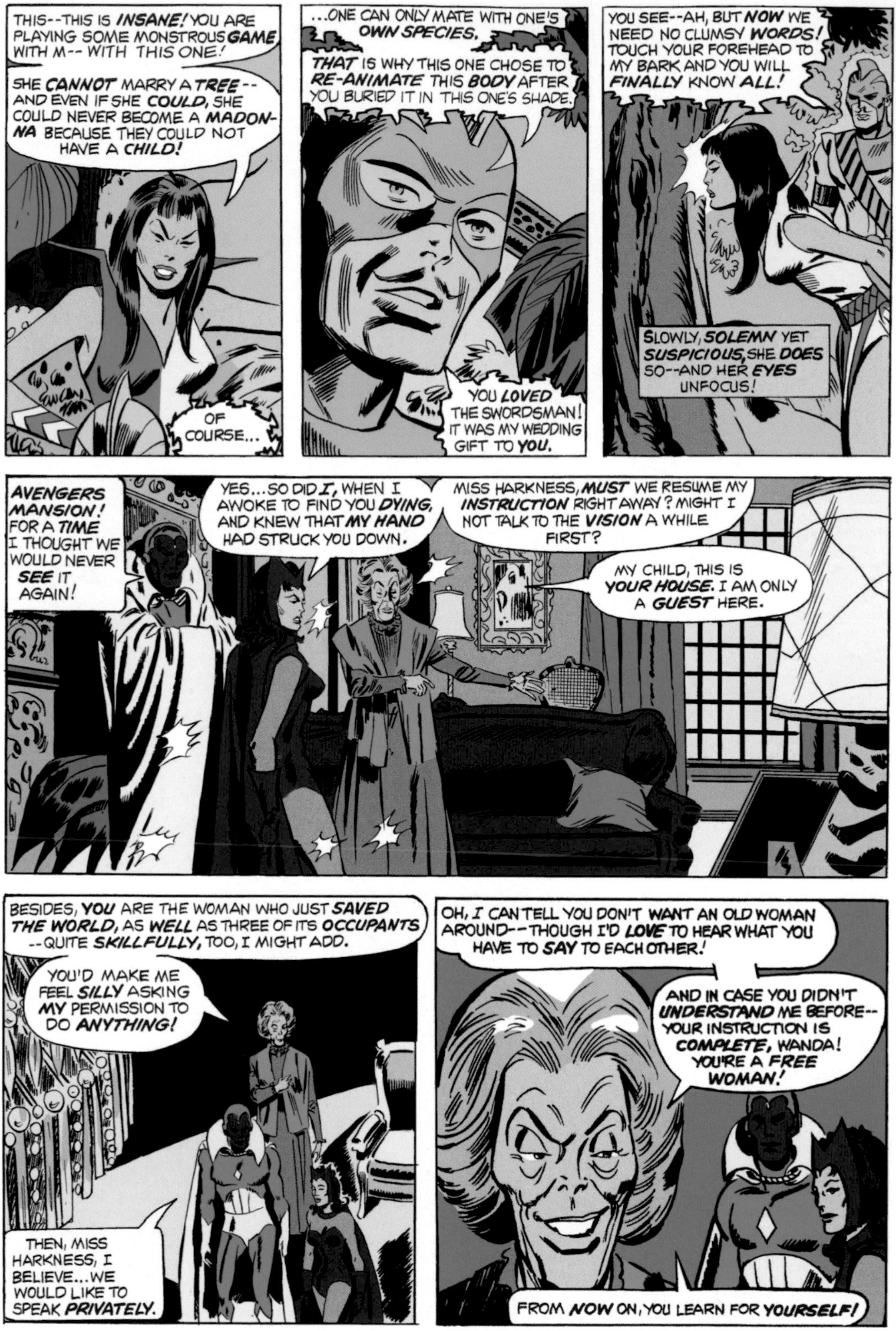
THIS--THIS IS INSANE! YOU ARE PLAYING SOME MONSTROUS GAME WITH M-- WITH THIS ONE!
SHE CANNOT MARRY A TREE-- AND EVEN IF SHE COULD, SHE COULD NEVER BECOME A MADONNA BECAUSE THEY COULD NOT HAVE A CHILD!
OF COURSE...
...ONE CAN ONLY MATE WITH ONE'S OWN SPECIES.
THAT IS WHY THIS ONE CHOSE TO RE-ANIMATE THIS BODY AFTER YOU BURIED IT IN THIS ONE'S SHADE.
YOU LOVED THE SWORDSMAN! IT WAS MY WEDDING GIFT TO YOU.
YOU SEE--AH, BUT NOW WE NEED NO CLUMSY WORDS! TOUCH YOUR FOREHEAD TO MY BARK AND YOU WILL FINALLY KNOW ALL!
SLOWLY, SOLEMN YET SUSPICIOUS, SHE DOES SO--AND HER EYES UNFOCUS!
AVENGERS MANSION! FOR A TIME I THOUGHT WE WOULD NEVER SEE IT AGAIN!
YES...SO DID I, WHEN I AWOKE TO FIND YOU DYING, AND KNEW THAT MY HAND HAD STRUCK YOU DOWN.
MISS HARKNESS, MUST WE RESUME MY INSTRUCTION RIGHT AWAY? MIGHT I NOT TALK TO THE VISION A WHILE FIRST?
MY CHILD, THIS IS YOUR HOUSE. I AM ONLY A GUEST HERE.
BESIDES, YOU ARE THE WOMAN WHO JUST SAVED THE WORLD, AS WELL AS THREE OF ITS OCCUPANTS --QUITE SKILLFULLY, TOO, I MIGHT ADD.
YOU'D MAKE ME FEEL SILLY ASKING MY PERMISSION TO DO ANYTHING!
THEN, MISS HARKNESS, I BELIEVE...WE WOULD LIKE TO SPEAK PRIVATELY.
OH, I CAN TELL YOU DON'T WANT AN OLD WOMAN AROUND--THOUGH I'D LOVE TO HEAR WHAT YOU HAVE TO SAY TO EACH OTHER!
AND IN CASE YOU DIDN'T UNDERSTAND ME BEFORE--YOUR INSTRUCTION IS COMPLETE, WANDA! YOU'RE A FREE WOMAN!
FROM NOW ON, YOU LEARN FOR YOURSELF!

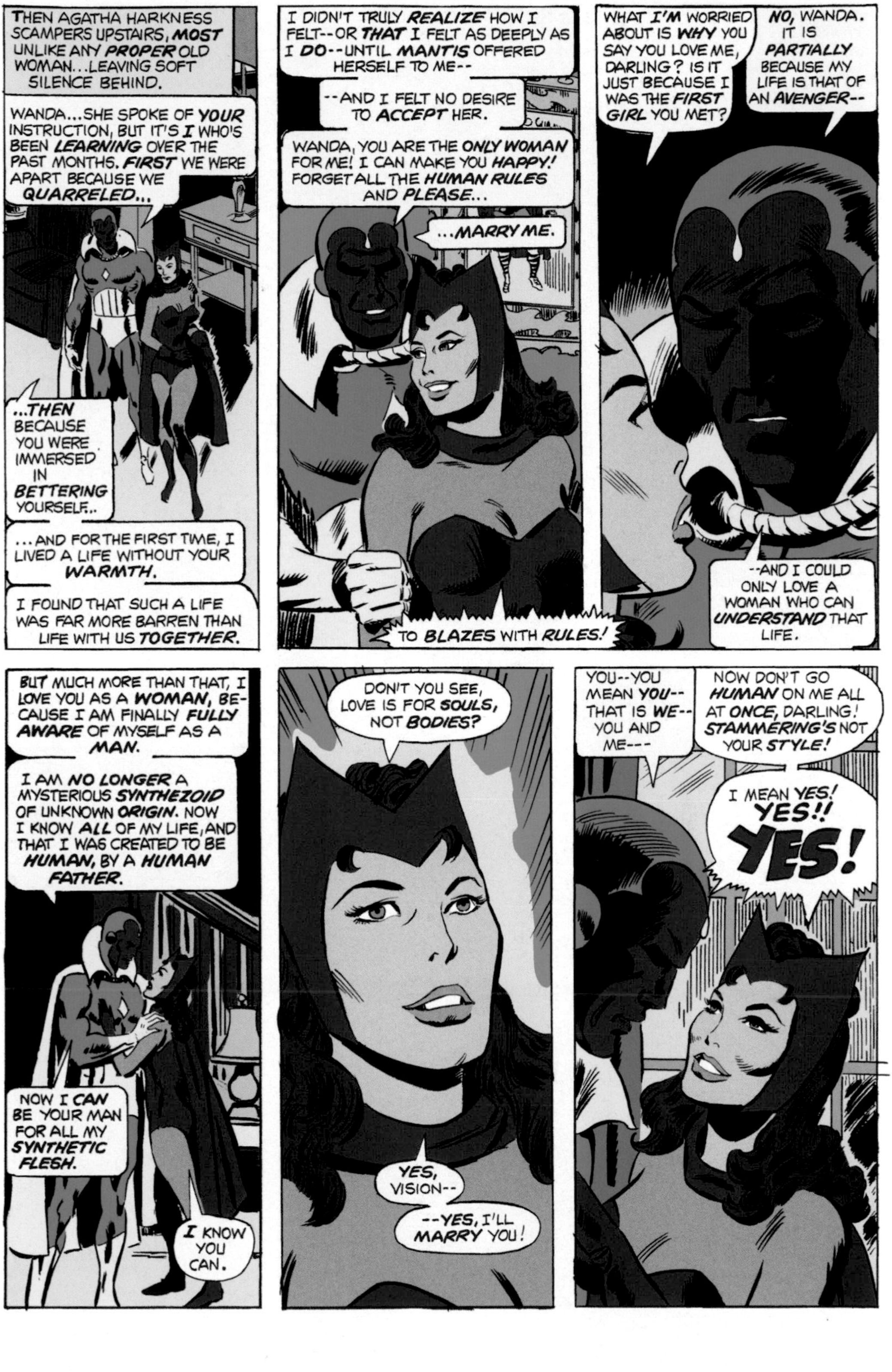
THEN AGATHA HARKNESS SCAMPERS UPSTAIRS, MOST UNLIKE ANY PROPER OLD WOMAN... LEAVING SOFT SILENCE BEHIND.
WANDA... SHE SPOKE OF YOUR INSTRUCTION, BUT IT'S I WHO'S BEEN LEARNING OVER THE PAST MONTHS. FIRST WE WERE APART BECAUSE WE QUARRELED...
...THEN BECAUSE YOU WERE IMMERSED IN BETTERING YOURSELF..
...AND FOR THE FIRST TIME, I LIVED A LIFE WITHOUT YOUR WARMTH.
I FOUND THAT SUCH A LIFE WAS FAR MORE BARREN THAN LIFE WITH US TOGETHER.
I DIDN'T TRULY REALIZE HOW I FELT--OR THAT I FELT AS DEEPLY AS I DO--UNTIL MANTIS OFFERED HERSELF TO ME--
--AND I FELT NO DESIRE TO ACCEPT HER.
WANDA, YOU ARE THE ONLY WOMAN FOR ME! I CAN MAKE YOU HAPPY! FORGET ALL THE HUMAN RULES AND PLEASE...
...MARRY ME.
TO BLAZES WITH RULES!
WHAT I'M WORRIED ABOUT IS WHY YOU SAY YOU LOVE ME, DARLING? IS IT JUST BECAUSE I WAS THE FIRST GIRL YOU MET?
NO, WANDA. IT IS PARTIALLY BECAUSE MY LIFE IS THAT OF AN AVENGER--
--AND I COULD ONLY LOVE A WOMAN WHO CAN UNDERSTAND THAT LIFE.
BUT MUCH MORE THAN THAT, I LOVE YOU AS A WOMAN, BECAUSE I AM FINALLY FULLY AWARE OF MYSELF AS A MAN.
I AM NO LONGER A MYSTERIOUS SYNTHEZOID OF UNKNOWN ORIGIN. NOW I KNOW ALL OF MY LIFE, AND THAT I WAS CREATED TO BE HUMAN, BY A HUMAN FATHER.
NOW I CAN BE YOUR MAN FOR ALL MY SYNTHETIC FLESH.
I KNOW YOU CAN.
DON'T YOU SEE, LOVE IS FOR SOULS, NOT BODIES?
YES, VISION--
--YES, I'LL MARRY YOU!
YOU--YOU MEAN YOU--THAT IS WE--YOU AND ME---
NOW DON'T GO HUMAN ON ME ALL AT ONCE, DARLING! STAMMERING'S NOT YOUR STYLE!
I MEAN YES! YES!! YES!

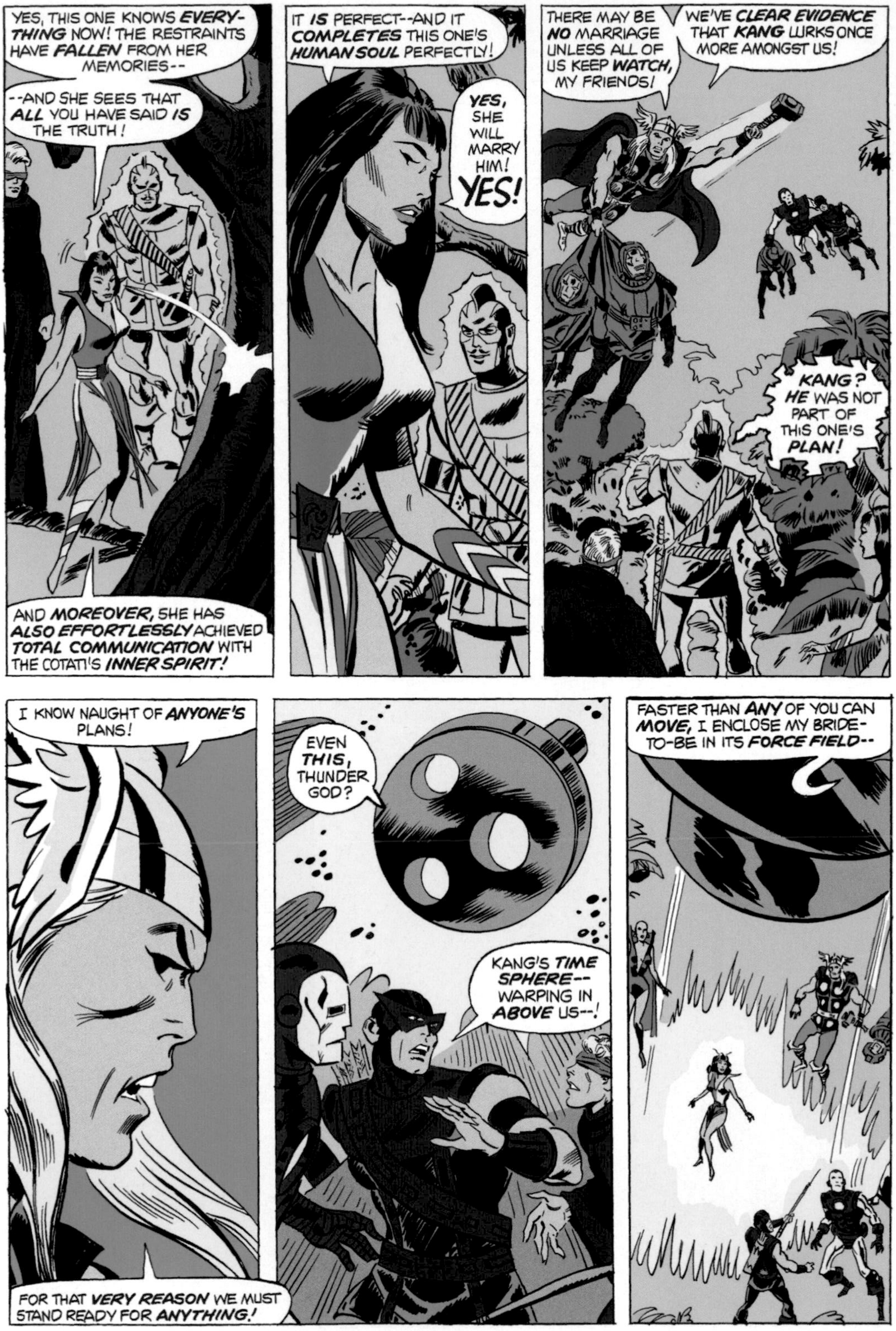

YES, THIS ONE KNOWS EVERYTHING NOW! THE RESTRAINTS HAVE FALLEN FROM HER MEMORIES--
--AND SHE SEES THAT ALL YOU HAVE SAID IS THE TRUTH!
AND MOREOVER, SHE HAS ALSO EFFORTLESSLY ACHIEVED TOTAL COMMUNICATION WITH THE COTATI'S INNER SPIRIT!
IT IS PERFECT--AND IT COMPLETES THIS ONE'S HUMAN SOUL PERFECTLY!
YES, SHE WILL MARRY HIM! YES!
THERE MAY BE NO MARRIAGE UNLESS ALL OF US KEEP WATCH, MY FRIENDS!
WE'VE CLEAR EVIDENCE THAT KANG LURKS ONCE MORE AMONGST US!
KANG? HE WAS NOT PART OF THIS ONE'S PLAN!
I KNOW NAUGHT OF ANYONE'S PLANS!
FOR THAT VERY REASON WE MUST STAND READY FOR ANYTHING!
EVEN THIS, THUNDER GOD?
KANG'S TIME SPHERE--WARPING IN ABOVE US--!
FASTER THAN ANY OF YOU CAN MOVE, I ENCLOSE MY BRIDE-TO-BE IN ITS FORCE FIELD--

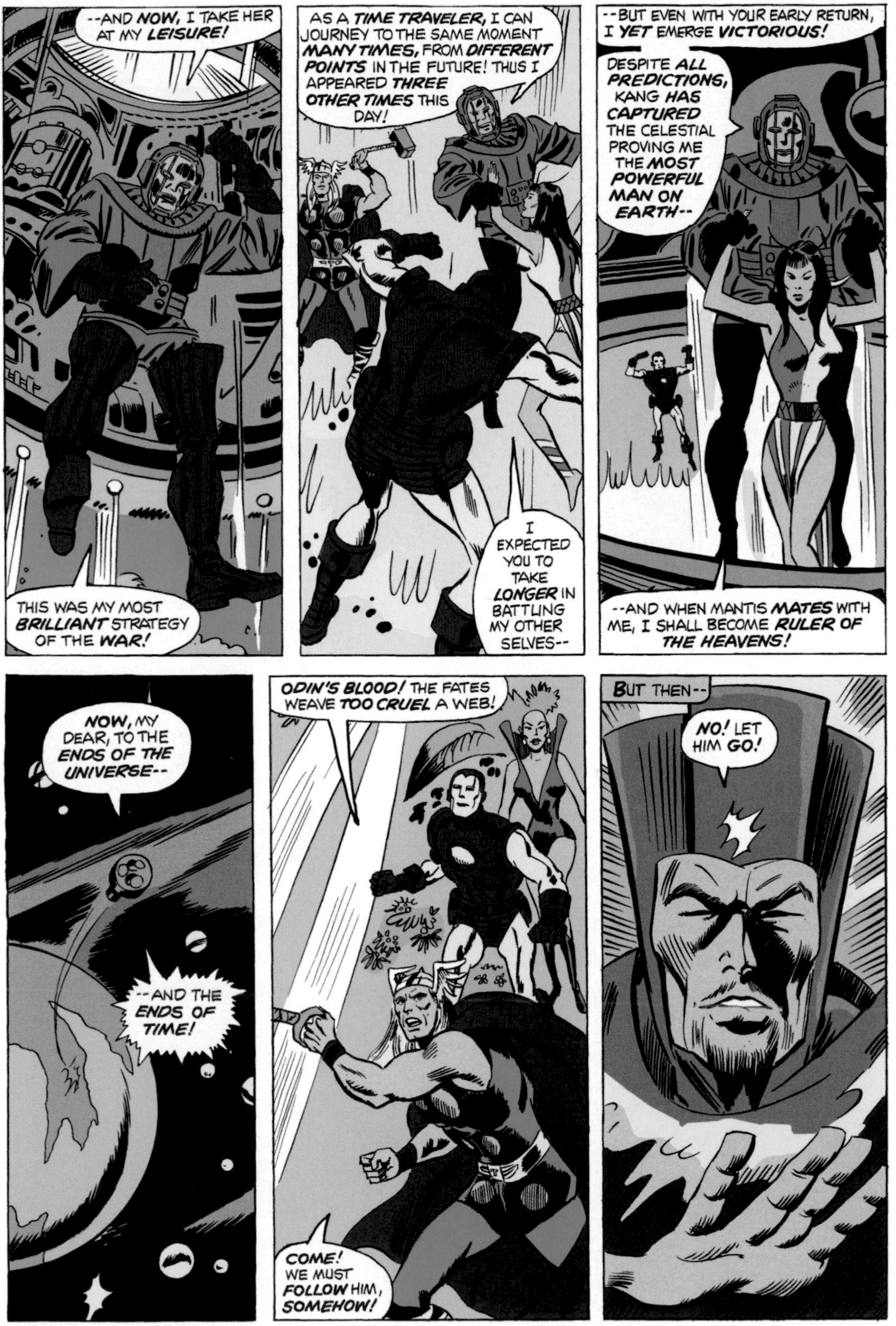
--AND NOW, I TAKE HER AT MY LEISURE!
THIS WAS MY MOST BRILLIANT STRATEGY OF THE WAR!
AS A TIME TRAVELER, I CAN JOURNEY TO THE SAME MOMENT MANY TIMES, FROM DIFFERENT POINTS IN THE FUTURE! THUS I APPEARED THREE OTHER TIMES THIS DAY!
I EXPECTED YOU TO TAKE LONGER IN BATTLING MY OTHER SELVES--
--BUT EVEN WITH YOUR EARLY RETURN, I YET EMERGE VICTORIOUS!
DESPITE ALL PREDICTIONS, KANG HAS CAPTURED THE CELESTIAL PROVING ME THE MOST POWERFUL MAN ON EARTH--
--AND WHEN MANTIS MATES WITH ME, I SHALL BECOME RULER OF THE HEAVENS!
NOW, MY DEAR, TO THE ENDS OF THE UNIVERSE--
--AND THE ENDS OF TIME!
ODIN'S BLOOD! THE FATES WEAVE TOO CRUEL A WEB!
COME! WE MUST FOLLOW HIM, SOMEHOW!
BUT THEN--
NO! LET HIM GO!

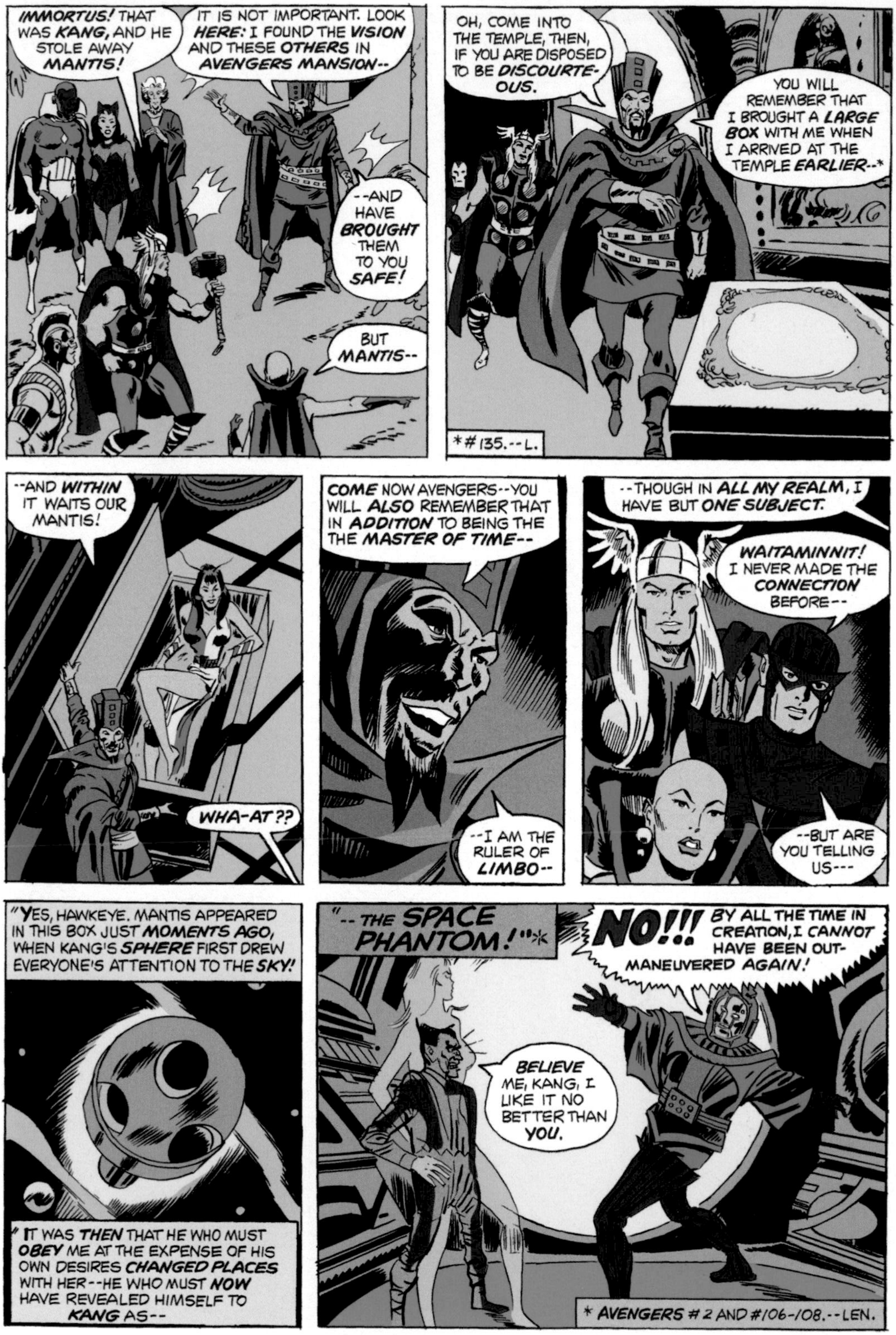
IMMORTUS! THAT WAS KANG, AND HE STOLE AWAY MANTIS!
IT IS NOT IMPORTANT. LOOK HERE: I FOUND THE VISION AND THESE OTHERS IN AVENGERS MANSION--
--AND HAVE BROUGHT THEM TO YOU SAFE!
BUT MANTIS--
OH, COME INTO THE TEMPLE, THEN, IF YOU ARE DISPOSED TO BE DISCOURTEOUS.
YOU WILL REMEMBER THAT I BROUGHT A LARGE BOX WITH ME WHEN I ARRIVED AT THE TEMPLE EARLIER--*
*#135.--L.
--AND WITHIN IT WAITS OUR MANTIS!
WHA-AT??
COME NOW AVENGERS--YOU WILL ALSO REMEMBER THAT IN ADDITION TO BEING THE THE MASTER OF TIME--
--I AM THE RULER OF LIMBO--
--THOUGH IN ALL MY REALM, I HAVE BUT ONE SUBJECT.
WAITAMINNIT! I NEVER MADE THE CONNECTION BEFORE--
--BUT ARE YOU TELLING US---
"YES, HAWKEYE. MANTIS APPEARED IN THIS BOX JUST MOMENTS AGO, WHEN KANG'S SPHERE FIRST DREW EVERYONE'S ATTENTION TO THE SKY!
"IT WAS THEN THAT HE WHO MUST OBEY ME AT THE EXPENSE OF HIS OWN DESIRES CHANGED PLACES WITH HER--HE WHO MUST NOW HAVE REVEALED HIMSELF TO KANG AS--
"--THE SPACE PHANTOM!"*
NO!!! BY ALL THE TIME IN CREATION, I CANNOT HAVE BEEN OUT-MANEUVERED AGAIN!
BELIEVE ME, KANG, I LIKE IT NO BETTER THAN YOU.
* AVENGERS #2 AND #106-108.--LEN.

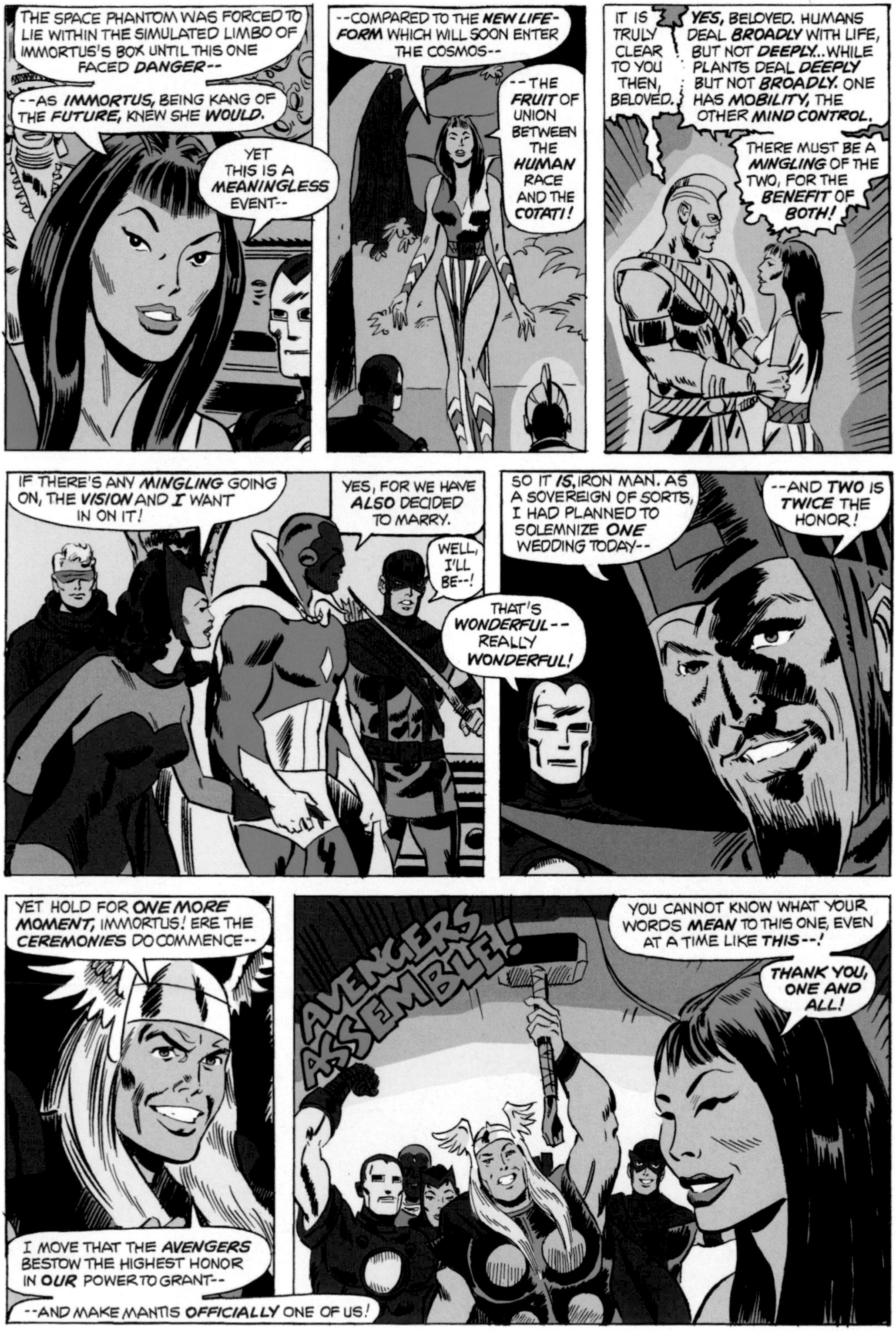
THE SPACE PHANTOM WAS FORCED TO LIE WITHIN THE SIMULATED LIMBO OF IMMORTUS'S BOX UNTIL THIS ONE FACED DANGER--
--AS IMMORTUS, BEING KANG OF THE FUTURE, KNEW SHE WOULD.
YET THIS IS A MEANINGLESS EVENT--
--COMPARED TO THE NEW LIFE-FORM WHICH WILL SOON ENTER THE COSMOS--
--THE FRUIT OF UNION BETWEEN THE HUMAN RACE AND THE COTATI!
IT IS TRULY CLEAR TO YOU THEN, BELOVED.
YES, BELOVED. HUMANS DEAL BROADLY WITH LIFE, BUT NOT DEEPLY...WHILE PLANTS DEAL DEEPLY BUT NOT BROADLY. ONE HAS MOBILITY, THE OTHER MIND CONTROL.
THERE MUST BE A MINGLING OF THE TWO, FOR THE BENEFIT OF BOTH!
IF THERE'S ANY MINGLING GOING ON, THE VISION AND I WANT IN ON IT!
YES, FOR WE HAVE ALSO DECIDED TO MARRY.
WELL, I'LL BE--!
THAT'S WONDERFUL-- REALLY WONDERFUL!
SO IT IS, IRON MAN. AS A SOVEREIGN OF SORTS, I HAD PLANNED TO SOLEMNIZE ONE WEDDING TODAY--
--AND TWO IS TWICE THE HONOR!
YET HOLD FOR ONE MORE MOMENT, IMMORTUS! ERE THE CEREMONIES DO COMMENCE--
I MOVE THAT THE AVENGERS BESTOW THE HIGHEST HONOR IN OUR POWER TO GRANT--
--AND MAKE MANTIS OFFICIALLY ONE OF US!
AVENGERS ASSEMBLE!
YOU CANNOT KNOW WHAT YOUR WORDS MEAN TO THIS ONE, EVEN AT A TIME LIKE THIS--!
THANK YOU, ONE AND ALL!

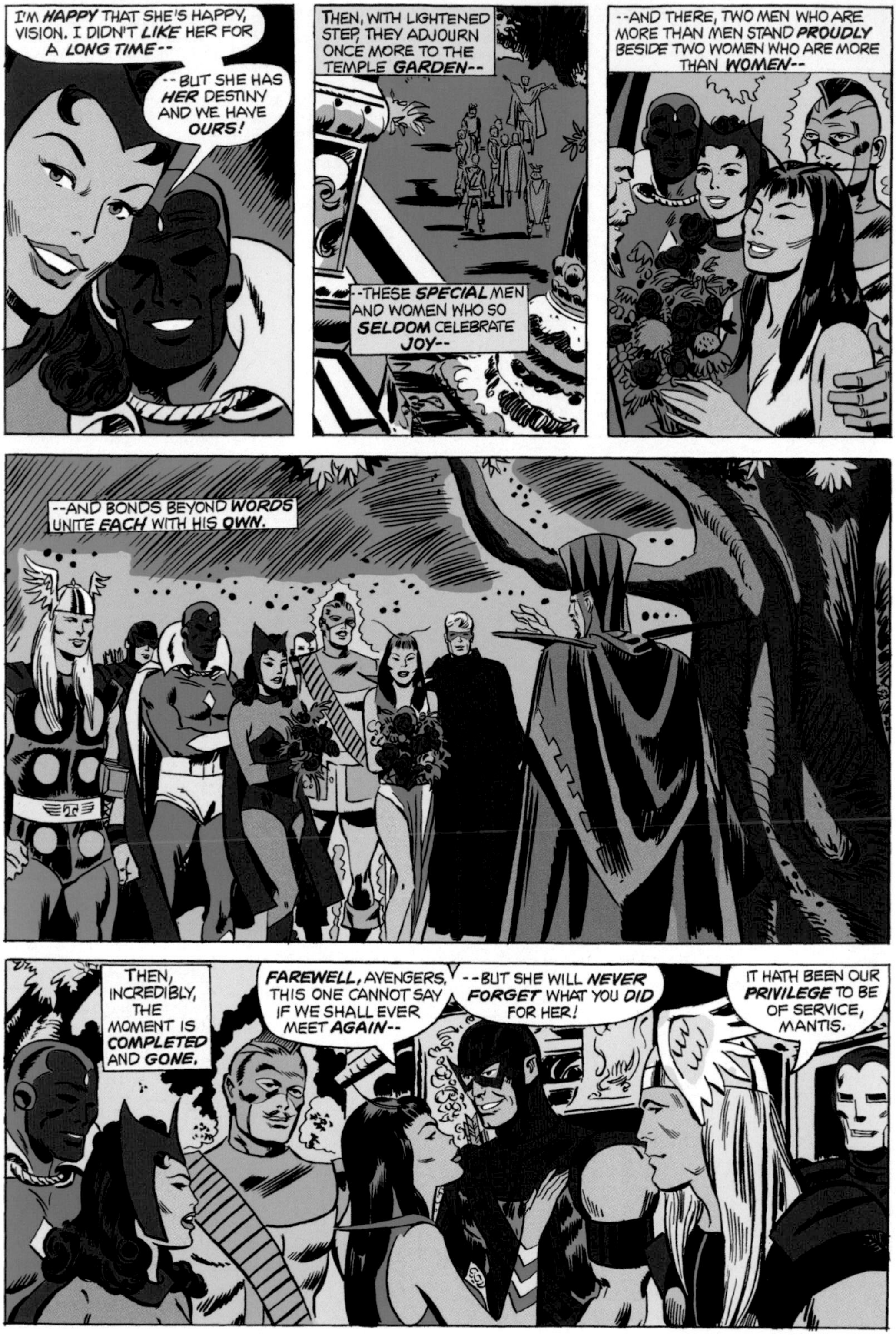
I'M HAPPY THAT SHE'S HAPPY, VISION. I DIDN'T LIKE HER FOR A LONG TIME--
--BUT SHE HAS HER DESTINY AND WE HAVE OURS!
THEN, WITH LIGHTENED STEP, THEY ADJOURN ONCE MORE TO THE TEMPLE GARDEN--
--THESE SPECIAL MEN AND WOMEN WHO SO SELDOM CELEBRATE JOY--
--AND THERE, TWO MEN WHO ARE MORE THAN MEN STAND PROUDLY BESIDE TWO WOMEN WHO ARE MORE THAN WOMEN--
--AND BONDS BEYOND WORDS UNITE EACH WITH HIS OWN.
THEN, INCREDIBLY, THE MOMENT IS COMPLETED AND GONE.
FAREWELL, AVENGERS. THIS ONE CANNOT SAY IF WE SHALL EVER MEET AGAIN--
--BUT SHE WILL NEVER FORGET WHAT YOU DID FOR HER!
IT HATH BEEN OUR PRIVILEGE TO BE OF SERVICE, MANTIS.

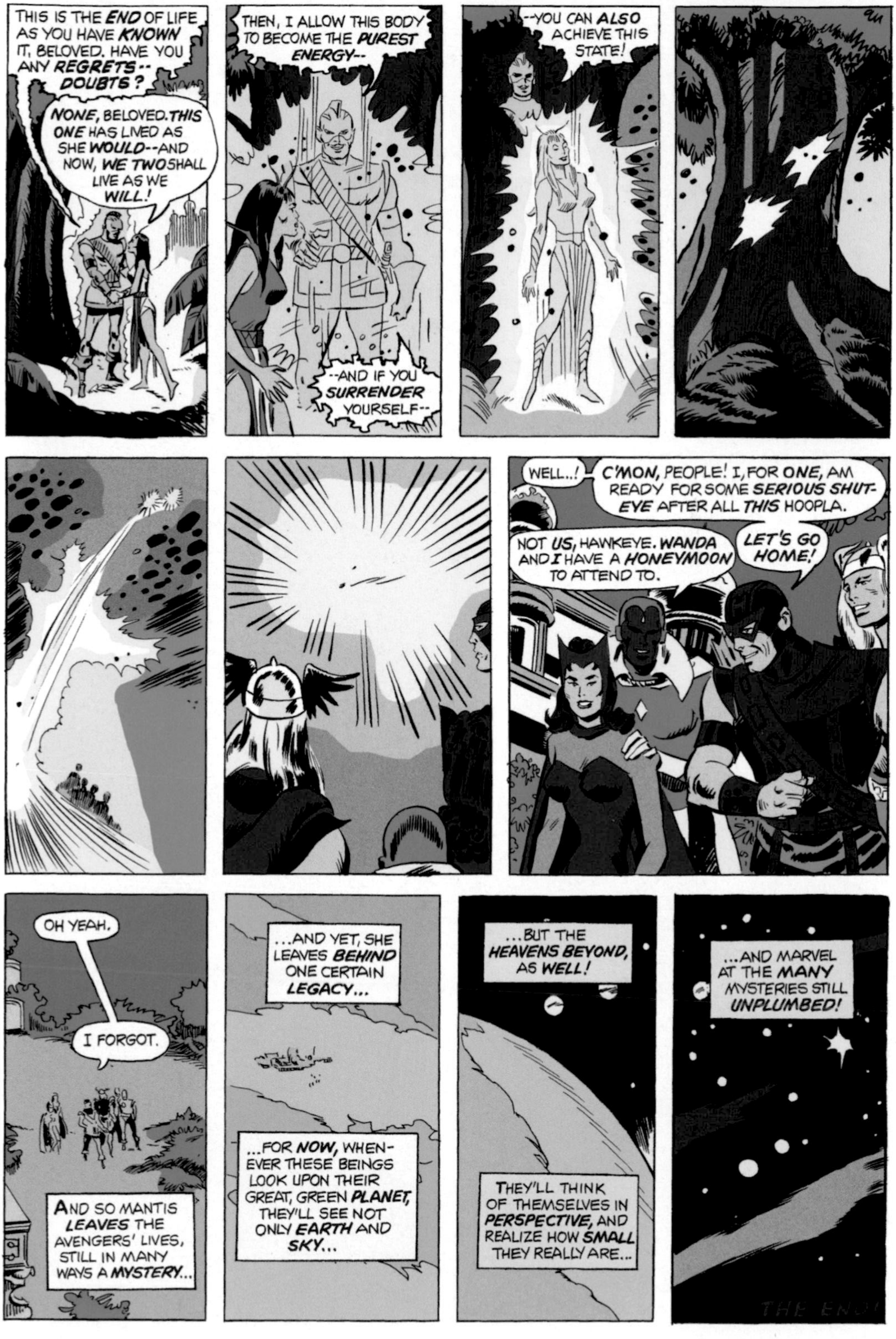
THIS IS THE END OF LIFE AS YOU HAVE KNOWN IT, BELOVED. HAVE YOU ANY REGRETS--DOUBTS?
NONE, BELOVED. THIS ONE HAS LIVED AS SHE WOULD--AND NOW, WE TWO SHALL LIVE AS WE WILL!
THEN, I ALLOW THIS BODY TO BECOME THE PUREST ENERGY--
--AND IF YOU SURRENDER YOURSELF--
--YOU CAN ALSO ACHIEVE THIS STATE!
WELL...!
C'MON, PEOPLE! I, FOR ONE, AM READY FOR SOME SERIOUS SHUT-EYE AFTER ALL THIS HOOPLA.
NOT US, HAWKEYE. WANDA AND I HAVE A HONEYMOON TO ATTEND TO.
LET'S GO HOME!
OH YEAH.
I FORGOT.
AND SO MANTIS LEAVES THE AVENGERS' LIVES, STILL IN MANY WAYS A MYSTERY...
...AND YET, SHE LEAVES BEHIND ONE CERTAIN LEGACY...
...FOR NOW, WHENEVER THESE BEINGS LOOK UPON THEIR GREAT, GREEN PLANET, THEY'LL SEE NOT ONLY EARTH AND SKY...
...BUT THE HEAVENS BEYOND, AS WELL!
THEY'LL THINK OF THEMSELVES IN PERSPECTIVE, AND REALIZE HOW SMALL THEY REALLY ARE...
...AND MARVEL AT THE MANY MYSTERIES STILL UNPLUMBED!
THE END

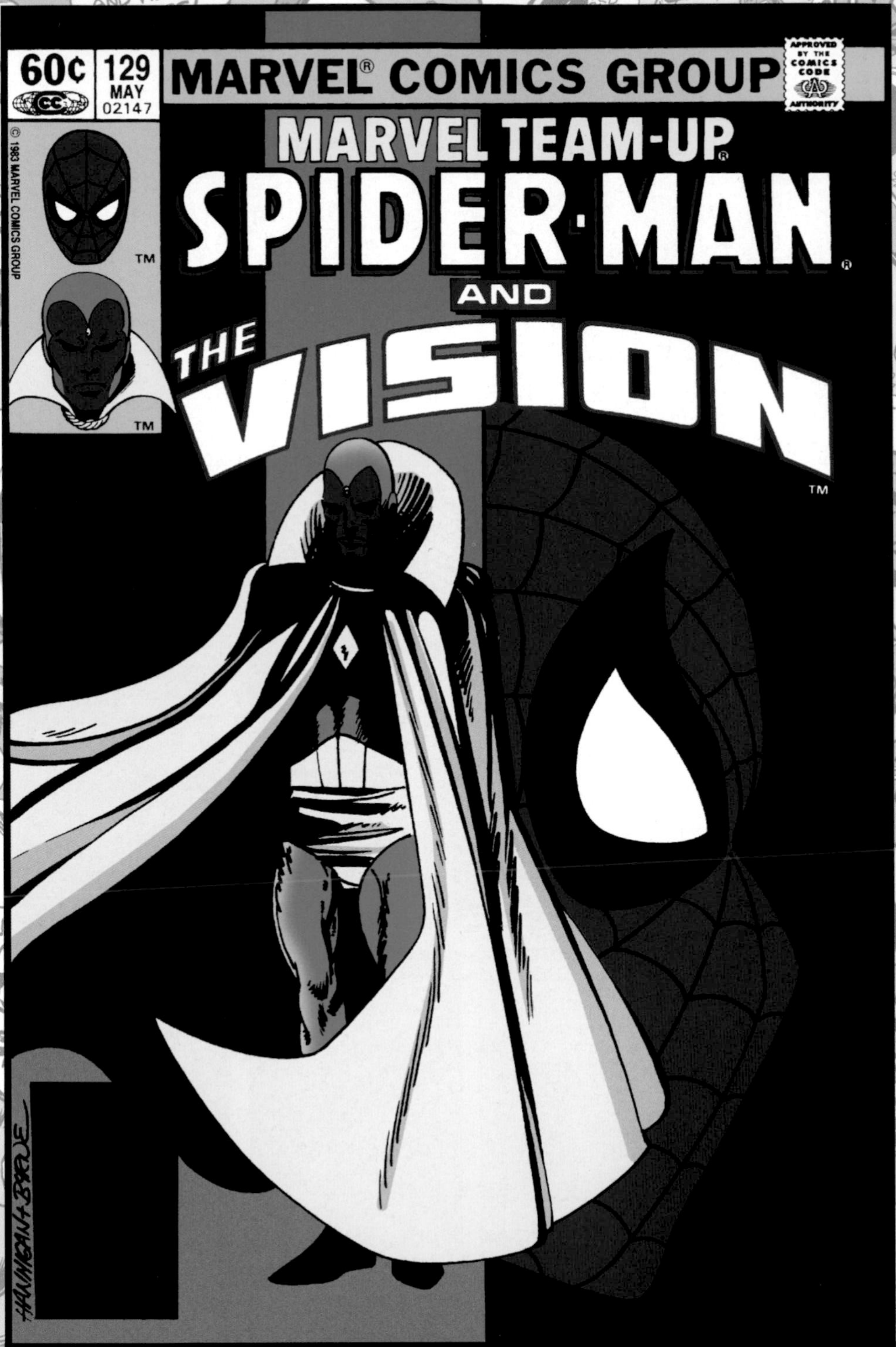
60¢
129
MAY
02147
MARVEL® COMICS GROUP
APPROVED BY THE COMICS CODE AUTHORITY
© 1983 MARVEL COMICS GROUP
MARVEL TEAM-UP®
SPIDER-MAN®
AND
THE VISION™

MARVEL TEAM-UP (1972) #129

IT'S A MIGHTY MARVEL TEAM-UP AS VISION AND SCARLET

STAN LEE PRESENTS: **SPIDER-MAN** *and the* **VISION**

J. M. DeMATTEIS SCRIPTER	KERRY GAMMILL PENCILER	MIKE ESPOSITO INKER	DIANA ALBERS LETTERER	BOB SHAREN COLORIST	TOM DeFALCO EDITOR	JIM SHOOTER CHIEF

LEONIA, NEW JERSEY, TWO A.M.

ASIDE FROM THE DISTANT ECHO OF A TELEVISION SET LEFT ON LONG AFTER ITS OWNER HAS DRIFTED OFF TO SLEEP, AND THE MEWLING OF A PRODICAL CAT RETURNING HOME FROM A WEEK'S GADDING, THIS SUBURBAN TOWNSHIP IS BLANKETED IN SILENCE.

IT IS A COMFORTING SILENCE, DEEP AND WARM, THAT SOOTHES THE SOULS OF DREAMERS.

BUT THERE ARE ALWAYS THOSE TO WHOM SLEEP IS DENIED; WHO SEE, IN NIGHT'S STILLNESS, NOT A COMFORTER, BUT A MOCKING ENEMY. THEY ARE THE RESTLESS SPIRITS WHO STAND, WIDE-EYED, AT WINDOWS, WITH LITTLE TO DO...

...AND MUCH TO PONDER BEFORE THE DAWN...

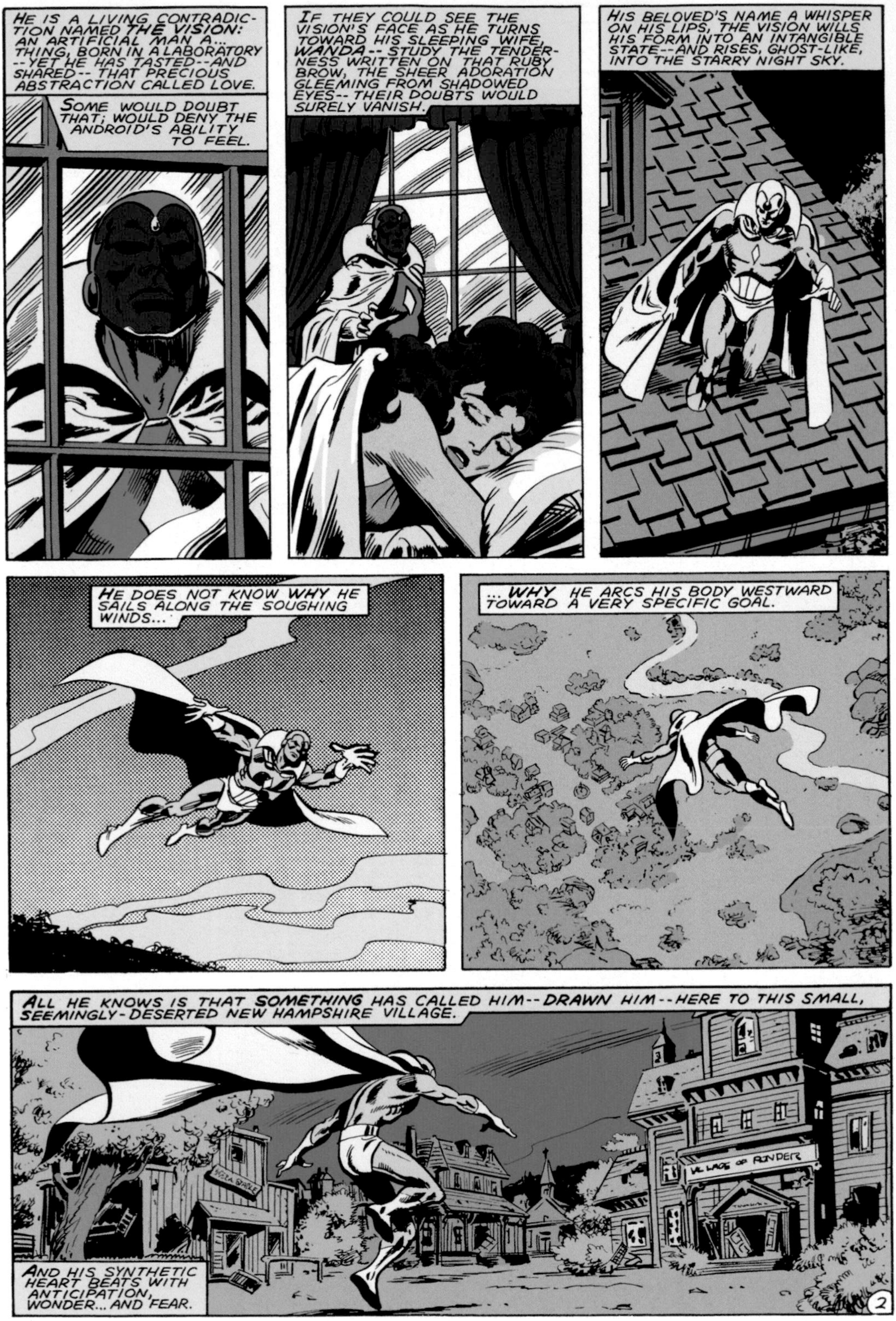
HE IS A LIVING CONTRADICTION NAMED THE VISION: AN ARTIFICIAL MAN A... THING, BORN IN A LABORATORY --YET HE HAS TASTED--AND SHARED-- THAT PRECIOUS ABSTRACTION CALLED LOVE.
SOME WOULD DOUBT THAT; WOULD DENY THE ANDROID'S ABILITY TO FEEL.
IF THEY COULD SEE THE VISION'S FACE AS HE TURNS TOWARD HIS SLEEPING WIFE, WANDA-- STUDY THE TENDERNESS WRITTEN ON THAT RUBY BROW, THE SHEER ADORATION GLEEMING FROM SHADOWED EYES-- THEIR DOUBTS WOULD SURELY VANISH.
HIS BELOVED'S NAME A WHISPER ON HIS LIPS, THE VISION WILLS HIS FORM INTO AN INTANGIBLE STATE--AND RISES, GHOST-LIKE, INTO THE STARRY NIGHT SKY.
HE DOES NOT KNOW WHY HE SAILS ALONG THE SOUGHING WINDS...
...WHY HE ARCS HIS BODY WESTWARD TOWARD A VERY SPECIFIC GOAL.
ALL HE KNOWS IS THAT SOMETHING HAS CALLED HIM--DRAWN HIM--HERE TO THIS SMALL, SEEMINGLY-DESERTED NEW HAMPSHIRE VILLAGE.
AND HIS SYNTHETIC HEART BEATS WITH ANTICIPATION, WONDER... AND FEAR.
2

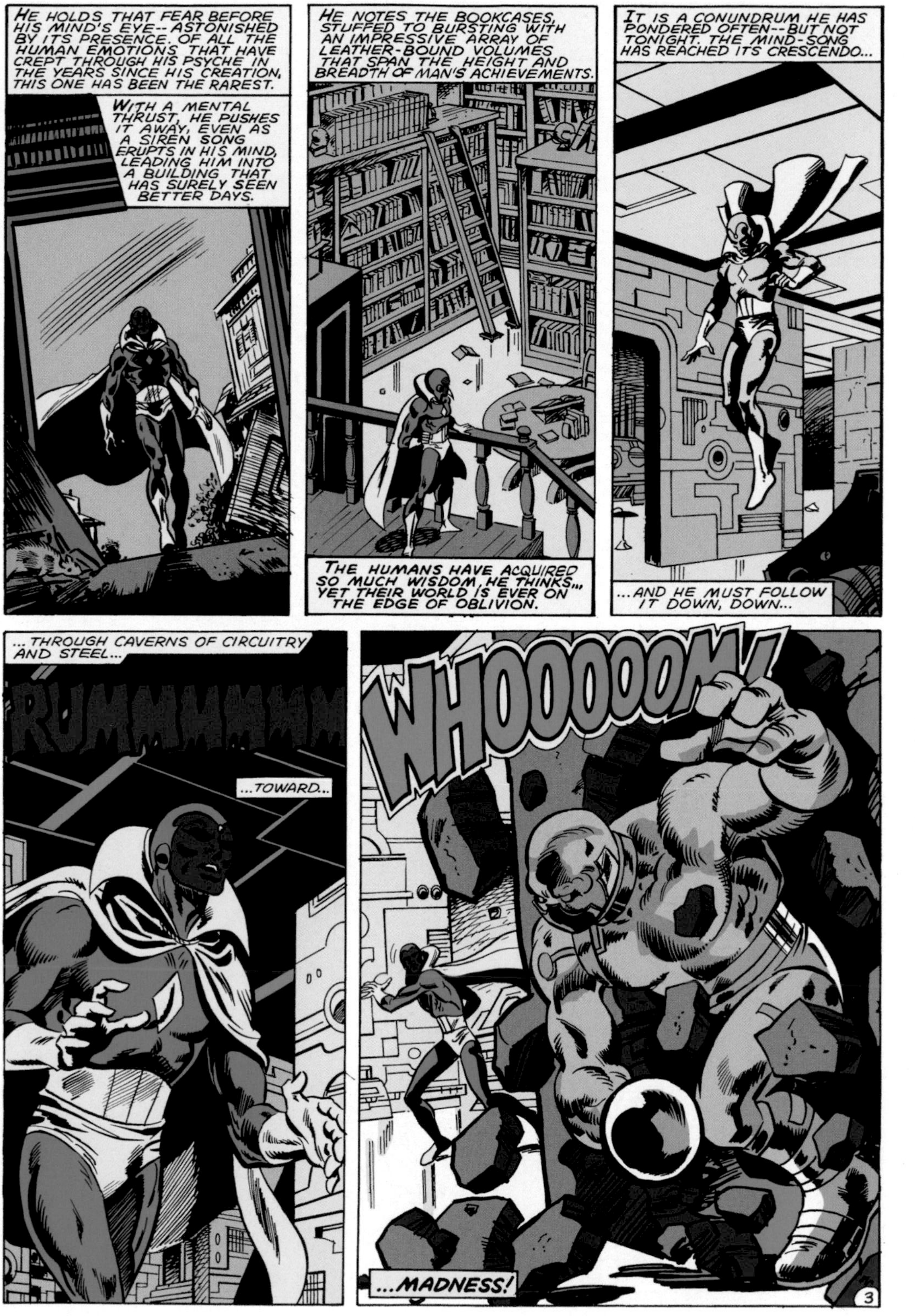
HE HOLDS THAT FEAR BEFORE HIS MIND'S EYE-- ASTONISHED BY ITS PRESENCE. OF ALL THE HUMAN EMOTIONS THAT HAVE CREPT THROUGH HIS PSYCHE IN THE YEARS SINCE HIS CREATION, THIS ONE HAS BEEN THE RAREST.
WITH A MENTAL THRUST, HE PUSHES IT AWAY, EVEN AS A SIREN SONG ERUPTS IN HIS MIND, LEADING HIM INTO A BUILDING THAT HAS SURELY SEEN BETTER DAYS.
HE NOTES THE BOOKCASES, STUFFED TO BURSTING WITH AN IMPRESSIVE ARRAY OF LEATHER-BOUND VOLUMES THAT SPAN THE HEIGHT AND BREADTH OF MAN'S ACHIEVEMENTS.
THE HUMANS HAVE ACQUIRED SO MUCH WISDOM, HE THINKS... YET THEIR WORLD IS EVER ON THE EDGE OF OBLIVION.
IT IS A CONUNDRUM HE HAS PONDERED OFTEN--BUT NOT TONIGHT. THE MIND-SONG HAS REACHED ITS CRESCENDO...
...AND HE MUST FOLLOW IT DOWN, DOWN...
...THROUGH CAVERNS OF CIRCUITRY AND STEEL...
RUMMMMMMM
...TOWARD...
WHOOOOOM!
...MADNESS!
3

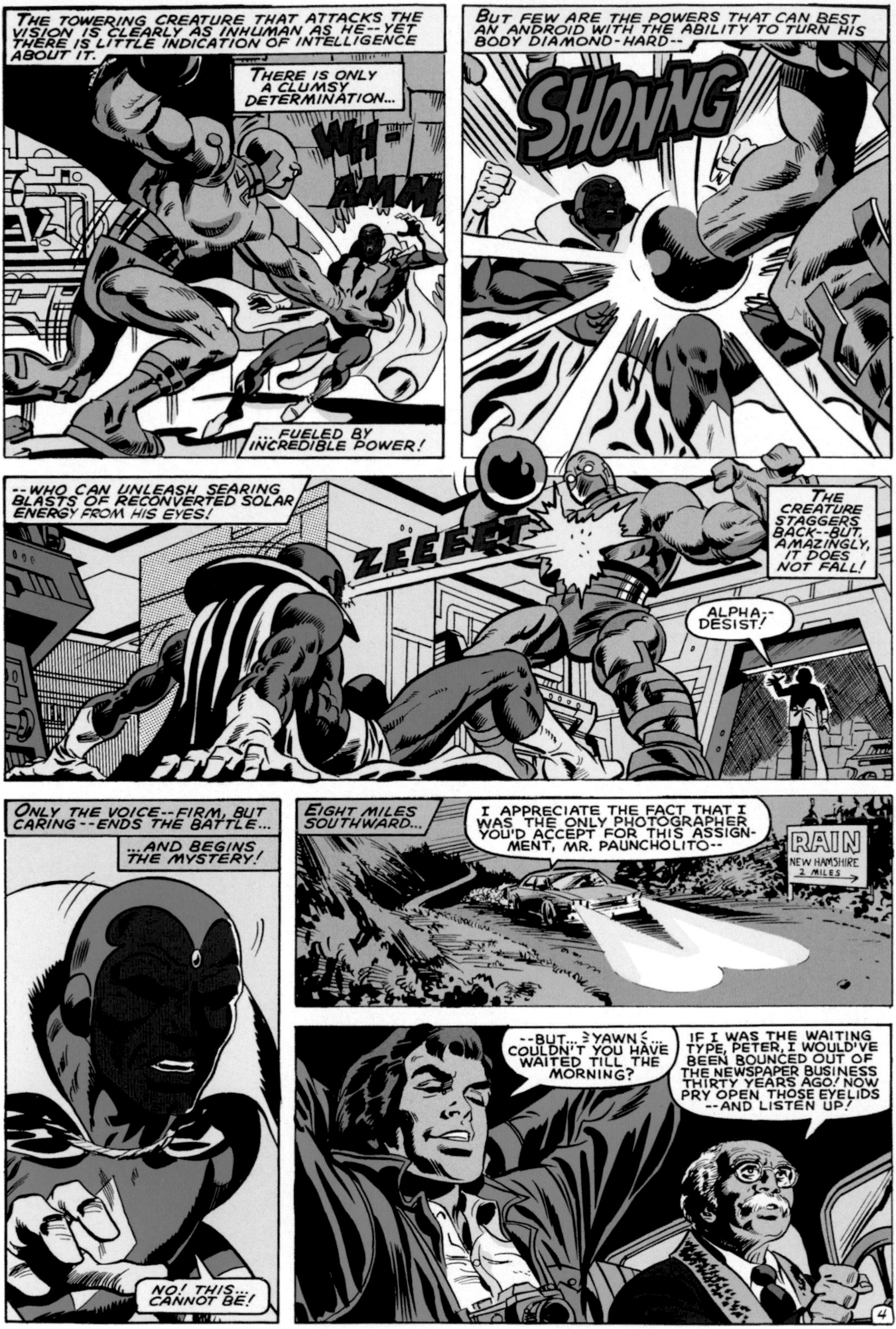
THE TOWERING CREATURE THAT ATTACKS THE VISION IS CLEARLY AS INHUMAN AS HE--YET THERE IS LITTLE INDICATION OF INTELLIGENCE ABOUT IT.
THERE IS ONLY A CLUMSY DETERMINATION...
WH-AMM
...FUELED BY INCREDIBLE POWER!
BUT FEW ARE THE POWERS THAT CAN BEST AN ANDROID WITH THE ABILITY TO TURN HIS BODY DIAMOND-HARD--
SHONNG
--WHO CAN UNLEASH SEARING BLASTS OF RECONVERTED SOLAR ENERGY FROM HIS EYES!
ZEEEET
THE CREATURE STAGGERS BACK--BUT, AMAZINGLY, IT DOES NOT FALL!
ALPHA--DESIST!
ONLY THE VOICE--FIRM, BUT CARING--ENDS THE BATTLE...
...AND BEGINS THE MYSTERY!
NO! THIS... CANNOT BE!
EIGHT MILES SOUTHWARD...
I APPRECIATE THE FACT THAT I WAS THE ONLY PHOTOGRAPHER YOU'D ACCEPT FOR THIS ASSIGNMENT, MR. PAUNCHOLITO--
RAIN
NEW HAMSHIRE
2 MILES
--BUT... YAWN... COULDN'T YOU HAVE WAITED TILL THE MORNING?
IF I WAS THE WAITING TYPE, PETER, I WOULD'VE BEEN BOUNCED OUT OF THE NEWSPAPER BUSINESS THIRTY YEARS AGO! NOW PRY OPEN THOSE EYELIDS --AND LISTEN UP!
4

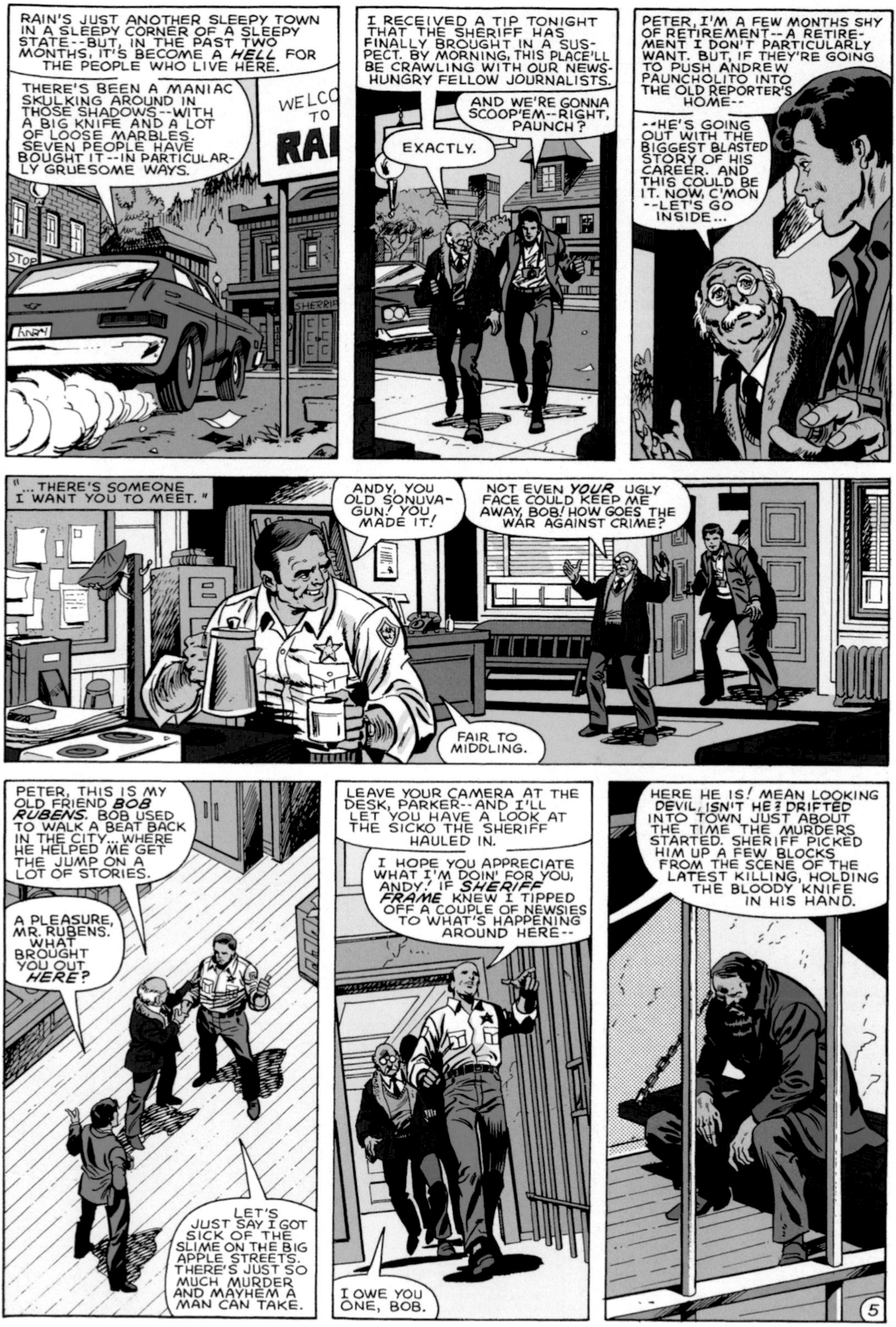

RAIN'S JUST ANOTHER SLEEPY TOWN IN A SLEEPY CORNER OF A SLEEPY STATE--BUT, IN THE PAST TWO MONTHS, IT'S BECOME A *HELL* FOR THE PEOPLE WHO LIVE HERE.
THERE'S BEEN A MANIAC SKULKING AROUND IN THOSE SHADOWS--WITH A BIG KNIFE AND A LOT OF LOOSE MARBLES. SEVEN PEOPLE HAVE BOUGHT IT--IN PARTICULARLY GRUESOME WAYS.
WELCO TO RAI
STOP
SHERRIF
I RECEIVED A TIP TONIGHT THAT THE SHERIFF HAS FINALLY BROUGHT IN A SUSPECT. BY MORNING, THIS PLACE'LL BE CRAWLING WITH OUR NEWS-HUNGRY FELLOW JOURNALISTS.
AND WE'RE GONNA SCOOP'EM--RIGHT, PAUNCH?
EXACTLY.
PETER, I'M A FEW MONTHS SHY OF RETIREMENT--A RETIREMENT I DON'T PARTICULARLY WANT. BUT, IF THEY'RE GOING TO PUSH ANDREW PAUNCHOLITO INTO THE OLD REPORTER'S HOME--
--HE'S GOING OUT WITH THE BIGGEST BLASTED STORY OF HIS CAREER. AND THIS COULD BE IT. NOW, C'MON --LET'S GO INSIDE...
"...THERE'S SOMEONE I WANT YOU TO MEET."
ANDY, YOU OLD SONUVAGUN! YOU MADE IT!
NOT EVEN *YOUR* UGLY FACE COULD KEEP ME AWAY, BOB! HOW GOES THE WAR AGAINST CRIME?
FAIR TO MIDDLING.
PETER, THIS IS MY OLD FRIEND *BOB RUBENS*. BOB USED TO WALK A BEAT BACK IN THE CITY...WHERE HE HELPED ME GET THE JUMP ON A LOT OF STORIES.
A PLEASURE, MR. RUBENS. WHAT BROUGHT YOU OUT *HERE*?
LET'S JUST SAY I GOT SICK OF THE SLIME ON THE BIG APPLE STREETS. THERE'S JUST SO MUCH MURDER AND MAYHEM A MAN CAN TAKE.
LEAVE YOUR CAMERA AT THE DESK, PARKER--AND I'LL LET YOU HAVE A LOOK AT THE SICKO THE SHERIFF HAULED IN.
I HOPE YOU APPRECIATE WHAT I'M DOIN' FOR YOU, ANDY! IF *SHERIFF FRAME* KNEW I TIPPED OFF A COUPLE OF NEWSIES TO WHAT'S HAPPENING AROUND HERE--
I OWE YOU ONE, BOB.
HERE HE IS! MEAN LOOKING DEVIL, ISN'T HE? DRIFTED INTO TOWN JUST ABOUT THE TIME THE MURDERS STARTED. SHERIFF PICKED HIM UP A FEW BLOCKS FROM THE SCENE OF THE LATEST KILLING, HOLDING THE BLOODY KNIFE IN HIS HAND.
5

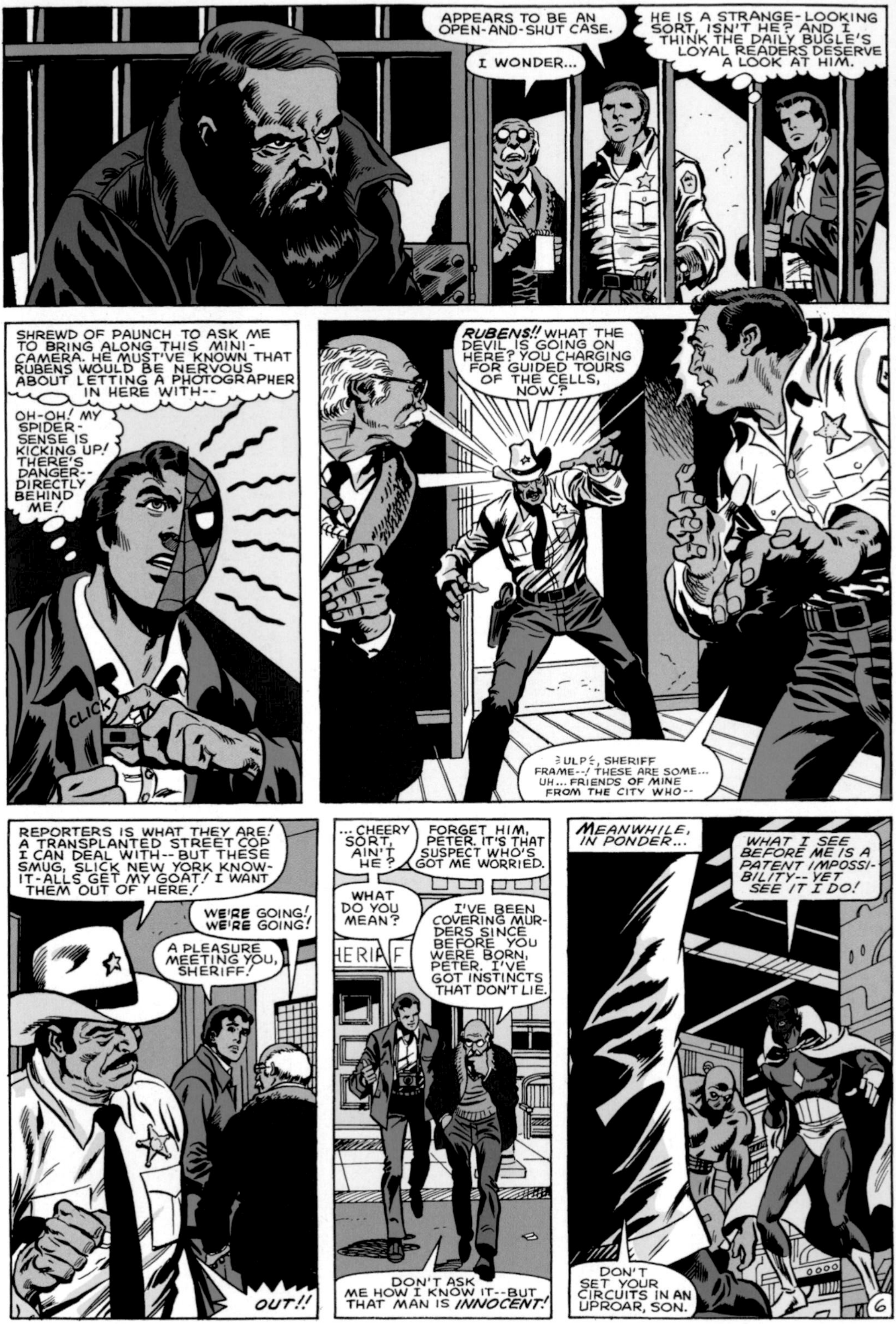
APPEARS TO BE AN OPEN-AND-SHUT CASE.
I WONDER...
HE IS A STRANGE-LOOKING SORT, ISN'T HE? AND I THINK THE DAILY BUGLE'S LOYAL READERS DESERVE A LOOK AT HIM.
SHREWD OF PAUNCH TO ASK ME TO BRING ALONG THIS MINI-CAMERA. HE MUST'VE KNOWN THAT RUBENS WOULD BE NERVOUS ABOUT LETTING A PHOTOGRAPHER IN HERE WITH--
OH-OH! MY SPIDER-SENSE IS KICKING UP! THERE'S DANGER-- DIRECTLY BEHIND ME!
CLICK
RUBENS!! WHAT THE DEVIL IS GOING ON HERE? YOU CHARGING FOR GUIDED TOURS OF THE CELLS, NOW?
GULP, SHERIFF FRAME--! THESE ARE SOME... UH... FRIENDS OF MINE FROM THE CITY WHO--
REPORTERS IS WHAT THEY ARE! A TRANSPLANTED STREET COP I CAN DEAL WITH-- BUT THESE SMUG, SLICK NEW YORK KNOW-IT-ALLS GET MY GOAT! I WANT THEM OUT OF HERE!
WE'RE GOING! WE'RE GOING!
A PLEASURE MEETING YOU, SHERIFF!
OUT!!
...CHEERY SORT, AIN'T HE?
FORGET HIM, PETER. IT'S THAT SUSPECT WHO'S GOT ME WORRIED.
WHAT DO YOU MEAN?
I'VE BEEN COVERING MURDERS SINCE BEFORE YOU WERE BORN, PETER. I'VE GOT INSTINCTS THAT DON'T LIE.
SHERIFF
DON'T ASK ME HOW I KNOW IT--BUT THAT MAN IS INNOCENT!
MEANWHILE, IN PONDER...
WHAT I SEE BEFORE ME IS A PATENT IMPOSSIBILITY--YET SEE IT I DO!
DON'T SET YOUR CIRCUITS IN AN UPROAR, SON.
6

...I'M JUST WHO I APPEAR TO BE. I AM *MARK TWAIN*...OR AT LEAST A REASONABLE ANDROID FACSIMILE!

I TRUST YOU RECOGNIZE MY SOMEWHAT BATTERED BRETHREN: CONFUCIUS, SHAKESPEARE, LINCOLN, SOCRATES...TOO MANY MORE TO MENTION!

WE JOINED OUR MINDS TOGETHER TONIGHT--AND REACHED OUT TO TOUCH A SPIRIT KINDRED TO OUR OWN...

TO TOUCH *YOU*, VISION.

I DO NOT UNDERSTAND. *WHO* CREATED YOU? *WHAT* IS THIS PLACE? *WHY* HAVE YOU DRAWN ME HERE?

"GOOD QUESTIONS, ALL--AND WORTHY OF EQUALLY-GOOD ANSWERS. OUR CREATOR WAS THE EVIL GENIUS CALLED *THE MAD THINKER.* SOME MONTHS BACK, HE TOYED WITH THE IDEA OF SPENDING THE REMAINDER OF HIS DAYS IN PURELY INTELLECTUAL PURSUITS. HE BUILT THIS TOWN--AND *US*: DUPLICATES OF HISTORY'S GREATEST MINDS; WORTHY COMPANIONS TO PROVIDE HIM WITH A LIFETIME OF MENTAL CHALLENGES. BUT HE SOON GREW BORED WITH US AND BEGAN KIDNAPPING THE WORLD'S GREATEST *LIVING* INTELLECTS...

"...TRANSFERRING THEIR MINDS INTO IMMORTAL ANDROID SHELLS. *

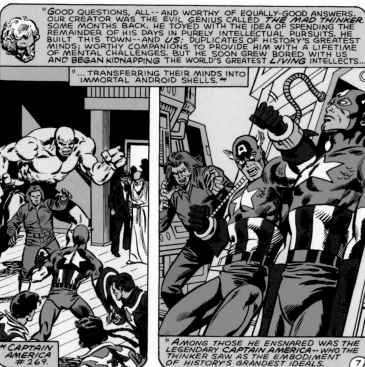

*CAPTAIN AMERICA #269.

"AMONG THOSE HE ENSNARED WAS THE LEGENDARY *CAPTAIN AMERICA*--WHO THE THINKER SAW AS THE EMBODIMENT OF HISTORY'S GRANDEST IDEALS.

7

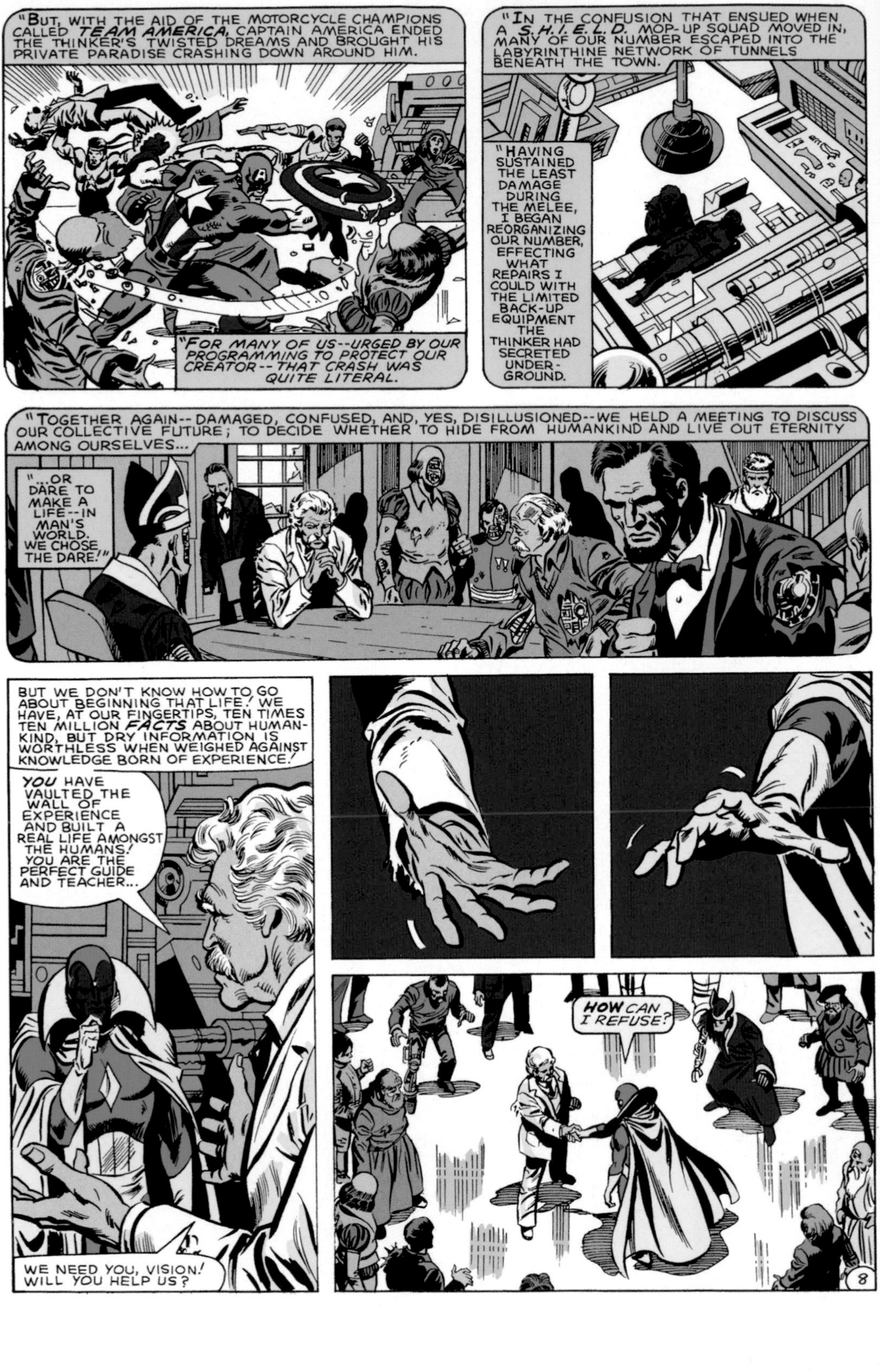

"BUT, WITH THE AID OF THE MOTORCYCLE CHAMPIONS CALLED TEAM AMERICA, CAPTAIN AMERICA ENDED THE THINKER'S TWISTED DREAMS AND BROUGHT HIS PRIVATE PARADISE CRASHING DOWN AROUND HIM.
"FOR MANY OF US--URGED BY OUR PROGRAMMING TO PROTECT OUR CREATOR--THAT CRASH WAS QUITE LITERAL.
"IN THE CONFUSION THAT ENSUED WHEN A S.H.I.E.L.D. MOP-UP SQUAD MOVED IN, MANY OF OUR NUMBER ESCAPED INTO THE LABYRINTHINE NETWORK OF TUNNELS BENEATH THE TOWN.
"HAVING SUSTAINED THE LEAST DAMAGE DURING THE MELEE, I BEGAN REORGANIZING OUR NUMBER, EFFECTING WHAT REPAIRS I COULD WITH THE LIMITED BACK-UP EQUIPMENT THE THINKER HAD SECRETED UNDER-GROUND.
"TOGETHER AGAIN--DAMAGED, CONFUSED, AND, YES, DISILLUSIONED--WE HELD A MEETING TO DISCUSS OUR COLLECTIVE FUTURE; TO DECIDE WHETHER TO HIDE FROM HUMANKIND AND LIVE OUT ETERNITY AMONG OURSELVES...
"...OR DARE TO MAKE A LIFE--IN MAN'S WORLD. WE CHOSE THE DARE!"
BUT WE DON'T KNOW HOW TO GO ABOUT BEGINNING THAT LIFE! WE HAVE, AT OUR FINGERTIPS, TEN TIMES TEN MILLION FACTS ABOUT HUMANKIND, BUT DRY INFORMATION IS WORTHLESS WHEN WEIGHED AGAINST KNOWLEDGE BORN OF EXPERIENCE!
YOU HAVE VAULTED THE WALL OF EXPERIENCE AND BUILT A REAL LIFE AMONGST THE HUMANS! YOU ARE THE PERFECT GUIDE AND TEACHER...
WE NEED YOU, VISION! WILL YOU HELP US?
HOW CAN I REFUSE?

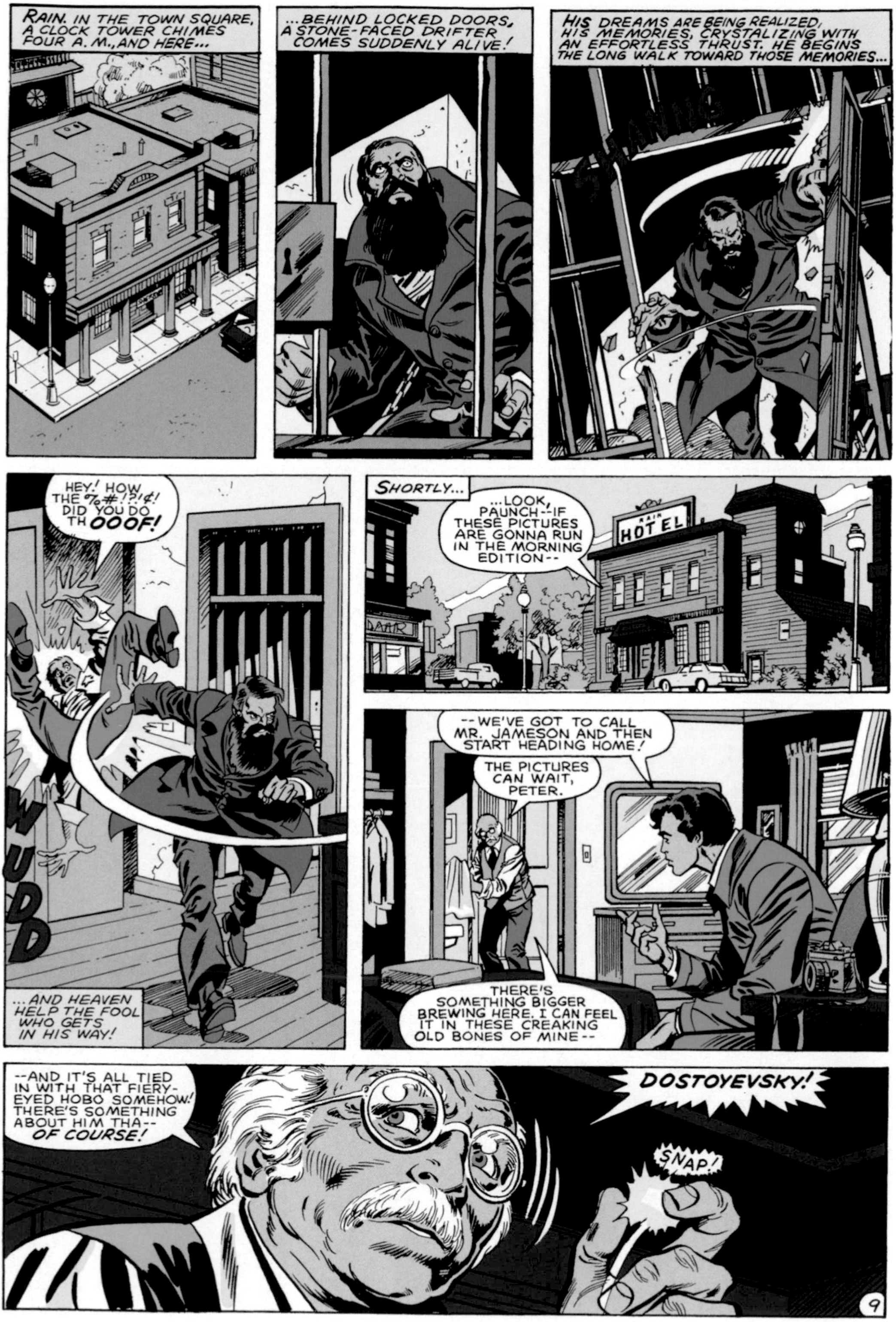
RAIN. IN THE TOWN SQUARE, A CLOCK TOWER CHIMES FOUR A.M., AND HERE...
...BEHIND LOCKED DOORS, A STONE-FACED DRIFTER COMES SUDDENLY ALIVE!
HIS DREAMS ARE BEING REALIZED, HIS MEMORIES, CRYSTALIZING WITH AN EFFORTLESS THRUST. HE BEGINS THE LONG WALK TOWARD THOSE MEMORIES...
HEY! HOW THE %#!?!¢! DID YOU DO TH OOOF!
WUDD
...AND HEAVEN HELP THE FOOL WHO GETS IN HIS WAY!
SHORTLY...
...LOOK, PAUNCH--IF THESE PICTURES ARE GONNA RUN IN THE MORNING EDITION--
RAIN HOTEL
--WE'VE GOT TO CALL MR. JAMESON AND THEN START HEADING HOME!
THE PICTURES CAN WAIT, PETER.
THERE'S SOMETHING BIGGER BREWING HERE. I CAN FEEL IT IN THESE CREAKING OLD BONES OF MINE--
--AND IT'S ALL TIED IN WITH THAT FIERY-EYED HOBO SOMEHOW! THERE'S SOMETHING ABOUT HIM THA-- OF COURSE!
DOSTOYEVSKY!
SNAP!
9

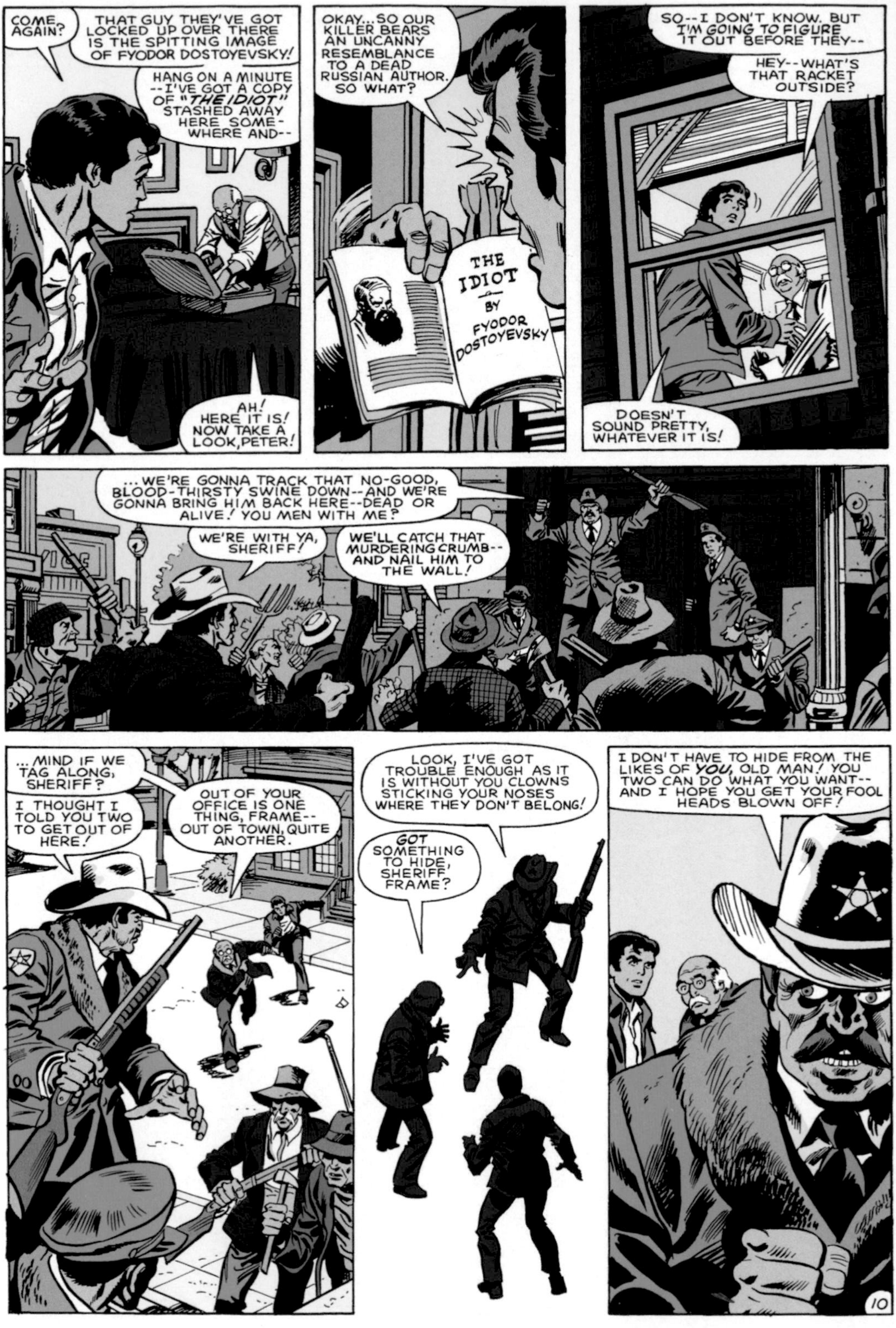
COME AGAIN?
THAT GUY THEY'VE GOT LOCKED UP OVER THERE IS THE SPITTING IMAGE OF FYODOR DOSTOYEVSKY!
HANG ON A MINUTE --I'VE GOT A COPY OF "THE IDIOT" STASHED AWAY HERE SOMEWHERE AND--
AH! HERE IT IS! NOW TAKE A LOOK, PETER!
OKAY...SO OUR KILLER BEARS AN UNCANNY RESEMBLANCE TO A DEAD RUSSIAN AUTHOR. SO WHAT?
THE IDIOT BY FYODOR DOSTOYEVSKY
SO--I DON'T KNOW. BUT I'M GOING TO FIGURE IT OUT BEFORE THEY--
HEY--WHAT'S THAT RACKET OUTSIDE?
DOESN'T SOUND PRETTY, WHATEVER IT IS!
...WE'RE GONNA TRACK THAT NO-GOOD, BLOOD-THIRSTY SWINE DOWN--AND WE'RE GONNA BRING HIM BACK HERE--DEAD OR ALIVE! YOU MEN WITH ME?
WE'RE WITH YA, SHERIFF!
WE'LL CATCH THAT MURDERING CRUMB--AND NAIL HIM TO THE WALL!
...MIND IF WE TAG ALONG, SHERIFF?
I THOUGHT I TOLD YOU TWO TO GET OUT OF HERE!
OUT OF YOUR OFFICE IS ONE THING, FRAME--OUT OF TOWN, QUITE ANOTHER.
LOOK, I'VE GOT TROUBLE ENOUGH AS IT IS WITHOUT YOU CLOWNS STICKING YOUR NOSES WHERE THEY DON'T BELONG!
GOT SOMETHING TO HIDE, SHERIFF FRAME?
I DON'T HAVE TO HIDE FROM THE LIKES OF YOU, OLD MAN! YOU TWO CAN DO WHAT YOU WANT--AND I HOPE YOU GET YOUR FOOL HEADS BLOWN OFF!
10

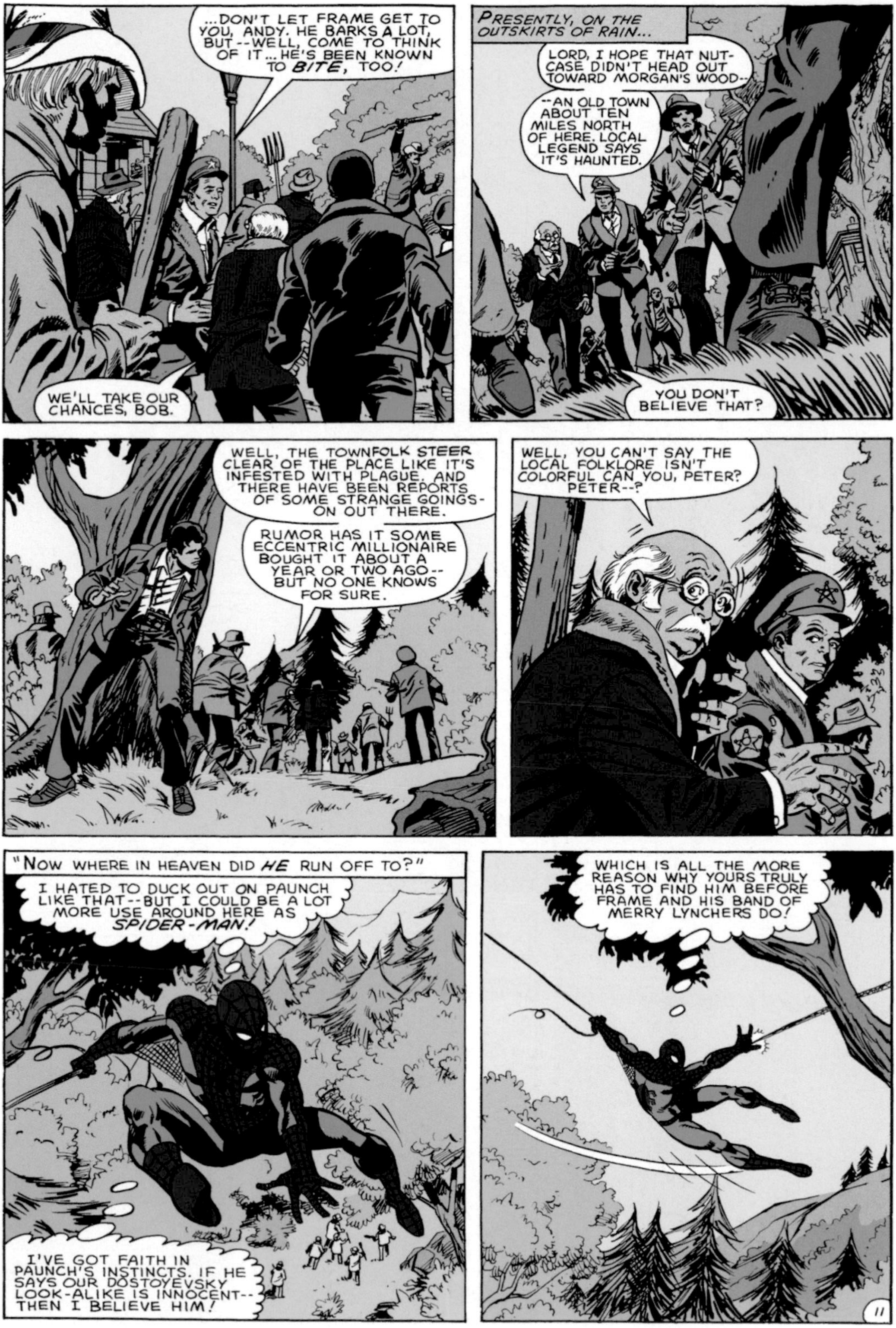
...DON'T LET FRAME GET TO YOU, ANDY. HE BARKS A LOT, BUT --WELL, COME TO THINK OF IT... HE'S BEEN KNOWN TO BITE, TOO!
WE'LL TAKE OUR CHANCES, BOB.
PRESENTLY, ON THE OUTSKIRTS OF RAIN...
LORD, I HOPE THAT NUT-CASE DIDN'T HEAD OUT TOWARD MORGAN'S WOOD--
--AN OLD TOWN ABOUT TEN MILES NORTH OF HERE. LOCAL LEGEND SAYS IT'S HAUNTED.
YOU DON'T BELIEVE THAT?
WELL, THE TOWNFOLK STEER CLEAR OF THE PLACE LIKE IT'S INFESTED WITH PLAGUE. AND THERE HAVE BEEN REPORTS OF SOME STRANGE GOINGS-ON OUT THERE.
RUMOR HAS IT SOME ECCENTRIC MILLIONAIRE BOUGHT IT ABOUT A YEAR OR TWO AGO-- BUT NO ONE KNOWS FOR SURE.
WELL, YOU CAN'T SAY THE LOCAL FOLKLORE ISN'T COLORFUL CAN YOU, PETER? PETER--?
"NOW WHERE IN HEAVEN DID HE RUN OFF TO?"
I HATED TO DUCK OUT ON PAUNCH LIKE THAT--BUT I COULD BE A LOT MORE USE AROUND HERE AS SPIDER-MAN!
I'VE GOT FAITH IN PAUNCH'S INSTINCTS. IF HE SAYS OUR DOSTOYEVSKY LOOK-ALIKE IS INNOCENT-- THEN I BELIEVE HIM!
WHICH IS ALL THE MORE REASON WHY YOURS TRULY HAS TO FIND HIM BEFORE FRAME AND HIS BAND OF MERRY LYNCHERS DO!

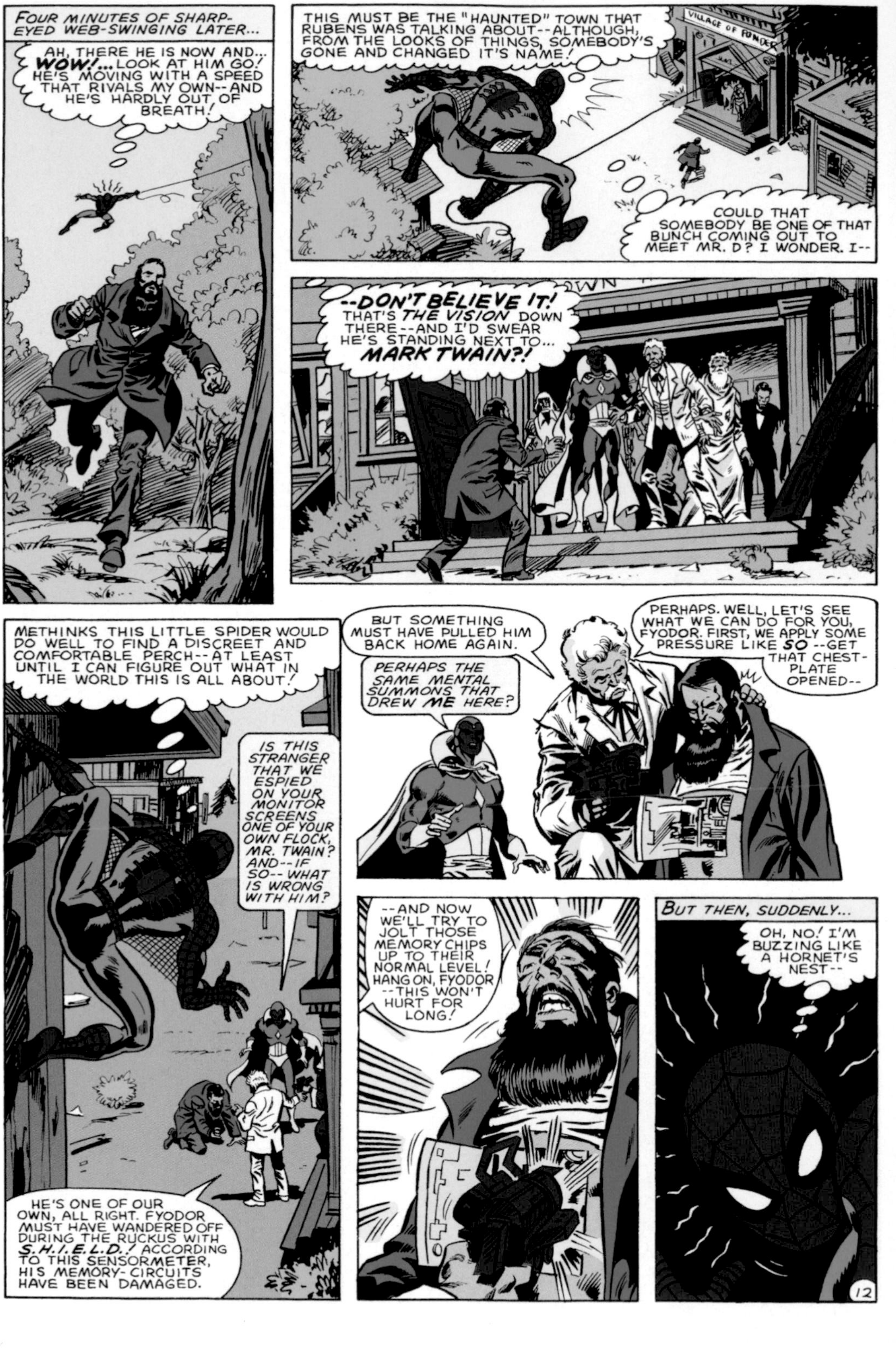
FOUR MINUTES OF SHARP-EYED WEB-SWINGING LATER...
AH, THERE HE IS NOW AND... WOW!... LOOK AT HIM GO! HE'S MOVING WITH A SPEED THAT RIVALS MY OWN--AND HE'S HARDLY OUT OF BREATH!
THIS MUST BE THE "HAUNTED" TOWN THAT RUBENS WAS TALKING ABOUT--ALTHOUGH, FROM THE LOOKS OF THINGS, SOMEBODY'S GONE AND CHANGED IT'S NAME!
VILLAGE OF FONDER
COULD THAT SOMEBODY BE ONE OF THAT BUNCH COMING OUT TO MEET MR. D? I WONDER. I--
--DON'T BELIEVE IT! THAT'S THE VISION DOWN THERE--AND I'D SWEAR HE'S STANDING NEXT TO... MARK TWAIN?!
METHINKS THIS LITTLE SPIDER WOULD DO WELL TO FIND A DISCREET AND COMFORTABLE PERCH--AT LEAST UNTIL I CAN FIGURE OUT WHAT IN THE WORLD THIS IS ALL ABOUT!
IS THIS STRANGER THAT WE ESPIED ON YOUR MONITOR SCREENS ONE OF YOUR OWN FLOCK, MR. TWAIN? AND--IF SO--WHAT IS WRONG WITH HIM?
HE'S ONE OF OUR OWN, ALL RIGHT. FYODOR MUST HAVE WANDERED OFF DURING THE RUCKUS WITH S.H.I.E.L.D.! ACCORDING TO THIS SENSORMETER, HIS MEMORY-CIRCUITS HAVE BEEN DAMAGED.
BUT SOMETHING MUST HAVE PULLED HIM BACK HOME AGAIN.
PERHAPS THE SAME MENTAL SUMMONS THAT DREW ME HERE?
PERHAPS. WELL, LET'S SEE WHAT WE CAN DO FOR YOU, FYODOR. FIRST, WE APPLY SOME PRESSURE LIKE SO--GET THAT CHEST-PLATE OPENED--
--AND NOW WE'LL TRY TO JOLT THOSE MEMORY CHIPS UP TO THEIR NORMAL LEVEL! HANG ON, FYODOR--THIS WON'T HURT FOR LONG!
BUT THEN, SUDDENLY...
OH, NO! I'M BUZZING LIKE A HORNET'S NEST--

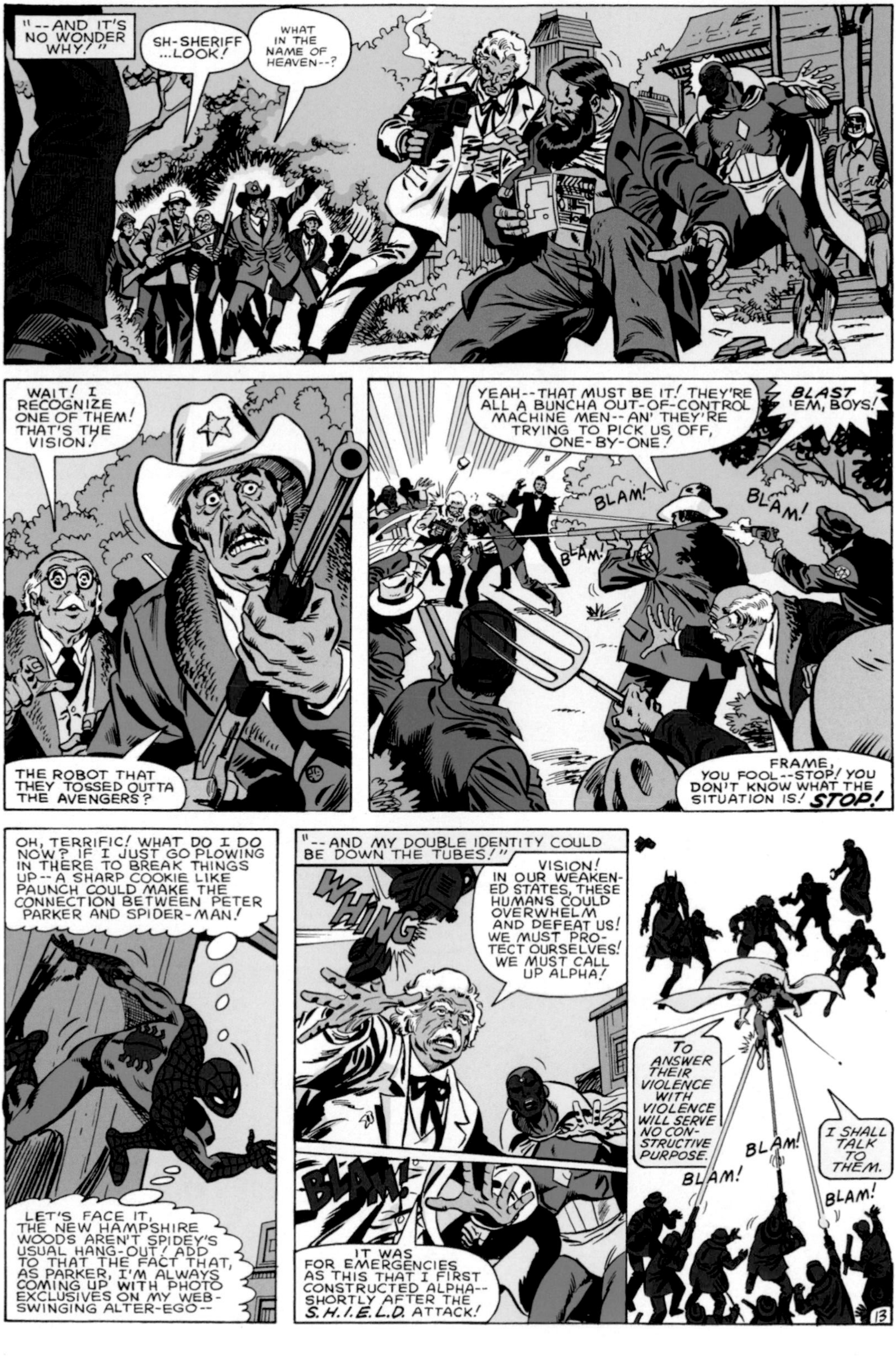

"--AND IT'S NO WONDER WHY!"
SH-SHERIFF ...LOOK!
WHAT IN THE NAME OF HEAVEN--?
WAIT! I RECOGNIZE ONE OF THEM! THAT'S THE VISION!
THE ROBOT THAT THEY TOSSED OUTTA THE AVENGERS?
YEAH--THAT MUST BE IT! THEY'RE ALL A BUNCHA OUT-OF-CONTROL MACHINE MEN--AN' THEY'RE TRYING TO PICK US OFF, ONE-BY-ONE!
BLAST 'EM, BOYS!
BLAM!
BLAM!
BLAM!
FRAME, YOU FOOL--STOP! YOU DON'T KNOW WHAT THE SITUATION IS! STOP!
OH, TERRIFIC! WHAT DO I DO NOW? IF I JUST GO PLOWING IN THERE TO BREAK THINGS UP--A SHARP COOKIE LIKE PAUNCH COULD MAKE THE CONNECTION BETWEEN PETER PARKER AND SPIDER-MAN!
LET'S FACE IT, THE NEW HAMPSHIRE WOODS AREN'T SPIDEY'S USUAL HANG-OUT! ADD TO THAT THE FACT THAT, AS PARKER, I'M ALWAYS COMING UP WITH PHOTO EXCLUSIVES ON MY WEB-SWINGING ALTER-EGO--
"--AND MY DOUBLE IDENTITY COULD BE DOWN THE TUBES!"
WHING
VISION! IN OUR WEAKENED STATES, THESE HUMANS COULD OVERWHELM AND DEFEAT US! WE MUST PROTECT OURSELVES! WE MUST CALL UP ALPHA!
BLAM!
IT WAS FOR EMERGENCIES AS THIS THAT I FIRST CONSTRUCTED ALPHA--SHORTLY AFTER THE S.H.I.E.L.D. ATTACK!
TO ANSWER THEIR VIOLENCE WITH VIOLENCE WILL SERVE NO CONSTRUCTIVE PURPOSE.
I SHALL TALK TO THEM.
BLAM!
BLAM!
BLAM!
13

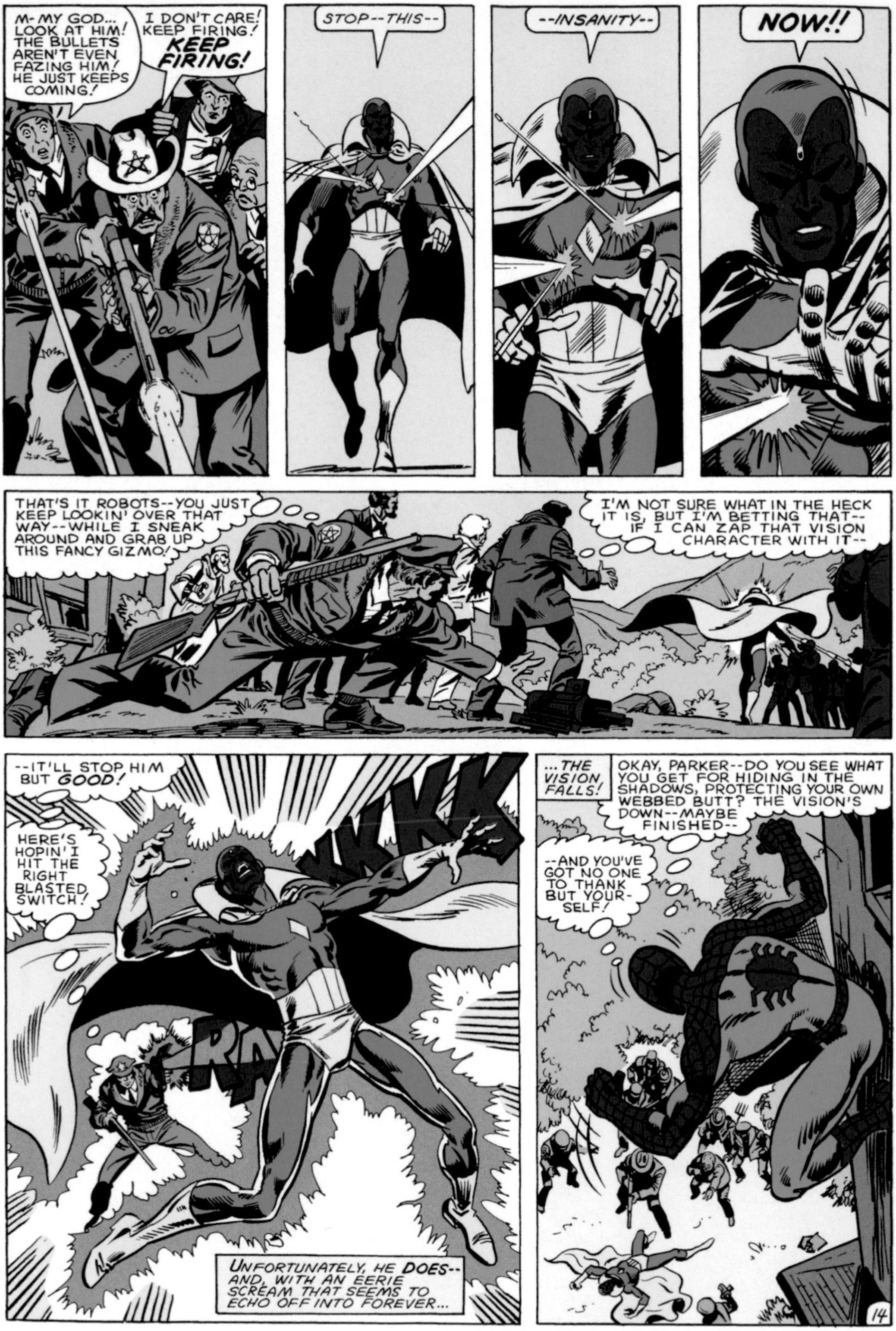
M-MY GOD... LOOK AT HIM! THE BULLETS AREN'T EVEN FAZING HIM! HE JUST KEEPS COMING!
I DON'T CARE! KEEP FIRING! KEEP FIRING!
STOP--THIS--
--INSANITY--
NOW!!
THAT'S IT ROBOTS--YOU JUST KEEP LOOKIN' OVER THAT WAY--WHILE I SNEAK AROUND AND GRAB UP THIS FANCY GIZMO!
I'M NOT SURE WHAT IN THE HECK IT IS, BUT I'M BETTING THAT-- IF I CAN ZAP THAT VISION CHARACTER WITH IT--
--IT'LL STOP HIM BUT GOOD!
HERE'S HOPIN' I HIT THE RIGHT BLASTED SWITCH!
KKK
RA
UNFORTUNATELY, HE DOES--AND, WITH AN EERIE SCREAM THAT SEEMS TO ECHO OFF INTO FOREVER...
...THE VISION FALLS!
OKAY, PARKER--DO YOU SEE WHAT YOU GET FOR HIDING IN THE SHADOWS, PROTECTING YOUR OWN WEBBED BUTT? THE VISION'S DOWN--MAYBE FINISHED--
--AND YOU'VE GOT NO ONE TO THANK BUT YOURSELF!
14

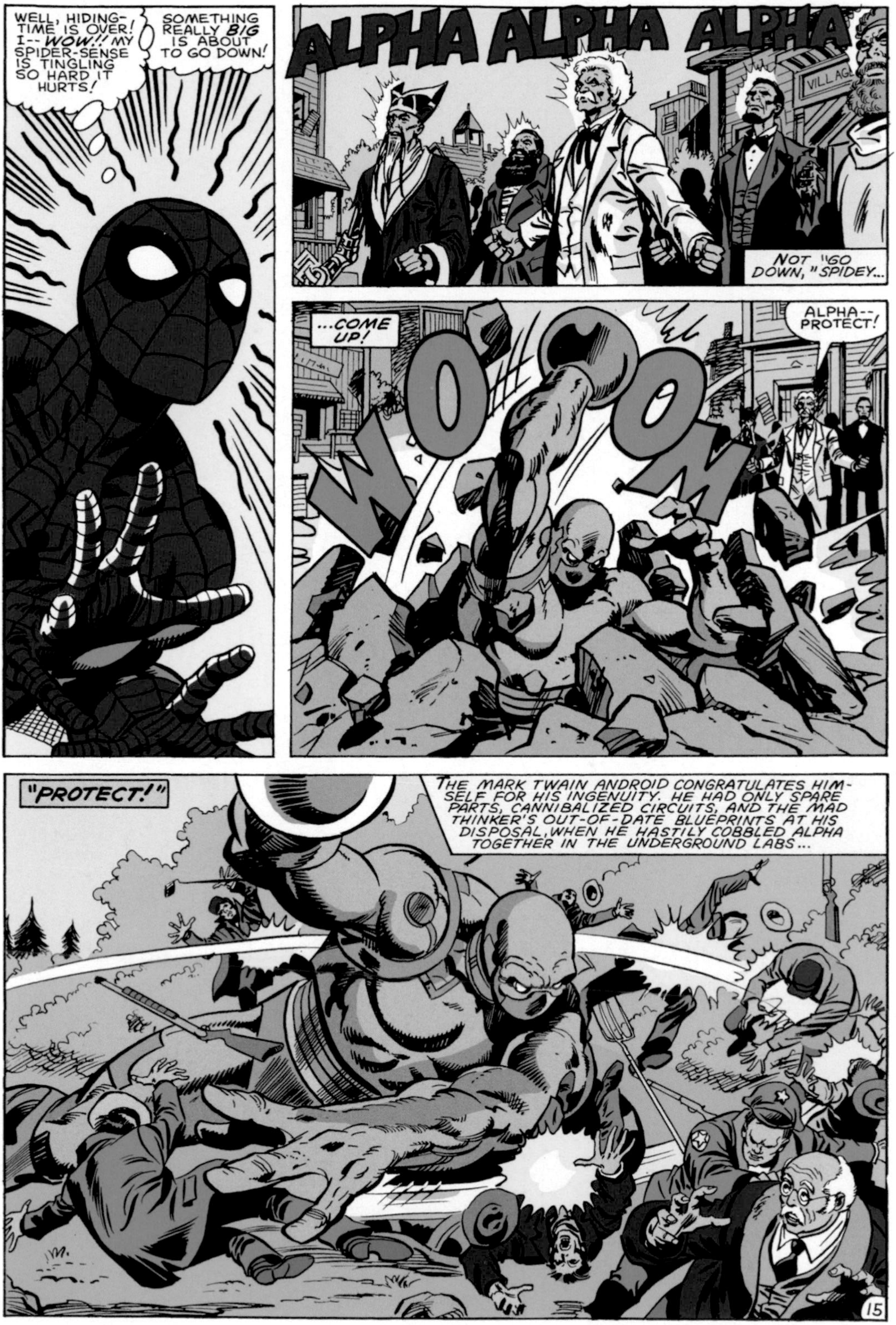

WELL, HIDING-TIME IS OVER! I-- WOW!! MY SPIDER-SENSE IS TINGLING SO HARD IT HURTS!
SOMETHING REALLY BIG IS ABOUT TO GO DOWN!
ALPHA ALPHA ALPHA
NOT "GO DOWN," SPIDEY...
...COME UP!
WOOOM
ALPHA-- PROTECT!
"PROTECT!"
THE MARK TWAIN ANDROID CONGRATULATES HIMSELF FOR HIS INGENUITY. HE HAD ONLY SPARE PARTS, CANNIBALIZED CIRCUITS, AND THE MAD THINKER'S OUT-OF-DATE BLUEPRINTS AT HIS DISPOSAL, WHEN HE HASTILY COBBLED ALPHA TOGETHER IN THE UNDERGROUND LABS...

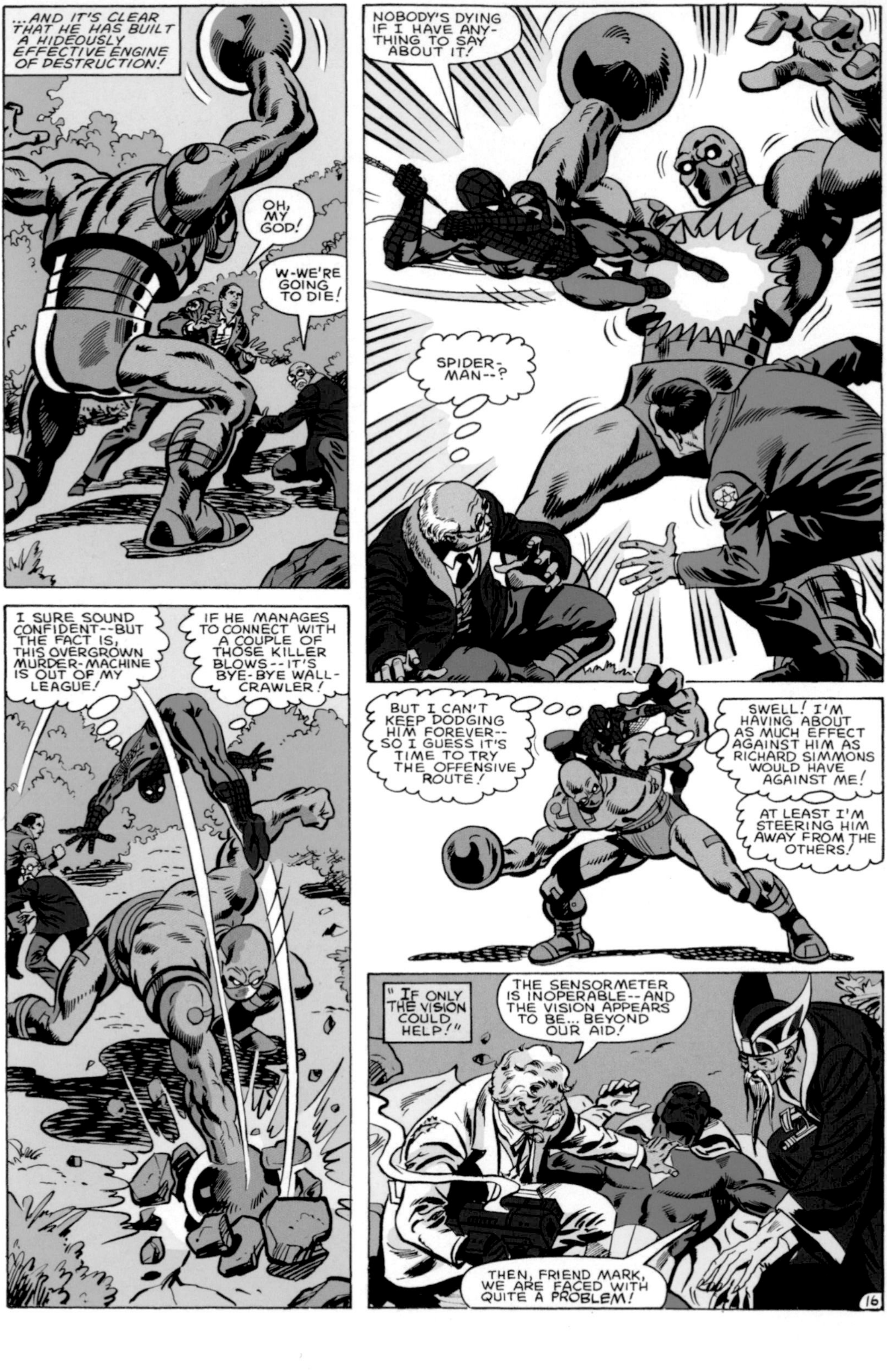
...AND IT'S CLEAR THAT HE HAS BUILT A HIDEOUSLY EFFECTIVE ENGINE OF DESTRUCTION!
OH, MY GOD!
W-WE'RE GOING TO DIE!
NOBODY'S DYING IF I HAVE ANYTHING TO SAY ABOUT IT!
SPIDER-MAN--?
I SURE SOUND CONFIDENT--BUT THE FACT IS, THIS OVERGROWN MURDER-MACHINE IS OUT OF MY LEAGUE!
IF HE MANAGES TO CONNECT WITH A COUPLE OF THOSE KILLER BLOWS--IT'S BYE-BYE WALL-CRAWLER!
BUT I CAN'T KEEP DODGING HIM FOREVER--SO I GUESS IT'S TIME TO TRY THE OFFENSIVE ROUTE!
SWELL! I'M HAVING ABOUT AS MUCH EFFECT AGAINST HIM AS RICHARD SIMMONS WOULD HAVE AGAINST ME!
AT LEAST I'M STEERING HIM AWAY FROM THE OTHERS!
"IF ONLY THE VISION COULD HELP!"
THE SENSORMETER IS INOPERABLE--AND THE VISION APPEARS TO BE... BEYOND OUR AID!
THEN, FRIEND MARK, WE ARE FACED WITH QUITE A PROBLEM!
16

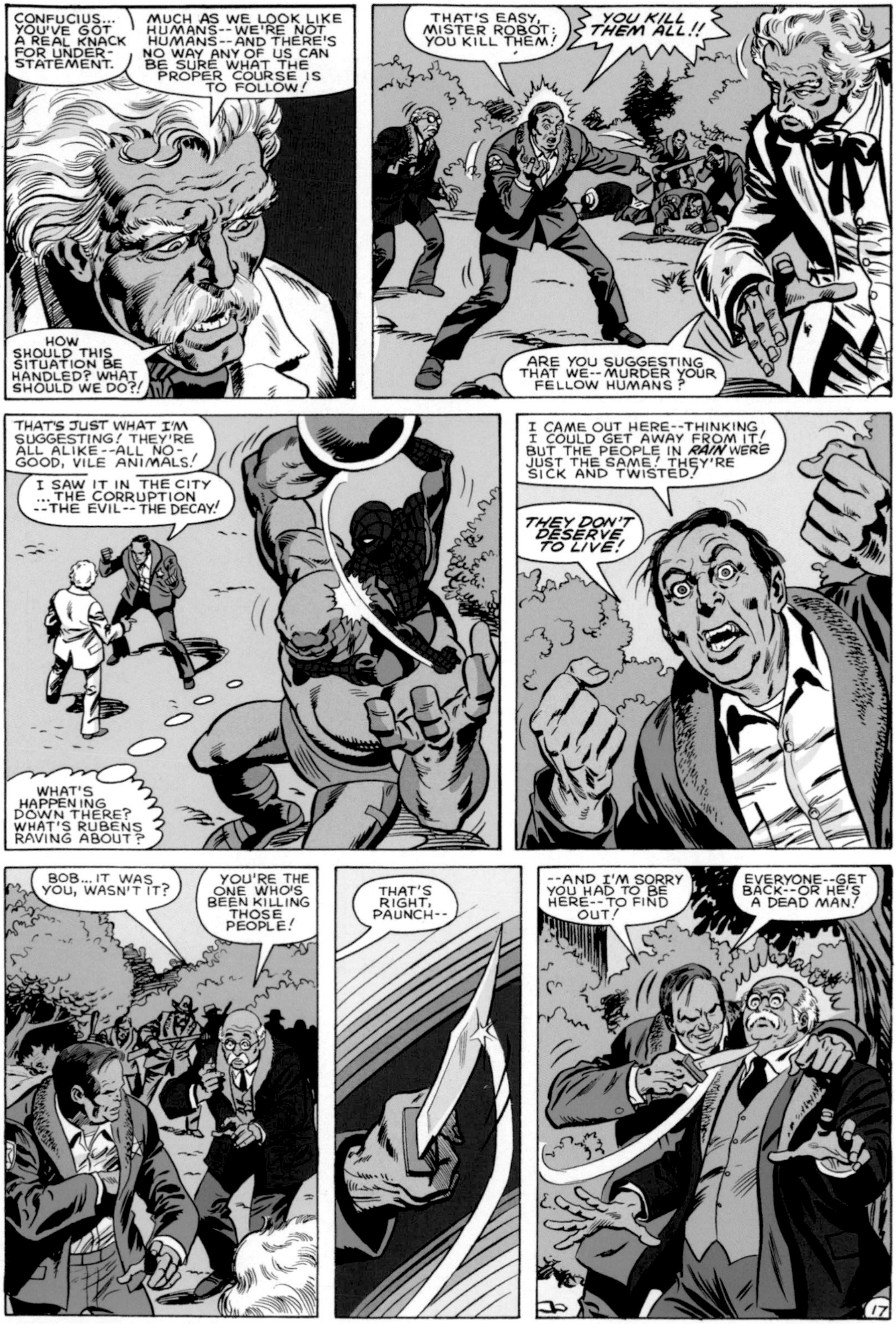
CONFUCIUS... YOU'VE GOT A REAL KNACK FOR UNDER-STATEMENT.
MUCH AS WE LOOK LIKE HUMANS--WE'RE NOT HUMANS--AND THERE'S NO WAY ANY OF US CAN BE SURE WHAT THE PROPER COURSE IS TO FOLLOW!
HOW SHOULD THIS SITUATION BE HANDLED? WHAT SHOULD WE DO?!
THAT'S EASY, MISTER ROBOT: YOU KILL THEM!
YOU KILL THEM ALL!!
ARE YOU SUGGESTING THAT WE--MURDER YOUR FELLOW HUMANS?
THAT'S JUST WHAT I'M SUGGESTING! THEY'RE ALL ALIKE--ALL NO-GOOD, VILE ANIMALS!
I SAW IT IN THE CITY ...THE CORRUPTION --THE EVIL-- THE DECAY!
WHAT'S HAPPENING DOWN THERE? WHAT'S RUBENS RAVING ABOUT?
I CAME OUT HERE--THINKING I COULD GET AWAY FROM IT! BUT THE PEOPLE IN RAIN WERE JUST THE SAME! THEY'RE SICK AND TWISTED!
THEY DON'T DESERVE TO LIVE!
BOB... IT WAS YOU, WASN'T IT?
YOU'RE THE ONE WHO'S BEEN KILLING THOSE PEOPLE!
THAT'S RIGHT, PAUNCH--
--AND I'M SORRY YOU HAD TO BE HERE--TO FIND OUT!
EVERYONE--GET BACK--OR HE'S A DEAD MAN!
17

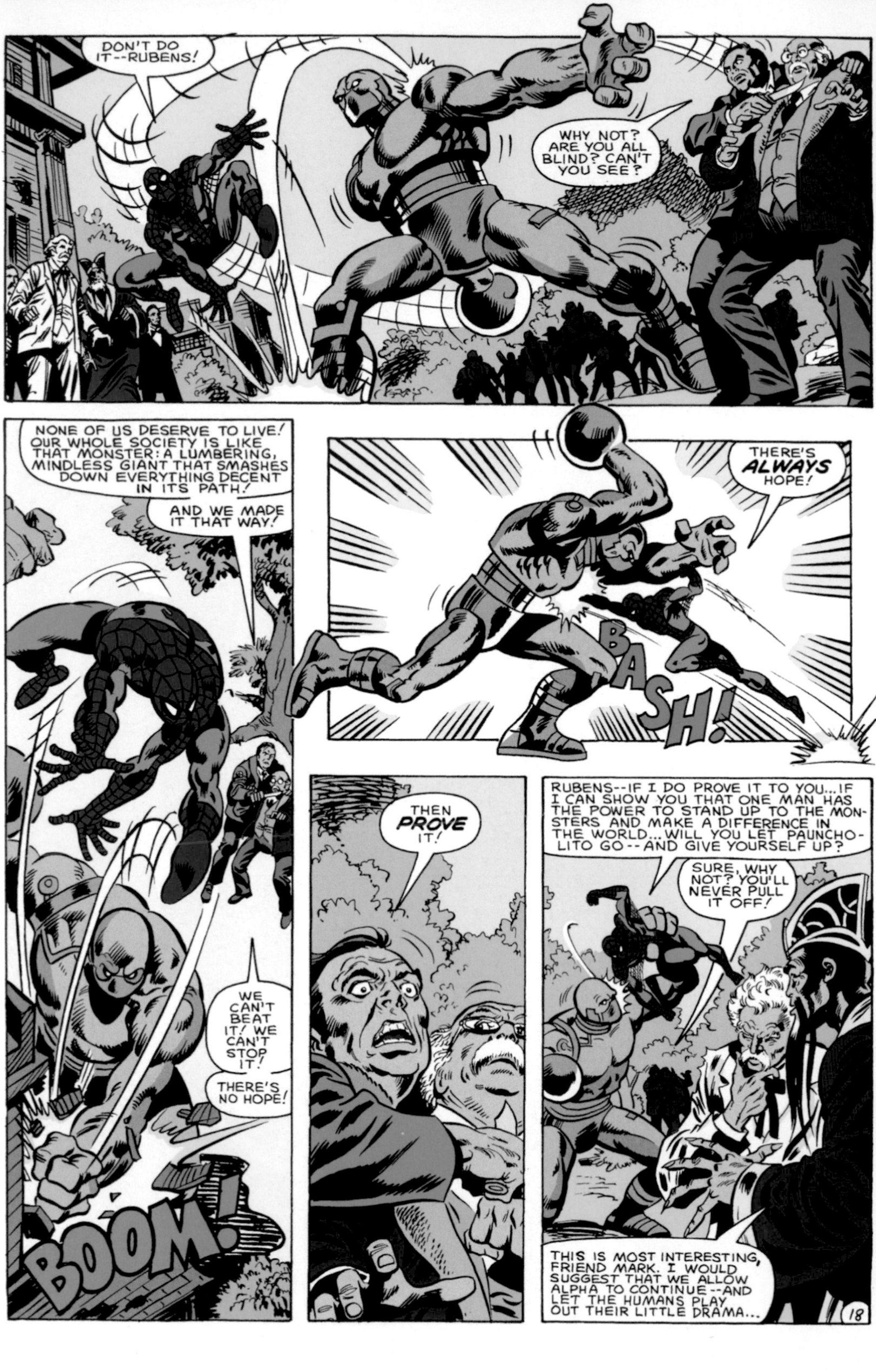

DON'T DO IT--RUBENS!
WHY NOT? ARE YOU ALL BLIND? CAN'T YOU SEE?
NONE OF US DESERVE TO LIVE! OUR WHOLE SOCIETY IS LIKE THAT MONSTER: A LUMBERING, MINDLESS GIANT THAT SMASHES DOWN EVERYTHING DECENT IN ITS PATH!
AND WE MADE IT THAT WAY!
WE CAN'T BEAT IT! WE CAN'T STOP IT!
THERE'S NO HOPE!
BOOM!
THERE'S ALWAYS HOPE!
BASH!
THEN PROVE IT!
RUBENS--IF I DO PROVE IT TO YOU... IF I CAN SHOW YOU THAT ONE MAN HAS THE POWER TO STAND UP TO THE MONSTERS AND MAKE A DIFFERENCE IN THE WORLD... WILL YOU LET PAUNCHOLITO GO--AND GIVE YOURSELF UP?
SURE, WHY NOT? YOU'LL NEVER PULL IT OFF!
THIS IS MOST INTERESTING, FRIEND MARK. I WOULD SUGGEST THAT WE ALLOW ALPHA TO CONTINUE--AND LET THE HUMANS PLAY OUT THEIR LITTLE DRAMA...

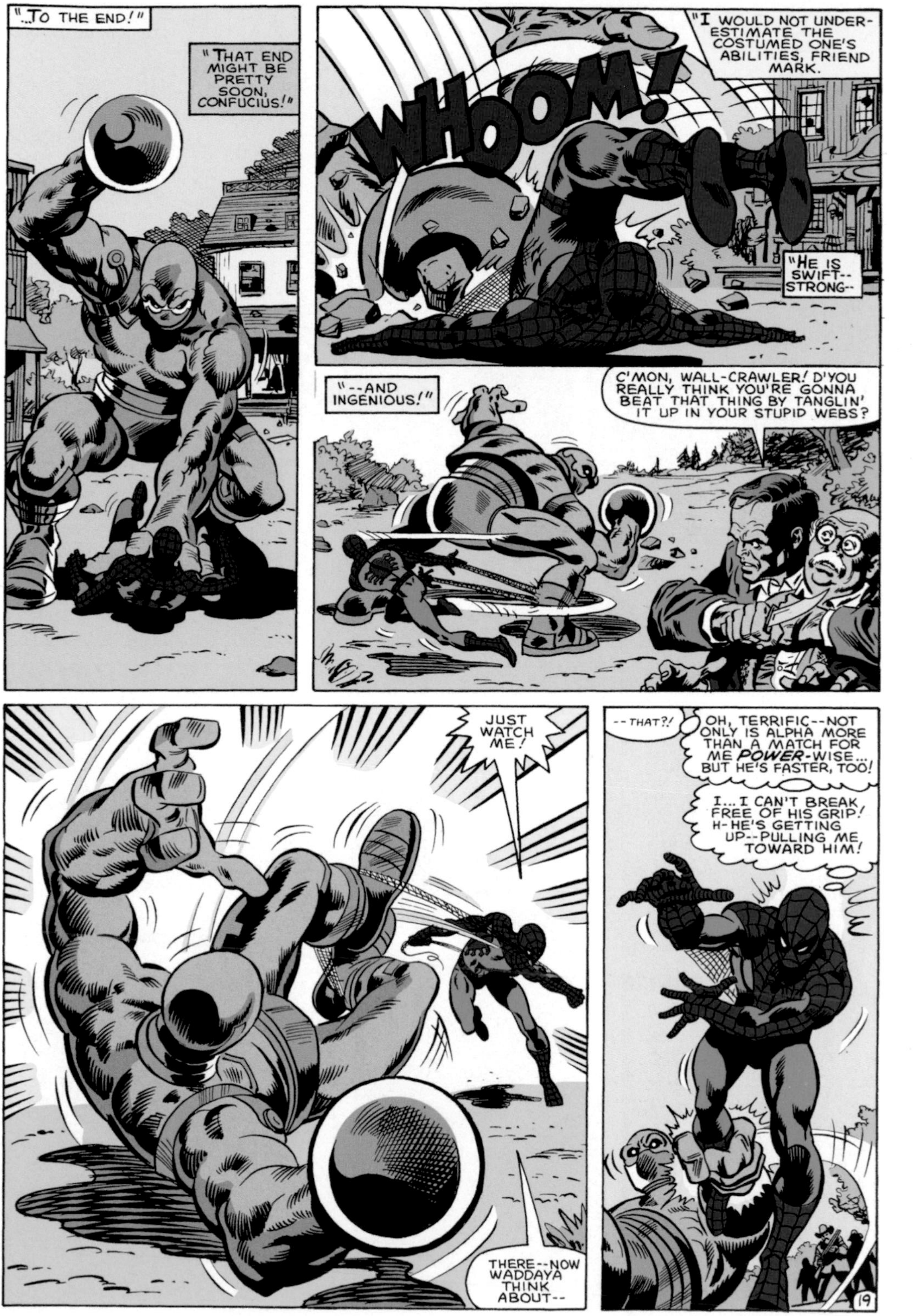
"...TO THE END!"
"THAT END MIGHT BE PRETTY SOON, CONFUCIUS!"
"I WOULD NOT UNDERESTIMATE THE COSTUMED ONE'S ABILITIES, FRIEND MARK.
WHOOM!
"HE IS SWIFT--STRONG--
"--AND INGENIOUS!"
C'MON, WALL-CRAWLER! D'YOU REALLY THINK YOU'RE GONNA BEAT THAT THING BY TANGLIN' IT UP IN YOUR STUPID WEBS?
JUST WATCH ME!
THERE--NOW WADDAYA THINK ABOUT--
--THAT?!
OH, TERRIFIC--NOT ONLY IS ALPHA MORE THAN A MATCH FOR ME POWER-WISE... BUT HE'S FASTER, TOO!
I... I CAN'T BREAK FREE OF HIS GRIP! H-HE'S GETTING UP--PULLING ME TOWARD HIM!

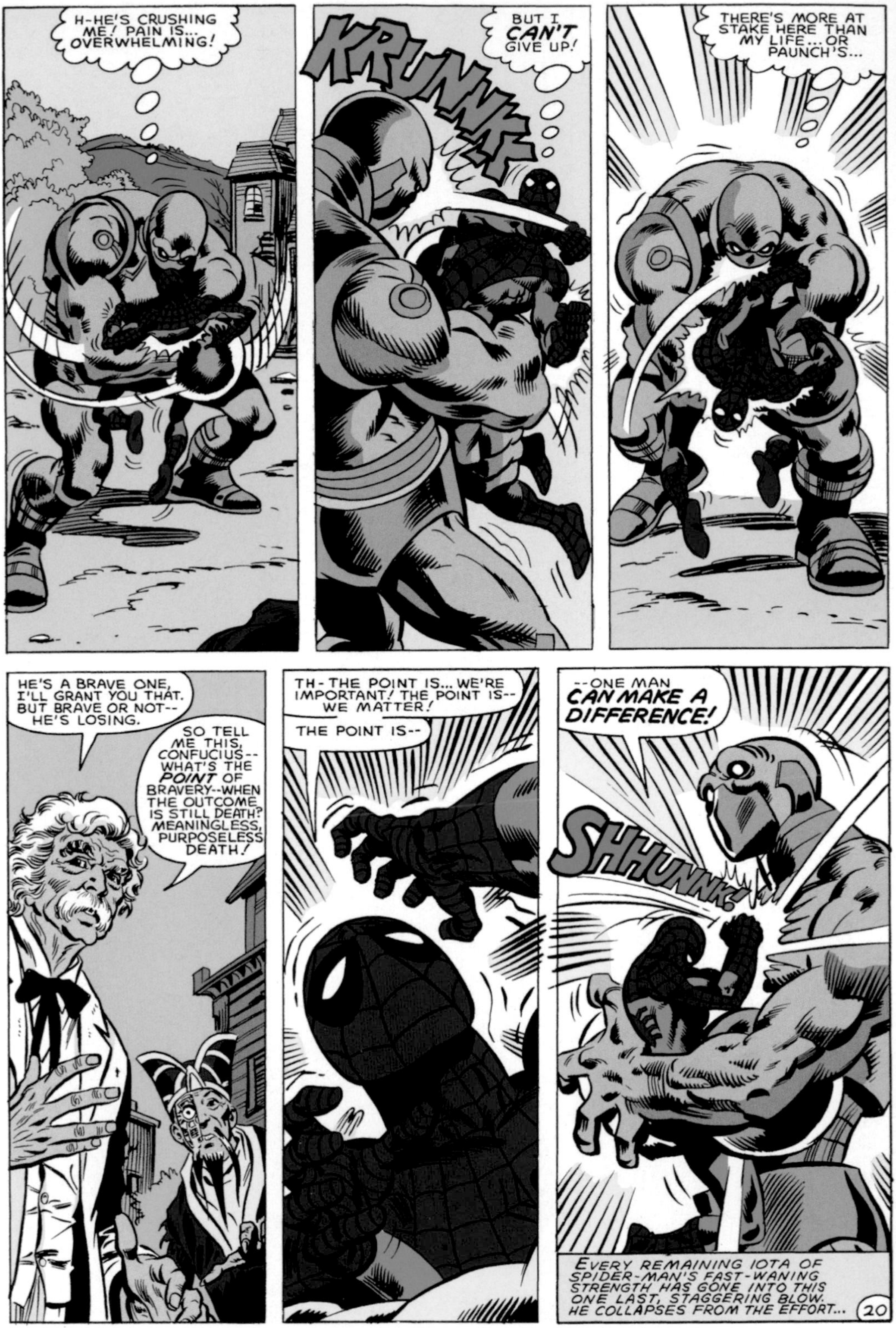

H-HE'S CRUSHING ME! PAIN IS... OVERWHELMING!
KRUNNK!
BUT I CAN'T GIVE UP!
THERE'S MORE AT STAKE HERE THAN MY LIFE... OR PAUNCH'S...
HE'S A BRAVE ONE, I'LL GRANT YOU THAT. BUT BRAVE OR NOT-- HE'S LOSING.
SO TELL ME THIS, CONFUCIUS-- WHAT'S THE POINT OF BRAVERY--WHEN THE OUTCOME IS STILL DEATH? MEANINGLESS, PURPOSELESS DEATH!
TH-THE POINT IS... WE'RE IMPORTANT! THE POINT IS-- WE MATTER!
THE POINT IS--
--ONE MAN CAN MAKE A DIFFERENCE!
SHHUNNK!
EVERY REMAINING IOTA OF SPIDER-MAN'S FAST-WANING STRENGTH HAS GONE INTO THIS ONE LAST, STAGGERING BLOW. HE COLLAPSES FROM THE EFFORT...
20

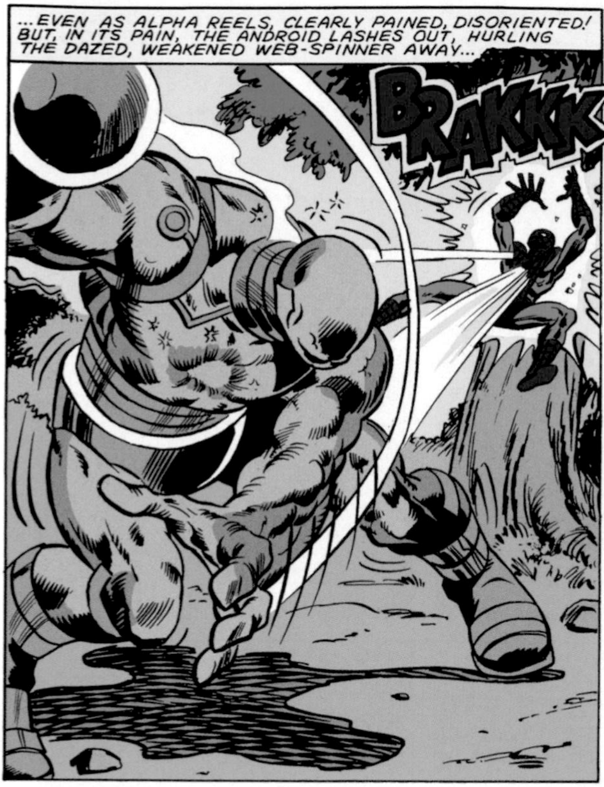
...EVEN AS ALPHA REELS, CLEARLY PAINED, DISORIENTED! BUT, IN ITS PAIN, THE ANDROID LASHES OUT, HURLING THE DAZED, WEAKENED WEB-SPINNER AWAY...
BRAKKK
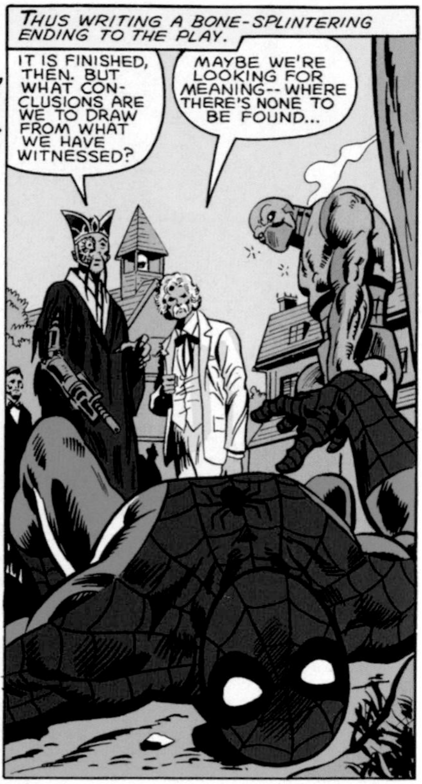
THUS WRITING A BONE-SPLINTERING ENDING TO THE PLAY.
IT IS FINISHED, THEN. BUT WHAT CONCLUSIONS ARE WE TO DRAW FROM WHAT WE HAVE WITNESSED?
MAYBE WE'RE LOOKING FOR MEANING-- WHERE THERE'S NONE TO BE FOUND...
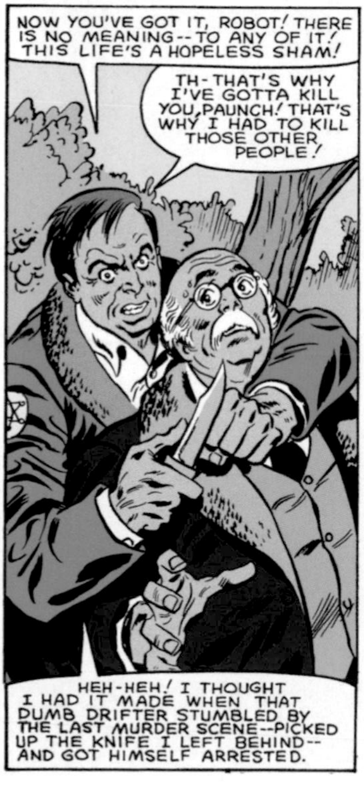
NOW YOU'VE GOT IT, ROBOT! THERE IS NO MEANING--TO ANY OF IT! THIS LIFE'S A HOPELESS SHAM!
TH-THAT'S WHY I'VE GOTTA KILL YOU, PAUNCH! THAT'S WHY I HAD TO KILL THOSE OTHER PEOPLE!
HEH-HEH! I THOUGHT I HAD IT MADE WHEN THAT DUMB DRIFTER STUMBLED BY THE LAST MURDER SCENE--PICKED UP THE KNIFE I LEFT BEHIND--AND GOT HIMSELF ARRESTED.
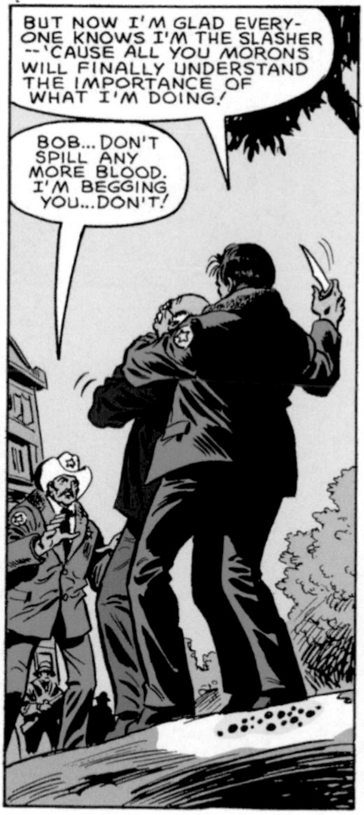
BUT NOW I'M GLAD EVERYONE KNOWS I'M THE SLASHER--'CAUSE ALL YOU MORONS WILL FINALLY UNDERSTAND THE IMPORTANCE OF WHAT I'M DOING!
BOB...DON'T SPILL ANY MORE BLOOD. I'M BEGGING YOU...DON'T!
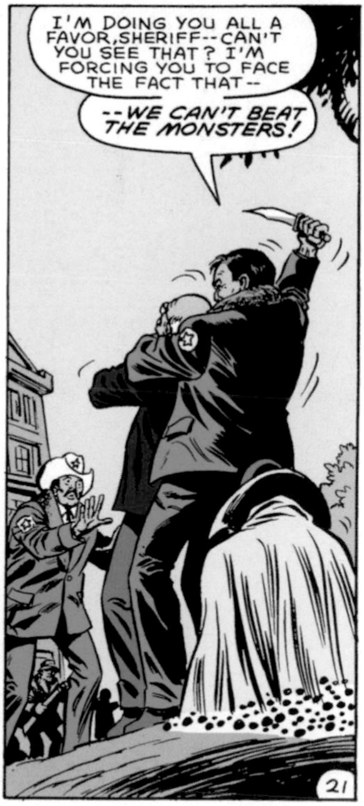
I'M DOING YOU ALL A FAVOR, SHERIFF--CAN'T YOU SEE THAT? I'M FORCING YOU TO FACE THE FACT THAT--
--WE CAN'T BEAT THE MONSTERS!

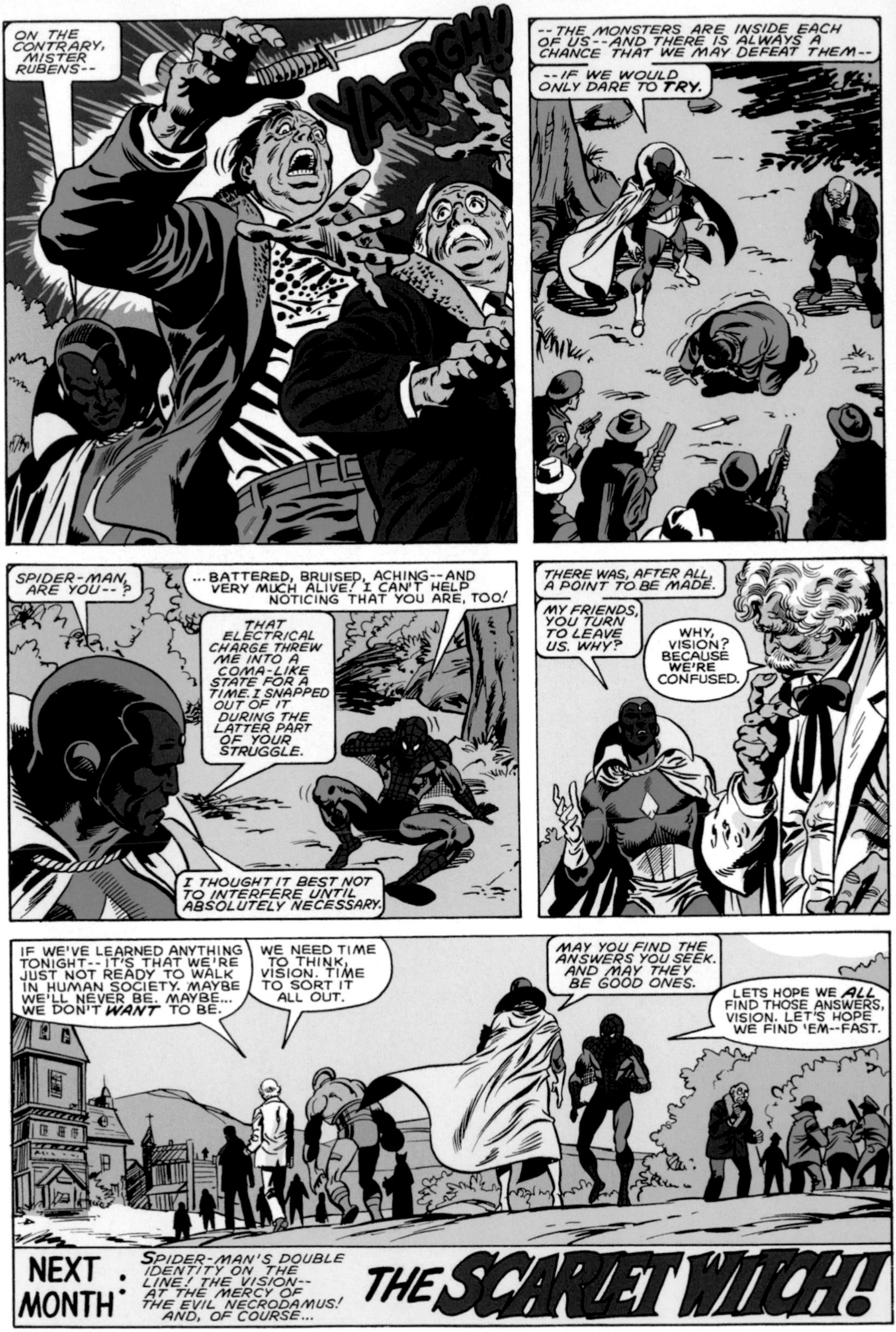
ON THE CONTRARY, MISTER RUBENS--
YARRGH!
--THE MONSTERS ARE INSIDE EACH OF US--AND THERE IS ALWAYS A CHANCE THAT WE MAY DEFEAT THEM--
--IF WE WOULD ONLY DARE TO TRY.
SPIDER-MAN, ARE YOU--?
...BATTERED, BRUISED, ACHING--AND VERY MUCH ALIVE! I CAN'T HELP NOTICING THAT YOU ARE, TOO!
THAT ELECTRICAL CHARGE THREW ME INTO A COMA-LIKE STATE FOR A TIME. I SNAPPED OUT OF IT DURING THE LATTER PART OF YOUR STRUGGLE.
I THOUGHT IT BEST NOT TO INTERFERE UNTIL ABSOLUTELY NECESSARY.
THERE WAS, AFTER ALL, A POINT TO BE MADE.
MY FRIENDS, YOU TURN TO LEAVE US. WHY?
WHY, VISION? BECAUSE WE'RE CONFUSED.
IF WE'VE LEARNED ANYTHING TONIGHT--IT'S THAT WE'RE JUST NOT READY TO WALK IN HUMAN SOCIETY. MAYBE WE'LL NEVER BE. MAYBE... WE DON'T WANT TO BE.
WE NEED TIME TO THINK, VISION. TIME TO SORT IT ALL OUT.
MAY YOU FIND THE ANSWERS YOU SEEK. AND MAY THEY BE GOOD ONES.
LETS HOPE WE ALL FIND THOSE ANSWERS, VISION. LET'S HOPE WE FIND 'EM--FAST.
NEXT MONTH:
SPIDER-MAN'S DOUBLE IDENTITY ON THE LINE! THE VISION--AT THE MERCY OF THE EVIL NECRODAMUS! AND, OF COURSE...
THE SCARLET WITCH!

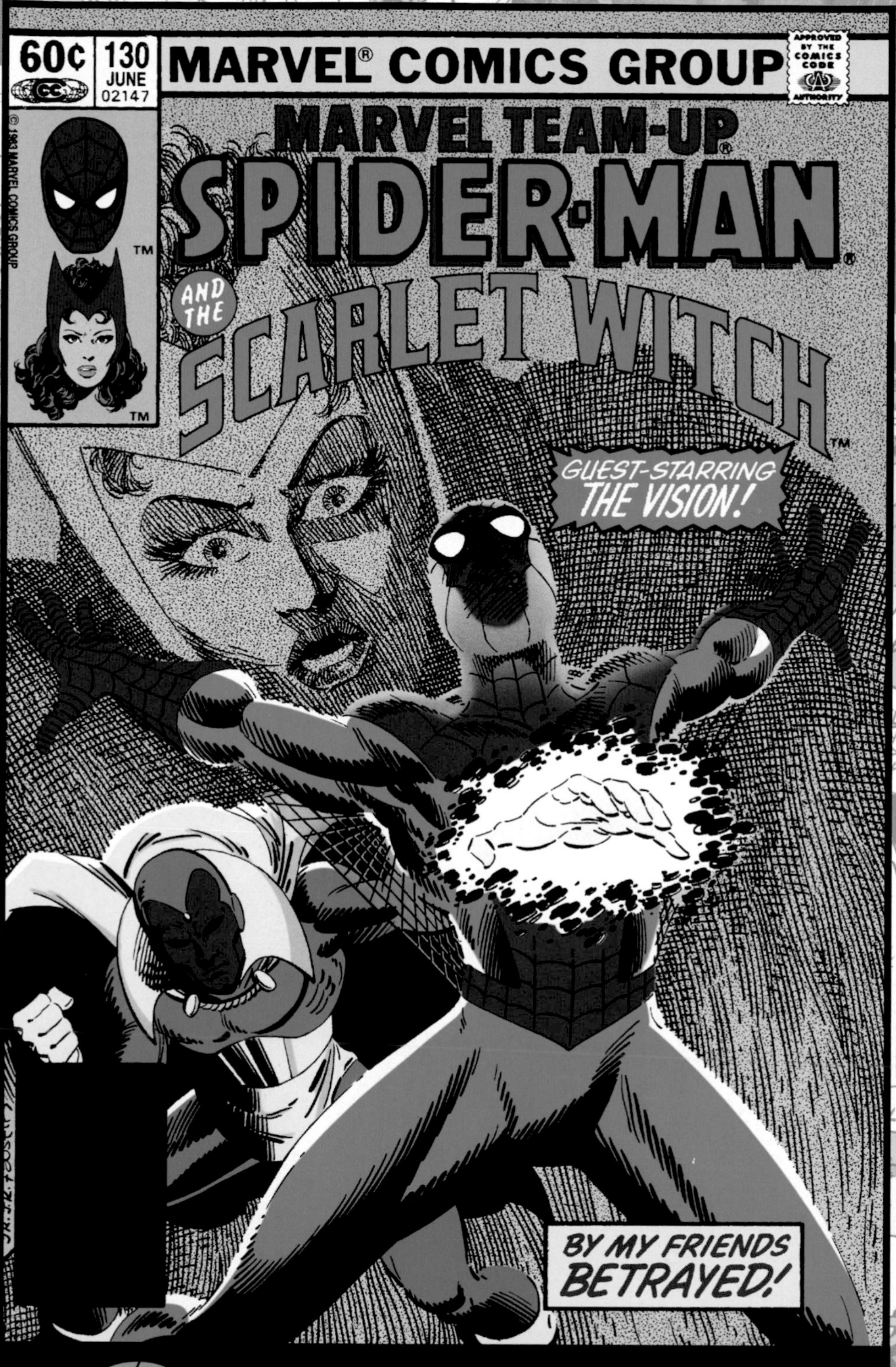
60¢
130
JUNE
02147
MARVEL COMICS GROUP
APPROVED BY THE COMICS CODE AUTHORITY
© 1983 MARVEL COMICS GROUP
MARVEL TEAM-UP
SPIDER-MAN
AND THE
SCARLET WITCH
GUEST-STARRING THE VISION!
BY MY FRIENDS BETRAYED!

MARVEL TEAM-UP (1972) #130

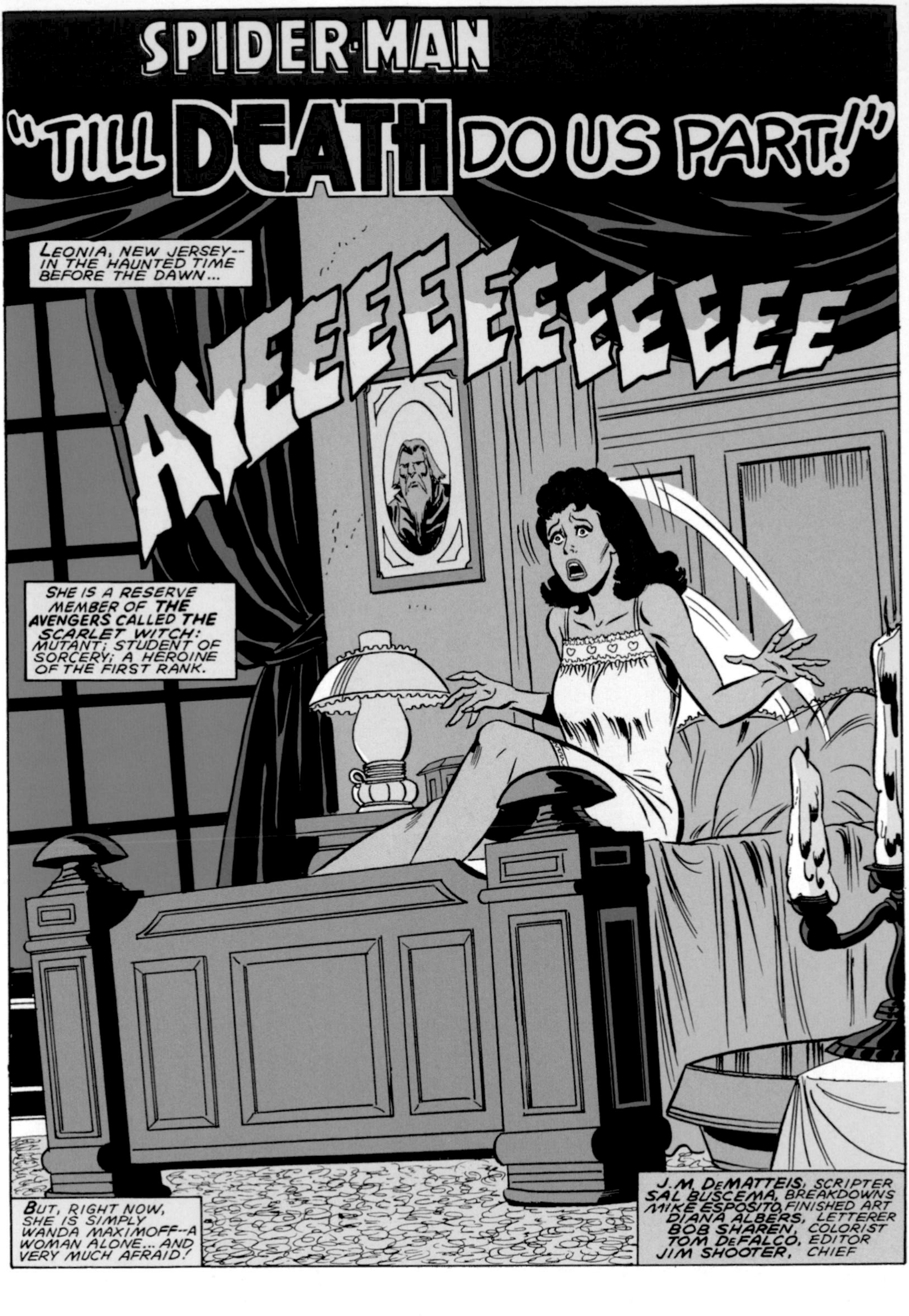
SPIDER-MAN
"TILL DEATH DO US PART!"
LEONIA, NEW JERSEY-- IN THE HAUNTED TIME BEFORE THE DAWN...
AYEEEEEEEEEEE
SHE IS A RESERVE MEMBER OF THE AVENGERS CALLED THE SCARLET WITCH: MUTANT; STUDENT OF SORCERY; A HEROINE OF THE FIRST RANK.
BUT, RIGHT NOW, SHE IS SIMPLY WANDA MAXIMOFF--A WOMAN ALONE... AND VERY MUCH AFRAID!
J.M. DeMATTEIS, SCRIPTER
SAL BUSCEMA, BREAKDOWNS
MIKE ESPOSITO, FINISHED ART
DIANA ALBERS, LETTERER
BOB SHAREN, COLORIST
TOM DeFALCO, EDITOR
JIM SHOOTER, CHIEF

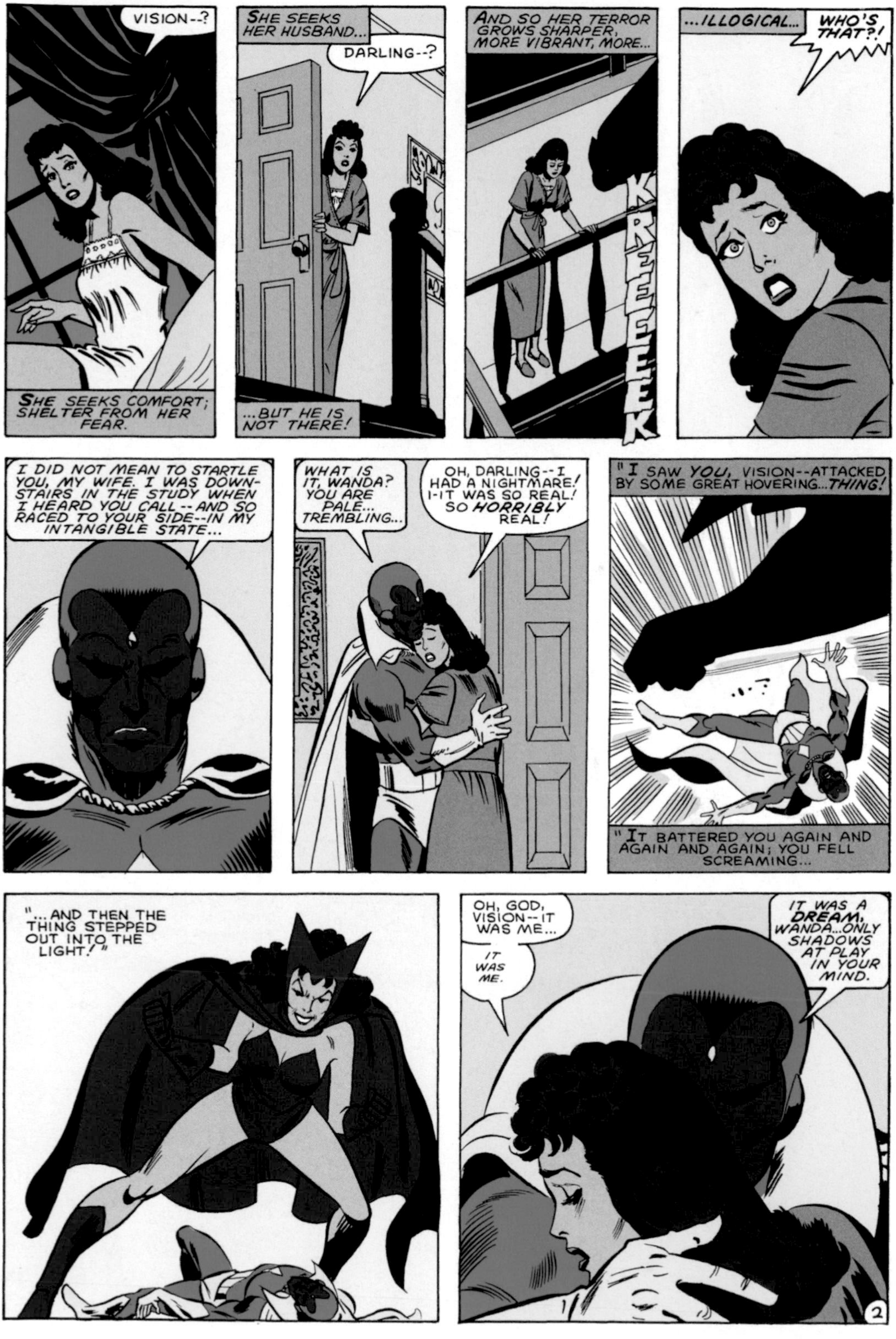
VISION--?
SHE SEEKS COMFORT; SHELTER FROM HER FEAR.
SHE SEEKS HER HUSBAND...
DARLING--?
...BUT HE IS NOT THERE!
AND SO HER TERROR GROWS SHARPER, MORE VIBRANT, MORE...
KREEEEEK
...ILLOGICAL...
WHO'S THAT?!
I DID NOT MEAN TO STARTLE YOU, MY WIFE. I WAS DOWN-STAIRS IN THE STUDY WHEN I HEARD YOU CALL--AND SO RACED TO YOUR SIDE--IN MY INTANGIBLE STATE...
WHAT IS IT, WANDA? YOU ARE PALE... TREMBLING...
OH, DARLING--I HAD A NIGHTMARE! I-IT WAS SO REAL! SO HORRIBLY REAL!
"I SAW YOU, VISION--ATTACKED BY SOME GREAT HOVERING...THING!
"IT BATTERED YOU AGAIN AND AGAIN AND AGAIN; YOU FELL SCREAMING...
"...AND THEN THE THING STEPPED OUT INTO THE LIGHT!"
OH, GOD, VISION--IT WAS ME...
IT WAS ME.
IT WAS A DREAM, WANDA...ONLY SHADOWS AT PLAY IN YOUR MIND.
2

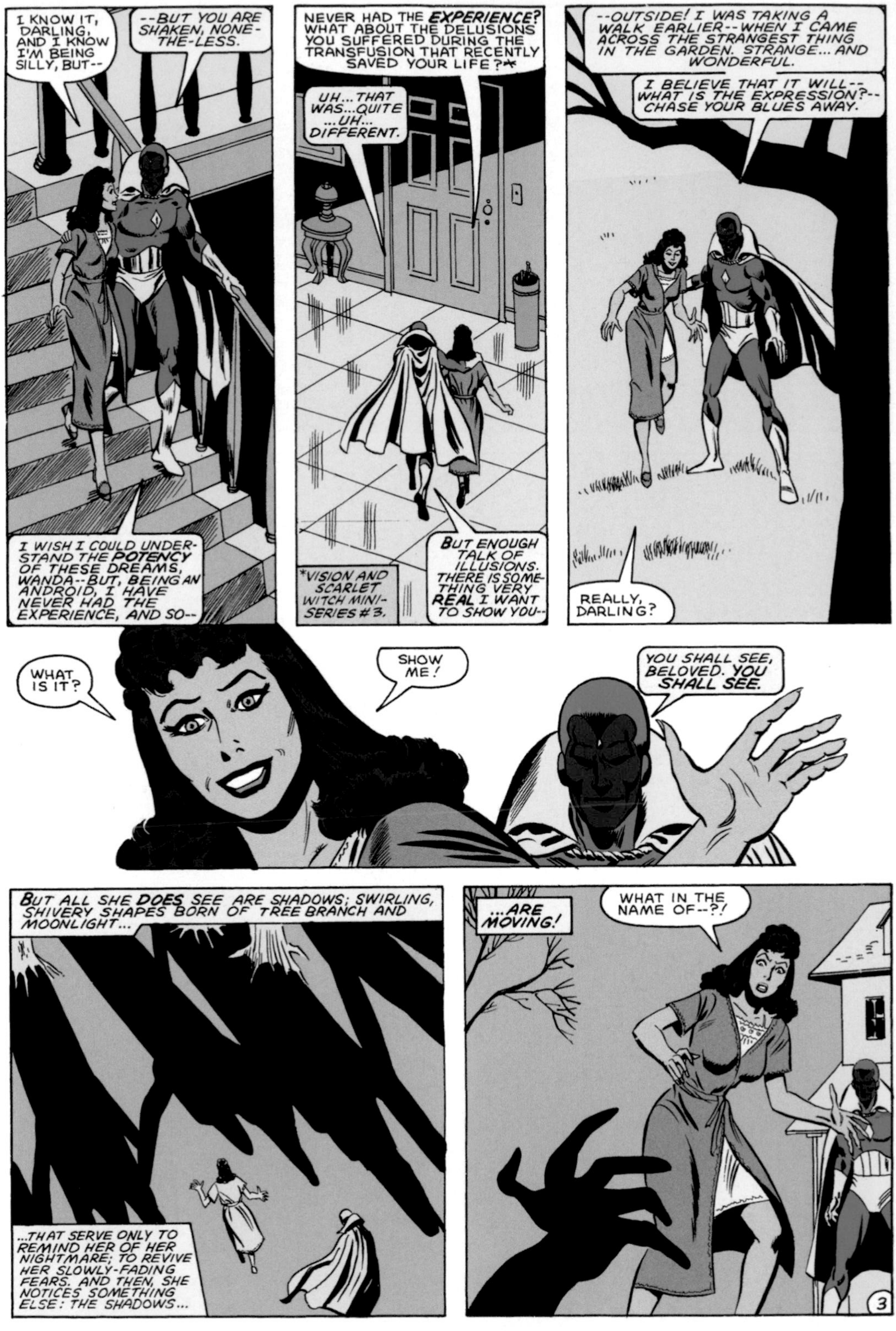

I KNOW IT, DARLING, AND I KNOW I'M BEING SILLY, BUT--
--BUT YOU ARE SHAKEN, NONE-THE-LESS.
I WISH I COULD UNDERSTAND THE POTENCY OF THESE DREAMS, WANDA--BUT, BEING AN ANDROID, I HAVE NEVER HAD THE EXPERIENCE, AND SO--
NEVER HAD THE EXPERIENCE? WHAT ABOUT THE DELUSIONS YOU SUFFERED DURING THE TRANSFUSION THAT RECENTLY SAVED YOUR LIFE?*
UH...THAT WAS...QUITE ...UH... DIFFERENT.
*VISION AND SCARLET WITCH MINI-SERIES #3.
BUT ENOUGH TALK OF ILLUSIONS. THERE IS SOMETHING VERY REAL I WANT TO SHOW YOU--
--OUTSIDE! I WAS TAKING A WALK EARLIER--WHEN I CAME ACROSS THE STRANGEST THING IN THE GARDEN. STRANGE... AND WONDERFUL.
I BELIEVE THAT IT WILL--WHAT IS THE EXPRESSION?--CHASE YOUR BLUES AWAY.
REALLY, DARLING?
WHAT IS IT?
SHOW ME!
YOU SHALL SEE, BELOVED. YOU SHALL SEE.
BUT ALL SHE DOES SEE ARE SHADOWS; SWIRLING, SHIVERY SHAPES BORN OF TREE BRANCH AND MOONLIGHT...
...THAT SERVE ONLY TO REMIND HER OF HER NIGHTMARE; TO REVIVE HER SLOWLY-FADING FEARS. AND THEN, SHE NOTICES SOMETHING ELSE: THE SHADOWS...
...ARE MOVING!
WHAT IN THE NAME OF--?!
3

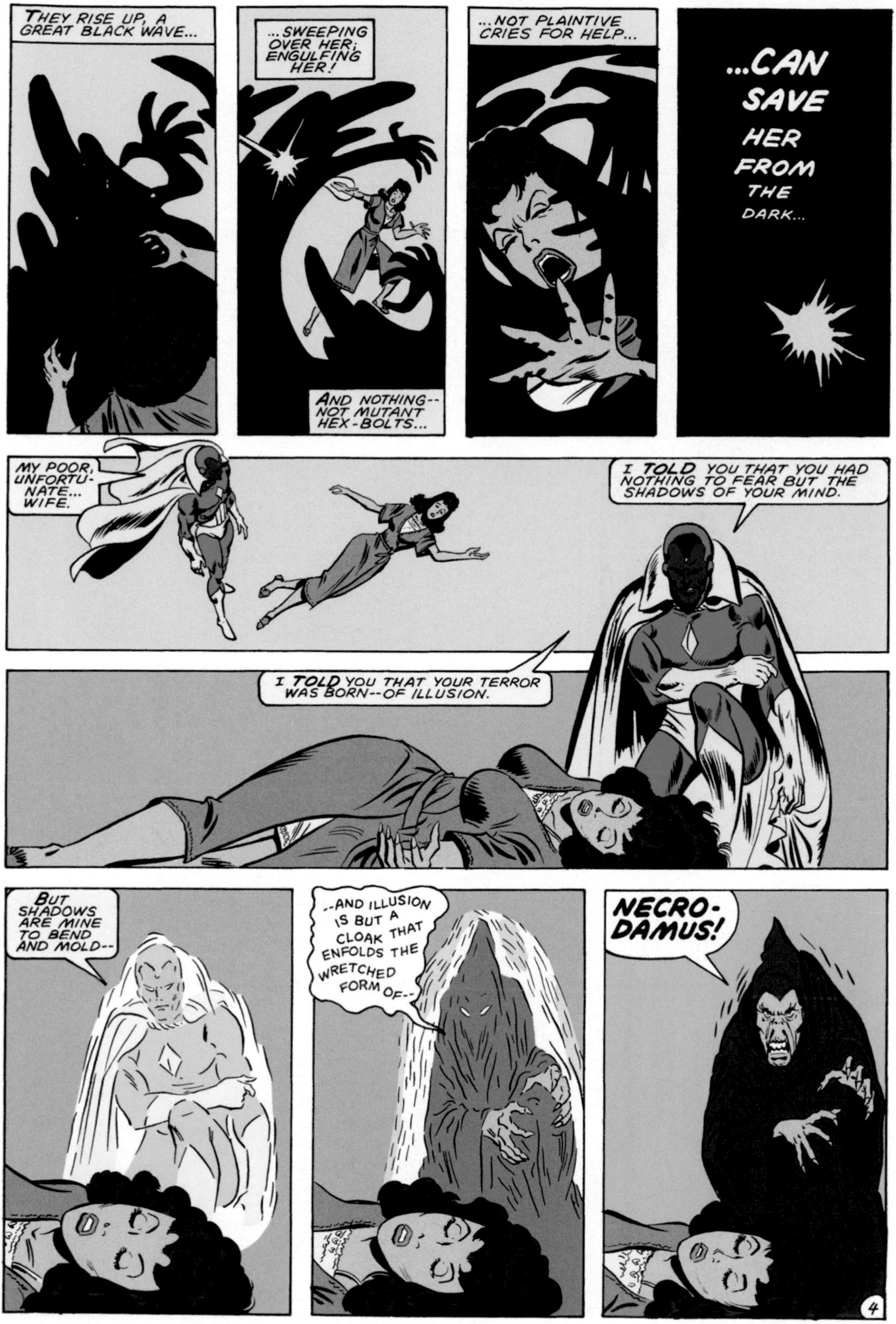

THEY RISE UP, A GREAT BLACK WAVE...
...SWEEPING OVER HER; ENGULFING HER!
...NOT PLAINTIVE CRIES FOR HELP...
AND NOTHING--NOT MUTANT HEX-BOLTS...
...CAN SAVE HER FROM THE DARK...
MY POOR, UNFORTU-NATE... WIFE.
I TOLD YOU THAT YOU HAD NOTHING TO FEAR BUT THE SHADOWS OF YOUR MIND.
I TOLD YOU THAT YOUR TERROR WAS BORN--OF ILLUSION.
BUT SHADOWS ARE MINE TO BEND AND MOLD--
--AND ILLUSION IS BUT A CLOAK THAT ENFOLDS THE WRETCHED FORM OF--
NECRO-DAMUS!
4

MEANWHILE, IN THE DESERTED NEW HAMPSHIRE VILLAGE OF *PONDER*, WHERE THE REAL *VISION* AND THE AMAZING *SPIDER-MAN* ARE RECOVERING FROM A DESPERATE BATTLE AGAINST BOTH HUMAN AND ANDROID INSANITY...*

LET ME HELP YOU UP, MY FRIEND.

U-UP--? HOW DID I GET *DOWN*? WH-WHAT HAPPENED?

YOU FAINTED, SON. I GUESS YOUR FIGHT WITH THAT *ALPHA*-CREATURE TOOK MORE OUT OF YOU THAN YOU REALIZED.

*LAST ISSUE.

SPIDER-MAN, IF YOU ARE IN NEED OF MEDICAL ASSISTANCE, I WILL GLADLY ESCORT YOU TO--

NAH, I'LL BE OKAY, VISION. AND THE IMPORTANT THING IS-- WE STOPPED A MANIAC FROM TAKING ANY MORE INNOCENT LIVES!

SOMETHING WRONG, MR. PAUNCHOLITO? YOU'RE STARING AT ME LIKE I'VE GOT THE MARK OF *CAIN* STAMPED ON MY FOREHEAD!

WRONG? NO, I... I NEVER *TOLD* YOU MY NAME!

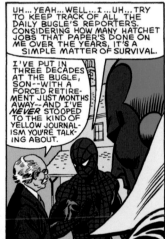

UH... YEAH... WELL... I... UH... TRY TO KEEP TRACK OF ALL THE DAILY BUGLE'S REPORTERS. CONSIDERING HOW MANY HATCHET JOBS THAT PAPER'S DONE ON ME OVER THE YEARS, IT'S A SIMPLE MATTER OF SURVIVAL.

I'VE PUT IN THREE DECADES AT THE BUGLE, SON--WITH A FORCED RETIREMENT JUST MONTHS AWAY--AND I'VE *NEVER* STOOPED TO THE KIND OF YELLOW JOURNALISM YOU'RE TALKING ABOUT.

I'M GLAD TO HEAR THAT!

NOW, IF YOU'LL EXCUSE ME, I'M LATE FOR THE ANNUAL COSTUMED ARACHNID'S CHARITY BALL, SO--

ONE THING BEFORE YOU GO, SPIDER-MAN.

I LOST TRACK OF MY PHOTOGRAPHER-PARTNER *PETER PARKER.* IF YOU SHOULD *SEE* HIM, WOULD YOU TELL HIM THAT I THINK I'VE FOUND THAT STORY I WAS LOOKING FOR--

--THE STORY SO BIG IT'LL MAKE THIS MANIAC THING LOOK LIKE A FILLER FOR PAGE SIXTY-FOUR? TELL HIM IF THEY'RE GOING TO RETIRE ME, I AIM TO GO OUT IN STYLE--

--AND I CAN'T LET *ANYTHING* STAND IN MY WAY.

5

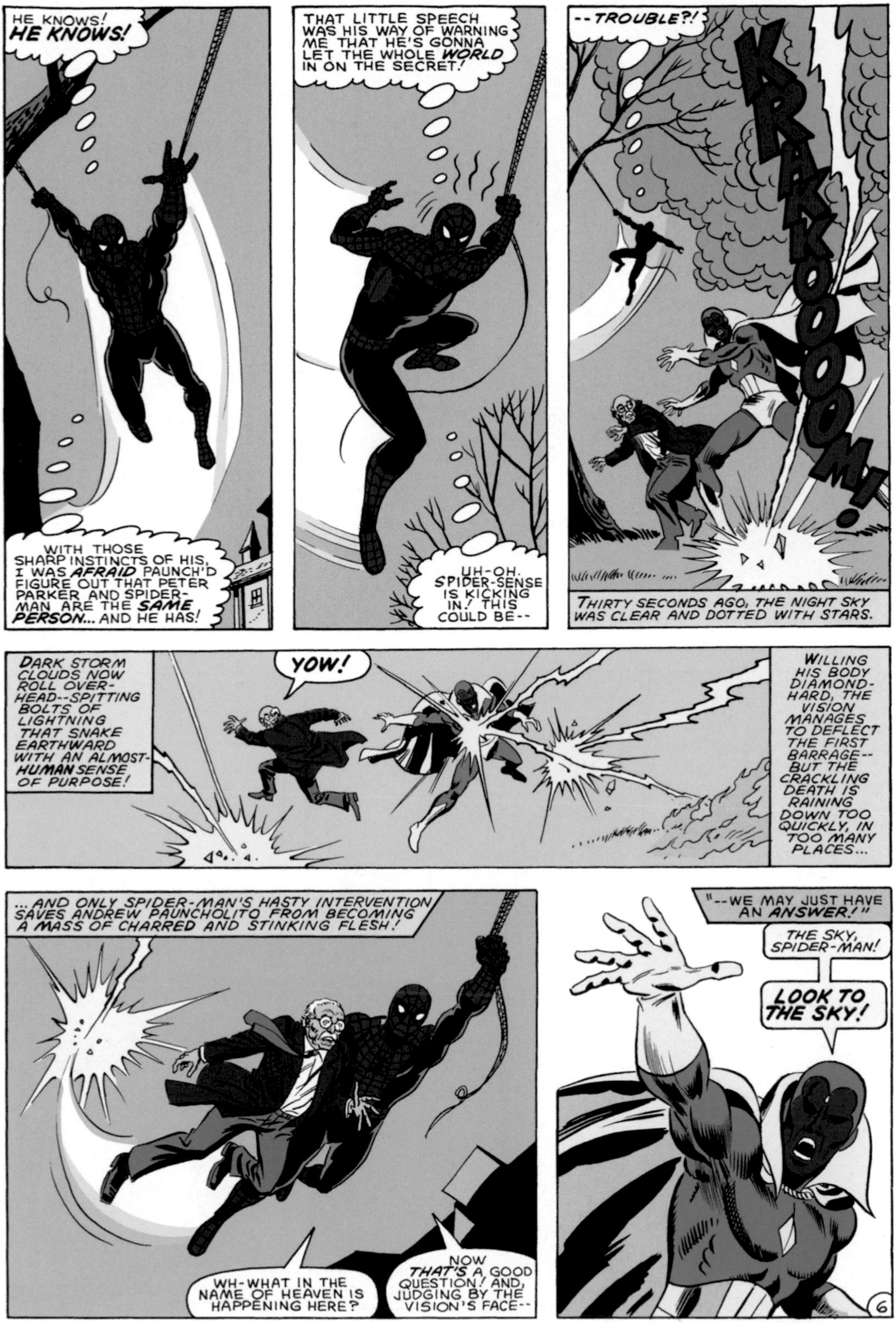
HE KNOWS! HE KNOWS!
WITH THOSE SHARP INSTINCTS OF HIS, I WAS AFRAID PAUNCH'D FIGURE OUT THAT PETER PARKER AND SPIDER-MAN ARE THE SAME PERSON... AND HE HAS!
THAT LITTLE SPEECH WAS HIS WAY OF WARNING ME THAT HE'S GONNA LET THE WHOLE WORLD IN ON THE SECRET!
UH-OH. SPIDER-SENSE IS KICKING IN! THIS COULD BE--
--TROUBLE?!
KRAKOOOOM!
THIRTY SECONDS AGO, THE NIGHT SKY WAS CLEAR AND DOTTED WITH STARS.
DARK STORM CLOUDS NOW ROLL OVER-HEAD--SPITTING BOLTS OF LIGHTNING THAT SNAKE EARTHWARD WITH AN ALMOST-HUMAN SENSE OF PURPOSE!
YOW!
WILLING HIS BODY DIAMOND-HARD, THE VISION MANAGES TO DEFLECT THE FIRST BARRAGE--BUT THE CRACKLING DEATH IS RAINING DOWN TOO QUICKLY, IN TOO MANY PLACES...
...AND ONLY SPIDER-MAN'S HASTY INTERVENTION SAVES ANDREW PAUNCHOLITO FROM BECOMING A MASS OF CHARRED AND STINKING FLESH!
WH-WHAT IN THE NAME OF HEAVEN IS HAPPENING HERE?
NOW THAT'S A GOOD QUESTION! AND, JUDGING BY THE VISION'S FACE--
"--WE MAY JUST HAVE AN ANSWER!"
THE SKY, SPIDER-MAN!
LOOK TO THE SKY!
6

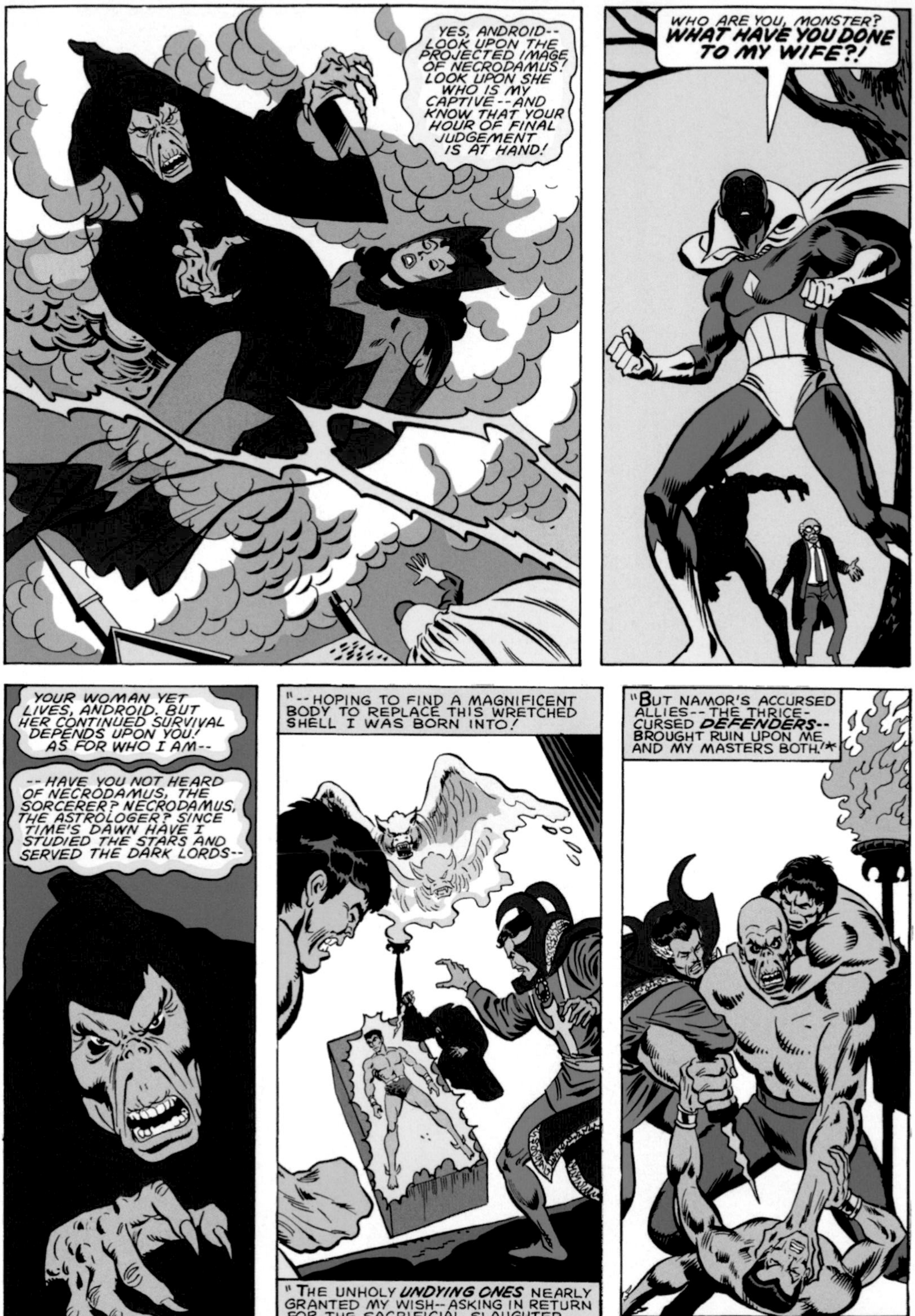
YES, ANDROID-- LOOK UPON THE PROJECTED IMAGE OF NECRODAMUS! LOOK UPON SHE WHO IS MY CAPTIVE--AND KNOW THAT YOUR HOUR OF FINAL JUDGEMENT IS AT HAND!
WHO ARE YOU, MONSTER? WHAT HAVE YOU DONE TO MY WIFE?!
YOUR WOMAN YET LIVES, ANDROID. BUT HER CONTINUED SURVIVAL DEPENDS UPON YOU! AS FOR WHO I AM--
--HAVE YOU NOT HEARD OF NECRODAMUS, THE SORCERER? NECRODAMUS, THE ASTROLOGER? SINCE TIME'S DAWN HAVE I STUDIED THE STARS AND SERVED THE DARK LORDS--
"--HOPING TO FIND A MAGNIFICENT BODY TO REPLACE THIS WRETCHED SHELL I WAS BORN INTO!
"THE UNHOLY UNDYING ONES NEARLY GRANTED MY WISH--ASKING IN RETURN FOR THE SACRIFICIAL SLAUGHTER OF PRINCE NAMOR OF ATLANTIS--THE FABLED SUB-MARINER!
"BUT NAMOR'S ACCURSED ALLIES--THE THRICE-CURSED DEFENDERS--BROUGHT RUIN UPON ME AND MY MASTERS BOTH!"*
*SEE DEFENDERS #1!
7

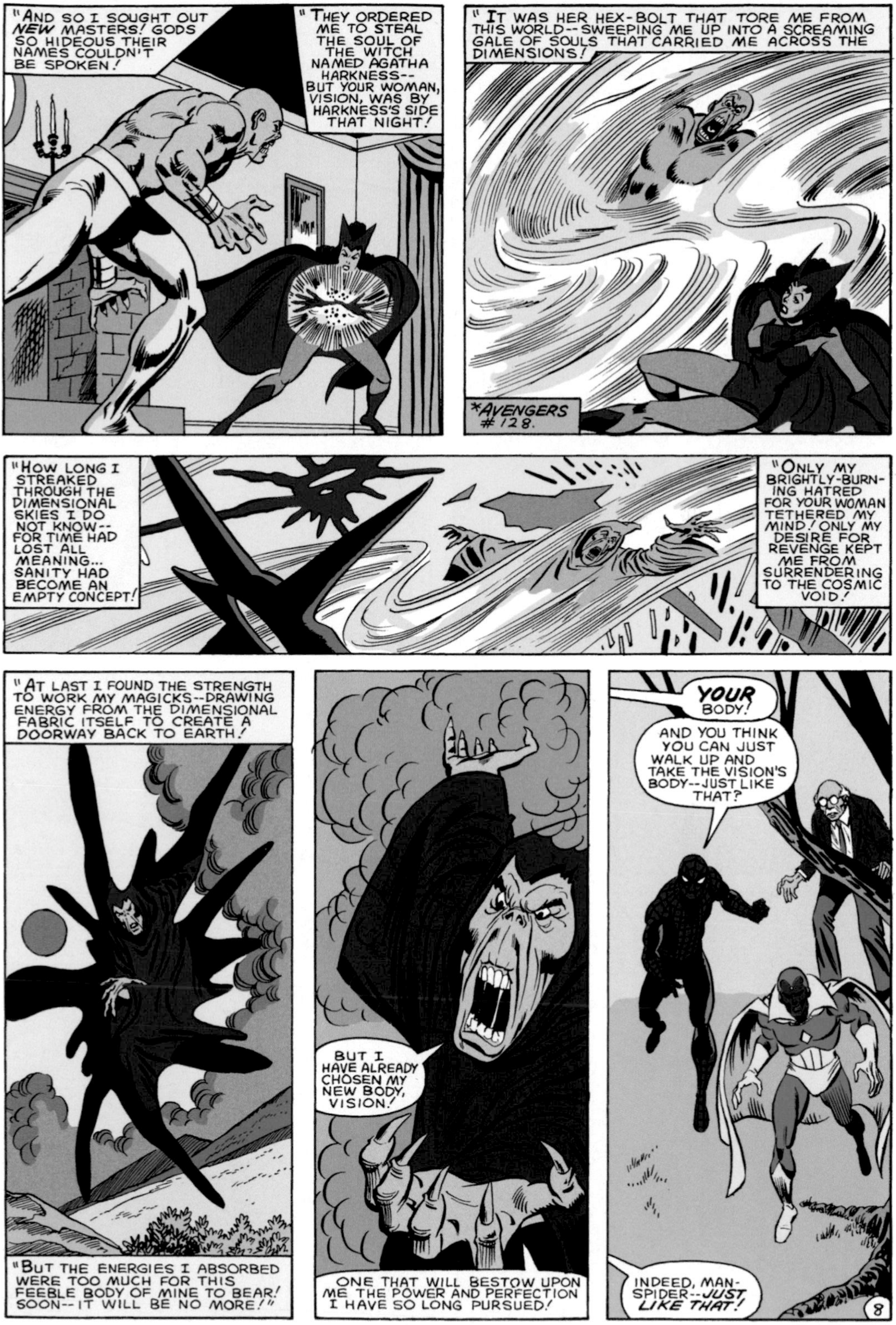
"AND SO I SOUGHT OUT NEW MASTERS! GODS SO HIDEOUS THEIR NAMES COULDN'T BE SPOKEN!
"THEY ORDERED ME TO STEAL THE SOUL OF THE WITCH NAMED AGATHA HARKNESS-- BUT YOUR WOMAN, VISION, WAS BY HARKNESS'S SIDE THAT NIGHT!
"IT WAS HER HEX-BOLT THAT TORE ME FROM THIS WORLD-- SWEEPING ME UP INTO A SCREAMING GALE OF SOULS THAT CARRIED ME ACROSS THE DIMENSIONS!
*AVENGERS #128.
"HOW LONG I STREAKED THROUGH THE DIMENSIONAL SKIES I DO NOT KNOW-- FOR TIME HAD LOST ALL MEANING... SANITY HAD BECOME AN EMPTY CONCEPT!
"ONLY MY BRIGHTLY-BURNING HATRED FOR YOUR WOMAN TETHERED MY MIND! ONLY MY DESIRE FOR REVENGE KEPT ME FROM SURRENDERING TO THE COSMIC VOID!
"AT LAST I FOUND THE STRENGTH TO WORK MY MAGICKS--DRAWING ENERGY FROM THE DIMENSIONAL FABRIC ITSELF TO CREATE A DOORWAY BACK TO EARTH!
"BUT THE ENERGIES I ABSORBED WERE TOO MUCH FOR THIS FEEBLE BODY OF MINE TO BEAR! SOON-- IT WILL BE NO MORE!"
BUT I HAVE ALREADY CHOSEN MY NEW BODY, VISION!
ONE THAT WILL BESTOW UPON ME THE POWER AND PERFECTION I HAVE SO LONG PURSUED!
YOUR BODY!
AND YOU THINK YOU CAN JUST WALK UP AND TAKE THE VISION'S BODY--JUST LIKE THAT?
INDEED, MAN-SPIDER--JUST LIKE THAT!
8

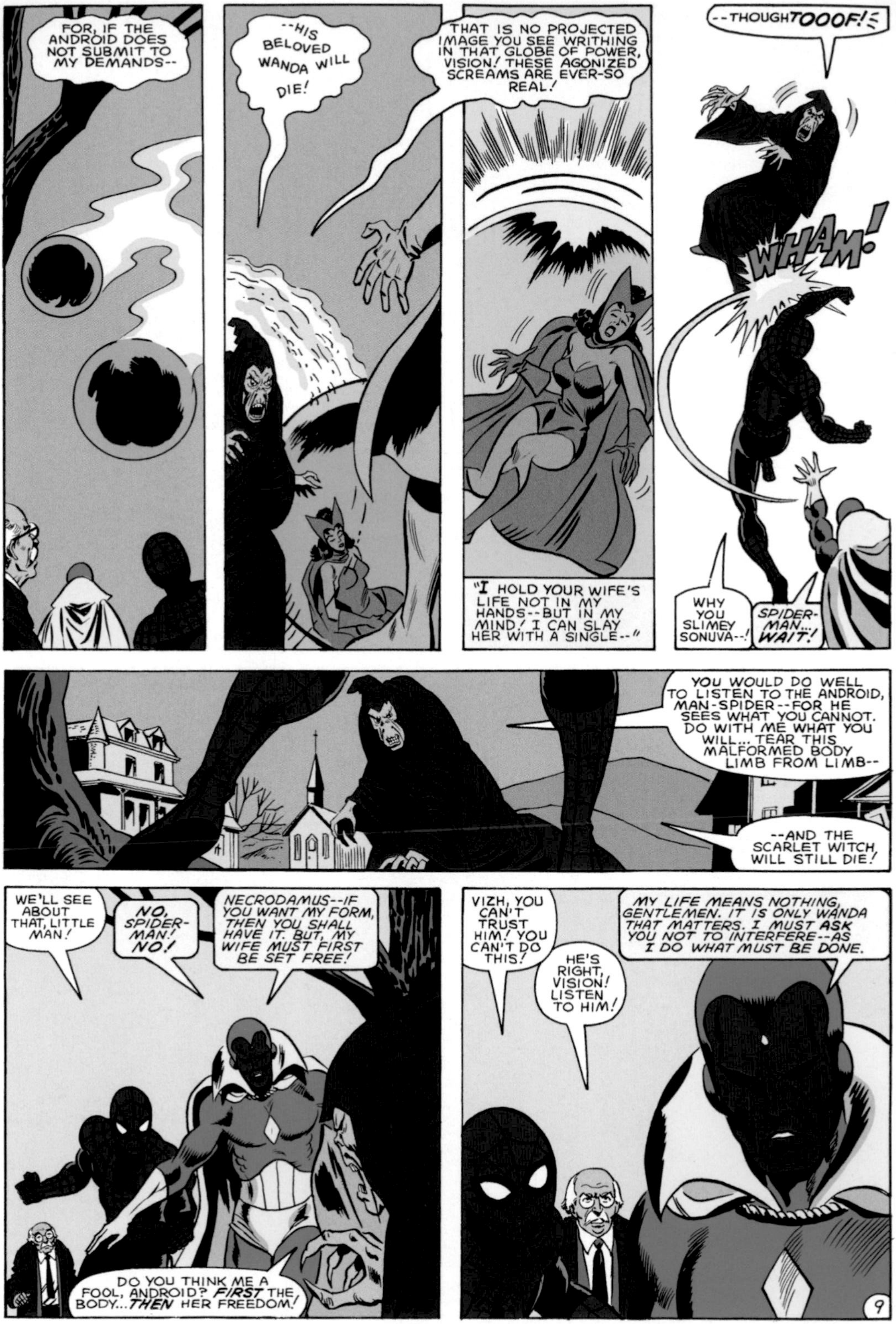

FOR, IF THE ANDROID DOES NOT SUBMIT TO MY DEMANDS--
--HIS BELOVED WANDA WILL DIE!
THAT IS NO PROJECTED IMAGE YOU SEE WRITHING IN THAT GLOBE OF POWER, VISION! THESE AGONIZED SCREAMS ARE EVER-SO REAL!
"I HOLD YOUR WIFE'S LIFE NOT IN MY HANDS--BUT IN MY MIND! I CAN SLAY HER WITH A SINGLE--"
--THOUGH TOOOF!
WHAM!
WHY YOU SLIMEY SONUVA--!
SPIDER-MAN... WAIT!
YOU WOULD DO WELL TO LISTEN TO THE ANDROID, MAN-SPIDER--FOR HE SEES WHAT YOU CANNOT. DO WITH ME WHAT YOU WILL... TEAR THIS MALFORMED BODY LIMB FROM LIMB--
--AND THE SCARLET WITCH WILL STILL DIE!
WE'LL SEE ABOUT THAT, LITTLE MAN!
NO, SPIDER-MAN! NO!
NECRODAMUS--IF YOU WANT MY FORM, THEN YOU SHALL HAVE IT. BUT, MY WIFE MUST FIRST BE SET FREE!
DO YOU THINK ME A FOOL, ANDROID? FIRST THE BODY...THEN HER FREEDOM!
VIZH, YOU CAN'T TRUST HIM! YOU CAN'T DO THIS!
HE'S RIGHT, VISION! LISTEN TO HIM!
MY LIFE MEANS NOTHING, GENTLEMEN. IT IS ONLY WANDA THAT MATTERS. I MUST ASK YOU NOT TO INTERFERE--AS I DO WHAT MUST BE DONE.

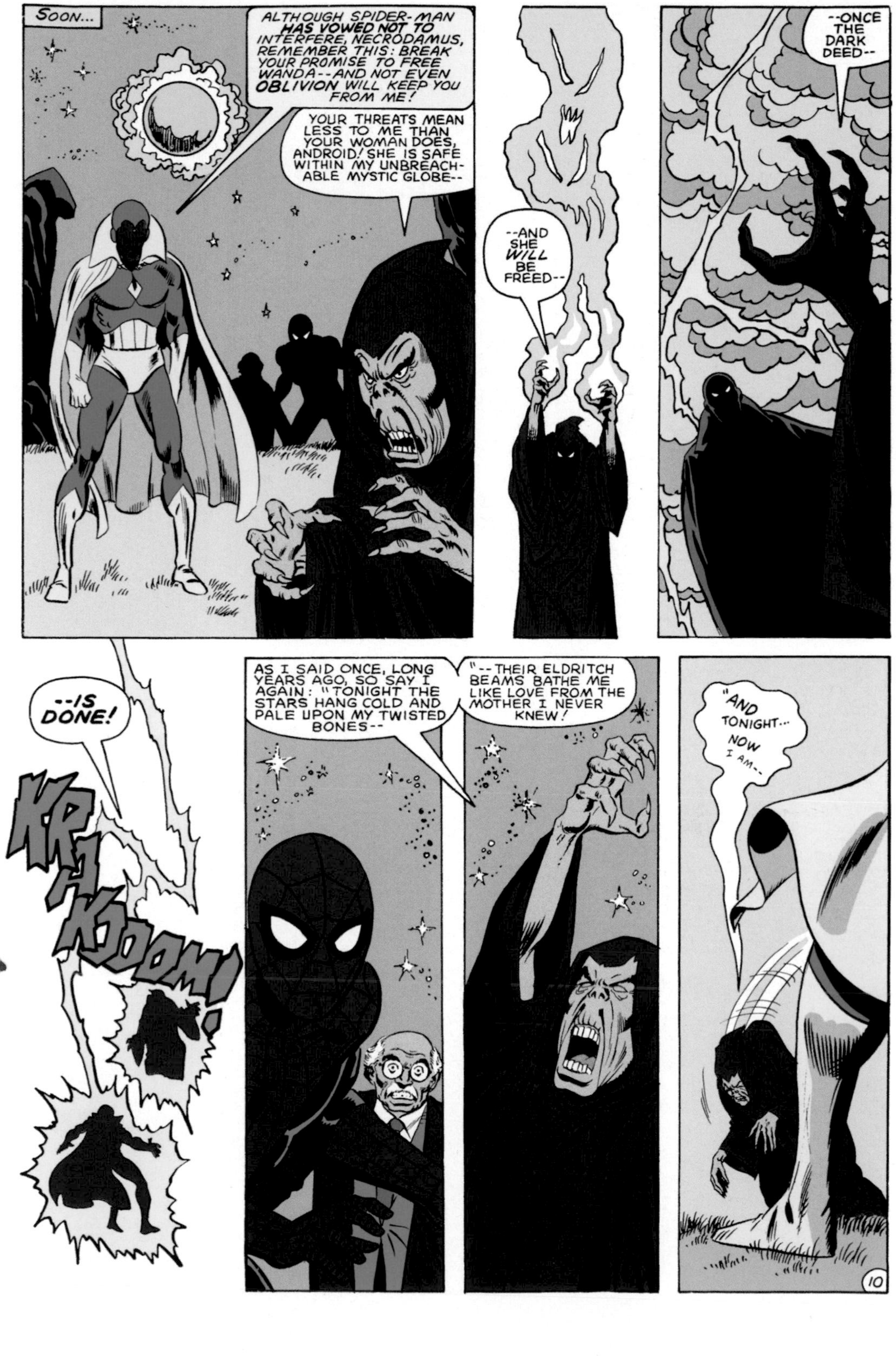
SOON...
ALTHOUGH SPIDER-MAN HAS VOWED NOT TO INTERFERE, NECRODAMUS, REMEMBER THIS: BREAK YOUR PROMISE TO FREE WANDA--AND NOT EVEN OBLIVION WILL KEEP YOU FROM ME!
YOUR THREATS MEAN LESS TO ME THAN YOUR WOMAN DOES, ANDROID! SHE IS SAFE WITHIN MY UNBREACHABLE MYSTIC GLOBE--
--AND SHE WILL BE FREED--
--ONCE THE DARK DEED--
--IS DONE!
KRAKOOM!
AS I SAID ONCE, LONG YEARS AGO, SO SAY I AGAIN: "TONIGHT THE STARS HANG COLD AND PALE UPON MY TWISTED BONES--
"--THEIR ELDRITCH BEAMS BATHE ME LIKE LOVE FROM THE MOTHER I NEVER KNEW!
"AND TONIGHT... NOW I AM--
10

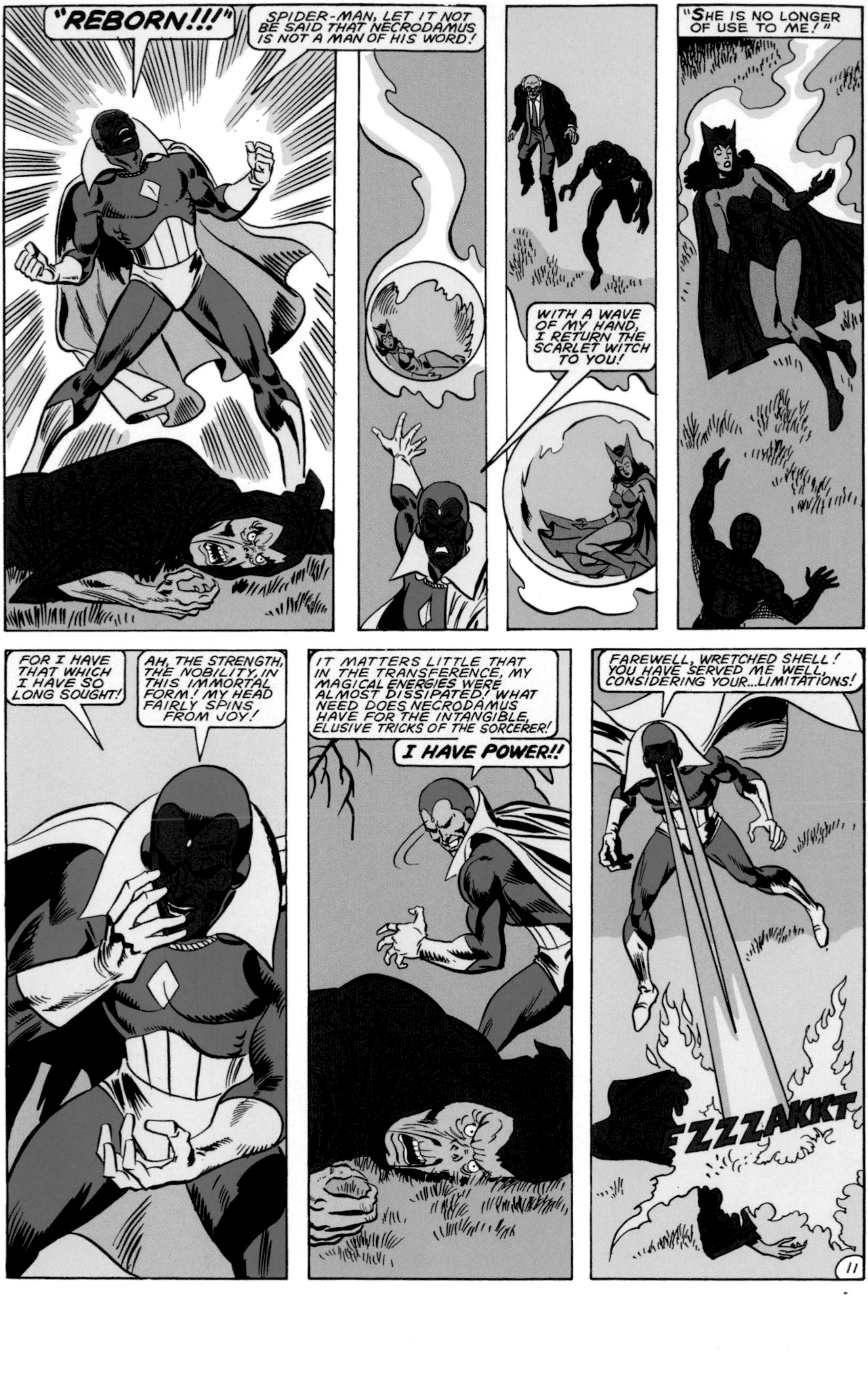
"REBORN!!!"
SPIDER-MAN, LET IT NOT BE SAID THAT NECRODAMUS IS NOT A MAN OF HIS WORD!
WITH A WAVE OF MY HAND, I RETURN THE SCARLET WITCH TO YOU!
"SHE IS NO LONGER OF USE TO ME!"
FOR I HAVE THAT WHICH I HAVE SO LONG SOUGHT!
AH, THE STRENGTH, THE NOBILITY, IN THIS IMMORTAL FORM! MY HEAD FAIRLY SPINS FROM JOY!
IT MATTERS LITTLE THAT IN THE TRANSFERENCE, MY MAGICAL ENERGIES WERE ALMOST DISSIPATED! WHAT NEED DOES NECRODAMUS HAVE FOR THE INTANGIBLE, ELUSIVE TRICKS OF THE SORCERER!
I HAVE POWER!!
FAREWELL, WRETCHED SHELL! YOU HAVE SERVED ME WELL, CONSIDERING YOUR...LIMITATIONS!
FZZZAKKT
11

OH, HOW I LOTHED YOU!

WHY YOU SLIMEY SONUVA--! DON'T YOU REALIZE WHAT YOU'VE JUST DONE?

THE VISION'S *SOUL* WAS IN THAT BODY!

WHAM!

HMMM... I SEE THAT ONE MUST CONCENTRATE TO MAKE THIS BODY IMPERVIOUS TO ASSAULT. THERE... *THAT* SHOULD DO IT.

AS FOR YOUR ERRONEOUS STATEMENT, SPIDER-MAN...

YOWWW!! MY HAND... NEARLY SHATTERED... WHEN I HIT 'IM!

YOU PROCEED FROM A FALSE ASSUMPTION! AN ANDROID HAS NO *SOUL*! IN TAKING THIS FORM, I HAVE SIMPLY WIPED OUT THE VISION'S PROGRAMMING! PULLED HIS IDENTITY-PLUG, SO TO SPEAK!

AND NOW THAT I HAVE EXPLAINED...

OH, NO! TOO STAGGERED FROM THE PAIN IN MY HAND... TO LEAP BACK IN TIME! HE'S MAKING HIS ARM INTANGIBLE... AND THEN PARTIALLY MATERIALIZING IT... *YARRGGH--*

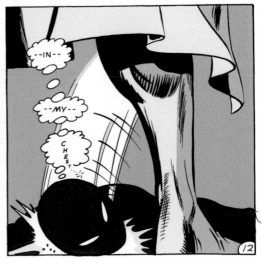

--IN--

--MY--

CHEST...

12

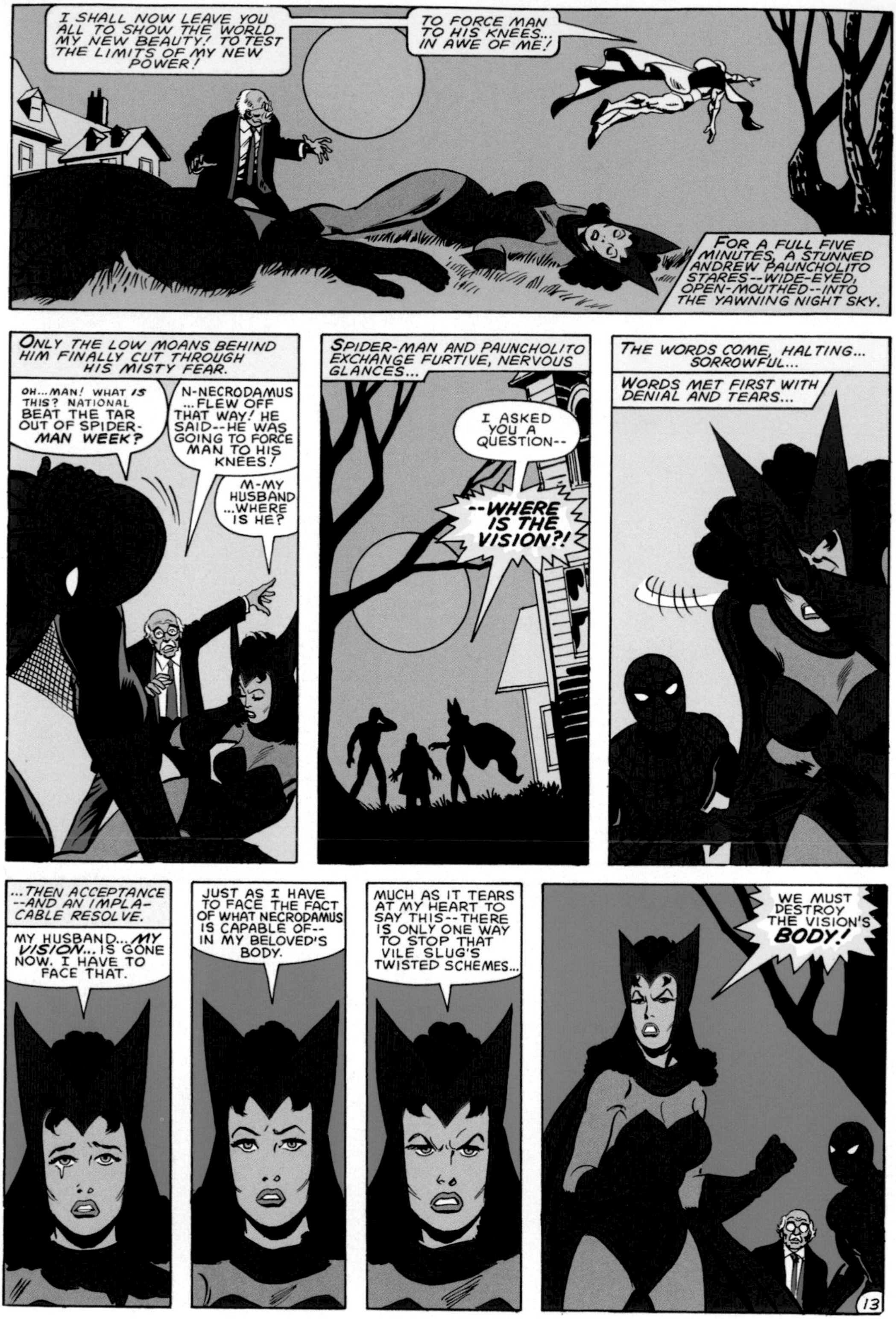

I SHALL NOW LEAVE YOU ALL TO SHOW THE WORLD MY NEW BEAUTY! TO TEST THE LIMITS OF MY NEW POWER!
TO FORCE MAN TO HIS KNEES... IN AWE OF ME!
FOR A FULL FIVE MINUTES, A STUNNED ANDREW PAUNCHOLITO STARES--WIDE-EYED, OPEN-MOUTHED--INTO THE YAWNING NIGHT SKY.
ONLY THE LOW MOANS BEHIND HIM FINALLY CUT THROUGH HIS MISTY FEAR.
OH...MAN! WHAT IS THIS? NATIONAL BEAT THE TAR OUT OF SPIDER-MAN WEEK?
N-NECRODAMUS ...FLEW OFF THAT WAY! HE SAID--HE WAS GOING TO FORCE MAN TO HIS KNEES!
M-MY HUSBAND ...WHERE IS HE?
SPIDER-MAN AND PAUNCHOLITO EXCHANGE FURTIVE, NERVOUS GLANCES...
I ASKED YOU A QUESTION--
--WHERE IS THE VISION?!
THE WORDS COME, HALTING... SORROWFUL...
WORDS MET FIRST WITH DENIAL AND TEARS...
...THEN ACCEPTANCE --AND AN IMPLACABLE RESOLVE.
MY HUSBAND...MY VISION...IS GONE NOW. I HAVE TO FACE THAT.
JUST AS I HAVE TO FACE THE FACT OF WHAT NECRODAMUS IS CAPABLE OF-- IN MY BELOVED'S BODY.
MUCH AS IT TEARS AT MY HEART TO SAY THIS--THERE IS ONLY ONE WAY TO STOP THAT VILE SLUG'S TWISTED SCHEMES...
WE MUST DESTROY THE VISION'S BODY!
13

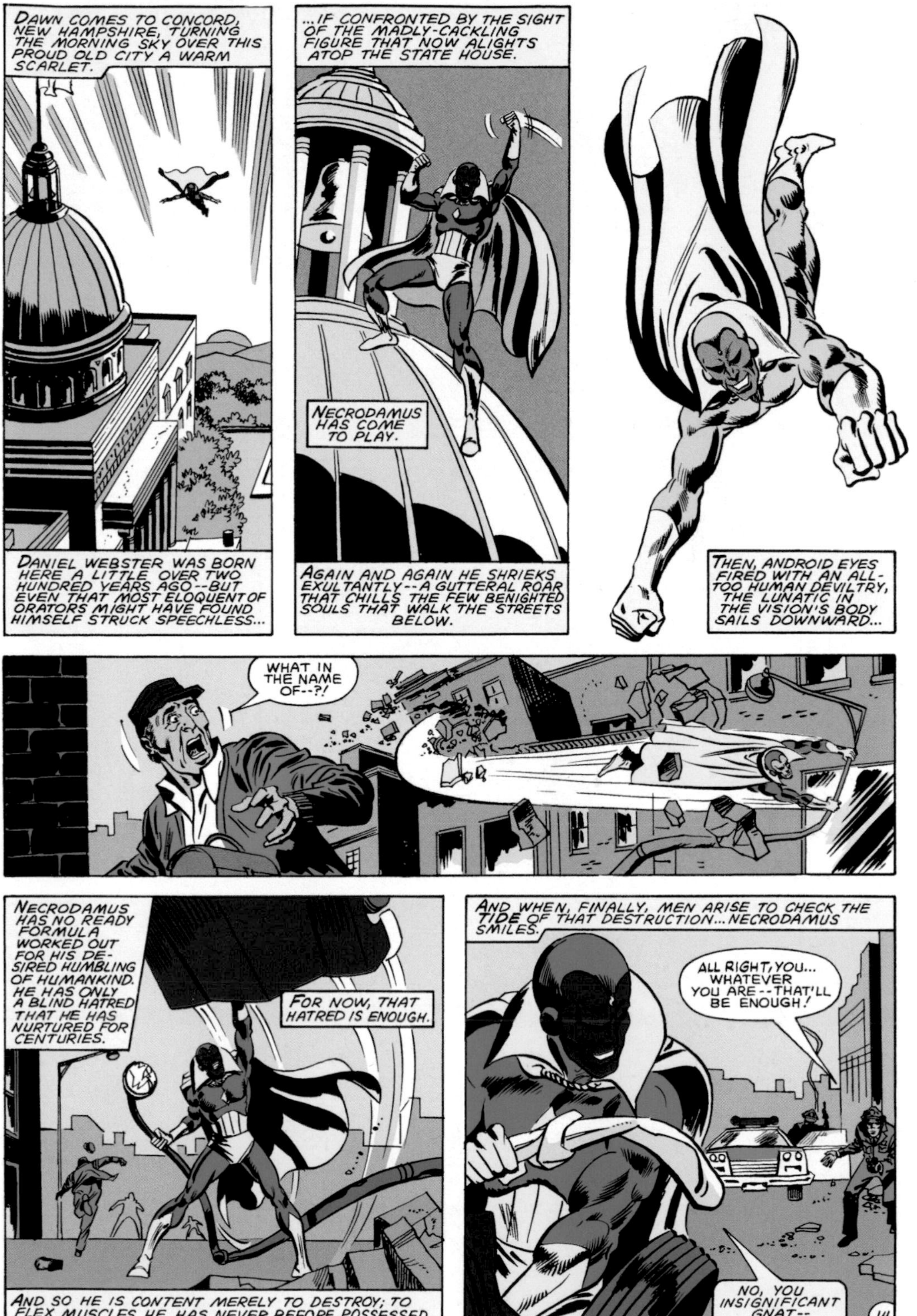
DAWN COMES TO CONCORD, NEW HAMPSHIRE, TURNING THE MORNING SKY OVER THIS PROUD OLD CITY A WARM SCARLET.
DANIEL WEBSTER WAS BORN HERE A LITTLE OVER TWO HUNDRED YEARS AGO--BUT EVEN THAT MOST ELOQUENT OF ORATORS MIGHT HAVE FOUND HIMSELF STRUCK SPEECHLESS...
...IF CONFRONTED BY THE SIGHT OF THE MADLY-CACKLING FIGURE THAT NOW ALIGHTS ATOP THE STATE HOUSE.
NECRODAMUS HAS COME TO PLAY.
AGAIN AND AGAIN HE SHRIEKS EXULTANTLY--A GUTTERAL ROAR THAT CHILLS THE FEW BENIGHTED SOULS THAT WALK THE STREETS BELOW.
THEN, ANDROID EYES FIRED WITH AN ALL-TOO HUMAN DEVILTRY, THE LUNATIC IN THE VISION'S BODY SAILS DOWNWARD...
WHAT IN THE NAME OF--?!
NECRODAMUS HAS NO READY FORMULA WORKED OUT FOR HIS DESIRED HUMBLING OF HUMANKIND. HE HAS ONLY A BLIND HATRED THAT HE HAS NURTURED FOR CENTURIES.
FOR NOW, THAT HATRED IS ENOUGH.
AND SO HE IS CONTENT MERELY TO DESTROY; TO FLEX MUSCLES HE HAS NEVER BEFORE POSSESSED...
AND WHEN, FINALLY, MEN ARISE TO CHECK THE TIDE OF THAT DESTRUCTION...NECRODAMUS SMILES.
ALL RIGHT, YOU... WHATEVER YOU ARE--THAT'LL BE ENOUGH!
NO, YOU INSIGNIFICANT GNAT--
14

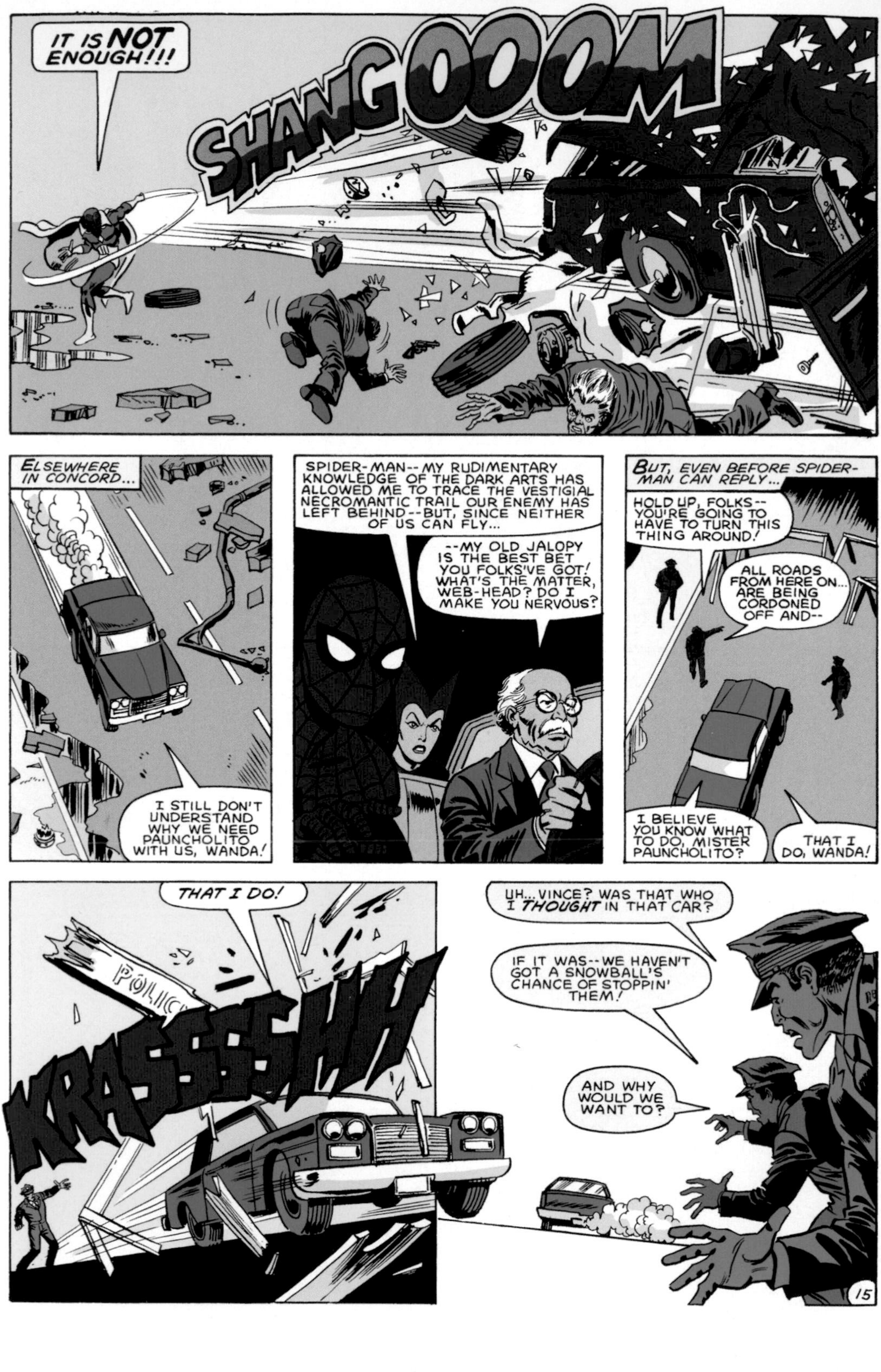

IT IS NOT ENOUGH!!!
SHANGOOOM
ELSEWHERE IN CONCORD...
I STILL DON'T UNDERSTAND WHY WE NEED PAUNCHOLITO WITH US, WANDA!
SPIDER-MAN--MY RUDIMENTARY KNOWLEDGE OF THE DARK ARTS HAS ALLOWED ME TO TRACE THE VESTIGIAL NECROMANTIC TRAIL OUR ENEMY HAS LEFT BEHIND--BUT, SINCE NEITHER OF US CAN FLY...
--MY OLD JALOPY IS THE BEST BET YOU FOLKS'VE GOT! WHAT'S THE MATTER, WEB-HEAD? DO I MAKE YOU NERVOUS?
BUT, EVEN BEFORE SPIDER-MAN CAN REPLY...
HOLD UP, FOLKS-- YOU'RE GOING TO HAVE TO TURN THIS THING AROUND!
ALL ROADS FROM HERE ON... ARE BEING CORDONED OFF AND--
I BELIEVE YOU KNOW WHAT TO DO, MISTER PAUNCHOLITO?
THAT I DO, WANDA!
THAT I DO!
POLICE
KRASSSSHH
UH... VINCE? WAS THAT WHO I THOUGHT IN THAT CAR?
IF IT WAS--WE HAVEN'T GOT A SNOWBALL'S CHANCE OF STOPPIN' THEM!
AND WHY WOULD WE WANT TO?

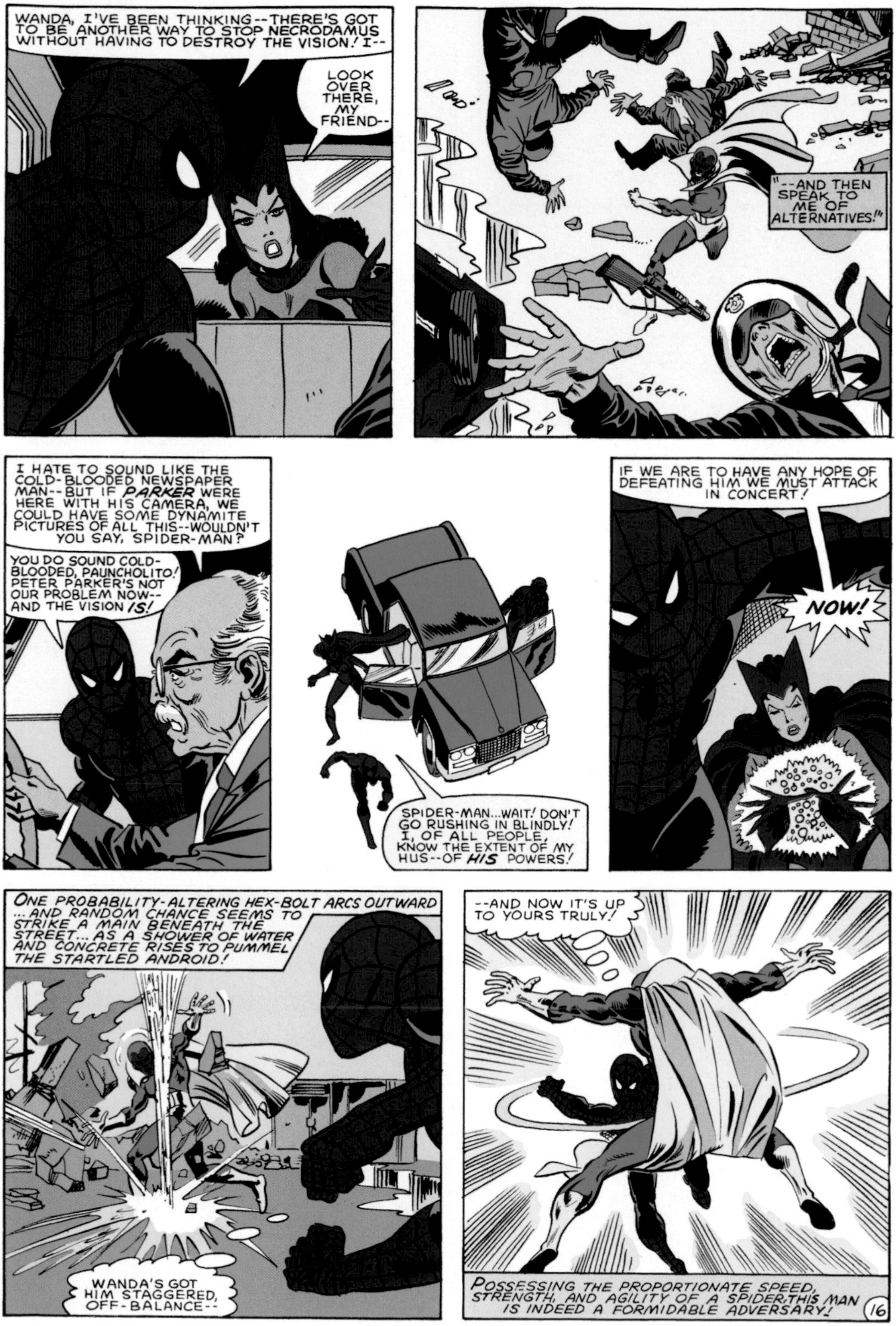
WANDA, I'VE BEEN THINKING--THERE'S GOT TO BE ANOTHER WAY TO STOP NECRODAMUS WITHOUT HAVING TO DESTROY THE VISION! I--
LOOK OVER THERE, MY FRIEND--
"--AND THEN SPEAK TO ME OF ALTERNATIVES!"
I HATE TO SOUND LIKE THE COLD-BLOODED NEWSPAPER MAN--BUT IF PARKER WERE HERE WITH HIS CAMERA, WE COULD HAVE SOME DYNAMITE PICTURES OF ALL THIS--WOULDN'T YOU SAY, SPIDER-MAN?
YOU DO SOUND COLD-BLOODED, PAUNCHOLITO! PETER PARKER'S NOT OUR PROBLEM NOW--AND THE VISION IS!
SPIDER-MAN...WAIT! DON'T GO RUSHING IN BLINDLY! I, OF ALL PEOPLE, KNOW THE EXTENT OF MY HUS--OF HIS POWERS!
IF WE ARE TO HAVE ANY HOPE OF DEFEATING HIM WE MUST ATTACK IN CONCERT!
NOW!
ONE PROBABILITY-ALTERING HEX-BOLT ARCS OUTWARD ...AND RANDOM CHANCE SEEMS TO STRIKE A MAIN BENEATH THE STREET... AS A SHOWER OF WATER AND CONCRETE RISES TO PUMMEL THE STARTLED ANDROID!
WANDA'S GOT HIM STAGGERED, OFF-BALANCE--
--AND NOW IT'S UP TO YOURS TRULY!
POSSESSING THE PROPORTIONATE SPEED, STRENGTH, AND AGILITY OF A SPIDER, THIS MAN IS INDEED A FORMIDABLE ADVERSARY!
16

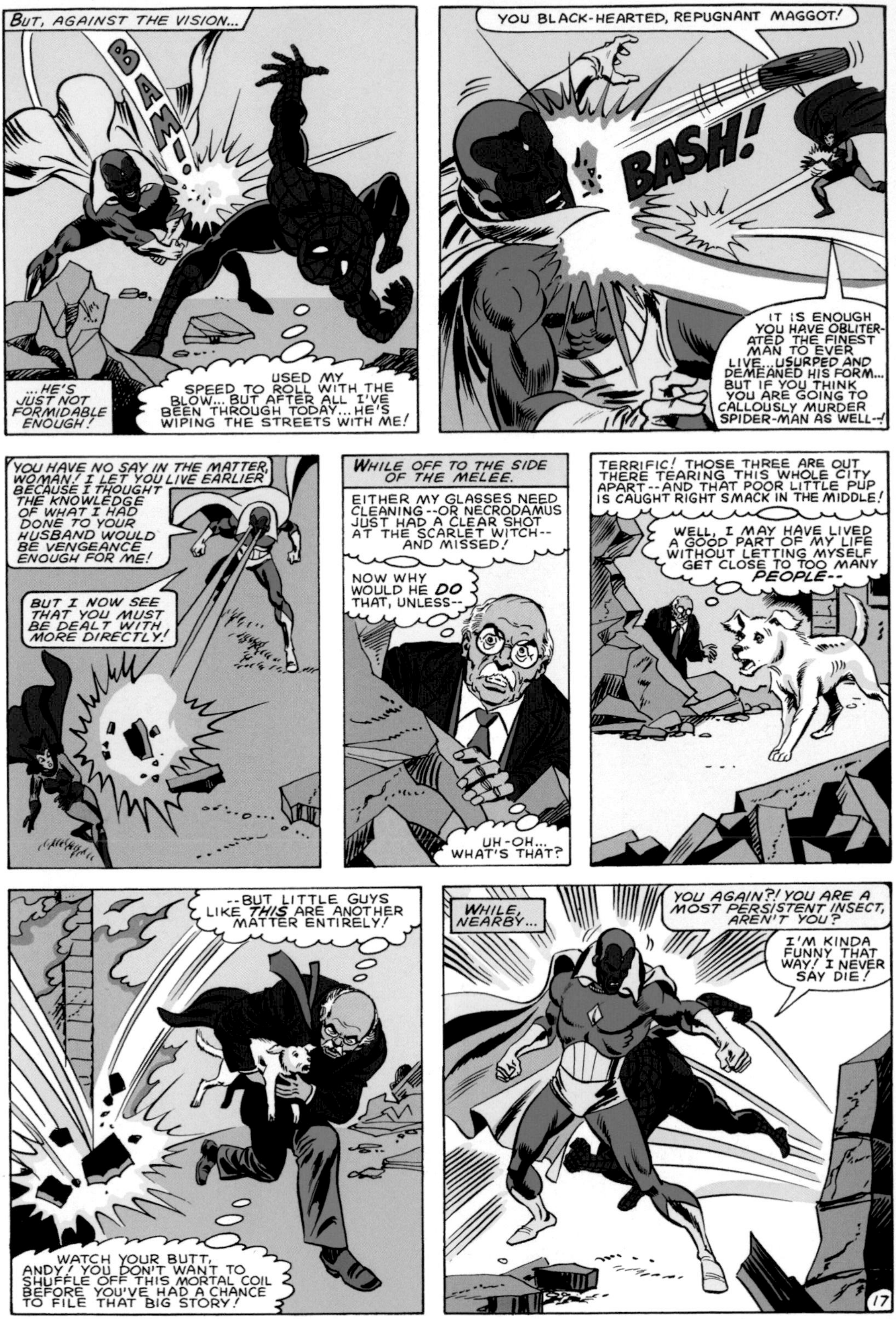

BUT, AGAINST THE VISION...
BAM!
...HE'S JUST NOT FORMIDABLE ENOUGH!
USED MY SPEED TO ROLL WITH THE BLOW... BUT AFTER ALL I'VE BEEN THROUGH TODAY... HE'S WIPING THE STREETS WITH ME!
YOU BLACK-HEARTED, REPUGNANT MAGGOT!
BASH!
IT IS ENOUGH YOU HAVE OBLITERATED THE FINEST MAN TO EVER LIVE...USURPED AND DEMEANED HIS FORM... BUT IF YOU THINK YOU ARE GOING TO CALLOUSLY MURDER SPIDER-MAN AS WELL--!
YOU HAVE NO SAY IN THE MATTER, WOMAN! I LET YOU LIVE EARLIER BECAUSE I THOUGHT THE KNOWLEDGE OF WHAT I HAD DONE TO YOUR HUSBAND WOULD BE VENGEANCE ENOUGH FOR ME!
BUT I NOW SEE THAT YOU MUST BE DEALT WITH MORE DIRECTLY!
WHILE OFF TO THE SIDE OF THE MELEE.
EITHER MY GLASSES NEED CLEANING--OR NECRODAMUS JUST HAD A CLEAR SHOT AT THE SCARLET WITCH--AND MISSED!
NOW WHY WOULD HE DO THAT, UNLESS--
UH-OH... WHAT'S THAT?
TERRIFIC! THOSE THREE ARE OUT THERE TEARING THIS WHOLE CITY APART--AND THAT POOR LITTLE PUP IS CAUGHT RIGHT SMACK IN THE MIDDLE!
WELL, I MAY HAVE LIVED A GOOD PART OF MY LIFE WITHOUT LETTING MYSELF GET CLOSE TO TOO MANY PEOPLE--
--BUT LITTLE GUYS LIKE THIS ARE ANOTHER MATTER ENTIRELY!
WATCH YOUR BUTT, ANDY! YOU DON'T WANT TO SHUFFLE OFF THIS MORTAL COIL BEFORE YOU'VE HAD A CHANCE TO FILE THAT BIG STORY!
WHILE, NEARBY...
YOU AGAIN?! YOU ARE A MOST PERSISTENT INSECT, AREN'T YOU?
I'M KINDA FUNNY THAT WAY! I NEVER SAY DIE!
17

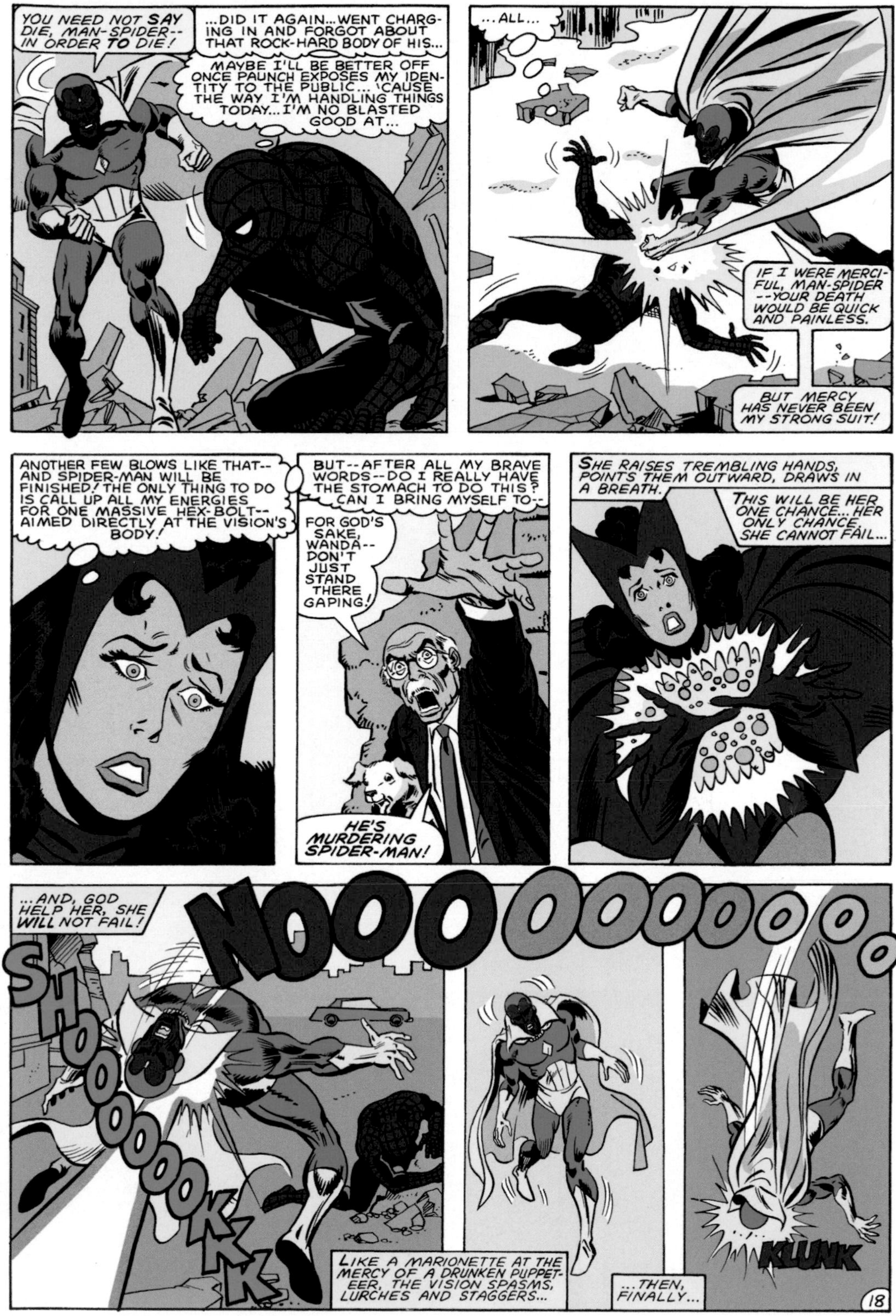
YOU NEED NOT SAY DIE, MAN-SPIDER-- IN ORDER TO DIE!
...DID IT AGAIN...WENT CHARGING IN AND FORGOT ABOUT THAT ROCK-HARD BODY OF HIS...
MAYBE I'LL BE BETTER OFF ONCE PAUNCH EXPOSES MY IDENTITY TO THE PUBLIC... 'CAUSE THE WAY I'M HANDLING THINGS TODAY...I'M NO BLASTED GOOD AT...
...ALL...
IF I WERE MERCIFUL, MAN-SPIDER --YOUR DEATH WOULD BE QUICK AND PAINLESS.
BUT MERCY HAS NEVER BEEN MY STRONG SUIT!
ANOTHER FEW BLOWS LIKE THAT-- AND SPIDER-MAN WILL BE FINISHED! THE ONLY THING TO DO IS CALL UP ALL MY ENERGIES FOR ONE MASSIVE HEX-BOLT-- AIMED DIRECTLY AT THE VISION'S BODY!
BUT--AFTER ALL MY BRAVE WORDS--DO I REALLY HAVE THE STOMACH TO DO THIS? CAN I BRING MYSELF TO--
FOR GOD'S SAKE, WANDA-- DON'T JUST STAND THERE GAPING!
HE'S MURDERING SPIDER-MAN!
SHE RAISES TREMBLING HANDS, POINTS THEM OUTWARD, DRAWS IN A BREATH.
THIS WILL BE HER ONE CHANCE...HER ONLY CHANCE. SHE CANNOT FAIL...
...AND, GOD HELP HER, SHE WILL NOT FAIL!
NOOOOOOOOOOOo
SHOOOOOOOKK
LIKE A MARIONETTE AT THE MERCY OF A DRUNKEN PUPPETEER, THE VISION SPASMS, LURCHES AND STAGGERS...
...THEN, FINALLY...
KLUNK

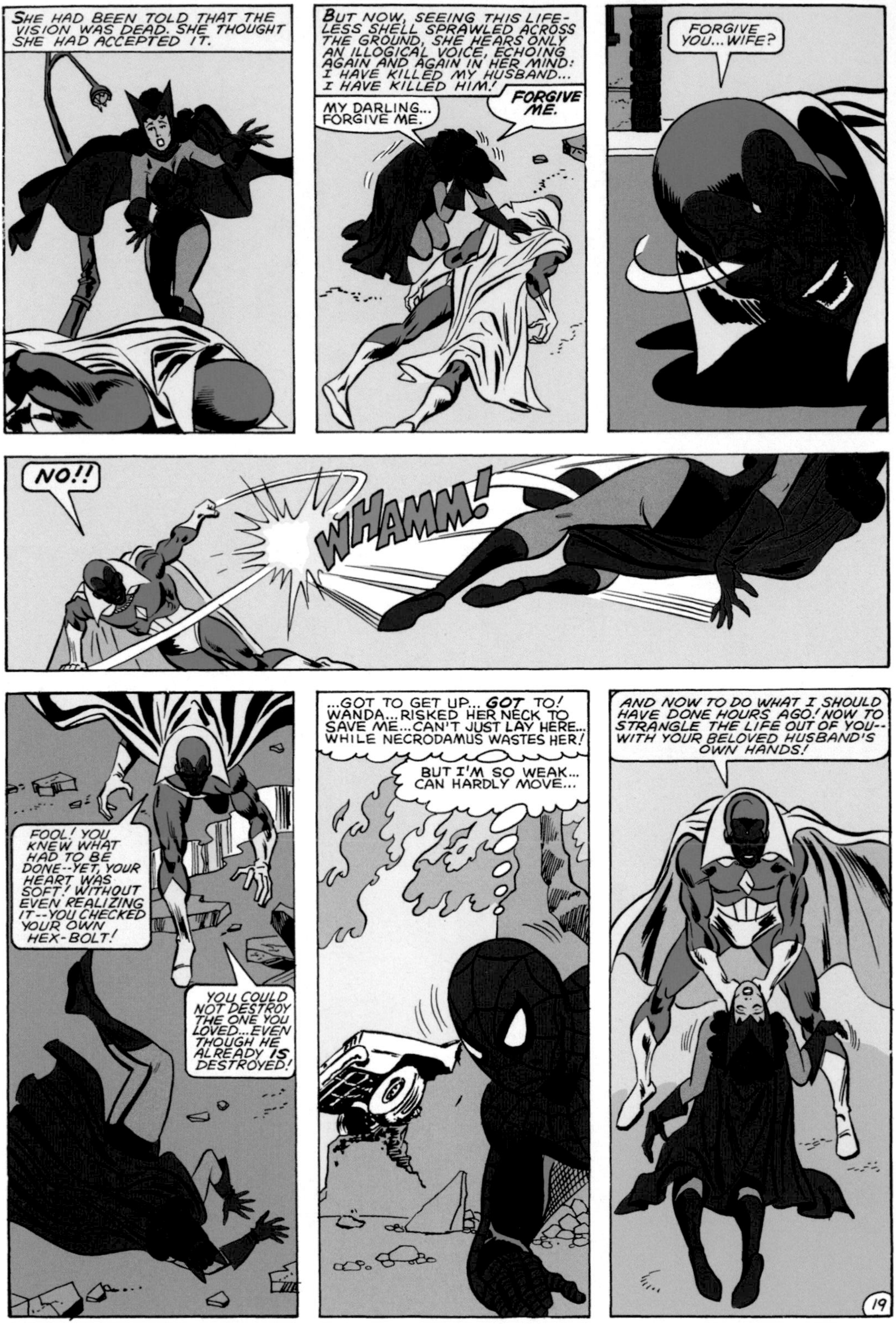

SHE HAD BEEN TOLD THAT THE VISION WAS DEAD. SHE THOUGHT SHE HAD ACCEPTED IT.
BUT NOW, SEEING THIS LIFELESS SHELL SPRAWLED ACROSS THE GROUND, SHE HEARS ONLY AN ILLOGICAL VOICE, ECHOING AGAIN AND AGAIN IN HER MIND: I HAVE KILLED MY HUSBAND... I HAVE KILLED HIM!
MY DARLING... FORGIVE ME.
FORGIVE ME.
FORGIVE YOU...WIFE?
NO!!
WHAMM!
FOOL! YOU KNEW WHAT HAD TO BE DONE--YET, YOUR HEART WAS SOFT! WITHOUT EVEN REALIZING IT--YOU CHECKED YOUR OWN HEX-BOLT!
YOU COULD NOT DESTROY THE ONE YOU LOVED...EVEN THOUGH HE ALREADY IS DESTROYED!
...GOT TO GET UP... GOT TO! WANDA... RISKED HER NECK TO SAVE ME...CAN'T JUST LAY HERE... WHILE NECRODAMUS WASTES HER!
BUT I'M SO WEAK... CAN HARDLY MOVE...
AND NOW TO DO WHAT I SHOULD HAVE DONE HOURS AGO! NOW TO STRANGLE THE LIFE OUT OF YOU-- WITH YOUR BELOVED HUSBAND'S OWN HANDS!
19

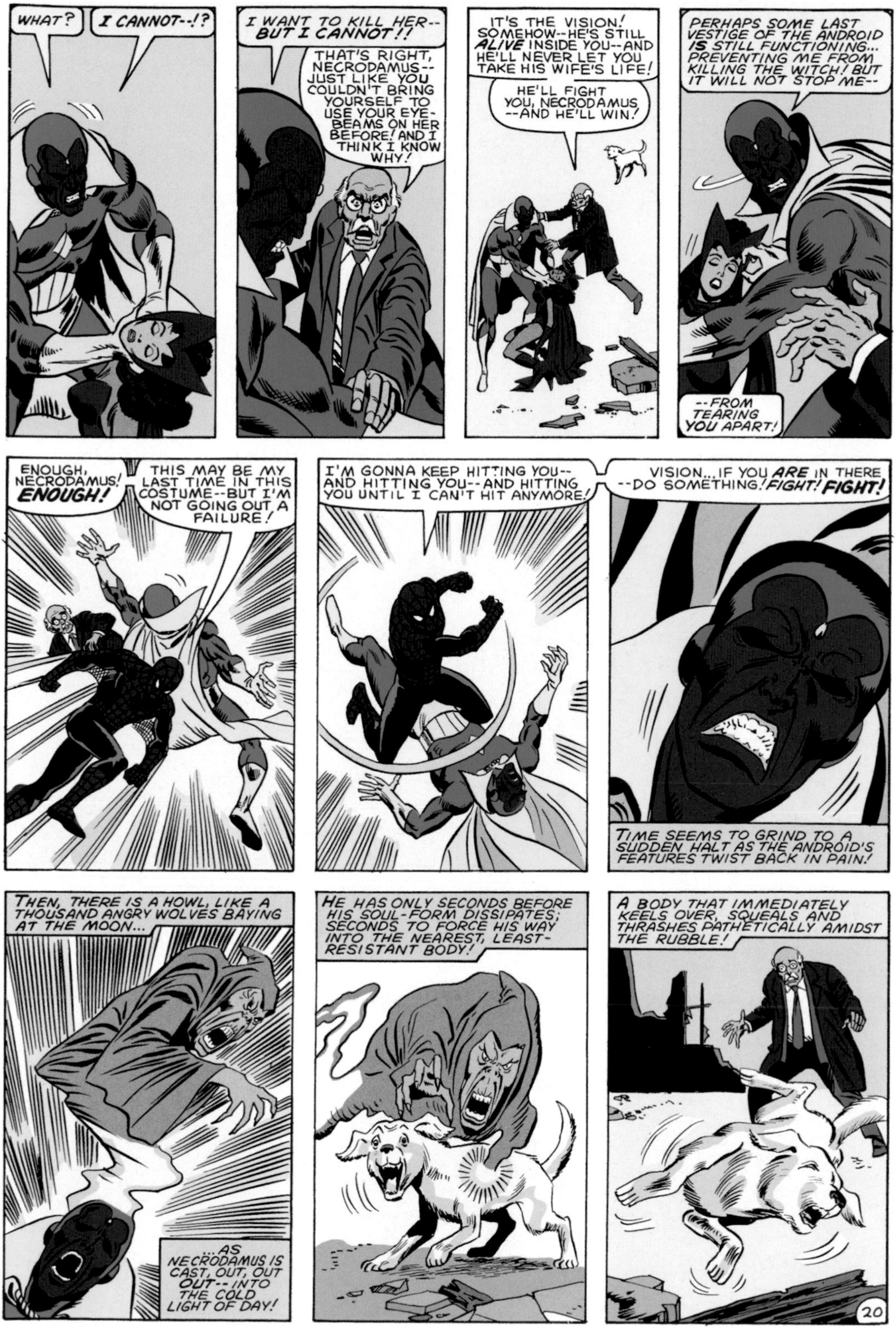
WHAT?
I CANNOT--!?
I WANT TO KILL HER-- BUT I CANNOT!!
THAT'S RIGHT, NECRODAMUS-- JUST LIKE YOU COULDN'T BRING YOURSELF TO USE YOUR EYE-BEAMS ON HER BEFORE! AND I THINK I KNOW WHY!
IT'S THE VISION! SOMEHOW--HE'S STILL ALIVE INSIDE YOU--AND HE'LL NEVER LET YOU TAKE HIS WIFE'S LIFE!
HE'LL FIGHT YOU, NECRODAMUS --AND HE'LL WIN!
PERHAPS SOME LAST VESTIGE OF THE ANDROID IS STILL FUNCTIONING... PREVENTING ME FROM KILLING THE WITCH! BUT IT WILL NOT STOP ME--
--FROM TEARING YOU APART!
ENOUGH, NECRODAMUS! ENOUGH!
THIS MAY BE MY LAST TIME IN THIS COSTUME--BUT I'M NOT GOING OUT A FAILURE!
I'M GONNA KEEP HITTING YOU-- AND HITTING YOU--AND HITTING YOU UNTIL I CAN'T HIT ANYMORE!
VISION...IF YOU ARE IN THERE --DO SOMETHING! FIGHT! FIGHT!
TIME SEEMS TO GRIND TO A SUDDEN HALT AS THE ANDROID'S FEATURES TWIST BACK IN PAIN!
THEN, THERE IS A HOWL, LIKE A THOUSAND ANGRY WOLVES BAYING AT THE MOON...
...AS NECRODAMUS IS CAST, OUT, OUT OUT--INTO THE COLD LIGHT OF DAY!
HE HAS ONLY SECONDS BEFORE HIS SOUL-FORM DISSIPATES; SECONDS TO FORCE HIS WAY INTO THE NEAREST, LEAST-RESISTANT BODY!
A BODY THAT IMMEDIATELY KEELS OVER, SQUEALS AND THRASHES PATHETICALLY AMIDST THE RUBBLE!
20

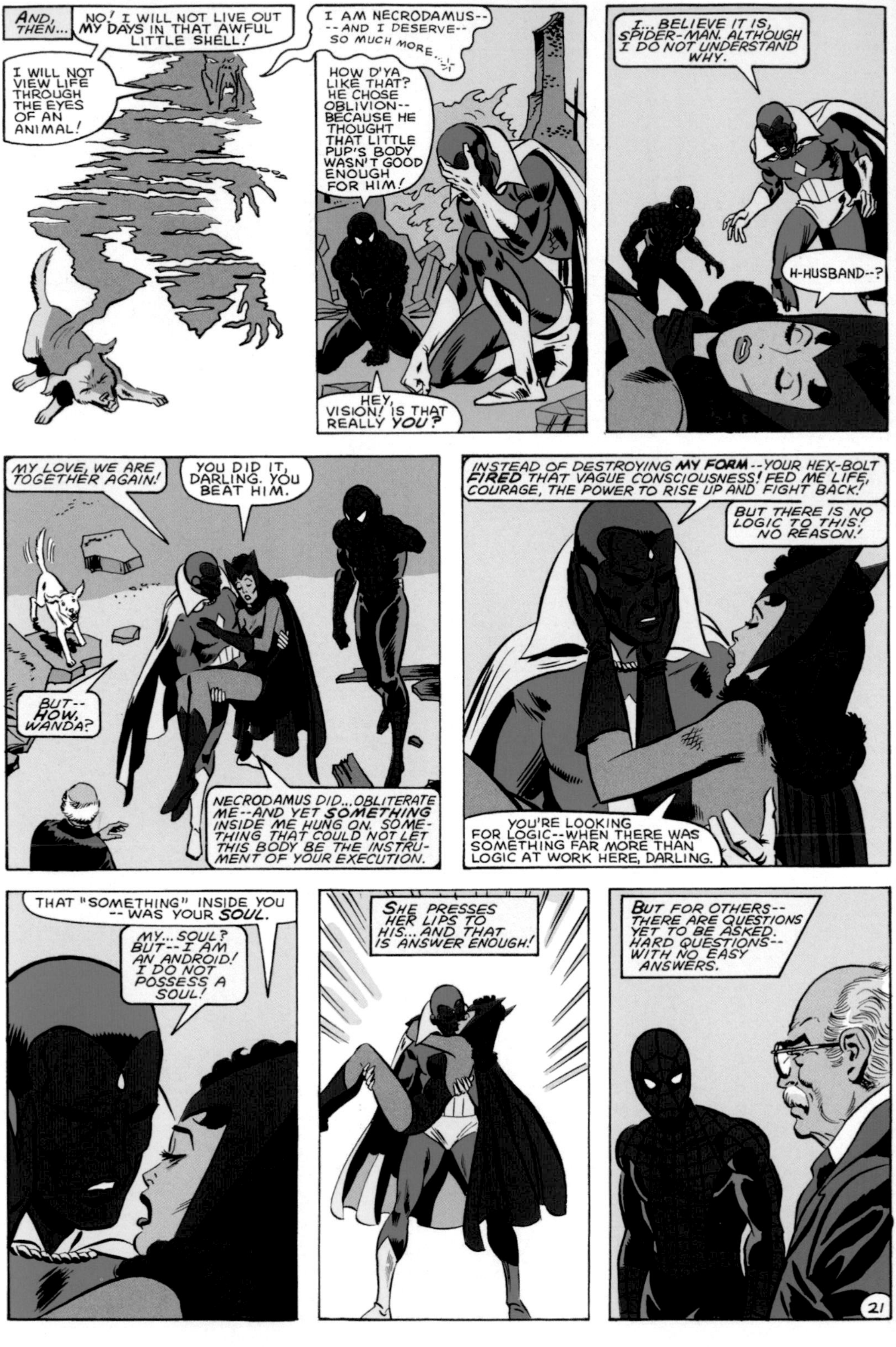
AND, THEN...
NO! I WILL NOT LIVE OUT MY DAYS IN THAT AWFUL LITTLE SHELL!
I WILL NOT VIEW LIFE THROUGH THE EYES OF AN ANIMAL!
I AM NECRODAMUS-- --AND I DESERVE-- SO MUCH MORE...
HOW D'YA LIKE THAT? HE CHOSE OBLIVION--BECAUSE HE THOUGHT THAT LITTLE PUP'S BODY WASN'T GOOD ENOUGH FOR HIM!
HEY, VISION! IS THAT REALLY YOU?
I... BELIEVE IT IS, SPIDER-MAN. ALTHOUGH I DO NOT UNDERSTAND WHY.
H-HUSBAND--?
MY LOVE, WE ARE TOGETHER AGAIN!
YOU DID IT, DARLING. YOU BEAT HIM.
BUT--HOW, WANDA?
NECRODAMUS DID...OBLITERATE ME--AND YET SOMETHING INSIDE ME HUNG ON. SOMETHING THAT COULD NOT LET THIS BODY BE THE INSTRUMENT OF YOUR EXECUTION.
INSTEAD OF DESTROYING MY FORM--YOUR HEX-BOLT FIRED THAT VAGUE CONSCIOUSNESS! FED ME LIFE, COURAGE, THE POWER TO RISE UP AND FIGHT BACK!
BUT THERE IS NO LOGIC TO THIS! NO REASON!
YOU'RE LOOKING FOR LOGIC--WHEN THERE WAS SOMETHING FAR MORE THAN LOGIC AT WORK HERE, DARLING.
THAT "SOMETHING" INSIDE YOU --WAS YOUR SOUL.
MY... SOUL? BUT--I AM AN ANDROID! I DO NOT POSSESS A SOUL!
SHE PRESSES HER LIPS TO HIS... AND THAT IS ANSWER ENOUGH!
BUT FOR OTHERS--THERE ARE QUESTIONS YET TO BE ASKED. HARD QUESTIONS--WITH NO EASY ANSWERS.
21

EPILOGUE

...NICE OF YOU TO DROP BY MY *PLACE*, PETER-- BUT MAKE IT QUICK, WILL YOU--

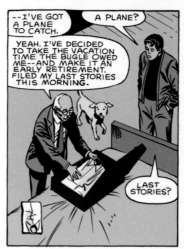

--I'VE GOT A PLANE TO CATCH.

A PLANE?

YEAH. I'VE DECIDED TO TAKE THE VACATION TIME THE BUGLE OWED ME--AND MAKE IT AN EARLY RETIREMENT. FILED MY LAST STORIES THIS MORNING.

LAST STORIES?

YOU KNOW--ABOUT THE NEW HAMP-SHIRE SLASHER-- AND THAT MESS IN CONCORD.

BUT I THOUGHT... I MEAN WHAT ABOUT YOUR *BIG* STORY?

THE ONE YOU WANTED TO GO OUT IN A BLAZE OF GLORY WITH?

LOOK, PETER--LET'S PRETEND--JUST *PRETEND*, MIND YOU--THAT I *DID* COME ACROSS A STORY SO BIG THAT IT'D BLOW ME RIGHT TO THE TOP OF MY PROFESSION.

JUST FOR EXAMPLE--LET'S SAY I KNOW WHO SPIDER-MAN REALLY IS.

WELL, LET ME TELL YOU SOMETHING, SON--I SAW SPIDER-MAN IN ACTION...UP CLOSE. I SAW A BRAVE, TIRELESS, SELFLESS YOUNG MAN. A REAL, HONEST-TO-GOD *HERO*.

THIS WORLD *NEEDS* HEROES, PETER--MORE THAN *I* NEED A PULITZER PRIZE.

A *LOT* MORE.

BUT--SINCE I DON'T *HAVE* THE STORY-- WHAT'S THE POINT OF US EVEN TALKING ABOUT IT, RIGHT?

C'MON, KID-- LEMME BUY YOU A BEER BEFORE I GO.

UH-UH, MR. PAUNCHOLITO--

--THIS ONE'S ON *ME*.

END

NEXT: WOULD YOU BELIEVE-- **THE FABULOUS FROG-MAN** BOUNCES BACK?!

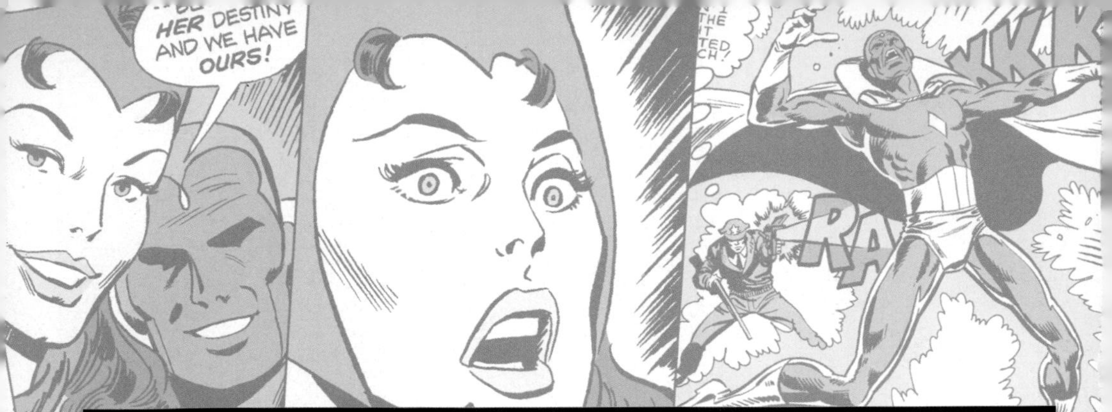
HER DESTINY
AND WE HAVE
OURS!

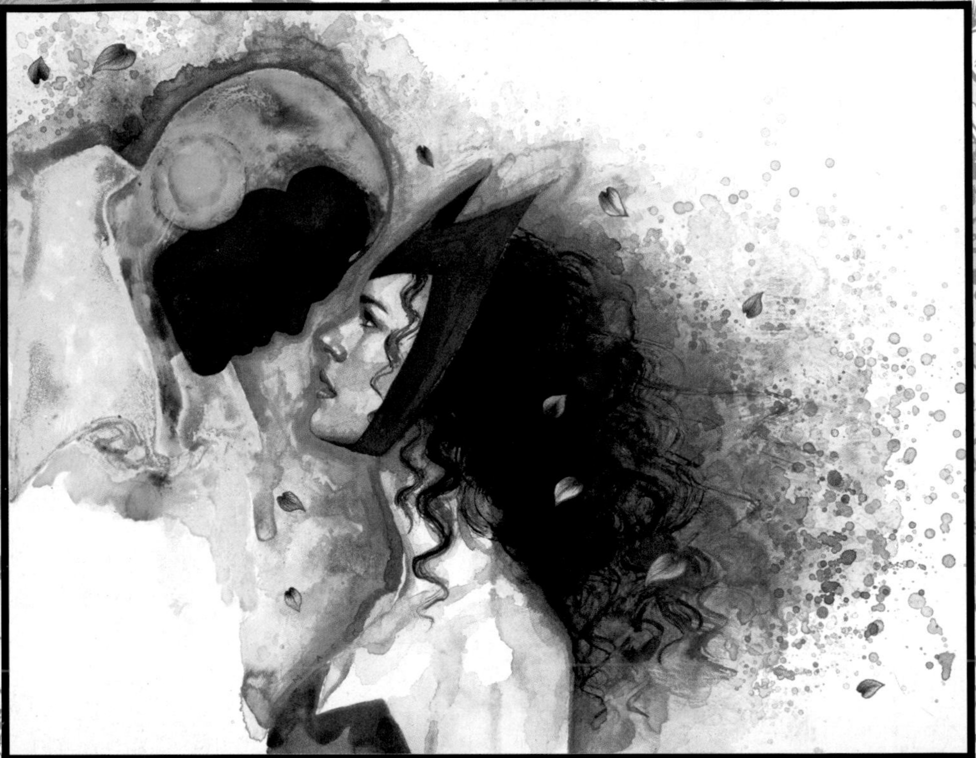

VISION AND THE SCARLET WITCH

BY DAVID MACK

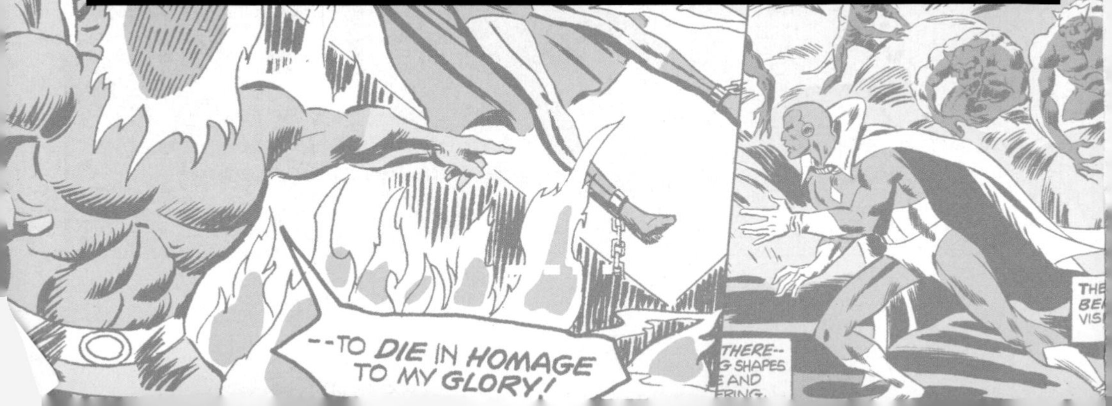
--TO DIE IN HOMAGE
TO MY GLORY!